CONFESSIONS OF A

WAYWARD
ACADEMIC

TOM CORBETT

Selected Praise for the Author's Nonfiction Works:

"Tom Corbett's *The Boat Captain's Conundrum* is a winning performance."

—Forward Clarion Book Review

"Corbett takes a topic often shrouded in numbers and dense writing and turns it into an intellectual, yet conversational memoir."

—U.S. Review of Books

"A long-time policy wonk delivers an engrossing look at his work fighting poverty in government and academic settings."

—Kirkus Review

"I enjoy his writing style, it was comfortable yet candid, like listening to a respected relative recount their own life with unabashed honesty."

—Pacific Book Review

"Corbett imparts an enormous amount of wisdom and humanity."

—Clarion Review

Reviews of the author's fictional works:

"*Palpable Passions* delivers a compelling story arc infused with historical fact that should appeal to readers . . ."

—Blue Ink Reviews

"The book feels like a screenplay; its dialogue is abundant and punchy, its landscapes well defined, and its characters have significant bonds. *Palpable Passions* uses bright, earnest characters to show that a microcosm can be as complicated as the big picture."

—Foreword Book Review

"*Tenuous Tendrils* by Tom Corbett is a compelling journey from exile to redemption. Like its characters, the book is quite clever and features an abundance of humor. Many heavy scenes are punctuated by conversations about the futility of war and the humanitarian failings of government also feature omniscient narrative wit that keeps the text from being bogged down by sentiment and allows the character's personalities to shine."

—Clarion Review

"Corbett has created a captivating novel. The book title perfectly describes the fragile thread that spirals around each individual . . . to create an enthralling story that anyone will love to read."

—U.S. Review of Books

"Corbett obviously loves to tell stories. *Tenuous Tendrils* by Tom Corbett is a captivating read with engaging vignettes which paint a picture of a retired professor, his life, and the connections which bind everything together."

—Pacific Review of Books

"This is . . . a fully rendered tale. Those interested in the complexity of relationships will find some rewards here."

—Blue Ink Reviews

Amazon Reader Reviews for *Tenuous Tendrils* and *Palpable Passions*.

"A penetrating look into the human soul and the fragility of relationships."

"*Tenuous Tendrils* is a conversational and meditative look back on a man's life. I really like the depth of detail that the author brought to these characters."

"This book was incredibly personal on so many levels. Overall, I found this to be an extremely touching and educational read."

"I personally loved this book. It was refreshing and thoughtful."

"The overall story is incredibly genuine, realistic to the time limits it covers and thoughtful. Each time I put down the book I found it moderately difficult since I wanted to know what would happen next."

"Excellent characterization and historical facts make this a compelling story as hope overcomes despair."

"Tom Corbett's "*Palpable Passions*" is the perfect combination of fact and fiction as it educates its readers about current events in our world today."

CONFESSIONS OF A
WAYWARD
ACADEMIC

TOM CORBETT

Other Books by the Author

Confessions of a Clueless Rebel (Hancock Press, 2018)

Palpable Passions (Papertown Press, 2017)

Tenuous Tendrils (Xlibris Press, 2017)

The Boat Captain's Conundrum (Xlibris Press, 2016)

Ouch, Now I Remember (Xlibris Press, 2015)

Browsing through My Candy Store (Xlibris Press, 2014)

Return to the Other Side of the World with Mary Jo Clark, Michael Simmonds, Katherine Sohn, and Hayward Turrentine (Strategic Press, 2013)

The Other Side of the World with Mary Jo Cark, Michael Simonds, and Hayward Turrentine (Strategic Press, 2011)

Evidence-Based Policymaking with Karen Bogenschneider (Taylor and Francis Publishing, 2010)

Policy into Action with Mary Clare Lennon (Urban Institute Press, 2003)

ACKNOWLEDGEMENTS

There are many people that contributed to the production of this book in big and small ways. I received input on an earlier version of his book from several colleagues including Karen Bogenschneider, Sheldon Danziger, Dennis Dresang, Mary Fairchild, Irv Garfinkel, Bob Haveman, Robert Moffitt, Joel Rabb, Ann Sessoms, Unmi Song, Matt Stagner, and Barbara Wolfe. Most were helpful in reading portions and making sure my faulty memory was not playing tricks on me, some provided encouragement. Robin Snell and Dana Connelly helped with various logistics. In addition, I want to thank Carol Lobes very much for reading through the whole draft and making numerous editorial suggestions, she is a trooper.

Finally, I would like to thank Mike Middleton and Eileen Snyder of Hancock Press for their encouragement and assistance in making this project come to life.

Additional Copies:

www.amazon.com

www.barnesandnoble.com

Published in the United States of America

ISBN hardcover: 9781948000239

ISBN softcover: 9781948000222

This work is dedicated to many people but mostly to my devoted spouse, Mary Rider, who put up with many absences over the years as I ran around the country tilting at just one more policy windmill. She and our adorable Cavalier King Charles, Ernie, who unfortunately is no longer with us, would greet each of my returns home with enthusiasm. I must admit though, Ernie greeted me with a good deal more enthusiasm than did my spouse. I suppose he knew no better. Now we have a cute black Shih Tzu appropriately named Rascal. He is wise enough to ignore me totally.

Sheldon Danziger, Irv Garfinkle, and Robert Haveman were early Institute for Research on Poverty (IRP) Directors who helped me a great deal as my career evolved. Frustrated, Sheldon finally kicking me out of the doctoral program with what I feel was an unearned terminal degree (a Ph.D.). Bob taught me much about thinking like a policy wonk, as we worked together on Wisconsin welfare reform issues in the late 1970s. Irv demonstrated for me a seminal truth that an academic could both be a scholar and be passionate about change in the real world. Another colleague, Karen Bogenshneider, has been extremely supportive of me as a purveyor of the written word, almost embarrassingly so.

In addition, there are three individuals important to my development who are no longer with us. Irv Piliavin provided me with an opportunity to transition from state government to the university. Robert Lampman was an iconic figure in poverty research, often thought of as a godfather of the War-on-Poverty and the man most responsible for the Institute for Research on Poverty being located at the University of Wisconsin. Despite his fame and stature, he was a wonderful and kind man who always treated me with far more respect than I deserved back when I had no academic standing whatsoever. Finally, Bill Prosser was a long-time official with the U.S. Department of Health and Human Services. He was a good friend of the Poverty Institute and to me personally.

While most of my academic colleagues were trained as economists, there are a couple of social work types I want to mention. Stephanie Robert, now director of the Wisconsin Social Work Program, has been supportive of my writing compulsion from the beginning. In addition, Jennifer L. Noyes, more a management guru than a social worker, proved a wonderful colleague toward the end of my career, and a good friend. Jennifer, along with Stephanie, insult me with sufficient regularity to prevent any sign of an ego from developing.

Ms. Unmi Song, as a project officer at the Joyce Foundation, consistently supported my rather crazy notions through several grants despite our tendency to bicker with one another, a fact that obscured much mutual affection. Finally, there were many public officials at all levels of government who taught me so much about doing public policy. I cannot thank them all, but I am indebted to each of them.

"Real knowledge is to know the extent of one's ignorance."
—Confucius

"Education is the most powerful weapon which
you can use to change the world."
—Nelson Mandela

"A perfection of means, and confusion of aims,
seems to be our main problem."
—Albert Einstein

"The ultimate authority must always rest with the
individuals own reason and critical analysis."
—Dalai Lama

"Your life has purpose. Your story is important. Your dreams
count. Your voice matters. You were born to make an impact."
—Someone who does not know me

CONTENTS

How To Read This Book.. 17

Preface 19

Chapter 1; A Candy Store 31

Chapter 2; The House Training Of A Policy Wonk.................... 64

Chapter 3; Welfare Wars: Storm Clouds Rising 110

Chapter 4; The Welfare Wars: Cracks In The Safety Net 148

Chapter 5; Welfare Wars: Ending Welfare As We Know It........ 190

Chapter 6; Searching For The Holy Grail................................. 247

Chapter 7; A Failure To Communicate..................................... 302

Chapter 8; To See Things, You Have To Go Out And Look 358

Chapter 9; Darkness And Light?... 416

Chapter 10; Values And Other Inconveniences 448

Chapter 11; A Wayward Academic Or The Cultural Disconnect 480

Chapter 12; The "Sheltered" Workshop.................................... 521

Postscript 578

Key Sources and Other Resources 589

About the Author 609

HOW TO READ THIS BOOK

I thought it wise to provide the reader with a few caveats before they plunge into the text itself. Be advised, this is not a text about the social safety net. It is not a manual for doing social policy, nor is it a history book. You will, however, learn quite a bit about the safety net, about doing policy, and about the history of the transformation of the welfare state and antipoverty policies over the past half century.

This is a personal memoir of my professional life based largely on what I can still remember. You will see a lot of quotes, some of which I draw from written material and many from memory. They cannot be taken verbatim, though I have not intentionally altered or fabricated anything. I report conversations and events as I recall them. I do provide a list of books cited in the text at the end, as well as a list of many papers, articles, and reports I have written on the topics covered in the text. These are organized by theme, though many products could be placed in more than one category. The book itself is structured in terms of the big themes covered by my professional life. Thus, on occasion, it will look as if I am backtracking at the start of a new chapter. I am merely picking up the thread of the new theme at the point I began (or believe I began) to focus on this specific set of issues. Unlike many academics that prefer to specialize, I was more of the dilettante who moved from topic to topic with the themes often overlapping with one another. Even though the text feels like a novel, at least I hope it does, there are serious lessons for current and would-be policy wonks. The overall tone is light, but the underlying issues and insights can be quite serious.

Finally, you will notice several articles of mine in the text that were published in *Focus,* a publication of the Institute for Research on Poverty at the University of Wisconsin. You will also find reports distributed through the WELPAN (Welfare Peer Assistance Network). You can find these papers and so much more on poverty, inequality, and the social safety net at the Institute for Research on Poverty's web site located at http://www.irp.wisc.edu. Have fun, which is precisely what I had in mind as I created this journey down memory lane.

PREFACE

Real knowledge is to know the extent of one's ignorance.

—Confucius

In 2014, I wrote *Browsing through My Candy Store,* a memoir of my career practicing the public policy arts. That book, though enjoying modest sales at best, was well received by members of the academy, by those members of the public who stumbled upon this gem, and by so-called book scouts who ferret out literary finds. That pleased me greatly. My intent was to develop a crossover work that might bridge both the real and the academic worlds. I tried to avoid being so technical that the average reader risked being driven into a deep coma. That is an unfortunate condition I too often witnessed among my university students, especially the undergraduates I taught in early-morning required courses.

More than once, I called in paramedics to check for signs of life among the apparently lifeless forms sitting in front of me. Chastened by such near-death experiences, among my hostage-like students at least, it became my firm conviction that works of substance do not have to be dreary tomes. In fact, one of my more enduring life goals has been to bring some wit and *savoir faire* to a policy world normally infused with way too much angst and anger. I think I may just have accomplished that in these pages though, in the final analysis, only the reader can judge my success or failure in that regard.

Still, why republish an updated version of *Browsing?* Three reasons: First, the initial effort was not well-marketed, something we hope to remedy this time around. Second, during the summer of 2017, I began receiving numerous phone calls from assorted marketing and publishing firms saying that book scouts loved the work while offering to help push *Browsing* in the marketplace. One caller breathlessly informed me that *Browsing* had scored a 90 percent mark in originality—whatever that means. Third, much has changed in the policy world over the past four years, especially at the national political and policy levels. I welcome the opportunity to comment on the dire public policy environment we now confront.

The original work did not materialize out of thin air. Rather, the birth of my professional memoir was the result of a rather fascinating gestation period. Over the Memorial Day weekend in May of 2009, Peace Corps (PC) volunteers from what was known as the India-44 group gathered in Oakland, California. It was the fortieth anniversary of our return home from service in either Rajasthan or Maharashtra, two provinces located in the western part of India. Whatever our expectations might have been, the reality of the get together proved remarkably personal and rewarding.

This sharing of experiences and feelings evoked memories and emotions long muted by time and the demands of our frantic lives. Those of us who wished would put thoughts and reflections to paper—what brought us to Peace Corps; what we experienced during training and service; how those experiences shaped our subsequent life; and what those subsequent lives looked like. These reflections served as a kind of palimpsest that uncovered a deeper set of memories for me and the others. Each specific recollection serving as a source for images and feelings long buried under the detritus of a life long-lived, if not well-lived.

Then it hit me. With a modest, or not so modest, expansion of effort and a slight alteration of focus, my India reflections could serve as inspiration for Tom's scintillating story as a policy guru or, as I prefer to say, a policy wonk. Such a narrative would surely compete on any futility scale with my fanciful efforts to single-handedly turn India into a developed country way back in the 1960s. With the right marketing, I might be able to hawk this rendition of my professional experiences to the Pentagon, perhaps as an insidious instrument of torture. Employed with sufficient care, my years in the trenches might replace the infamous waterboarding technique that fell into such disrepute after Vice President Cheney left office.

I often have ideas, however, which excite me in the moment, yet never see the light of day. Perhaps this vision would be another of those. I was blessed, though, when a couple of people inadvertently pushed me along. One was Michael Simonds, one of my Peace Corps colleagues who helped in developing the two volumes capturing our experiences in India. Michael also wrote a set of personal reflections, one based on his triumphs and tragedies (mostly the latter, in his view) with the women he met through online dating services after his divorce. He asked me to read an early draft, which I found moving, sometimes sad, occasionally humorous, but always entertaining. *This is good stuff,* I thought.

Besides, I am eternally grateful for the way Michael pictured me in a chapter of his draft that went all the way back to our final Peace Corps days. He apparently despaired of lucking out with some of the PC gals at a final "going home" party in New Delhi. Unbelievably, he feared competition from me for the affections of the young ladies. He went on to describe me as "tall and dark, with the rugged good looks of someone who could adorn the cover of a romance novel." Of course, this was just hours before it was discovered that he had a detached retina and was whisked off to a U.S. military base in Germany for emergency eye surgery.

But the specific origins for this tale of woe may well go back further, to the early days of this century. I was headed to Washington, D.C. for a National Governors Association meeting. At the airport, I ran into the woman who headed the highly touted welfare reform program in Wisconsin known as W-2 or "Wisconsin Works." Jennifer Noyes had formerly been a policy advisor to Governor Tommy Thompson who, at the time of this trip, was serving as Secretary of Health and Human Services under

President George W. Bush. I was then the Associate Director of the Institute for Research on Poverty at the University of Wisconsin. Now, Secretary Thompson, the former Governor of Wisconsin, did not like the Institute. He did not like me. By extension, Jennifer was required to dislike me as well. But, since we were headed to the same destination, we struck up a conversation.

This turned out to be the trip from hell though not because she and I found ourselves traveling together, at least not on my part. Cancelled flights, bus trips from Madison to Milwaukee, sitting on the tarmac waiting for the weather to clear for what seemed like days, and sundry other hurdles turned a four-hour trip into a twelve-plus-hour ordeal. To avoid talking about welfare, politics, or other sensitive subjects, I regaled her with stories of my life. After all, my life just happens to be one of my favorite topics.

By the time we reached the Washington hotel at 3:00 AM or so, she was in desperate straits. Importantly, she had agreed to help repair the State's relationship with the Institute (well, not quite true just yet) and to give me her firstborn, anything to avoid hearing any more about Tom's early years. I was struck with an insight at that very moment. The power of an excruciatingly boring story cannot be overestimated. Exposed to endless repetitions of my life, I suspect even Sarah Palin would break down and willingly sign on as an Obamacare fan.

As much fun as it might be to torture others, there are more defensible reasons for setting down my recollections. My story, if truth be told, is not terribly unusual or dramatic. Variants of my journey from an ethnic working-class childhood to modest success as a policy wonk, and even some limited success as an academic, is neither exciting nor remarkable. Countless others have tread down similar paths. And yet, each of us, no matter how humble or unremarkable, has a story to tell. Each life contains moments of drama, despair, joy, sadness, triumph, failure, roads that should not have been taken, and redemptive moments that, on occasion, set things right. Looking back, even my ordinary tale has all these elements.

I also came to realize that if my memories are not retrieved and recorded, they will soon surely be lost. Clearly, no one else will document my journey through life, neither for commercial gain since there would not be any, nor for historical justification since not that much of note occurred.

And so, it is up to me to set my story down before all is lost amidst cognitive decay and mental confusion. This narrative, in effect, serves as my personal journey through a series of social policy challenges that dominated the past half century or so of our political history. It encompasses such topics as poverty, welfare reform, and the growing inequality in social opportunities.

I do not cover everything. That would be too daunting, and even I can take pity on others. But this work does touch upon many of the highlights and lowlights which I have shared with others verbally when necessity required that they endure my company.

You will soon understand why I have so few friends. The chapters that follow permit the reader to journey through what I often call my policy candy store. I characterize my professional career as such because, despite everything, it was a pure delight and a joy to experience. This remained true despite the many frustrations, the failures, and the grueling hours.

There were many nooks and crannies in my professional candy store and I get to many of them. In addition, I do spend time talking about my ill-fated tenure as a wayward academic which I touch upon obliquely toward the end, but which remained an irresolvable tension throughout my career. For the most part, I tried to focus on those topics representing the more thematic and substantive narratives of my career as a policy wonk. More to the point, these issues are the inspiration for much that I have learned about doing public policy and about the joys attached to such professional pursuits.

I typically start a narrative about one of my topical themes with the phrase, "I am reminded of the time that my phone rang" or "I saw a message" or something similar that would alter the trajectory of my professional life. The course of my professional life owes much to fortune and serendipity. In short, I have been very fortunate to stumble upon some of the biggest social policy issues of the past four-plus decades, largely without any forethought whatsoever. It was as if some invisible hand were guiding my career. Perhaps this serendipity has something to do with the luck of the Irish, though it could be argued that, in truth, this just might be more of a curse?

In all honesty, I am not the brightest bulb on the marquee. Still, even I eventually realized that I was blessed with a few gifts. I could sit among diverse audiences, whether government officials or academic types or social workers or think tankers or ordinary folk and really feel the contours of the dialogue about me. I could quickly drive to the core of what was being said, often weaving a central story out of diverse and seemingly unrelated threads. I could conceptualize a pattern out of the separate strands of complex narratives, sometimes in ways that took the conversation in an unexpected direction. At some point, I realized that many people, including prominent academics and key public officials, listened to what I had to say. I had come a long way from my rough-and-tumble working class origins.

It is a good thing I had such skills since I had few others. If I were required to make my way through life doing real work, it would have been a pitiful sight indeed. I have often felt like one of those scribes in ancient Egypt, scribbling testimonies all day to inflate some Pharaoh's ego. Like those ancient scribes, my work was inconsequential. Still, it kept me occupied and sufficiently busy to keep me from doing real harm in the world. Surely, had I been born into an earlier era, I would have starved had I been required to till a field or build a pyramid. And heaven forbid that I would be expected to go into battle for the Pharaoh. That would be a short-lived endeavor as demonstrated by the gaping wound in my back suffered as I ran from the battlefield in total panic.

Obviously, you do not need to be a genius to contribute to the policy world. I am exhibit one! Still, in my experience, a lot of young promising policy types shy away from the challenges because they assume that doing policy is terribly arcane and technical and thus will be as boring as waiting for paint to dry or watching a lopsided curling match. Let me say from the outset that this book should paint a very different picture of what policy is all about, a picture that stresses the human element in the exercise of the policy arts.

I think doing policy should be fun. I believe whatever we do in life should be fun. Otherwise, it would be work, a terrible four-letter word. I warn you now that my better half has spent our married life trying to beat the wit out of me to no avail. If someone asks me whether I need help with my bag upon entering an upscale hotel with my spouse, I am likely to respond with "no, thanks, my wife is capable of getting up to the room by herself." Or when the waiter asks where I would prefer to sit, my likely response is, "Today, I think I will try a chair." There is no off-switch. Wit or no, I find it difficult to imagine going through life without finding some humor even in very serious situations. If we do not laugh, we just might cry.

Throughout this book, I wax exuberantly on the joys and rewards of doing policy work. True enough, my love for the policy arts is, in my mind, warranted and justified. Still, let me end this introductory essay with a confession. If my first love was not being a conventional academic, and it wasn't, it probably does not lie in being a policy wonk either. As I look back over a long life, I see more clearly that my passion was in self-expression, the act of writing. This is what I wanted to do as a young lad. While my working-class delinquent friends dreamed of being cowboys or athletes, I fantasized about being the next Hemingway or Joyce. I was an oddball right from the get-go.

Discretion prevailed, though, and I decided that a paid job as an academic would guarantee three squares a day and a roof over my head. I do like to eat. Besides, pretending to be an academic meant I could pretty much do what I wanted. What freedom! Moreover, I never got past my amazement that someone would pay you, with real money, for having fun struggling with society's more intractable problems. Who would have thought? Doing policy mostly has been a joy, even with the impossible impediments, the brutal hours, and the tensions that interfered with sound sleep. I recall jolting awake before dawn most mornings, worried about being behind in everything. I recoil with horror at those Friday evenings getting stuck in O'Hare airport on my way back to Madison. I still relive the many failures and frustrations as the best of intentions went unrealized. In the end, none of that seems to matter.

Longevity and experience as a policy wonk has brought home one lesson about finding one's way in life. I recently had lunch with my cousin who has two grand-daughters. Her eldest takes after her grandfather, Jack, who loved mathematics and computers, and who self-taught himself the early computer language, Fortran, when he was a high school teacher in the early 1960s. As computers spread, he had rare skills and was hired to teach the subject at a local college. On the other hand, the younger grand-daughter takes after my cousin who is an avid reader. My cousin even reads all my works but, like me, can barely operate a smart phone.

Guess what? The elder grand-daughter went to a very good technical college and is a successful engineer in Boston. The younger offspring, who responded enthusiastically to the writing muse, attended an excellent liberal arts college and now works for a New York publishing house. I am convinced the genetic dispositions of each parent is reflected separately in their two grand-children. This vignette suggests to me that we each possess a niche that is within us from the moment of conception. The trick is to figure out what it is and where we belong. Since my retirement from policy work and the academic world, I have gone back to my abandoned first love. The lesson I have fully embraced is to never forget about those inner muses. Find them, even if later in life when you are one short step from the nursing home.

Tom Corbett
Madison Wisconsin
June 2018

CHAPTER 1

A CANDY STORE

Success is going from failure to failure
without losing your enthusiasm.
—Winston Churchill

I will be very direct. This chapter, this book in fact, is not about any candy store, which is a labored metaphor designed to capture the fun I had during my policy career. Rather, these pages embrace selected recollections touching upon my struggles and joys as a rather addicted policy wonk. In the subsequent chapters, the reader is taken on a compelling, often witty, journey as I grappled with some of the more challenging policy issues of the past few decades—poverty, welfare reform, and our efforts to create a more just and workable society. While those issues are deadly serious, my efforts to address them often were futile and quite inept. Not surprisingly, my bumblings about the policy world afford me a rich vein of needed humor and comic relief, a needed antidote when one continuously butts his head against impossible social challenges.

Best of all, it is a journey that takes you directly into the trenches of doing policy. So, if you have ever wondered what it might be like to do public policy from an insider's perspective, or at least close to the inside, keep reading. This will get you as close as you are likely to get without getting your hands dirty, soiling yourself, or perhaps experiencing irritating bouts of nausea.

My hapless journey takes you along into the heart of those complex and contentious policy challenges that defy easy answers, and which often generate heated ideological and partisan passions. Because of this, or perhaps despite this, each of these societal problems has become a treasured counter in my metaphorical sweets shop. Thus, any trip through my allegorical confectionary business can be dramatic, stimulating, humorous, seductive, frustrating, and hopefully rewarding at times. From my perspective, it was a heck of a journey, and a wonderful place to browse around for unforgettable memories. The best thing is that no calories are involved, a good thing since I already have consumed far more than my lifetime quota.

Let me start the journey rather late in my career. The phone in my University of Wisconsin office rang one day, in the latter part of the 1990s. The voice on the other end asked if I would come to a significant national event to be held in Chicago. Would I be willing to participate in something called an electronic focus group comprised of various national welfare experts and officials?

As a "reward," I would get special seating for a "town hall" meeting featuring President William Jefferson Clinton.

I waffled. I was getting so many requests to give talks, participate on panels, or consult on policy issues that my daily rounds of teaching, research, consulting, and administration often suffered. In the end, though, I relented. The university-based research institute I helped manage at the time needed public exposure to keep needed resources flowing. So, perhaps I could accommodate them. That was a weakness of mine, having trouble saying no—squeezing in just one more event. Besides, they would pay the bill and I liked Navy Pier, the site of this big event.

I was never quite sure how some of these calls came my way in the first place. Oh sure, most callers were members of a familiar crowd. They were the academics, think tank scholars, government officials, philanthropists, evaluation firm experts, social welfare trade organization types, advocacy group representatives, and media folk that were bound together by an interest in poverty and social welfare. I would repeatedly run into such folk at conferences and workshops and meetings and other such venues. Some I had worked rather closely with over time. Others were simply familiar faces in a crowd that toiled in the welfare war trenches.

Some calls, though, left me perplexed. How did such and such a person find me? I never thought of myself as famous or noteworthy. I was rather a failure as a conventional scholar and never much of a traditional researcher. Yet, the calls kept coming to give talks, attend workshops, consult, or provide comment to media types. When the national newspaper, *U.S.A. Today*, had a series called "know your expert" where they highlighted one so-called expert from various fields, they selected me as the national welfare and poverty specialist. They did a full article on me with a picture and all. I mean, we are talking *U.S.A. Today*, a publication read in more bathrooms around the country than any other newspaper. How in the world did they find me? Even more perplexing is why they selected me. Most of my colleagues were even more perplexed than I.

So, off to Chicago it was. The high-tech focus group was fun, though the purpose eluded me even after it was finished. After an informal chat with the economics editor for the *New York Times*, who had earned his doctorate at MIT and wanted to chat about a prior colleague of mine, Sheldon Danziger (also an MIT grad), an event official approached me. She handed me a special badge for the following days' big event. "Thanks for helping us out," she said, "and don't forget to wear this badge to the town hall meeting tomorrow morning." "Sure," I responded, and gave the matter not a second thought, stuffing her offering in my pocket.

And so, I arrived at the big "town hall" session the next day, the highlight of the conference. I was stunned at the size of the crowd. Welfare, and its reform, was big business in the 1990s and the President was clearly a draw. Still, I was used to conference crowds in the dozens or hundreds at best, not the thousand or two that had gathered in Chicago. When I reached the first security checkpoint, they glanced at my badge and waived me on. I got to the second, and then the third checkpoint, each time I was waived on. Then I get to the stage. *Surely, I will be stopped at this point,* I thought. But no! "Dr. Corbett, please take one of the chairs on the stage." *Oh snap,* I thought, *I would have worn clean underwear if I knew I would be this close to the President.*

And so, one fine day in the late 1990s, I found myself on a stage in a large conference hall at Navy Pier in Chicago. With me on that stage were, among others, President Clinton, a few Fortune 500 CEOs, and a few former welfare recipients who were now successful members of the workforce. The event was a major celebration of the welfare reform legislation passed in 1996 that created TANF, the Temporary Assistance to Needy Families program. The purpose of the legislation was to move those nondisabled adults thought to be dependent on cash assistance into the workforce. This event was to celebrate how well the law was working. Thus, we had the Fortune 500 CEOs and the exemplar former recipients who went from abject dependency to regional VP of marketing in some major corporation, all in less than six months. The audience loved the rags-to-riches stories. It was like one of those old-style revival meetings where the lost sinners were being saved to the exuberant huzzahs of the true believers.

I can still remember shaking Clinton's hand as he looked directly at me. What should I say? Perhaps I should mention the role I played in developing his welfare reform bill, the one that never made it out of committee. Or perhaps I should plug my research institute, which received considerable federal funding. Surely, I can mention how the governor of my home state (a Republican who often challenged the President on his approach to reform) had also publicly attacked me on occasion for being a total numbnuts on welfare issues, and for not always supporting his own approach to reform. Surely, we can bond over this common antagonist. But like so many others before me, I stood mute, a state that many colleagues had longed hope might become my permanent condition.

Years later, after my retirement, my next-door neighbor told me he was going to an event in New York, where he would meet former President Clinton. Jokingly, I told him to give Bill my regards. I was jesting since the Big Guy could not possibly have any idea regarding who the hell I was. After all, I only met him one other time. That was during my year-long sabbatical of sorts in the Department of Health and Human Services (HHS) while working on his welfare reform legislation. The meeting was in a very large group setting, where my only notoriety was setting off the security device several times while trying to enter the room. I was almost down to my BVDs before I made it through.

Anyway, my neighbor returned from his New York soiree to insist that Bill, indeed, did remember me from those days. I scoffed, concluding that the former President is just a smooth politician who tells people whatever they might want to hear. But you never know, a fair amount of my work, and even my actual language, made it into the final version of the President's welfare proposal as submitted to Congress in 1994. Moreover, his memory is the stuff of legend. I think I will go with the totally unlikely story that he did recall me.

Later in the town hall meeting, many of the attending academics, researchers, policy wonks, and public officials whom I knew from various prior projects wandered up to ask, "How did you get up on the stage?" I could hear the unstated query, "When did you get so important?" *Good questions,* I thought. As a kid, there was no promise of anything other than a most ordinary life for me. I grew up in a working-class neighborhood; spending my early years hanging around street corners with dissolute buddies clearly headed, I thought at the time, for the same kind of nondescript life as I. Now that I think on it, it is where most of them ended up.

Perhaps part of the motivation for putting all this down on paper is to figure out how I managed to get on that stage. Just how did I become one of those policy wonks? Surely, my only accomplishments from that most ordinary of childhoods was to stay out of juvenile hall. There was nothing, absolutely nothing, to suggest a professional tenure among the better social policy minds of my generation. Surely, it was never part of any plan. I grew up simply hoping to find some way to support myself that did not involve heavy lifting or an extended prison term.

Yet, there is another, more compelling, motivation for this rehashing of my professional life. It goes back to the many years I spent teaching policy courses to eager (and not so eager) students at the University of Wisconsin. Some of those students kept raising questions that have stayed with me to this day. Perhaps it is time that I answer them . . . better late than never.

The 600-level Social Work course that I taught for many years was what we called a practicum experience for advanced graduate students interested in doing policy work from a social work perspective. Permit me to make a brief distinction between the acts of doing policy and studying policy. You typically attack the latter challenge through a rigorous curriculum of course work and readings and mathematical exercises. You are expected to absorb a large amount of information on programs and policies designed to help people, and to develop a command of technical skills designed to carry out rigorous analyses of issues and policy options. You study policy to become a better technician.

Doing policy is somewhat different. I am reminded of a sociology professor way back in college who kept insisting that all of us students should be "doing" sociology. I thought that a stretch, but doing policy makes more sense. Here, you want to help nurture or learn a set of skills and attitudes that make you an effective player in the larger policy arena. These skills and dispositions are less precise than the microeconomics and benefit-cost analysis skills that technical policy folk master. But they are so very important for engaging what we call "wicked" policy issues where disputes over ends, theories, design, and evidence are severe and clouded by competing values and ideologies.

The "doing" policy skills include things like listening well, interpreting what is going on around you, integrating diverse and seemingly unrelated facts into meaningful wholes, and communicating well with others. You must see issues and interactions in a larger frame of reference, not just how something affects a single family, but how aggregates of families are affected by society's rules and protocols. You must be able to absorb arguments that challenge your belief system with a modicum of grace, and to debate points in ways that suggest respect for the positions of others. In short, you must be a special kind of person, whose core attributes I will describe more fully later.

Each second year Social Work masters student interested in doing policy was placed in what was called a practice internship with real policymakers. In such a setting, they hopefully would experience policy work at the ground level. Their real-world practice experience was supported by weekly group meetings where I would astound them with my brilliant insights on a range of related topics. Well, that is my story, at least, and I am sticking with it. It was a small group (eight to fourteen students), and I would have them for a full academic year . . . great fun, for me at least.

So, each September, a small band of intrepid second year masters students would troop into my office with various degrees of conviction. They faced a big decision—their choice of a second year "concentration." In effect, they were facing that terrible decision each of us has faced at some point in our life—what do we want to do, and be, when we grow up? I myself plan on tackling that question next month, if I am not too pooped by then.

In many ways, this choice was much like a medical student deciding on whether to be a brain surgeon or a urologist—the decision to focus on the body's central processing unit, or its internal plumbing. This decision, whether made by a future doctor or social worker, could well decide their future as a professional. Social workers selecting a policy practicum over more conventional choices such as personal counseling or child welfare, signaled their disciplinary interest in a way that would likely narrow future career prospects. Policy was a choice for the intrepid few.

For virtually all aspiring social workers, counseling various angst-ridden middle-class clients or perhaps aspiring juvenile delinquents, proved more appealing than tackling seemingly intractable and abstract issues such as poverty, social dysfunction, and political paralysis. Besides, any expression of interest in policy would be met with incredulity by several members of the social work faculty of that era. Students told me that some responded to their interest in policy by asking, "Tell me again why you don't want to be a real social worker?" Fortunately, most remained undaunted by such expressions of ill-disguised contempt.

Some of these policy wannabes were the "I want to change the world" types. Those already committed to righting wrongs, to tilting their unbounded reservoirs of optimism at various societal windmills. But most were far less certain or committed. What is social policy? What would I do? Can I learn to do this stuff? Could I get a job, really? I want to make a difference, but isn't it all hopeless anyway? Isn't doing this stuff very mysterious and complicated? But policy is all about boring numbers and such, wouldn't I be happier working with real people? And then they would circle back to the most pressing concern of all, what kind of job could I possibly get? Such questions and concerns would go on in one form or another, but you get the drift.

Whatever I told them must have been somewhat convincing since virtually all eventually signed on. I can yet recall some of my spiel. I would talk about the need for smart, tough people willing to take on the critical macro issues of the day. I would remind them of the historic role that social work once played in rectifying social wrongs. Surely, they remember Jane Adams. And did they ever hear of Harry Hopkins, the social worker who lived in the White House while helping President Franklin Delano Roosevelt pull the country out of the Great Depression?

I might even touch upon an embarrassment or two for the discipline. There was the time President John Kennedy called on social work and social workers to tackle what was perceived as an emerging welfare crisis in the early 1960s. It was an assignment that, within a fairly short time, the profession would abandon to the dismal science of economics and to those dry, humorless economists, a disciplinary retreat to be regretted for sure. At some point, I would resort to the ever-handy metaphor about whether it was better to pluck endangered individuals from the raging river one by one and/or head upstream to curb the river's tempest in the first instance.

I would typically end with a challenge, "If not you, then who? Surely not those heartless economists!" Now, I feel comfortably denigrating acolytes of this dismal science, since many of my professional colleagues were trained as economists. In the academy, they typically were my closest colleagues even though my doctorate was in Social Welfare, the advanced degree in Social Work, and I was attached to the School of Social Work in my awkward and futile attempt to play at being an academic. In fact, I worked so closely with economists that I picked up quite a bit of their world view and their everyday vernacular. Many from outside the university assumed I was a devotee of the dismal science, until I set them straight.

Despite my playful comments about them, most economists I worked with ranged from damn smart to outright brilliant. But as a group, they did have one or two rather annoying traits—they took themselves way too seriously and tended to look at things from an overly narrow perspective. All that mattered was costs and benefits and incentives all expressed through the metric of money. All our understanding of issues was to be pursued through sophisticated, quantitative techniques. Thomas Picketty, the acclaimed economist put it this way in his highly regarded book on inequality:

> To put it bluntly, the discipline of economics has yet to get over its childish passion for mathematics and for purely theoretical and often highly ideological speculation, at the expense of historical research and collaboration with the other social sciences. Economists are all too often preoccupied with petty mathematical problems of interest to themselves. This obsession with mathematics is an easy way of acquiring the appearance of scientificity (sic) without having to answer the more complex questions posed by the world we live in .

But I digress! There were times, after these young students left my office full of newly found conviction and purpose, that I would sink into a shallow pool of guilt and remorse—a dark pool well-known to those of Irish persuasion. I am reminded of an aphorism attributed to Dave Powers, a member of the Irish Mafia that counseled President Kennedy. It went something like this, "We Irish know we must pay for any good we experience, we just don't know when the price is to be paid."

Was I a snake oil salesman? Would these students one day return to sue me for ruining their lives? After all, I knew just how demanding and difficult the challenge of achieving policy goals can be. I was fully aware of how intractable most social problems remained. So why did I continue urging them on? Then I would calm myself. My culpability likely was limited. To win a lawsuit, they would probably have to establish malicious intent on my part. In truth, I was not exactly evil, just a little misguided.

In a weak, pre-emptive strike against the inevitable guilt that would follow, I would touch upon the difficulties they would face. Doing policy was often a marathon, not a sprint. Success was often hard to identify, never mind achieve. I would warn that right and wrong often blurred in indefinable ways, that tradeoffs were everywhere, and that it was almost a certainty that new policies and programs would involve losers as well as winners. Victory was seldom clean and neat, if it could be achieved at all. Purveyors of the policy arts must be prepared for a life of partial successes at best.

I would even suggest that their emotional experience of the coming year would be curvilinear. They would start out with enthusiasm and commitment. That upbeat period would slowly erode as they confronted the glacial speed at which policy often occurs, the paralysis imposed by political or ideological confrontations, and the sheer difficulty of deciding what is right and wrong in many situations. Even when you have the problem correctly identified, it is not always obvious what to do about it. Still, these caveats often struck me as insufficient.

I would sometimes sit in my office and ponder the following: knowing what I knew by that time in my career, would I do it over again? If I were facing the choice that these students were, would I now say, "Thanks, but no thanks . . . I think I will see what they are offering down the hall." After all, doing policy was not only challenging, it was exhausting. Victories typically were uncertain, opaque, and ephemeral. The policy wars seemed interminable and intractable. Bottom line, doing policy was hard and frustrating work. For the most wicked of problems, there never seemed to be an ultimate solution.

And when you add the fact that I was trying to be both an academic and a policy wonk at the same time, the challenge of being a policy wonk struck me as exhausting and overwhelming. I can recall, one year, when I was the associate director of the Institute for Research on Poverty (IRP), a major research unit at the University of Wisconsin-Madison. I also was carrying what was considered a full-time teaching load, was the principle investigator on several projects, and had a full schedule of talks and presentations to make across the country. Some of the additional burdens during that period could be attributed to the fact that IRP was in danger of losing its federal support. In response, I accepted more opportunities to give talks than I typically might to keep the institute visible nationally, particularly in Washington.

In addition, I was playing at being an assistant professor of social work, which meant accommodating the demands of an academic department, including those interminable faculty meetings and committee responsibilities. In retrospect, it probably was the equivalent of at least two full-time positions or more—an impossible schedule even for one with ambition and clear professional goals, which certainly was not me. While that year was a bit of an outlier, it was close to the norm in the latter part of my career. Most years were zany and taxing in one way or another.

It got so bad that I had no time to prepare for talks or class lectures. Hell, I hardly had time to take care of my bodily functions. Since this was back in the days when transparencies were still used, I gradually collected a large file of these useful aids covering a variety of social policy topics. I would start preparing for most off-site presentations when I boarded the plane to wherever the event was located. First, I would recheck what kind of talk I was supposed to give. Next, I would sort through my pile of transparencies, select a subset, and begin organizing that subset into a sequence that might conceivably serve as a coherent narrative. Then, I would cross my fingers, hoping the talk would be reasonably on target and good enough to fool the audience that my story line was relevant.

For years, I had a recurring nightmare that I would be introduced by a conference moderator as an expert on toxic waste disposal or some other equally exotic topic I knew nothing about. But who knows, perhaps being thought of as a so-called expert gives you an inherent comparative advantage. You know, the audience would think, "Gee, this sounds like total bull-hockey, but the guy must know what he is talking about since he is an expert." In any case, I would stand before those assembled, say a brief prayer to a deity I assumed had long since given up on me, and then wing it. It must have worked since invitations kept on coming.

Often, on the return flight, I would turn to an upcoming class lecture, one of which (a Program Evaluation course for Public Policy masters students) was a new course for me. Thus, I could not just slide through on the previous year's notes. Way too often, there was simply no time to get ready for the upcoming lecture. I would kid myself that, if needed, there would always be a spare hour or two to prepare right before the appointed hour. That anticipated opportunity inevitably would slip away as unavoidable phone calls, administrative crisis, and unexpected project-related demands intruded. At the last minute, I would panic and jot down a few basic thoughts before bracing myself for a room full of expectant students. Disaster stared me in the face.

What a fraud, I thought to myself, *surely, they will sue to get their money back or mercifully stone me with their textbooks to escape this misery.* Ironically, however, I often sensed I did better on those days when I was least prepared. The lecture seemed to flow effortlessly. I could always call on my limitless supply of personal and professional vignettes to fill in the silences, many of these stories you will have an opportunity to suffer through in subsequent chapters.

Such a frantic life is not enjoyed without some cost, however. One fine day during this period, I noticed several of those yellow slips used back then in my mailbox. They contained increasingly frantic notes to contact my doctor whom I had seen the day before for a routine exam. *Wow, this looks serious,* I thought, *perhaps I have a half hour to live.* When I called his office, he was home for lunch, but had left a message for me to call him there. *Oh shit,* I thought, *perhaps I only had a few minutes left.* Turns out there were anomalies in my EKG and he wanted me checked out by a cardiac specialist at the university hospital right away, even before getting on a plane for my next D.C. trip that was coming up, a fact that somehow had come up as we chatted.

After getting the Cadillac of cardiac exams by the top heart man at University Hospital, he sat me down to ask about my work and my lifestyle. Then, he gave me the lecture. Ever get the lecture? It is about getting priorities straight and scaling back. Time to think about my health and not what I falsely thought was important. No one is as important, nor as essential, as they believe they are. He told me he had reached the same conclusion about his own career. He had started to find a heathier balance in his life.

Though I assume he was right, I pretty much ignored him. If you have not already, you will soon conclude that I am not too bright. I would still get on planes to fly around the country to knock my head repeatedly against a figurative wall composed of impossible policy questions. Fortunately, I escaped all subsequent medical catastrophes. In addition, I am happy to report that no student ever sued me for dereliction as an instructor. More amazingly, I can't even recall any (well, not many at least) complaints. A declining memory can be a blessing. In fact, the opposite occurred. I recall one public policy student from the LaFollette School who later held a congressional staff position in Washington D.C. She told Health and Human Services (HHS) officials, with whom I worked closely with, that I was the best professor she had at Wisconsin. My friends in HHS were incredulous. So was I.

I cannot forget one undergraduate student who constantly complained about my 'Intro to Social Policy' course, how demanding it was, and about how much she had to study for it. She appeared sufficiently stressed that I considered getting her some counseling. Her name stuck with me back then, at least, a very rare occurrence. Perhaps I feared one day coming across an article saying a certain young student had jumped to her death in despair over this course taught by some diabolical, uncaring professor.

At a conference several years in the future, an economics professor from Johns Hopkins University asked me if I recalled a certain student. It was her. It turned out that he was her stepfather. I winced, thinking that he would next tell me she had been in therapy for the intervening decade or so and that I had ruined her life. This revelation would be followed by a demand that I pay the full cost of her rehabilitation. But no! To my amazement, he went on about how much she loved my course and, amazingly, that she had kept her class notes from those many years ago. Again, go figure!

I have always been shocked by unexpected feedback coming directly from former students. Years after being in my class, one masters-level social work student emailed the following:

I remembered thinking, when you described your convictions and philosophy in seminar, that those ideas were something I would aspire to. It made me so much intellectual, spiritual, and emotional sense. It makes the same sense today and I am proud that they have become my heartfelt convictions and philosophy. You made and continue to make a difference in my life and worldview every day . . .

At the time, I thought I was failing them miserably, mostly because I felt I was doing everything haphazardly, and on the run. But eventually, I realized something. You never really know what kind of impact you are having. Those undergraduates apparently asleep in the back rows might well have been absorbing my brilliance, at least that is the story I am sticking with. The comatose figures slumped over their desks, whose inert forms had me on the verge of calling in EMTs to check for signs of clinical life, might really have been in the throes of inspiration. Not bloody likely, but you never really know. Guess what, the same is true for doing social policy. You seldom can measure your impact in any visible manner. You might make a point, perform an act, or develop a proposal that might change the course of a debate or the character of a decision, a small step toward significant effects down the line. You just never know.

It was also during this period that many of my more treasured policy initiatives were languishing. The ideological and political winds had begun to blow in a different direction. The governor of Wisconsin at the time, renowned welfare reformer Tommy Thompson, attacked me in a public forum in Chicago because, I suspect, some of the many interviews I gave to the media seemed critical of his reform efforts, at least in his eyes. Even more depressing, a working relationship I had painstakingly helped develop between the Institute for Research on Poverty at UW and the state of Wisconsin was on life support, and in danger of totally falling apart.

Worse, the Institute for Research on Poverty (IRP), where I served as associate director at the time, was in crisis. IRP had been a federally funded, university-based research entity since the onset of the War-On-Poverty (WOP) in the mid-sixties. Over the subsequent three decades, it had generated full-throated and sophisticated research and analysis agenda as well as trained or supported a generation or two of talented researchers.

Once, when I testified before U.S. Senator Daniel Patrick Moynihan, the avuncular and sometime irascible welfare expert in Congress, he noticed that I was from the institute. He announced to those assembled that IRP was just about the best thing that had come out of President Johnson's WOP. But now, in the mid-nineties, possibly because of the personal animus of one external reviewer of the institute's refunding proposal, IRP tottered on the verge of extinction.

Those, indeed, were trying times. Most mornings, I would spring awake at 4:00 AM, only to be met by overpowering feelings of dread and anxiety. Too many Friday nights I would be stuck in O'Hare airport—surely the armpit of the American air transportation system—waiting for a connecting flight to Madison, Wisconsin, amid a milling mob of weary and anguished travelers. I could never escape the feeling of being behind, the specter of never being able to catch up, the sense that doom and failure were everywhere. The policy headwinds were pushing against me and threatening much of what I had worked on over the prior two decades. My Irish sense of perpetual gloom surely was in full bloom during those days.

Where was the fun in this? I often asked myself. I recall watching as my parents labored at real jobs in dirty, dangerous pre-OSHA factories, or waited on tables for crabby patrons. Their experiences taught me an invaluable life lesson—never take a real job, particularly one involving heavy lifting. Early on, I devoted myself to avoiding such a fate. Now, however, I began fantasizing about jobs like roofing houses, tilling fields, life on the road as a long-haul truck driver, or perhaps doing some mindless, repetitive task on an assembly line. Maybe I could work the night shift in one of those highway tollbooths. That seemed mindless enough that even I could handle it. *Damn,* I thought to myself back then, *if I had been smarter as a kid, I could have had a career doing a job with real value to America, like serving up ice cream cones at Dairy Queen.*

And yet, here I was, hawking a career of doing social policy to impressionable young students who really could not be expected to know any better. Was I a sadist, a perverse ghoul? I don't recall wandering around my neighborhood as a young boy, pulling the wings off butterflies, and kicking stray dogs. Perhaps I had repressed those memories. At a minimum, I could not escape the sense that my efforts to pimp social policy careers would make me guilty of malicious indifference to human happiness.

And yet, at the end of the day, I had to admit that I loved it all. Despite all these downsides, the pervasive sense of not doing enough and surely not doing it well, I did love it. Have I ever told you I loved doing social policy work? What I probably enjoyed most was flying around the country to work with the best and the brightest from academia, research firms, think tanks, the philanthropic community, the government at all levels of authority from local sites to Washington, D.C., and from human service providers of all stripes. With these bright and talented men and women, I was fortunate enough to engage many of the most vexing social issues of my generation, and at a time when these issues also consumed national attention and concern.

Given that I was considered an expert of some sort, I always had access to the newest ideas and reform initiatives. This enabled me to see change as it happened; up close and personal, as they say. I could always keep abreast of what was happening in the social policy world on a real time basis. Not bad for a kid from a lower income working-class family, whose parents' fondest hope was that I stay out of jail, at least until I was old enough that they could legally boot me out the door.

One set of questions from my social work students would stump me more than the others. It usually went something like this: What does it take to do policy? I know so little, so how can I do something like that? I mean, really, isn't it all about numbers and boring technical stuff and incomprehensible mathematics? What kind of person do you have to be to do this crap well? And the final kicker went something like this: Do I really have what it takes?

I never knew what to say at this point. Any reasonably intelligent person can learn the technical tools associated with doing policy work, though some of the advanced estimation techniques are daunting indeed. With some diligence, you can absorb the skills essential to creating data sets, drilling down into those data to elicit useful information, developing policy alternatives, advocating for specific options, and implementing or managing those new policies and programs. But it is quite another thing to do the more subtle and demanding aspects of policy work. That takes place on a different level.

I discovered that you could always find others to do the boring technical work. Doing policy in a more complete sense, however, involves many subtle human qualities and capacities not always present in those pursuing this avocation. You must possess a capacity to work well with people of diverse backgrounds and perspectives. You should be able to engage in what we think of as lateral thinking, where you integrate seemingly disconnected facts in new or clever ways. You must stay with the course when all seems desperate and lost. And there are other demands!

I believe you need a set of softer skills and personal strengths since doing policy in the real world is a bit like going to war. Often, there is a fog of confusion and a distinct sense of conflict. In the real-world values and interests clash, ends are difficult to agree upon, and competing theories of how the world operates confuse even well-meaning observers. Data can be manipulated and massaged to defend numerous conclusions. Values and ideology subvert rational discourse. Power trumps the public good. In effect, the most interesting policy challenges can be thought of as "wicked social problems." They defy easy solution.

It took me a long time before I realized I could do policy well, even without the advanced technical skills. It took me even longer to understand that I brought something essential and unique to the policy table. It took me a lifetime to comprehend the nature of the less obvious attributes and skills that are essential to taking on society's more wicked problems at an advanced level. Want to know what they are? Well, you will have to read the whole book before I tell you. One teaser attribute I will reveal now is that you must be just a bit of a masochist. As I have said, doing this stuff is damn hard.

I am reminded of the scene from the movie *A League of Their Own,* a delightful movie about a professional girl's baseball league that was created during World War II when there was a danger that men's baseball might be closed for the duration of the conflict. The scene in question involves the character played by Geena Davis, who was the star of the team managed by Tom Hanks. When her wounded husband returned from the war, she decides to leave the team just before the start of the new league's playoff series.

Jimmy, the Hanks character, tries to change her mind. "Baseball is what gets inside you. It's what lights you up, you can't deny that."

"It just got too hard," Dottie, the Davis character, responds.

Jimmy glowers for a moment before spitting out a memorable line. "Baseball . . . is supposed to be hard. If it wasn't hard, everyone would do it. It is the hard that makes it great."

Similarly, it is the very fact that doing policy well is hard is what makes it worth doing. It also means that not everyone can do it, at least not well. I would look at the (mostly) young students across from me, looking so earnest yet uncertain. Who could tell if they had the right stuff? Not me. So, I would typically end my conversation with them with something like the following:

At the end of the day, no one can tell you whether this is the right choice for you. You must look within yourself for the answer to that. Policy is about the large questions . . . about the rules and protocols that regulate and shape societal and human interactions. If you look around and don't like what you see, then maybe you have a chance at making a difference. But you must possess a certain fire inside, a passion to change the things about you. You not only need to make individuals better, but also make communities better . . . make society work better. It might be easier, though not much, to change one person or one family at a time, but tackling the big problems promises change through a more macro-set of programs and policies that will impact many people, few of whom you will ever know personally. If you can pull that off, the potential rewards are inestimable. The challenges, however, are equally as daunting.

Then I might throw out a few facts about the American challenge to cement my argument. If I were talking to them today, I likely would point out the following.

We talk easily about American *exceptionalism*, but the raw reality is that we are doing exceptionally poor relative to other advanced countries. For example:

We have poverty rates in the U.S. that are the highest among our peer countries. And our child poverty rates have run four or five times that found in some Scandinavian counties, inexplicable in such a wealthy country.

The so-called "American dream," a term first used by historian James Thurlow Adams in 1931, has faded. Income and wealth inequality in America is as high now as it was just before the onset of the Great Depression in the late 1920s. The six Walmart heirs alone have more wealth than the bottom 41 percent of all households.

Children born in Denmark in the bottom quintile of household ranked by income are twice as likely to rise to the top quintile as adults than American kids. In fact, class mobility in America is now less than virtually all our peer nations, so much for that part of the American dream.

We spend far more than any other advanced country on health care, yet our health outcomes are about average, ranking just above Romania. Our amenable mortality rate (deaths that could be prevented by timely and effective medical intervention) in 2007 was 103 per 100,000 people, which put us 21 out of 25 countries examined. France, by comparison, had a measured rate of 55 per 100,000. In a recent study, the U.S. ranked dead last among 11 rich countries on the value, efficiency, and effectiveness of its health care system.

In another example, American women are twice as likely to die in childbirth relative to our neighbors to the north (Canada).

Our rate of early childbirths is embarrassingly high while our non-marital birth rates in the U.S. are among the highest among advanced countries. The rate of births to teens in the U.S. has fallen by half since 1991, a rare bright spot.

We incarcerate our citizens at the highest rate anywhere in the world, and still execute some prisoners, a practice outlawed in most (but not all) countries. The U.S. has 5 percent of the world's population and 25 percent of its prison population. Yet, we still have 80 to 90 gun-related deaths per day whereas such deaths in our peer countries run about 80 to 90 per year and often sometimes fewer.

We have inordinately high rates of child abuse and neglect.

We have the best colleges in the world. But the cost of going to college is far outpacing the ability of the middle class to cover these expenses. Thus, many young people start out in life with crippling student debt. Most of our competitor countries subsidize college costs more than we do, sometimes footing the entire bill.

Our young people (ages 16-24) rank poorly relative to comparable peers in other advanced countries in numeracy and scientific knowledge, suggesting a comparative disadvantage for our economy in the future. In science and math, our kids do far worse than better performers such as Finland, Singapore, and Poland.

This list could go on, but the point is clear. We make choices as a society that determine who wins and who loses. Those rules can provide opportunities for all or build in unfair advantages for the few. Between the onset of the Great Depression and the early 1970s, inequality in America fell sharply and opportunity increased dramatically. After World War II, real incomes doubled over the next generation with all income quintiles participating in that growth. Since the early 1980s, trends have moved in the opposite redirection . . . the middle-class ideal that defined the American dream has faded.

Rising inequality is found everywhere. But the American story has been bleaker than almost anywhere else. The truth is that there will always be winners and losers in society. Not everyone is born with the same intelligence, motivation, character, or ambition to be a success. Nor can government equalize social or economic outcomes across individuals or groups without damage to the aggregate economy. At the same time, inequality today approaches levels that easily can destabilize the social fabric of our society. Research being done at present appears to confirm that extreme inequality slows economic growth by reducing consumer demand and thwarting opportunities for the less fortunate. We can do much to ameliorate these imbalances threatening our futures. We simply need the will.

Thus, the rules governing society do matter . . . a lot. That is why economic elites and other interest groups spend outrageous sums on tilting the rules in their favor. That is how indefensible tax policies such as the "carried interest" provision are enacted. This permits hedge fund managers to pay less proportionately in taxes than working class stiffs trying to get by in life. Skewed tax policies are just one way for the top 1 percent of the population to accumulate as much wealth as the bottom 90 percent. Billionaire investor Warren Buffet has complained that he pays less (again proportionately) in taxes than the secretary that works for him. "Yes," Warren has pointed out many times, "there has been a class war going on, and my class has won."

I am retired now, and no longer send young idealists off on policy careers. But maybe I can do the next best thing, put down what I learned and experienced over some four decades of fighting in the trenches . . . well, maybe mostly in the rear lines. It is not much but better than nothing. Besides, it might be the best I have to offer. I do share many of my better academic and intellectual thoughts in another of my literary masterpieces titled *The Boat Captain's Conundrum*, well worth the price. The truth, however, is that I spent most of my professional life in academia without fully embracing the culture of an academic. That didn't mean I did not have many great thoughts or develop innovative ways of looking at things. I am very clever indeed. But my first love was always policy. I was, alas, a wayward academic but a first-class policy wonk. There is, therefore, an upside to my professional misadventures. I have much to share about the policy arts which rather explains why this book is so damn long.

In the end, however, no book or classroom lectures can adequately communicate what doing social policy really entails. I am reminded of my days as a Peace Corps volunteer so long ago. Our training was long and arduous. When our group gathered together four decades after completing our service, we recalled how transformative our training and Peace Corps experience had been. To a person, we all agreed that Peace Corps had profoundly changed our lives. At the same time, we all recognized how unprepared we were for the rigors of living in the alien culture of rural India. No matter how well we were trained, the reality of being in an Indian village was a shock.

There was a phrase we heard often from the locals, "It is just now coming." We were fully prepared intellectually to understand that the promised bus would probably arrive in five minutes. Then again, it might not arrive for five hours or five days. Still, not to worry, Sahib, ". . . it is just now coming." And so, with our western cultural expectations fully in place, we would dutifully wait in the blazing noon day sun for a bus that never seemed to arrive.

If nothing else, we provided great amusement to the locals with whom we worked.

Still, a hard lesson was eventually understood, not from a training lesson but from reality. You must experience something first hand to really know it. Similarly, you must do social policy to truly appreciate what it is and what it takes to do it well. However, if you don't have an opportunity to do that now, reading about it might be the next best thing. So, let us get started.

CHAPTER 2

THE HOUSE TRAINING
OF A POLICY WONK

A person who never made a mistake never tried anything new.

—Albert Einstein

My introduction into the policy world started with a phone call one summer night in 1971. I had accepted the unacceptable . . . I would have to get a grown-up job. Then, however, I bumped up against an irritating reality. People were not falling all over themselves to offer me positions that would support even my modest lifestyle while realizing my firm ambition to never accept a job that demanded heavy lifting. Shockingly, I found that there appeared to be little to no demand for my talents or my services. How could that be? After all, I was a legend in my own mind.

For a while, I had survived as a ticket-taker at the Downer Theatre . . . a kind of artsy neighborhood venue located not far from campus on the east side of Milwaukee. It did not pay much, but the perks were great. I got all the free popcorn and soda I could consume. Even better, I was in charge on Thursday nights and would let in my friends for free. My popularity surged to new heights during this period but, I must confess, from a very low base.

In truth, I was not a total deadbeat. Frank Besage, a professor of education at the University of Wisconsin-Milwaukee (UW-M), was kind enough to give me a research assistantship (RA) even though technically I was no longer a student, having already completed my master's in urban affairs. He saw some semblance of talent in me that most others overlooked. That sinecure was temporary at best, you don't see many elderly RAs running around.

My ticket-taker career also was fraying at the edges. Recent events suggested that longer-term career prospects in the movie world might be inadvisable. There had been several theater robberies in Milwaukee that summer. The manager called me aside one night. We need a plan, he somberly intoned, which he then laid out for me. If I was forced upstairs to the office at gunpoint, I was to use a secret knock which would signal him not to open the locked door. I paused a moment to consider his plan before responding, "Listen, you better come up with a plan B . . . no freaking way am I going to stand like an idiot outside the locked door with a gun at my back. You are going to open the damn door and give them the money." He agreed, though reluctantly and after some thought. I sensed it was time to get a real job, as much as the very thought grieved me.

Back to the phone call, it was from Professor Besage telling me that I had a job interview in Madison (the state capital) the next morning. "Great," I responded, "what is the job?" Unfortunately, he had no idea other than it was a state civil service position of some kind. All he had was a time and a location for an interview. I was desperate, though, and could not ignore this very dubious prospect.

Frank had asked me to accompany him to some meetings in Madison some weeks earlier to meet with several State officials regarding policy issues now long forgotten. Over lunch, my bleak career prospects came up, and one of the Wisconsin officials asked if I might be interested in working for State government. I barely knew we had a State government, but probably mumbled something to the effect that this had always been my life's dream. Before heading back to Milwaukee, he procured some forms for me to fill out, which I did, and promptly returned to him. Then I forgot about the whole thing. My other desultory attempts to secure an adult job had led nowhere, why should this be different.

Upon arriving in Madison that day, I entered the designated interview room to find I was about to take an oral civil service examination for the position of research analyst-social services. Three inquisitors waited to grill me. *Wonderful*, I thought, *I know virtually nothing about research and less about social services. This ought to be quick and mercifully short as soon as they realized I was a total fraud.* However, I can be loquacious, even when I am clueless about the topic at hand. *The interview was rather fun*, I thought.

Sometime later, I found I was third on the hiring list, the last position the hiring supervisor could legally interview. Initially, I had been fourth, but one candidate dropped out. If they had not, my life might have been radically different. Perhaps I would still be ripping up movie tickets at some theater. Huge consequences attend to the smallest events. In any case, I was still relaxed when I met Shirley Campbell, a unit supervisor in the research section for the Wisconsin Department of Health and Family Services. Surely, she will hire one of the two more qualified candidates.

Shockingly, she chose me. There really is no accounting for some of the atrocious decisions made by otherwise sensible people. So, in September of 1971, I began my career as a social welfare researcher, whatever the hell that was. In my mind I knew less than zip about the things necessary to do this job. But really, what is the worst that could happen? I figured I would get paid for a while until they realized the error of their ways and chucked me out the door.

My career as a state-level policy wonk in Wisconsin, it turned out, really was a close-run thing. The day after I got a call from Shirley offering me the position, I was contacted by an official with the Model Cities Program in Jersey City, NJ. This program was a WOP (War-On-Poverty) initiative designed to coordinate services in distressed areas, which surely applies to Jersey City. I had been interviewed by this guy several weeks earlier but assumed nothing would come of it after hearing nothing more. He now offered me a position as a planner in that program. I often wondered where my life would have gone had the calls arrived in the opposite order. When you have no plan for life, your trajectory is often driven by idiosyncratic and seemingly serendipitous events.

One of my favorite mantras is that you don't know something until you experience it and, even better, try to explain it to others. Now, I would truly be learning on the fly. On many days in the beginning I felt like that new puppy in the house. I sort of knew that it was important where I pooped, but I hadn't quite gotten the drill down yet. My ever-present infirmity known as the "imposter syndrome" was in full bloom. I always expected that the adults, finally realizing their error in judgment, would swoop down and take me back to that same breeder where they made the mistake of selecting me in the first instance.

My supervisor, Shirley, was patient, however. She taught me several lifelong lessons . . . the first was to curb my tendency to write in a flowery, literary style. "From now on," she instructed me, "no more sentences longer than ten words, and no more than a couple of four-syllable words to a paragraph." While such rules were a challenge for me at first, I got better over time.

One day, she confessed that the second applicant for my position was better than the first and that I was better than the second-place candidate. The civil service review committee had ranked people on the wrong attributes, in her opinion. "Good thing you could not get to number four," I responded, "they must have been dynamite." In those early days, I often thought on my being hired. I wondered if Shirley had been taken with my Irish charms. That hypothesis seems preposterous, but I have no other explanation for why I was hired. I doubt it involved any observable talents for the position nor any knowledge on the topic. Indeed, a mystery!

On paper, I was to be the analyst for the "quality control" program, a federally-mandated initiative to control waste and fraud in the Aid to Families with Dependent Children program (AFDC). Now known as the Temporary Assistance to Needy Families (TANF), AFDC was the singular cash-assistance program for low-income families with children. Though other income tested programs existed, this one was synonymous with the word "welfare" and had always been tainted in the public's eye.

AFDC caseloads were growing. Even more ominous to many, the complexion of the caseload was shading toward a darker hue. This added to the negative animus associated with the program. What once had been a system for helping sympathetic widows and other worthy poor had morphed into a worrisome trough of the public's generosity that was being exploited by the lazy and the morally lax.

Enter Quality Control (QC), a strategy designed both to curb abuse and enhance public confidence. Using methods adopted from manufacturing assembly lines, a monthly random sample was drawn from the statewide AFDC population. QC reviewers, stationed in regional offices across the state, would conduct a "review" of each selected case. Home visits were done to check on the household composition. In addition, birth records were reviewed; financial documents and bank accounts scoured; and any possible employment sniffed out. The review compared the local welfare worker's handling of the case against existing rules and protocols to determine if the family was, indeed, eligible and that they were getting the correct amount of benefits for that review month. A deviation of five dollars or more, above or below the correct amount, would constitute an error. And to make sure the states were not incompetent or cheating, federal QC reviewers rechecked a random subsample of the original sample.

This was serious business and quite an administrative expense to the state. It could be more expensive to the state if certain tolerance levels were not met. A tolerance level was a proportion of error cases which, if exceeded for a specified period, could result in very bad publicity at the least and heavy federal fines at the worst. The tolerance levels were 3 percent for eligibility levels and 5 percent each for underpayments and overpayments. Of course, states were given time to analyze what might be going wrong if tolerance levels had been exceeded before the other shoe dropped. For example, they would be expected to develop what were called profiles of error-prone cases, and to remedy the patterns of excess errors through targeted corrective action plans. If not, the threat of fiscal penalties and bad publicity loomed large. This was a program accountability initiative writ large.

Now, remember the kerfuffle of a few years ago over the IRS use of profiling strategies to target suspicious non-profit agencies for tax audits to determine if they really were legitimate charities and not political organizations. They used certain identifiers or markers such as "Tea Party" or "Up with Marxism" in the organization's title to identify programs for intensive audits. It seemed rational to tax officials that such programs just might be a bit more likely to claim tax exempt status as a charity even though they primarily were involved in partisan-driven activities. Conservatives went nuts with their usual conspiracy theories but with was just good strategy.

In fact, this is the exact same principle that was used in welfare QC. You don't want to select 100 random cases on which to focus corrective action efforts where the hit rate for an error-plagued case might be one in twenty. Rather, you want to select those cases with certain known propensities for error on which to apply your labor-intensive corrective action tactics ... let us say with a hit rate of three-in-five or 60 percent. Basically, you wanted to identify error-prone cases. This is simply efficient management, which the private sector does all the time, or at least should do, to ensure that quality products go out the door.

Anyways, here is where I came in. I would collect data from all the reviews over a six-month period, create a data base (using the long-forgotten Hollerith cards), and then prepare an analysis. There were two kinds of products. The simple one was a straightforward analysis that pretty much focused on aggregate error rates, comparisons to tolerance levels, and a global discussion of why the state was doing such a crappy job. The second was more creative and involved digging into the data to figure out why errors were occurring, where they were occurring, and what might be done about them.

In the beginning, I was slogging my way through a lot of this stuff... getting comfortable with Hollerith cards, punching up my own data, figuring out the best way to code and store information, and learning basic data manipulation commands to run simple computations. They should have hired an eight-year-old for this stuff since, at the time, I could not reset the time on my VCR if it was blinking 12:00 AM after a brief power outage. Come to think of it, I still can't reset the time on those damn machines. But I struggled through this early learning period, and no one seemed to notice my incompetence. People liked me even then, and that trait excuses many sins.

I did figure out that I was rather clever on the bigger, more conceptual stuff. For example, I developed my own way of coding data that apparently was sufficiently attractive to catch on with other states when the feds picked up on my innovation. I also argued that the QC system should be used to collect data for broader management purposes since you had all these well-paid case reviewers driving around the state poking into a representative sample of the welfare population. I had some success with that broader vision for the system, but not as much as I had hoped.

My great success came in getting our error rate down, and here I do justifiably take considerable credit. Many states exceeded the federal tolerance rates in the beginning and faced the "threat" of federal sanctions. Now the feds did a lot of talking about doing these error profiles, and then spending a lot of time and money training local workers to handle such cases better. And we did play along, developing a research proposal to assess the effect of alternate training regimens on error rates. I probably pushed this research project along just to see if I could pull it off.

One distinct memory remains from this attempt at a conventional strategy. My phone rang. It was a call from a colleague named Louise Bakke. "The feds are on my line," she sounded a bit panicked, "they like our training ideas, but want to know more about our research design." They are not the only ones, I mused silently, but told her I would come down to her office. Fortunately, this was located at the other end of the building which gave me time to collect my thoughts. I grabbed a copy of that thin classic (for that era) volume on research methods by Stanley and Campbell (or was it Campbell and Stanley), and slowly walked down the hall as I flipped through the book. On getting to her office I said to Louise, "I'll handle this." I took the receiver from her and laid out a methodology as if I had given the matter far more thought than the four or five minutes it took to reach her office. While my ploy seemed to work for the moment, we eventually had to fly out to D.C. to agree upon a more rigorous experimental design. We did get the money, though. It was my first success at bringing in research money. *Now, that was fun.* I thought.

I quickly concluded that all this interest in training was for show. The real action would be elsewhere. My reasoning was simple, and I won't claim to be the only one to see this rather obvious point. Calculating eligibility and especially grant levels were very complicated tasks back then. If you were to look at the manual governing welfare case decision-making, the detail was daunting. To calculate what was called the benefit guarantee, each need item (or necessary expenditure) was calculated separately— clothes, rent, utilities, and so forth. The same for work expenses, if there were any, that would be offset against available income. How much for gas, parking, uniforms, child care, or whatever? As the decision points mounted, the probability of error in a given month (since circumstances change all the time) grew exponentially.

Two options presented themselves. Increasing local discretion was one. That is, change all "shalls" in the manual to "mays." If a rule is discretionary, how can there be an error? Since there already were "mays" in the rule books of that era, why not add a few more? How could a rule be violated if it were discretionary? Then, it wasn't really a rule, at least in the conventional sense. But that gave too much leeway to locals who could easily abuse it, that approach was a non-starter. The second option proved more alluring—reduce the number of decision points. This was an approach clearly within state control and less likely to raise the eyebrows of the feds who were always looking over the State's shoulders looking for nefarious schemes.

But let me start with one of my more intriguing stratagems. As I looked at the data, and chatted with the case reviewers in the field, I noticed something interesting. Welfare used an asset test for determining eligibility, an amount of accumulated resources which, if the permitted maximum were exceeded, got you kicked off the rolls. The intent was to ensure that only the truly destitute obtained aid and thus meet the goal of target efficiency where benefits were directed to the truly needy. Federal rules permitted states to set the limit as high as $2,000 but Wisconsin had a much more stringent test of $1,000.

This more stringent standard caused a problem. A family might obtain a modest amount of money, through part-time work for example, and put it in the bank to cover upcoming expenses. If the QC reviewer happened to check on a day after a deposit to the bank had been made, they might find assets that ran over the allowable limit by a few dollars and thus rendering the case ineligible for assistance. The case would remain in error even if the situation was rectified the next day when more bills were paid. It was just like the rules of golf, rigid and inflexible. There were no do overs.

So, I made the following argument—raise the limit to the federal level. Then variations in cash resources during a month would be less likely to exceed the asset limit at an inopportune moment. This resonated with management, and the change was made. On paper, the eligibility error rate went down, which was duly reported as a savings to the state. No one mentioned that caseloads probably rose since additional families could now meet the more liberal asset standard. In welfare, perception was everything. I suppose we could have advised clients to hide excess money under the mattress, but I doubt the feds would have considered that an appropriate corrective action. Interesting philosophical point, though. Is an error an error if it is never discovered?

The big changes, though, involved a push toward a reduction in the number of decision points used in determining benefit levels. Two main types of computations were involved—calculating need and then determining available resources. We simplified the need calculation first. Complexity was slashed away by eliminating the individual need items like clothes, utilities, and rent. When all those items were aggregated into an averaged lump sum, we were left with what was called a flat grant. If you had a family of a given size, then you got a grant of a certain amount. No consideration would be given to the actual needs of the family or any special circumstances. Under the old system you could get a special need payment if an appliance broke down or a car needed for work went kaput.

Next, I focused on the rules governing the calculation of work expenses. As suggested above, workers were required to look at an array of expenditures associated with work which were then offset from earnings. The resulting net amount was then deducted from need to determine if they were still eligible and how much they would get for the month. In truth, it was a bit more complicated than that when you considered the so-called work incentive provisions built into the rules, but you get the drift.

It did not take a rocket scientist to figure out that, with the calculation of need highly simplified, cases with working adults remained the most error-prone cases. Calculating net resources is where the remaining complexity was located. Now, being a witty and mischievous guy, my first instinct was to go in and argue we needed to stop all clients from working. While this was before the big "get recipients to work" push that would come around about a decade in the future, even I backed off that dubious idea.

What I did do involved the following ingenious strategy. I grabbed a sample of working cases; and examined them closely, particularly the volatility of the employment-related expenses over time. Not surprisingly, these cases were an administrative nightmare. Then, I went a step further. I calculated the average expenses across these working cases. Let's say this exercise came up with expenses totaling 35 percent of earnings, on average. I argued that we should just use that rate for all cases irrespective of the actual numbers . . . a kind of flat rate for what it costs to earn money. Not only did this become policy, but my haphazard analysis of a quite small sample of cases caught on and somehow even made it into the Congressional Record.

Of course, more than reducing error rates went into the push for simplified rules and protocols. Caseloads kept growing. It was no longer feasible to micromanage each case. I still remember one longtime bureaucrat summarizing the general feeling as follows. "We simply cannot tend to each case as if it were some precious, exotic plant." Increasingly, there was a growing consensus that we had to make welfare management way more efficient.

It is a truism, however, that no (very few at least) new policy directions are unambiguously positive. True, simplified rules enhanced efficiency and lowered errors. They also took away from local workers the kind of discretion that could be abused in the wrong hands . . . punishing clients they don't like while rewarding the ones they do. These were obvious positives.

On the other hand, it is far from clear which approach optimized what is called horizontal equity (treating equals equally), another goal of your welfare guru. A flat grant seems fair and understandable. At the same time, it makes no pretense to meeting the actual needs of families that may look similar on the surface (for example, same family size) but whose circumstances differ dramatically in reality. The cost of living in the city, for example, might easily be higher than country living. Getting to a job in a rural area might involve more work expenses since public transportation would not be available.

The real problems associated with simplified grant calculations lay elsewhere and would not be realized for several years. Flat grants, it turns out, proved much easier to cut than those based on the actual needs of families. As welfare grew more unpopular and as welfare-motivated migration concerns increased, grant levels began to fall, slowly at first and then ever more quickly. The connection between benefit guarantees and what it took to survive had been severed. Later, I would work on conceptualizing a basic needs study that would systemically address the need issue, but even back then norms and values were superseding science in policymaking. By the time I went to D.C. to work on Clinton's Reform Bill in 1993, I oft repeated one of my standard quips, "Damn, we better reform AFDC soon or there will be nothing left to reform." The real value of welfare guarantees had been falling since the early 1970s.

Even with all this going on, I was quickly getting bored and looking for other mischief to get into. I was like the new puppy in the house. Just where was the next pair of shoes for me to rip apart? I am not sure why I was bored. I sometimes went to QC meetings with other states that the feds sponsored. I was stunned to see that some of these states had several people doing what I handled on my own. Perhaps I should have relaxed. But I suspect I already sensed that most of the counters of my imaginary policy candy store were still bare and needed filling up. I didn't realize just how challenging the next counter would be.

Probably without fully appreciating it at the time, I felt a lot of cross currents going on in my bureaucratic environment. The department I worked in was a new so-called "super" agency that housed formerly separate programs. It was hoped that more collaboration might take place if these distinct programs were physically collocated. So, welfare and social services were now supposed to talk to one another, maybe even work together. In the words of that great Roman wit, Cicero, that would be a *mirabilis dictu;* roughly translated as a marvelous sight to behold. Or, in my words, not bloody likely!

As raw as I was, I sensed that this institutional marriage was doomed. The cultural gap between officials from the welfare and service sides of the new agency simply was too wide. Many years in the future, my separate work with several colleagues, Karen Bogenschneider, Larry Mead, Jennifer Noyes, and Michael Wiseman would lead me to refine the concept of an "institutional cultural disconnect." Put in its simplest terms, people functioning in different organizational milieus over time experience increasing difficulty understanding one another though they cannot always see this disconnect on a conscious level.

Unfortunately, the feds were simultaneously pushing the separation of aids and services at the local or operational level, thereby severing the tie between the giving out of income support benefits and any efforts to habilitate these families so that they might function better. Might it be that the left and right hands (the feds and the states) were working at cross-purposes? Shocking!

The reasons for this separation at the agency or local level were many. There was a growing sense that welfare was an entitlement and that client sovereignty was to be respected. You know, keep those meddling social workers away. Besides, there was still a chance we would get what was called a Negative Income Tax. If enacted, this would establish an income floor under all Americans, federalize cash assistance, and likely eliminate a whole bunch of touchy-feely service programs purportedly designed to help poor people cope.

The next counter in my candy store touched indirectly on these cross-currents. Ever since the Kennedy amendments to the Social Security Act in the early 1960s, the feds supported a host of service strategies oriented toward helping welfare clients toward independence. When I started in the department, funding for these services was sum-sufficient. The feds would supplement whatever the states spent under rather loose guidelines, and at quite generous levels. Over time, the feds expanded which groups the states could help. The original focus had been on current welfare families, but the funding spigot gradually expanded to encompass help to former clients and even to persons who might become clients in the future. Hell, by those loose criteria, I desperately needed counseling (probably still do). My lack of command over basic life skills has always put me at risk of a future on public aid or, much more likely, a stint in an assisted living facility. Under the rules at the time, we could argue that my counseling ought to be paid for by Washington.

Again, it is not rocket science to see that states would manipulate the system to maximize the flow of federal dollars. The exploitation race was heating up, alarming federal officials. They first tried tightening up the purposes for which services could be provided, and next sought to push states to document or justify that these resources were being appropriately spent. The Goal-Oriented Social Services (G.O.S.S.) concept briefly emerged. Nothing burns those who hand out money more than not knowing what they are getting for it. This is especially true when they are dubious about the program in the first place. Here is where I come in to at least try to save the day.

If I knew nothing about welfare when I started, I knew less about human services. And yet, I was asked to put together a system for collecting data from public (State and County) social workers across Wisconsin so that the State might demonstrate the prudent and effective use of federal dollars. If not that, were the dollars at least being spent on the right stuff? *This should be fun,* I thought. It turned out I was wrong about the fun part. On the other hand, it was the start of another adventure, and the filling up of yet another candy counter!

Initially, I had to do some quick study cramming to get an inkling of what these social services were all about. What the hell do social workers do? It was in that process that I stumbled upon one of my enduring strengths. It turns out that I was able to develop a decent conceptual framework for collecting and organizing the data describing service activities. The basic challenge associated with this task was to capture activities related to a discrete set of larger tasks that, in turn, were being delivered to achieve overall program purposes, sort of a tiered approach to thinking about the provision of services. The data was to be collected at the case level but then aggregated all the way up to the state level. I worked long and hard with the computer nerds to make it all come together. Well, the framework seemed coherent to me. Then again, I often fall in love with my own ideas. In truth, I almost always love them even when they are not appreciated by mere plebeians.

That was the easy part. Shirley, my direct supervisor, then told me to go out and train all these social workers around the state in how to record what they were doing on this form I had designed. Now, it had not been that long since I had fallen off the turnip truck but even I sensed a problem. "I don't know," I recall suggesting, "some of them may be kind of ticked off at doing all this paperwork." She brushed off my concerns by instructing me to tell complainers that "I represented the state and that they would simply have to do this." I was dubious but, as the old poem goes,

"Ours is not to question why, ours is but to do and die." In fact, my demise turned out to be a close-run thing.

They gave me some help, a new hire by the name of Peter Albert. Here we were, two veteran bureaucrats with about a year's worth of experience between us. We were heading out to demand that social workers do something that they loathed and thought superfluous at best, utterly ridiculous at the worst. Even more reprehensible, we were asking them to collapse what they considered to be a therapeutic treatment regimen into a set of preformed categories that would be boiled down to numbers to be inserted into a bunch of boxes on a single sheet of paper for each case. They saw their world as infinitely complex and one demanding considerable professional judgment. Now, we waltz in asking them to oversimplify their professional work. Anyone see a problem here? But at least Peter had a masters level degree in Social Work, even if he earned it only two months earlier.

At the first training session, I saw that it would be far worse than I imagined. Up to this point in my life, I had survived exactly two near-death experiences involving rabid mobs. The first was in my college days at Clark University in Worcester Massachusetts. My very close friend, Carol Simon (who in later life would serve as Dean of the Department of Education at Rutgers University) and I decided to join an anti-Vietnam war rally in front of City Hall. This was early in the anti-war movement, and the first such event in the Worcester area. Probably about a 100 or so fellow protesters carried signs and such in a circle gathered in front of City Hall. We were surrounded by what seemed like thousands of enraged patriots who thought we were Commie pigs and traitors getting our directions straight from Moscow.

But I sucked it up and held to my convictions at least until our circular movement ground to a halt. Out of the corner of my eye I could see Hell's Angels devotees wearing their best biker outfits. The hate in their eyes was palpable. Eggs and other debris rained down on us. My remaining conviction drained away as I heard one of them say, "Let's beat the shit out of the tall one with glasses." My first reaction was to check to see if I had wet myself. Satisfied that I was okay in that department, I whispered to Carol, "I think we only have seconds left, maybe we should make the most of it." She might have taken pity on me, but the line started moving again and the prospects of my immediate death receded for the moment though I read the next day that one or two other protestors did later fall into harm's way.

My second near-death experience happened during my training for the Peace Corps in the mid-1960s. We spent a brief time in Houston, Texas, not exactly the citadel of enlightenment. One night, we found out that some of our fellow Black trainees had been denied access to a club where you could purchase alcoholic drinks. Apparently, Houston was dry (alcohol prohibited) back then except for "private" establishments where you could conveniently buy a nightly membership for a nominal fee. Well, we huffed, they can't get away with that; and off we marched to confront this injustice. While noble in intent, this turned out to be a "back-forty" idea. A "back-forty" idea is one so stupid that you ought to brought-out to the back-forty acres of the farm and shot since you were obviously too dense to continue breathing on your own.

Anyways, we arrive at the club! Some of my white Peace Corps colleagues paid the fee and made it into the establishment. I stood next to the first Black trainee to reach the door. I saw the eyes of the burly gatekeeper narrow menacingly as he said to the young man next to me, "The fee for you is twenty dollars." An outrageous sum back then. When the volunteer made a move to pay this transparently fabricated sum, the bouncer snarled, "No, for you it is a million dollars." The message was clear. No Blacks were getting in that club. This soon led to much shoving and shouting as we were herded out onto the street. A crowd of patrons poured out of the club to confront us. I finally realized where the term redneck comes from—their necks were red with pure vitriol.

While I desperately tried to remember that Perfect Act of Contrition that might get even a lapsed Catholic like me into heaven, I saw a patrol car cruise down the street. I desperately waived it over thinking that we were saved. "Officer," I gravely intoned, "there has been a violation of the Civil Rights Act here." His response is yet burned into my memory. He looked at me as if I had just dropped out of an alien space craft, and said with ill-disguised contempt, "I don't give a fuck about civil rights," before rolling up his window and cruising off up the street. Once again, though, I managed to survive an early and tragic demise. Perhaps, though, I would have gotten a statue in front of the Peace Corps building in D.C., a fitting tribute to that martyred trainee stupid enough to get himself killed even before going overseas.

And yet, nothing in my past prepared me for what I now faced. In that first training session for our new whizz bang concept for reducing social work practice to a one-page form filled with tiny boxes, I looked out over a sea of hate unlike any I had encountered before. Nothing I said seemed to be working—the need for accountability, the possible loss of federal funds, feedback to be used to improve services. None of these compelling and coherent arguments worked. You really can't please all the people all the time.

They kept throwing out impossible real-life situations which, while probably rare, did undoubtedly happen. "Okay, Mr. Madison expert, just how would you code the following case on your stupid form?" As my colleague, Peter Albert, and I stumbled for responses that made sense, the tension in the room grew. Wishing that I had left the car running to make a quick dash to safety, I felt we had precious little time left. The real problem was, as I saw it, that all their hatred was directed at me. I had made the rookie mistake of appearing to be in charge.

I then knew what had to be done. "Okay," I said with conviction, "when my colleague Peter here brought this scheme to me, I pointed out all these problems. But he insisted on going ahead with this anyways." Immediately, all the hateful stares turned away from me and toward him. There is a valuable lesson here for all would-be policy wonks: "When the going gets tough . . . the spineless blame the other guy." Yes, I really did say all that but then quickly tried to turn it into a weak joke before they lunged from their chairs to rip out his throat.

Well, we did survive the tour and got better at it as we went. I never did use Shirley's fallback line about "we are the state, so shut up and do it!" Surprisingly, the data eventually poured in, and we dutifully filled out the required federal reports. There was no stomach for a second run, so I concocted some brilliant way of updating the information for future reports. No one complained even though I had some sleepless nights thinking about the federal data police sweeping in to take me off to some penitentiary for submitting reports so transparently stupid that they could not pass the most primitive smell test.

In the end, sum-sufficient funding was doomed . . . no one could have saved it. A sum-certain formula was adopted which is also known as a block grant. In effect, the feds were saying forget about Goal-Oriented Social Service schemes and accountability-driven approaches to helping families. Here is a lump sum of money, have fun. While this flexibility seemed good in the moment, there is always a price to pay. The catch was that the given sum would never be increased. It simply would decline in value over time even as need increased. This is just like the flat grants for welfare guarantees. Both are easy to cut (in real or nominal terms) when the amounts are not tied to anything related to reality.

That is the short story. The longer story is much more fascinating. Back in Madison, after licking our wounds and boring anyone who would listen with our near-death experience in the field, we began to get serious about what we had learned. In our minds, there remained a desperate need for good data to document what was being done, and to use as feedback for systems design, accountability, and management improvement purposes.

Well, it was on my mind at least. Peter had the good sense to leave to do real social work. As his civil service probationary period came to an end, he submitted a letter saying that the employment probation process was a two-way street and the department had failed. Since they did callously put him in harm's way, I did see his point. And despite my own efforts to get him killed, we became good friends. He even served as best man at my wedding. Later, it hit me that this was his perfect revenge for the hell I had put him through. In the end, though, I forgave him for facilitating my marriage ceremony.

Decades later, when I resigned from my university position, Peter and his lovely wife, Sue, showed up. We had not seen each another in many years. I expressed surprise that he was there. "Well," he replied, "I was there at the beginning, and I thought I would be there at the end." I think near-death experiences help you bond at a closer level. On a serious note, I thought Peter an amazing character. Over time, he would take sabbaticals or even leave jobs to run off and climb the highest peaks in the world, including Everest. His two daughters are named Logan and McKinley, after the two mountains he had climbed just before their births.

But I digress again. Back to the longer story. I began talking up the fact that we could no longer run modern service and welfare programs with pen and paper technologies from the nineteenth century. We needed state-of-the-art automation to exploit computer technologies that were growing in sophistication by the day. I managed to convince some lower level colleagues that automated systems management was the wave of the future. Upper management was not so easily convinced. We became such pains in the butt that they formally shut us down. Get back to doing your real jobs, we were told.

We were so stubborn back then. We had all the zealous conviction that only the young and foolish possess. We could not meet at work or during normal work hours, so we started meeting in our homes after work and on the weekends. This kind of dedication takes an advanced form of idiocy. Obviously, given that management had not sanctioned our vision, our lobbying could not be overt. We had to be quite subtle. Eventually, we found a champion for our cause, a smart and charismatic young manager named Bernard (Bernie) Stumbras. He had now risen far enough in the bureaucracy to make a difference. He had one condition,

we would start by automating the three major welfare programs—
AFDC, Food Stamps, and Medicaid. *Oh goody,* I thought, *now I
can torture welfare case workers for a while.*

As we began, we had no idea how utterly difficult and
transformative this project would be. By the end, welfare
administration looked nothing like it was at the beginning. Despite
the challenges, and the emotional and personal toll this exacted on
some people, Wisconsin would once again blaze the trail into a
new era of public sector management. I only got to board this train
for the early part of the journey, but it was an exciting trip indeed.

I remember several fun tasks. Yes, perhaps my idea of fun is just
a bit odd. I recall scouring each required federal and state report
to identify information redundancy. Rather than collecting the
same data many times to complete separate reporting requirement,
we would collect data once and use it multiple times for many
purposes. Nothing is easy, though, and seemingly similar data
often was defined slightly differently for distinct reports.

I recall doing county level agency site visits around the state to
document how local staff currently completed mandated reporting
requirements. We also hoped to assess how the new system might
help locals in the future. This was a version of the old refrain that
"we are from Madison and we are here to help you." People were
polite, but I could see the cynicism in their expressions. "Help us?
Sure, when pigs fill the sky and the Stanley Cup is contested on an
ice rink somewhere in hell."

I recall working on what was called the "combined" application form. Previously, applicants had to negotiate three separate forms and three distinct application processes to get a complete menu of help. In the future, there would be one form and one process with calculations and key decisions done by computer. Efficiency would rise, and the practice of abusive discretion would decrease. This was to be bureaucratic heaven. Well, that was the plan anyways.

Alas, pitfalls abounded. One day, we were sitting around a big conference table doing the final review of the combined application form. I personally did not think it was as innovative as my one-page box-filled form for social workers, but I may be just a bit biased. In any case, excitement prevailed around the table. Another milestone was about to be achieved. In addition, the length of the document appeared reasonable, which was just a bit of a surprise. We could sense the finish line was in sight.

Then someone said, "Wait, something is wrong here. The AFDC and Food Stamp programs use different accounting units." That is, in some instances you needed to aggregate information for separate sets of people within the household to determine eligibility and benefits for each program. This meant that we had to collect data at the individual and not the family or household level. We had been used to the latter approach and initially designed the application form accordingly.

By collecting personal information at the individual level, we could aggregate the data based on different groups within the household to conform the rules governing each program. That small wrinkle should have been obvious to us; but we were, after all, trying something that no one else had done. After what seemed like a very long pause to let the bad news soak in, someone moaned, "Well, back to the drawing board." Wow, sometimes it takes a two-by-four upside the head to see the obvious.

We finally got it right. Technical contractors had been brought in to help with the effort. They kept arguing for things that would make the form even longer. For example, they wanted a separate question (to be asked of each adult and older child member of the household) for each conceivable source of income, no matter how unlikely it might occur in the real world. "How about a question on whether they have any winnings from the Irish Sweepstakes?" they would suggest. I would groan, seeing an application growing to fifty pages or more . . . a tome that might well dissuade less educated or desperate applicants to give up despite their need. Though I won a number of these battles, the final product ultimately topped out at some thirty-seven pages.

One final task proved the most vexing; this really was a group project, not a solo effort. An automated case management system could brook no ambiguity. Each decision point had to be binary, yes or no. There could be none of the professional discretion central to the AFDC program of former years. Early on, caseworkers were expected to use their judgment to determine if a family was "fit" for support or worthy of public largesse. While assessing fitness had been was frowned upon by the 1970s, a lot of fuzzy language persisted.

I recall sitting in long meetings where the group would plow through page after page trying to decide whether a "may" should be turned into a "yes" or a "no." These could be marathon sessions with many a dispute dotting long afternoons while we poured over tedious manual material. These sessions became an enervating ordeal as the afternoon sun turned the pre-airconditioned depression-era cement mausoleum called the State Office Building (SOB) into a furnace. You can well imagine that many thought the acronym SOB stood for the people working inside the building and not the building itself.

Sometime after I left state service, what was known as the Computer Reporting Network or CRN was unveiled. The system profoundly transformed the administration of welfare. Case level data was entered by workers in seventy-two different counties. The system crunched the data and determined eligibility and benefits for the three major programs simultaneously. Client notices and worker reminder messages were spit out effortlessly. Reports were routinely generated without labor intensive effort by the locals.

I still remember visiting one county in the early days of the project. I asked what they did to complete various required reports. A bubbly clerk showed me a huge (a very huge) notebook kind of thing with a lot of colored ribbons running through it. What is this I asked? She then launched into an exhaustive description of how she used the different color ribbons to navigate the data to find what was needed for each state and federally-mandated report. I kept nodding despite being totally lost. At the end, she proudly mentioned that she bought all her ribbons after Christmas when they were at half price. I put on my best Irish smile and said, "That is great. But when we get the new system up, you won't have to do all that anymore, the reports will be completed automatically." My optimistic words did not have the intended effect. She looked crestfallen. My image of myself as a savior on a white horse existed only in my own mind.

The impact went way beyond administrative efficiencies. People were affected as well. Caseworkers were stripped of any remaining professional judgment. They became more like clerks who simply collected and entered data. Once, they had been more like social workers, making real decisions. Now, they tended to function as cops defending the integrity of the public purse. Many could still recall the time when a caseworker managed relatively few cases with each demanding personal scrutiny and attention. Caseload numbers now multiplied by factors of two and three and four. Overhead costs plummeted in Wisconsin, reaching less than 5 percent of total expenditures at one point, best in the nation as I recall.

One consequence of the power of technology jumped out at us. About half the counties never had what were known as an AFDC-U case on their rolls. The U stood for unemployed parent.

These were cases where two adults with children could get benefits if the breadwinner had lost their employment. Eligibility for this special program required a recent work history and an adult (typically the male) who would accept any work available.

In addition, there were no child care issues since there was always an adult in the home to care for the children. For a variety of reasons, the AFDC-U caseload numbers were always much lower than the lone-parent caseload. Still, to never have such a case in a county raised suspicions. After CRN went into effect, these cases popped up all over the state. Many county boards and directors simply disapproved of the program and previously had found ways to deny or discourage applicants. In one small county, for example, a director was known to send the male in every applicant family to a friend of his who ran a chicken farm, and always needed someone to pluck the chickens. It was horrendous work that paid little but, if refused, was an immediate excuse to declare the family ineligible for AFDC-U help. Now, with a computer located in Madison making the decisions, it was more difficult for them to advance their private agendas.

My training (housetraining if you will) perhaps can be described as a series of epiphanies throughout my early professional life. I clearly remember one from this period. I was working with a small planning group. We were struggling to come up with a conceptual framework for collecting and organizing a set of data . . . a classic policy wonk concern though the specifics of this specific project now escape me after so many years. I recall vividly preferring an organizing framework that was shared by no one else in the group. This was not my first isolated and lonely stand. This time, though, I was certain I was correct. I dug in and kept arguing my position. Now, I am wrong a lot, but this was not one of those times. Still, despite my brilliance, I was overruled by the others who were just as adamant that I was full of crap. What was I missing?

Shortly thereafter, we brought the plan to the big man, Bernard Stumbras, whom I mentioned earlier. As the others explained the agreed upon framework to Bernie (as he was universally known), I sat silently. Okay, perhaps I was pouting just a bit. But I noticed he was silent and his brow was furrowed. *Hmm,* I thought, *maybe he sees the same problem that I did.* When he finally spoke up, he essentially laid out the conceptual approach for which I had been arguing. Yes, vindication! I was elated and just a bit puffed up with a slight case of excess hubris.

Then, without a beat, the others began to nod and say things like, "Oh, that is brilliant, why didn't we think of that?" For a moment I was stunned. "That is exactly what I had been arguing all morning, really for the past week." Of course, I made this complaint only to myself. I was paralyzed with disbelief that they could not see what they were doing, pivoting 180 degrees without missing a beat. And then the epiphany hit. Where you sit really does mean more than where you stand. The lesson learned made the aggravation of the day well worth it. Besides, if ever I made any progress toward sitting at a higher bureaucratic elevation, I now knew that I would suddenly turn brilliant without changing one whit.

In any case, I really was sorry that I did not have an opportunity to see CRN through to the finish. After all, in an indirect way it all started with my near-death experience trying to turn social workers into bureaucrats. Apparently, good things can emerge from the most desperate of situations.

I must have become a veteran bureaucrat at some point since I was asked to break-in a new employee one day. I took this responsibility seriously and gave his orientation to the place my best shot. At lunchtime I asked if he wanted to join me, but he begged off saying he had errands to run. We agreed to get together right after the break. When he failed to show I looked around for a bit before noticing a note left on his desk. He was resigning . . . after four hours! What happened, I wondered? Did I offend him? Did I emit some strange body odor? It usually takes people at least a week before they realize they cannot stand me. Perhaps he was a quick learner. His only expressed reason was that he could see the job was not for him. I remained sure it was me. In any case, I noticed that they never assigned another new employee to me for the initial orientation.

At another point, I managed to get myself elected as the union representative of the research and statistics bargaining unit. State employees had won expanded bargaining rights, and in 1975, five bargaining units represented by AFSCME (the Association of

Federal, State, County, and Municipal Employees) were locked in a contentious set of negotiations with the state. Of the five bargaining units, the intrepid band of researchers and statisticians were virtually a joke. In no way were we going to bring the State to its knees. On the other hand, the public safety unit (state cops, prison guards, the capitol police and the like) had real clout even without carrying their guns into the negotiating sessions.

I have racked what is left of my brain to recall how I managed to let myself get trapped into this position but cannot. I certainly did not seek it out. Now, there are many things I liked about unions, having grown up in a union household. I was not, though, exactly a true believer. The public safety unit I mentioned above, for example, felt that seniority was a nonnegotiable principle. The longer you were there, the more protected you were and the more perks you should enjoy. In addition, they argued for stringent work rules. If you were a box-filler and the other guy was a box-emptier, no boss could tell you to empty a box, ever.

My little unit thought of themselves as professionals. We wanted more flexibility and respect. I strongly suspected, however, that it was not prudent to confront the prison guards. They were big and tended to drool on occasion and to snarl a lot. But it was the occasional growl that really put me on edge. And, of course, most of them were used to carrying weapons. Still, I loved it when we sat around singing "Solidarity Forever." I kept looking for a barricade to defend.

For me, as someone who loves to observe life, seeing the negotiating process from the inside was priceless. Two vignettes deserve mention. One day, the union heads told us to pack a bag since we were going to D.C. to see Jerry Wurf, the head of AFCSME and a power in the union world. He was impressive, I must admit. I can still see him expressing shock and outrage that a great Democrat like then Governor Patrick Lucey was not bargaining in good faith. I took this to mean that the governor was not caving into all the union demands.

As promised, Wurf arrived in Madison to meet with the governor. After the pleasantries, he launched into an attack. "How could you, as someone who was elected by the working men and women of Wisconsin, treat hardworking public servants with such cavalier disregard . . ." and on he went, as the governor's face turned deeper shades of red. But to his credit, Pat Lucey remained civil throughout. I cannot imagine President Trump remaining so composed. All in all, this was a pretty good exposure to hardball politics.

A couple more candy counters caught my attention before I headed out the door for that mile journey down State Street, transitioning from government to the academy. One candy counter involved one final tweak to the AFDC QC system, but a tweak with interesting consequences. The size of our small state-level QC unit (not including the field reviewers) was small . . . about three or four people. It was time to utilize computer technology to increase the efficiency of our small band. When I started, I would use a card reading machine located with the computer nerds after hours and on weekends when no one else was using it. That now seemed silly. What we needed was our own computer terminal. Then, we could directly enter data and analyze it during the working day. It seemed so sensible.

The pushback was immediate. The central computer nerds do that kind of work. Program staff does not, and certainly they do not need any esoteric computer technology. All such work must go through the nerds located somewhere up on the sixth floor which, in truth, was closer to heaven than the QC unit. It was worse where my wife worked at the time. There was a very simple tabulating tool called WISTAB which could be used to create tables and do simple calculations. Even a moron like me could learn how to use it in twenty minutes or less. But the computer gods refused to let program staff in her department even see the manual. I did give my spouse a contraband copy I had purloined and, once again, waited for the data police to pounce.

What kind of crap is this, I thought as I reflected on the stance of the technical wizards. The typical drill might go something like this. You send up some simple analytical task. Three weeks later, you get a printout back. You look at it and then say, oh shit. I should have run this a slightly different way. Or maybe the first pass suggests a second pass. Up into technology heaven one more time and another three-week wait. Okay, I probably am exaggerating the wait times involved, but you get my drift.

It struck me what the problem was. I believe the technology wizards thought that if they let go of complete control, they would run out of work. Maybe they would lose their jobs. I was astounded. Even a technical moron like myself could easily see the future. Computer-related work would continue to expand exponentially. Centralized staff could never keep up with the increasing demand. Unacceptable bottlenecks would ensue along with outraged mobs attacking the citadel of technology looking for their technical output. I was offering them an out from a terrible fate, and likely a horrible demise. Just before I left, I won my battle. We got a terminal, the first in any program unit. It was not long that I would walk into that building and see terminals on every desk. Apparently, once the dam was breached, the onrushing waters could not be turned back. I would just smile.

Another counter involved the expansion of the QC methodology into the Food Stamp program. If the system worked for the AFDC program, it should work for this other assistance system. So, officials in the Department of Agriculture (DOA), the federal bureaucracy responsible for Food Stamps, simply borrowed what was being done by the Department of Health, Education, and Welfare (HEW as it was labelled at the time) for cash welfare assistance. Seemed simple enough! It was not. It seldom is.

As they launched the new initiative, the responsible feds brought to Washington representatives from as many states as they could lure to the big city. They wanted high-level people. From Wisconsin, they got me instead. You could see the disappointment written on their faces. Perhaps their desire for high-level officials was strategically self-serving. People that high up might not have enough detailed knowledge about reality on the ground. They would not notice problems as I would.

As I sat there listening to what they were proposing, I was appalled. The Food Stamp program was incredibly complicated. In addition to the usual complications, the process of establishing the household unit was bizarre. You put together groups that shared eating facilities and bought food together irrespective of familial relationships. Then you had need assessments and earnings considerations and what was called a purchase requirement. Based on your net income, you were expected to pay a certain amount for your stamps. It was so complicated that federal rules allowed states to average need and income and purchase requirements over reasonable time periods. That made sense even though the circumstances for a given month might deviate from the average used.

I assumed that the FS-QC system would be tweaked to accommodate the conceptual and structural differences between AFDC and FS. But such was not the case. The reviewers were expected to go in and use the AFDC monthly accounting period.

If need or income or the purchase requirement varied from the average used by the caseworker for the QC review month, the case would be in error. They used the same five-dollar fudge factor as AFDC, and the same error tolerance levels—3 percent for eligibility errors and 5 percent for over and underpayments.

The longer they talked, the closer my chin got to the floor. Finally, losing my patience, I spoke up, "Look, I pointed out. Your methodology is very flawed. Even well-run programs will have extraordinarily high error rates that have nothing to do with fraud and not that much to do with management deficiencies. When these rates are reported in the press, however, Congress and the public will read fraud, not inconsequential deviations due to a faulty method for assessing error. This will taint the program and cause much unnecessary grief for state program administrators, for clients already under public suspicion and, I might add, for you." I pleaded, "Get the methodology right before launching what will surely be a disaster."

I recall that a few federal officials rushed up to me at the break and praised me for my great insights. *Insights!* I thought to myself. A retarded chimpanzee should have been able to figure this out. Alas, there were no chimps in the room . . . retarded or not. Unfortunately, this train simply was too far down the tracks to be stopped. It was launched as planned. The disaster occurred as any reasonable observer would have guessed. There were error rates of 50 and 60 percent and more in the early going, and the press used the words fraud and abuse as was their want. After the fact, one Ag official from the regional office privately confided to me that he was suspicious of any case review in which an error was not found.

One more humorous memory remains. The man who headed our QC unit was very nice but not the sharpest knife in the drawer. Sometime after the Food Stamp review system was launched, the expected intolerable error rates were found, as expected. The press found this man at home and asked for a statement. Apparently, they woke him from a nap, and he responded to their sharp questions about the bad Wisconsin numbers (they were bad everywhere) without thinking. Now, all he could remember was calling the Dept. of Agriculture a nickel-and-dime operation. He was moaning and groaning the next morning at work, convinced he would be fired as soon as the top managers found his sorry ass. When they did, they congratulated him on calling as it is. They feds running Food Stamps were a nickel-and-dime operation. Why this program was located within the Department of Agriculture and not with the other need-tested income assistance programs raised many questions.

My days of State service were running out, however. Why did I leave amid such fun? It started with another phone call, this one from Irving Piliavin, a professor in the School of Social Work at the University of Wisconsin. He was also an affiliate of the Institute for Research on Poverty (IRP). He asked if I would come to IRP and help him run a large project that would look closely at discretion in the patterns of decision making by welfare caseworkers. He needed someone with an inside perspective who knew how things worked in state government.

I had gotten several unsolicited offers of employment in the first half of the 1970s, both from consulting firms and from other states. In fact, in no other comparable period over the rest of my career did I experience such a flattering demand for my services. This offer from Irv was different, however. The others required relocating to other states and my wife giving up her job. When I told one of the consulting firms that my wife's career was an impediment to a move, they immediately offered her a position without even an interview. That would have been like getting quarterback Aaron Rogers as a throw in for failed QB in a trade package, Tim Tebow. She was the talent in the family.

This offer to work at the university was not totally out of the blue. Weeks earlier, Irv had approached the state about a research proposal he was developing. The federal source of funds required that a state agency submit the proposal. He made the argument that his research would help the state better manage its welfare programs. I suspect this promise was met with general skepticism by the powers that be. Most of the managers could not conceive that any egghead could tell them anything of use.

Though the distance between the state bureaucracy and the university is only one mile on the map, it is much further in reality . . . thus the pervasive skepticism on the part of State officials.

So, they assigned a low-level schlep like me to work with him. After all, I was expendable. I am sure they hoped that Irv would eventually just go away. In any case, I set about working with him and his graduate student, Tom Macdonald. Together, we turned the proposal into something that could sound useful to the sponsoring federal agency and to State officials.

Then I forgot about it until the call. The university! Hmmm, that sounds better than working for a living. So, I did what I usually do in making a big decision. I thought about it for four or five seconds and said, "Sure, why not." Big decisions were always the easiest. In buying our first home, my spouse and I looked at one house on a rainy winter evening when we could not see anything. We returned to our apartment with the real estate agent. My wife and I looked at one another and I casually said, "What the hell, let's buy it." We did.

I continued to work with the state of Wisconsin off and on over the succeeding decades but my full-time employment as a state worker was over. I think back on those days fondly. I worked with some very smart and dedicated people. Public service was respected back then, at least for the most part. And Wisconsin was looked upon as a model for honest, competent government. Good people still work for the state, but our respect for what public workers do is largely gone. Much of the best talent from the earlier days left, it is hard to do good work in a highly political atmosphere. The demise of public service in Wisconsin brings me great sadness.

In September of 1975, exactly four years after getting the shocking news that I was to be a research analyst-social services, I took that one mile walk down State Street. I was now house broken as a policy wonk. I looked forward to the beginning of a new professional life working in the academy with a bit of anticipation and a whole lot of trepidation.

We now fast forward to 1977. The error project I managed for Irv Piliavin was coming to an end, at least the data collection phase was. I felt a little bad for Irv. He really wanted to research the use and abuse of discretion in the welfare system. To do so, we collected data on everything that moved from frontline workers all the way through the bureaucracy to the top people in Madison. We reviewed case files and created measures tapping a host of organizational factors and on and on. At the beginning of the project I used all that I had learned about project planning and management to lay out a plan. I taped pages of circles and diamonds and squares lengthwise across two walls of my office. This effort was a management nightmare, but we pulled it off.

Unfortunately, the primary dependent measure was flawed. I and others had been successful in rooting out most ways that workers could exercise discretion. This is exactly what I had spent a good deal of my tenure in the state bureaucracy doing. It would have been a great study a decade earlier. Still, I learned a lot about running a large project. I will touch on Irv's project later in the book so will skip over it here.

The late 1970s is also the period when I decided to go for my doctorate in social welfare at UW. It was clear to me by now that staying in the academy was far preferable to working for a living. Of course, it would be easier to stay if I had the proper union card, a Ph.D. Moreover, a terminal degree in social welfare sounded perfect since no one knew what that meant. Hell, I could pass myself as an expert in so many areas. Given my usual short attention span, it took me over a decade to get the darn thing, and then only by ginning up some scam conceived by then IRP director Sheldon Danziger to kick me out of the program with a degree. I must have become an embarrassment to them. Sadly, I am one of those pathetic creatures that would never allow my schooling to interfere with my lifelong education. In any case, let us not dally too long here. Rather, let us return to my policy candy store so that we can begin our journey through the welfare wars.

CHAPTER 3

WELFARE WARS: STORM CLOUDS RISING

If you cannot make it good, at least make it look good.

—Bill Gates

What I call the "welfare wars," at least as I experienced them, started in 1977 with a call from Mary Ann Cook, a relatively high-ranking Wisconsin state official. Mary Ann knew me socially through my wife, who also worked for the state. For some unfathomable reason, she thought I would be a good starting place for an important project she had been handed. The Wisconsin Legislature had authorized the creation of a Welfare Study Committee to examine state public assistance programs, and to recommend any reforms deemed appropriate. The committee would have two years to do its work.

Mary Ann had two requests. First, would I consider shepherding the staff that would be assigned to the committee? Second, would I recommend an IRP affiliate who might serve as committee chair? To the first I said with conviction and emphasis . . . no can do! For once in my life, I was determined to be a serious student as I started out for my doctorate. To the second request I suggested Irv Garfinkel, current IRP director; or Bob Haveman, the former director. Either would have been wonderful for the role, and I gave my assessment of their comparative strengths. For whatever reason, they tapped Bob for the honor; perhaps because he evinced an avuncular air of wise authority. Their request for his services did not exactly make his day. Public service is not prized in the academy, even if done at the federal level. Doing a favor for state government would garner him little credit among his academic peers. He worried this would be a no-win assignment for him. I had to work on Bob a bit before he signed on. I was already a schmoozer.

It is not surprising that the state would turn its attention to welfare at this point. Caseloads had begun to rise in the 1960s, which caused local officials to look on with increasing alarm. Reform fever, however, was held at bay by the promise of federal action. In the early years of the 1970s, the Nixon administration sponsored the Family Assistance Plan (FAP); which purportedly would solve all the state's problems. During my state employment days, I vividly recall Wilbur Schmidt, then secretary of the Wisconsin Department of Health and Family Services (HFS), assert to a large audience of state and local officials that federal relief was on the way. It was a guarantee coming directly from

Wilbur Cohen, a long-time power on the Washington scene who had graduated from UW sometime in the 1930s. Apparently, this fact enhanced the credibility of his prognostication. It was treated as inside information that Wilbur was sharing with a few hundred intimate friends.

Funny thing, Wilbur turned out to be dead wrong. FAP, a kind of negative income tax or guaranteed income floor, came close but didn't quite make it. When President Carter assumed office, he launched another major reform initiative, the Program for Better Jobs and Income (PBJI). But this time around, there was more skepticism at the local level about any possible federal rescue. The feeling emerged that the state should probably save itself rather than wait any longer for outside help. Thus, the study committee was authorized; the one that I was absolutely, positively, without question, not going to get sucked into no matter how sumptuous those delights might look in my candy store.

You guessed it. I folded like a cheap suit. If I had been born in the Philippines, my nickname surely would have been the manila folder. In my defense, I did hold out a bit, a very little bit. It took some more pleading from Mary Ann and three calls from Terry Wilkom, the deputy secretary of the department. Terry had been the majority leader in the Wisconsin State Assembly before moving to a top administrative position in the state bureaucracy. He had also been my spouse's supervisor in state government for a while, so I knew him socially as well. If Terry was anything, he was persuasive. Softened by a mixture of flattery and appeals to doing the public good, my dedication to the scholarly life wilted, and I signed on the dotted line. It was sign of things to come in my struggle for a professional identity. Good thing, it was a better learning environment than most of the classes I would try to squeeze in at the same time.

The committee was small. In addition to Bob, the other members of note were a close aide to the governor, a rising member of the State Assembly (Tom Loftus), and a welfare advocate. I was able to slip out of the top staff job but did supervise the work of two Economics research assistants at the U.W. The state-located staff included Susan McGovern, the daughter of George McGovern, the 1972 Democratic presidential candidate. With the structure in place, the fun began.

As the work got underway, there were no clear instructions about how to proceed. Peter Tropman was a high-ranking official in the department. Trained as a social worker, he represented a portion of Milwaukee in the legislature before moving into the executive branch of government, and thus had formed strong opinions about what was wrong with welfare. As I recall, he pushed for much stronger work requirements, perhaps anticipating themes that would emerge with considerable strength in a few years. He did not seem to do so with great conviction, however. The work theme was only gaining strength, and he might have held concerns that he was straying a bit from his Democratic roots. There were occasional murmurs from conservatives about the rising dependency crisis, and the need to get tough on the so-called welfare crisis; but their grumblings had not yet coalesced into a coherent or organized attack. Storm clouds were rising but were not yet ominous.

In general, it appeared we would be given a relatively free hand. I can recall checking with Mary Ann on more than one occasion to confirm that we really were free to consider radical changes. She kept giving me a green light, repeatedly noting that she went after me so hard because I was considered an idea man. I guess that meant I was to come up with some ideas. This was clearly a "beware of what you ask for" moment. Warning to all current and future managers: never let the lunatics take over the asylum.

Don Percy was the secretary of the department at the time. He had been a vice president in the U.W. system, a position he achieved without a doctorate . . . an almost inconceivable achievement in any classist university system. Having gone as far as he could in that system, his move to an executive agency made sense.

Don was considered an intellectual, a creative and imaginative manager, and someone who sought to delegate important responsibilities to staff. I recall once going into his office to have him sign off on some research proposals that were going off to the federal government. As he began to sign them I asked him if he needed more time for review or perhaps a verbal summary. "No," he said, "I trust you. Besides, I know where to find you." Another time he told me that he wanted us to take chances, to be creative. When I looked at him with incredulity, he did add a caveat. "The only thing I ask is that if you really screw up, come and tell me first. I will back you, but I don't want to be blindsided." In effect, he had also given us a green light.

Okay, I thought, *I have just fallen down the rabbit hole and come up in policy wonk heaven.* Hell, we appeared to be free to dream up whatever mischief our imaginations might spawn, and our courage would permit. It was just a little like being a teenager who was given the keys to Dad's car and his credit card to boot. Could a trip to juvenile court be far behind?

Many of the details are lost to history and a decaying memory. But I do recall a pattern that emerged. Bob and I would meet at IRP and brainstorm some possibilities. Basically, we scoured existing ideas that were in play in Washington or could be borrowed "off the shelf" from the existing academic literature. So, we looked at the tax structure to see if it might be altered to be more favorable to low income families. We started playing with the Earned Income Tax Credit concept that was still in its policy adolescence back in the 1970s. Could that concept somehow be imported into Wisconsin as a state reform initiative to help the working poor? What about tax credits for employers to hire job seekers with less skills and experience. These so-called wage bill subsidies were theoretically persuasive even though their performance in improving targeted labor demand was questioned by many. And what about the progressivity of the state tax code at the low-end of the income distribution. Were we exposing the poor to positive tax liabilities?

We also looked at what was going on with Carter's reform effort, what became known as the Program for Better Jobs and Income (PBJI). Several IRP affiliates were involved in that effort, Eugene Smolensky for one. While PBJI was destined to falter and fail, as so many others had in the past, there had been a lot of attention paid to jobs programs for welfare-type families. These were the first ripples in what would soon become a tidal wave of change.

Beyond that, we had access to some of the best thinking that had been done on the large scale Supported Work projects and the so-called Income Maintenance Experiments (IME). These were rigorous studies on the effects of alternate welfare guarantees and work incentives on seminal client behaviors like labor supply, marriage, and related outcomes of societal interest. It was hoped they would answer fundamental concerns about the behavioral consequences built into welfare programs. IRP had been instrumental in developing the experimental designs used to evaluate the IME interventions. You must remember that this was an era, now long past, when even some politicians looked to experimental research for answers.

Other suggestions might come from IRP affiliates. For example, John Bishop, a labor economist and post-doc at IRP, gave generously of his time on labor market issues. Finally, Sue McGovern did an exhaustive study of the General Assistance program, an income transfer for impoverished individuals and childless couples. And there were the usual subjects covered by every reform effort, how high child care costs; and the possible loss of health care after leaving welfare for work might impede a sustained move to independence. In a relatively short time, we had a smorgasbord of challenges, ideas, and possibilities.

The question was, what should we do with all these possibilities? There was a lot of back room vetting with staff and with key officials like Mary Ann. I do recall one meeting with Don Percy and some of his top staff. I personally was looking for some feedback on what would sell or not. Where were the boundaries? So, I started throwing out modest ideas first. Don lapped them up. Emboldened, I started throwing out bigger ones. He seemed to get even more excited. With each one, he would ask questions and then turn to Ron Hunt, his top budget analyst and say something like, "Ron, come up with some figures on that one." Each time, Ron's head would drop just a little more.

At one point, I recall thinking, *this is not working! I am getting zilch useful feedback here.* So, I threw out the stupidest idea I could think of, at least from a political feasibility perspective. "And maybe we could envision a State Health Service for poor people, sort of like the British System." When he turned to Ron for numbers on that one, I realized I had better avoid this poor budget guru for the next month or so. My final image of Ron that day was as he slowly walked down the hall, his head shaking in disbelief. In any case, it was clear that no one was going to put us on a short leash.

On occasion, we did reach out to other state departments, like the Department of Industry, Labor, and Human Relations (DILHR), which now is the Department of Workforce Development (DWR). We also talked with the tax people, the Department of Revenue (DOR). One day, I discovered that the deputy of DOR was attending the IRP holiday party. Pat Lipton was an ABD from the UW Economics Department and her spouse was on the UW faculty. So, I introduced myself and suggested that I meet with her and her boss. It struck me as wise to chat with them before recommending all kinds of crazy changes to the state tax system.

Her boss, the secretary of the department, was Dennis Conta. Ironically, he was my former Peace Corps training director just a little over a decade earlier. When I returned from India to Milwaukee, I helped him get reelected to the State Assembly. The only time I have ever done hands-on politicking. I was beginning to think this was a small world indeed. In any case, we nominally had a sympathetic ear at DOR.

Unfortunately, we did run into some headwinds there. A comparable study group was looking at the state's tax system. Another IRP affiliate, Martin David, was on that one. They were beginning to argue that the state taxation function should focus only on collecting revenue and not stray toward extraneous policy purposes. The tax system was fair game for all kinds of reformers who wished to motivate desired behaviors without expanding the size of government. I sympathized with those arguing for a policy neutral tax system except, of course, when it impinged on the policy purposes of interest to me. I chatted with Martin about my concerns, but inexplicitly he chose to stick to his own principles. Go figure!

But some of the best fun was selecting ideas and running them past the committee. Bob couldn't do it because he was a member of the committee. The person hired as nominal head of the committee staff was an ABD student in Sociology named Sandy Wright. She was competent and hardworking and smart, but also quite reserved, even shy. So, I typically (always) got the nod to do the staff talking at official meetings. At some of the meetings I might go on for extended periods in what was a give-and-take tutorial. For example, I would explain what wage bill subsidies were, why they might be important, and some of the pros and cons. Then I would review the glazed looks on some of the panelist's faces.

Except for Bob, few on the committee were terribly conversant with what was, even back then, a substantial litany of possibilities on welfare reform. Besides, nothing was straightforward, even the simplest idea had pros and cons that had to be carefully assessed. The process proved a wonderful learning opportunity. To repeat my favorite bromide from Bud Bloomberg, my old UW-M professor, you don't really understand something until you need to explain it to others. Thus, my original hope that this project would prove an effective heuristic opportunity for me proved quite prescient. Surely, I learned more doing this than in many of my classes.

Some of the real fun came out of the blue. One day, I was walking through the hallowed halls of IRP when Irv Garfinkel, the director at the time, and Maury Macdonald, an IRP affiliate, cornered me by the receptionist's desk. Now Irv was rather striking looking. He was thin and angular of stature, bearded with his hairline receding from what always struck me as a slightly larger than life forehead. He would never be confused with a Fortune 500 CEO but looked great as the slightly mad scientist. That aside, he was passionate about both good research and good public policy. He was also a scholar of great integrity who would be led by the data even when it conflicted with his priors. When he did grab onto an idea, though, he quickly became a runaway train. I could see it in his eyes, he had an idea. *Oh no*, I thought.

With considerable excitement, he launched into a discussion of a set of child support reforms. Not only did he have ideas for improving child support collections for needy children, he was proposing that the government, in effect, guarantee a minimal amount of child support; even if the obligations from the absent parent were never collected. He would eventually sweep all this up under the mantle of the next evolutionary stage of social insurance. We had social insurance for the elderly, why not for vulnerable children?

I don't think I absorbed it all in that moment. For one thing I knew immediately where he was going with all this. He got there soon enough. "Could I sell this to the Wisconsin Reform Committee?" My mind had already begun to frantically search for ways that this might be packaged in a politically saleable way. Despite Irv's enthusiasm, my initial reaction basically was "this is nuts." In a way, though, he did have some say over my future in IRP even though, in the academy, notions of hierarchy are loose at best. Still, I thought it best to say, "Irv, this certainly sounds promising, and I will think hard on it." Little did I know at the time that this hallway meeting eventually would launch a child support revolution in Wisconsin and beyond. It would also add fuel to future welfare conflagrations that would beset the state.

I certainly needed additional tutoring from Irv but eventually got around to vetting the child support ideas with the powers that be. I can still remember the initial look on Mary Ann Cook's face. It clearly read, "This is nuts." I always found Mary Ann one of the more engaging public servants I have met. She had an inexhaustible font of knowledge about programs, and about how government worked. She also had this agile mind that typically operated at warp speed. I thought I was a quick study, but she would exhaust me in a half hour as she careened from subject to subject making insightful comments and issuing lightening quick witticisms. Her "this is nuts' expression was not to be sneezed at. I also could hear her unstated comment, "Sure, I brought you in as an idea guy, but not to be the totally nutty idea guy."

Funny thing about new and nutty ideas! With time and massaging, they begin to make sense. Mary Ann, with that quick and agile mind, soon absorbed the main elements of the proposal. Irv could be persuasive. I am not sure she bought it as much as gave the green light to try it out on the committee. When we did present it, with ample help from Irv, at least one important member responded with considerable enthusiasm. Tom Loftus, our rising legislative star, eventually took it on as part of his future legislative agenda.

In 1979, we published a final report though, if you looked carefully, you would see the year 1978 on the front cover despite numerous edits. If that were our only error! For its time, I would say that it was a remarkable document. In one way or another it covered most of the issues that grabbed and kept our attention. The press we received was also positive for the most part. Over time I wondered why there had not been more negative reactions. Perhaps the comprehensiveness of the ideas muted latent animosity as readers got lost in the labyrinth of ideas and proposals.

Simple reform ideas such as let's impose workfare or let's raise cash guarantees invite easy ideological categorization and attack. Our report had something for everything. Among other things, the report contained ideas for reducing poverty among low-income populations, for incentivizing the poor to work more and for employers to hire them, for ensuring that absent parents meet their obligations to their children, and for agencies administering public assistance and workforce programs to collaboratively work together. There was something for individuals drawn from various parts of the political spectrum to love and to hate. It probably helped that the hard lines that were to develop around the welfare debate had not set yet congealed into bitter, ideological camps.

Our work touched on the elements of welfare that make the doing of policy so seductive and compelling. There are no easy answers. It is almost impossible to propose solutions that can satisfy all objectives satisfactorily. In addition, you cannot simultaneously appease all the stakeholders involved. You must deftly weave through the politics without doing too much harm. As the old saying goes…if it were easy to do, it would have already been done.

Some of the contributing complications are technical in character. Take, for instance, the iron law of welfare, a challenge that forced economists to run up the white flag of surrender by the 1970s. In theory, most early reforms of income support programs wanted to accomplish three goals: 1) improve the economic well-being of poor families; 2) improve labor supply through properly incentivizing work, and 3) satisfy target efficiency objectives by targeting benefits only on poor families. Other worthy policy goals might be added such as cost, target population saturation, and administrative efficiency among others; but let us keep this relatively simple.

In the real world, there were inevitable tradeoffs. Perhaps we could start with improving the economic well-being of our struggling families. We might consider raising welfare guarantees . . . the amount a family will receive if they have no other income. Immediately, we begin to worry that our generosity will take away the adult client's incentive to work. No problem, we can lower the tax rate on earnings (the benefit reduction rate) by reducing their benefits in the face of earnings by less than a dollar for every dollar earned, maybe by much less. Such a policy would make work more economically attractive. But that increases the break-even point or the effective income level at which welfare benefits fall to zero. Damn it, we would now discover that too many non-poor families are getting welfare. This sacrifices the target efficiency goal. We can play around with other policy options that involve different welfare guarantees and varying marginal tax rates on earnings, but we never seem to be able to satisfy all three objectives simultaneously. The lesson here is simple. Welfare reform, like all "wicked" policy issues, involves tough choices and often irresolvable conundrums.

The stakeholder issue is equally confounding. Joseph Califano, secretary of the U.S. Department of Health and Human Services which housed welfare reform called welfare the Mideast of domestic policy. There were many players in this political sandbox, and most were digging themselves into inflexible ideological or partisan positions. You wanted a political fight back, then take a shot at welfare reform. And the queen of contention in the welfare world was the Aid to Families with Dependent Children program (AFDC).

In AFDC, we were giving out cash to low-income families with children. The federal government first got involved as part of the Social Security Act passed in the depths of the Great Depression, largely to provide fiscal relief to states that had been running small relief programs for "deserving" widows. In the beginning, that noncontroversial program was dominated by white widows. By the sixties and seventies, however, the complexion of the caseload had darkened considerably; and a majority of the caseload now were single women with children who had never been married. In addition, the labor force participation of women was rising by one percentage point a year, year after year. People began to ask, why is this one groups of women exempt from the workplace when other women had been flocking into the labor market?

In budgetary terms, AFDC was pocket change, costing the federal government about $16 billion at its peak. The emotional juice generated by the program, however, was outsized and almost irrational. The program had become a proxy for all manner of concerns to Americans—poverty, work, family responsibility, sex, community decay, family stability, teen pregnancy, domestic violence, and a list that goes on and on. Worried about communism, pollution, sunspots, aliens from outer space, your waistline, a low testosterone level, blame AFDC. Okay, I exaggerate here but not by much. The program was blamed for many ills and was becoming the source of almost obsessive concern, which was only to accelerate in the coming years.

In any case, our report was now public. What next? The history of study committee reports is not encouraging. Most disappear under the waves without a search plane even being sent out to rescue them. The political news after our report was released was not encouraging. Almost immediately, a Republican governor assumed power taking over from the Democratic predecessor, Marty Schreiber. Surely, given the change in administrations, we would be playing taps over our work by the evening news.

The new Republican governor, Lee Dreyfus, turned out to be a maverick. He came out of nowhere as the former chancellor of a UW campus in central Wisconsin. He was a great communicator, traveling around the state in a bus wearing a red vest and not sounding anything like a politician, nor like a Republican. It was (he was) very refreshing. Shortly after his election, he stunned everyone (well, me at least) first by saying that he would not balance the budget on the backs of the poor, and second by retaining Don Percy as head of the welfare system. Perhaps we might check our pulse to detect any continuing life for our reform ideas.

Bob had decided that he had made enough of a contribution to the public good. I recall the day we walked down State Street (which bridged government and academia) shortly after the report was out. He went on about how much this commitment had cost him among his colleagues. Now he would have to buckle down and make up for "lost" time. Irv Garfinkel, on the other hand, was determined to struggle on. He was committed to the set of child support reforms he had championed. Sometime later, he told me that before committing himself further, he polled several of his closest colleagues about whether his academic prospects would suffer if he committed a lot of time and energy to promoting his child support innovations ideas in the public arena. He told me no one, not a single colleague, encouraged him to do so. The conventional wisdom in the academy is that public service is where scholarly careers go to die. He ignored them all and made it work.

Before discussing child support further, let us look at some of our other ideas. The concept of the Earned Income Tax Credit (EITC), once having been planted in the state public arena, eventually took hold and became law in Wisconsin. I don't recall us doing much further work on the idea, I suspect it sold itself. The EITC provided a refundable tax credit to low-income workers. The return increased proportionately to a pre-established level of earnings (a kink point) before beginning to decline to zero as earnings increased further (a break-even point).

Some of the virtues of the EITC are as follows. It is administered through the tax system and thus does not require an expansion of the dreaded welfare bureaucracy. By tying the state EITC to the federal program (the local version would be a percentage of whatever the federal refund was), its administration was relatively efficient. It only went to working low-income families with children though; years later, a small version for single workers was introduced by the feds. Thus, it was tied to work and was believed to encourage labor market participation. This appealed to conservatives. Finally, unlike cash welfare, people could combine earnings plus the federal and state EITC benefits (up to a point, at least) and have a legitimate shot at escaping poverty. This was less true of conventional cash welfare assistance.

There were downsides as there were with all reform ideas, even the appealing ones. It increased the "error rate" among tax returns. I have heard U.S. Treasury officials claim that it is the single most error prone element of tax returns. Many low-income workers did not think they needed to file a tax return, so it took a massive marketing effort to spread the word that doing so was to their advantage. The program was suspected of discouraging marriage since two-earner couples filing jointly may earn too much to get a refund while they would as non-married single filers. Finally, the economists worried (they are a worrying lot) about work being discouraged during the phase out range; particularly when other benefits like Food Stamps, might also be facing cuts during that same earnings range. What economists called marginal tax rates could exceed those faced by millionaires even back then, before we started redoing the tax code to give unconscionable tax breaks to the Koch brothers, the Walton family, and filthy rich hedge fund managers. Some of these issues were not fully appreciated at first, and the attraction of this concept remained reasonably high throughout this period.

At this point, let me interject a vignette that perfectly illustrates the chasm between the world of the policy wonk and the world where real people reside. One day, the welfare director of a smaller northern Wisconsin county accosted me. I think this was in a bar and back in my drinking days, so my judgment might not have been the best. "Tom," she said excitedly, "would you please come up north to give a talk to a group of welfare directors and county board chairs about the welfare study and the report's recommendations." Her request made sense. Counties back then had a budgetary stake in the welfare system and would (or should) be interested in what kind of mischief we were cooking up. Though my instincts told me that "this is not good," she wore me down after some more abject pleading and perhaps a couple more drinks. I should have stamped out that people-pleasing instinct I inherited early on in life.

Shortly, I was looking over the audience. I knew the welfare director part of the audience well . . . the county board chairs were a different animal. They struck me as old, white, male, and sporting a demeanor of mistrust across their faces. Too many of them looked as if they had just taken a break from working their alfalfa field and could not wait to get back to doing something worthwhile. I could see it in their eyes . . . surely this Communist sympathizer from Madison (a known den of left wing nut cases) had nothing of note to say. Bravely, however, I launched into my talk with soaring rhetoric and sweeping vision. The plan, if adopted, would transform the very foundations in the way we help poor families. I was so moved by my rhetoric that tears were forming in my own eyes.

Perhaps I should have paid more attention to the glazed eyes out there and the furtive glances at their watches. It eventually dawned on me that the noon hour was approaching. Oh my god, I was keeping them from lunch and, more importantly, the bar. I finally wound down to polite applause, the kind that says, "damn glad that is over." *Well,* I mused, *this was at least better than facing that bunch of social workers early in my state career.* My solicitation of questions was met with deafening silence. Finally, a grizzled board chair tentatively raised his hand. "Yes," I responded enthusiastically. "Well," he started, "I don't understand a lot of what you were saying but I can see that if a young girl gets pregnant the first time, we give her a little help. On the other hand, if it happens a second time, we sterilize her." Uh-uh, I think I might have missed this audience by just a smidge.

Try as I may, I could not recall one mention of sterilization in our report or in my remarks. I recalled, though, that this is exactly what happened to my wife's aunt in northern Minnesota back in the 1930s. She had a child out-of-wedlock and St. Louis County had her sterilized. After a couple more anemic questions and responses, someone gave a signal and the rush to the bar was on. Fortunately, I was not between them and their destination or my career as policy wonk would have come to a bloody end as my body was ground ingloriously into the floor. Many of my experiences result in personal epiphanies and this talk was no exception. In the future, I would never underestimate just how far my world is from the real world. As I would repeatedly tell my future students that what we consider to be the real world is vastly overrated. Avoid it at all costs, not leaving the protection of the university is one way of doing just that.

One other lingering piece of business from the report was the use of wage bill subsidies. These are subsidies to employers for hiring workers whose human capital or motivation might be less than that of a typical hire. Longer-term welfare recipients, those applicants with mild physical or mental impairments, others with criminal backgrounds or checkered employment histories might be targeted by these efforts. Economic theory would argue that a subsidy of the wage costs to employers would compensate for perceived deficiencies in an applicant, resulting in a positive marginal productivity contribution by the otherwise disadvantaged employee. Now that is a mouthful of jargon. Put more simply, lousy job applicants would look better if they cost less to the employer in wages. Some extended the basic argument by suggesting that the credits be generally available in softer labor markets to spur hiring that might not otherwise take place. When profit margins are squeezed, the availability of a wage subsidy might help maintain the demand for labor that would not otherwise exist given overall economic conditions. All this certainly sounded good on paper.

Variants of the wage bill subsidy concept flowered during this period including the New Jobs Tax Credit, the Targeted Jobs Tax Credit, the WIN (Work Incentive Program, notice they avoided the more accurate acronym of WIP) credit program. I think there also may have been a credit program for hiring displaced race jockeys from Lower Bessarabia. The problem was that we were hearing rumors on the policy grapevine that these initiatives were undersubscribed. That is, they were not being used as often as expected. Could economic theory be flawed? Perish the thought.

The question did intrigue me, however, though the thought crossed my mind that I should consider getting a real life as opposed to worrying about such things. Perhaps I should finish up my degree. Unfortunately, silly impulses to do the wise thing never stayed with me long. Be that as it may, I decided to look at this conundrum more closely. Now, economists generally prefer observational studies using large data sets and fancy econometric tools for teasing out causality. Unfortunately, I always had trouble with things like basic algebra. I could never figure out how long it took the boat captain to eat his lunch when the river was flowing in one direction at Y miles per hour, and the boat was chugging along in the opposite direction at Z miles per hour. Therefore, I concluded we should do something different. Let's ask employers directly! I can still hear the cries. This man should be shot for academic heresy.

Most acolytes of the dismal science would scoff at this approach. People lie. They give socially desirable responses. They cannot be trusted. Observed behavior, not verbalized intent, was the best path to the truth. Only devotees of the lesser pretend sciences, like sociologists and social workers, would ever ask people direct questions. As someone who had no ego left to defend, sarcasm was lost on me. I wanted to find out what was on people's minds.

With help from the Wisconsin Labor Department, we went about trying to answer that question. Stan Masters, an open-minded economist and IRP post-doc, signed onto the project along with Jim Moran, a Social Work doctoral student. Then we developed a complicated set of survey instruments including brief telephone surveys, in-depth personal interviews, focus groups, and so forth. We picked random samples from carefully selected sample frames representing sectors of the economy likely to use such subsidies. Like most people who spend their lives desperately avoiding reality, I found the opportunities to interact with real people surprisingly stimulating.

When we pulled all the data together, the picture was clear. I will reduce a rather complex narrative down to a simple story. Tax credits often did not work because the person doing the hiring was not the same person who worried about the firm's taxes. The former wanted the best applicant possible. If the tax person later found that a potential hire was eligible for a credit, great. In such a situation, the subsidy had no influence on the hire. It was a mere windfall to the employer, an unexpected benefit.

Even when the hiring decision and the wage-subsidy decision were codetermined, there were numerous issues. The largest problem involved stigma. If an applicant walks into an interview with a voucher in hand (used in some programs), too many employers told us this would set off a red flag. What is wrong with this person? Why does he or she need a subsidy? Many told us a variant of the following, no subsidy was worth hiring someone who would be unreliable, who would offend their customers, who would destroy their capital machinery, or who would unintentionally (or even intentionally) burn their business to the ground. Sometime later, our conclusion was verified by a true experiment in which a random sample of applicants bearing a wage subsidy voucher, which they showed to hiring supervisors, were less likely to be hired than those applicants without the subsidy.

The other big problem was the stigma associated with government. There were widespread feelings that participating in the program would be labor intensive, involve crushing red tape, and worst of all, would result in government looking over their shoulders. Again, a common refrain was that if I signed on, surely the government would tell me that I can't fire this person who just burned down my business and put me on food stamps. For me, the results persuaded me not to push the wage bill subsidy notion in Wisconsin even though we had spoken positively about the concept in our report.

My parting shot to state officials was that even if what I called "naked' subsidies did not work well (a subsidy that is not accompanied by any other information on the client from the sponsoring agency), work on developing the use of subsidies along with direct employer contact might be worth a try. Interacting with employers about specific clients might counteract general suspicions and stereotypes. But I would let others do the pursuing on that one. Sometime down the road, Sheldon Danziger pulled me aside and said that Gary Burtless, a Brookings scholar and IRP affiliate, had mentioned how useful he thought that wage bill study was. I respected Gary immensely, one of the brighter people I have met in this business, so this was high praise indeed. I got to know him much better a decade down the line when we worked together on revising the official poverty measure.

We now return to child support. Some of the best fun in the aftermath of the welfare study involved a push to reform the child support system in Wisconsin. This initiative started out small, but eventually evolved into a multifaceted set of reforms that, on occasion, erupted into fierce stakeholder debates, political controversy, and near-death experiences for some involved. The welfare wars were soon to pick up in intensity. I cannot do justice to the whole story here so will only touch upon selected highlights.

The core set of child support reforms, as first articulated by Irv Garfinkel, contained three main elements. I will start with the most controversial. Government should assure the payment of child support. That is, if government failed to collect what was due, then a guaranteed amount (set in law) would be forwarded to the child(ren). This "assured" child support payment, as it came to be called, was not without precedent. Variants could be found in a couple of Scandinavian countries and Harold Watts, first IRP director, apparently had floated a similar concept about two decades earlier.

Before the audience could scream about government overreach and excessive program cost, Irv would move on to his collection-side reform ideas. First, we needed a better way of setting child support amounts. The existing approach was subjective, incomprehensible, and largely based on who had the better lawyer. Awards varied from case to case on no transparent basis. With so much subjectivity, those expected to pay often did not, partly based on the notion that they were getting hosed since they knew other noncustodial parents in similar circumstances who paid much less.

After much thought and study, we proposed that a simple proportional formula be adopted. Absent parents would pay 17 percent for one child, 24 percent for two, 27 percent for three, and so on. Some modifications were made for shared custody arrangements, but the basic approach was highly simplified in most cases. When in place, this approach would respond to variation in earnings or cessation of earnings. After all, 17 percent of nothing is nothing. The percentage approach also would ensure that children would enjoy levels of support commensurate with what they enjoyed before the family dissolution.

The next step was to collect what was owed more efficiently. Existing practice would simply order the absent parent to pay. When they did not, a common occurrence, they would be warned; or a lien imposed on their earnings or, in the extreme, they would be thrown in jail where their ability to support their offspring was really challenged. It is rather hard to pay child support when you are making about eighty cents an hour stamping out license plates.

Why wait for default? We argued that the use of automatic wage withholding should be universal. Orders would immediately be deducted from earnings and forwarded to the child support agency in all cases where it was feasible. It would be a rebuttable presumption in legal jargon. While this is common practice now, it was revolutionary in the early 1980s.

As Irv put it, we were proposing a three-legged stool. Government would guarantee child support, or at least a minimal amount of support. But the public exposure would be minimized by sound improvements to the setting and collection of support orders. The second leg would be setting the amount of the obligation is a straightforward and uniform manner, while the final leg improved the collection process. Moreover, government would be highly motivated to go after what was owed since they were on the line if they failed on the collection side of things.

Even better, the guaranteed child support payment was *not* like welfare. A key characteristic of welfare is that benefits fall as earnings rise, a perverse incentive indeed. The child support guarantee did not operate that way (at least as we envisioned it). It would complement earnings, not act as a substitute for earnings, thus properly incentivizing work. This approach would help single-parent families escape poverty.

Going from where we were at the starting line to where we wanted to be at the finish would take much study, time, and effort. To do this we needed money (don't we all?). Remember that the two most important motivations driving research are a thirst for truth and the availability of money, and not in that order. We did get some help from outside sources. For example, with the help of Prudence Brown, the Ford Foundation kicked in with some early planning money. The primary source of support, however, came out of a much more imaginative idea and has supported a long-standing state-university partnership.

Simply put, whenever the federal government had a public assistance program that matched state dollars, there was an opportunity for a university-state partnership to maximize those federal dollars. It would work like this. Let us say the feds matched state contributions on a 3-1 basis, for each state dollar put up the feds put up three. Now, there was nothing in the law that said the university could not put up the state match since we are a state agency, though few of the faculty would see it that way. The genius of our approach was in developing new ways of coming up with the university match. Fortunately, the financial guy at IRP at the time, Jack Sorenson, was quite creative and rather devious. Bill Wambach, who followed Jack in the position, was equally talented.

I will let one example suffice as an illustration of the alleged creativity. The university had negotiated with the federal government a 44 percent overhead rate for research. That is, out of each federal research dollar, forty-four cents went to pay for stuff like lights, office space, janitorial services, and other costs to the university for maintaining a research capacity. A state agency paid nothing, or a nominal amount, toward these overhead costs when they contracted with IRP, or any university entity, for such analytical work. Therefore, Jack came up with the notion of declaring that this hypothetical overhead contribution by the university was a legitimate state match against which federal dollars could be leveraged. That is, the university's presumed overhead contribution was construed as a real contribution to the research effort. At a 3-1 match rate, you did not need much funny money to draw down a lot of real federal dollars.

I recall Mary Ann Cook, always the quick wit, saying that the university could somehow use a tree located in lot 34 (a university parking lot near IRP) as match for federal dollars. Eugene Smolensky was IRP director at the time. Geno, as he was known, later went on to be dean of the Public Policy School at Berkeley and was one of the funniest men I have ever met, which is hard to believe since he is an economist. Anyways, I recall Geno walking around muttering, "I just know I am going to jail. I just know I am going to jail." The problem was we had no precedent for such a state-university arrangement at the time. Since I was the state guy, it was up to me to negotiate something.

One day, therefore, I sat down with Sherwood "Woody" Zink, the lead attorney for the Wisconsin child support program and other such programs. Neither one of us can recall when we first met, but we have remained good friends to this day. Woody is a memorable character. While he occasionally could be a bit irascible, he was always loquacious and very entertaining. Best of all, he was smart as a whip. He tended to think out loud, and to keep changing his mind as he worked through some problem. Deep down, Woody was a warm, big-hearted guy, and a fine attorney, almost becoming the first public attorney to become the president of the Wisconsin Bar. Even more important, he had a risk-taking personality and enjoyed interacting with the weird folk from the university; an almost incomprehensible lapse in judgment.

On that day, it was clear that Woody was uncomfortable. We were setting about establishing this relationship for which no existing framework existed. In short, we were creating a contractual relationship. The problem in his mind was that he was an attorney negotiating with a non-attorney . . . me!

The first thing he did was define a contract for me. Then we started. Soon, a negotiating pattern emerged. I would suggest a certain provision or idea for inclusion in the contract. His initial reaction typically was an emphatic, "We can't do that." I would lean back and say something like, "Well, I am not an attorney so maybe you can explain what the problem is here." Then Woody would launch into a long monologue in which he eventually arrived at a point where that provision, or a slightly modified alternative, became acceptable. We would finally agree to that point and move on to the next, and the next, and the next. Some form of repetition of that basic script continued throughout the process.

There were some sticky issues that remained at the end of the day. For example, proprietary ownership over project products took a while to settle. The "right" of the state to review and request changes also proved sticky, bumping up against the academic freedom principle. But we wanted this to work, and eventually settled on language we could sell to both sides of State Street. The framework we developed that day has worked for a long time. For many years, I would write extensions of the initial agreement by deleting, amending, or adding new substantive provisions. Best of all, Geno never went to jail.

With a contract in hand, the work proceeded. We brought on board a marvelous group of students and faculty. One of the more memorable was Margo Melli, who sadly passed away last year. When she graduated from UW Law School, she was just one of a handful of females in her graduating class and in the law in general. She told me that the Law School Dean at the time told her that no top-level law firm would even consider hiring her. Females were not yet accepted within a male dominated legal profession. So, in due course, she became the first female faculty member of the Law School. Beyond being an expert in Family Law, she evidenced an unwavering commitment to children and an inner strength, which would be expected of the first female in any endeavor. But she also had a warm smile and generous laugh. She was a delight as a colleague.

I will greatly abbreviate a long story here. To repeat, there were three main pushes to this project: (1) the Assured Child Support benefit or public guarantee; (2) the collection side of the equation or the Percentage Income and Asset Standard for setting awards along with the Automatic Wage-Withholding provision for collecting the awards; and (3) the creation of a large child support data set upon which to do the basic research needed to design current and future reforms.

Ideally, we would have done the first two together, but that proved politically infeasible. Considerable progress, however, was made on the collection side. Those provisions contained less fiscal risk. The basic approach was to introduce the new provisions to first establish through our simplified formula and then collect awards through universal wage withholding in ten counties. We also picked ten matched counties to compare the outcomes on several measures of interest. Okay so far!

Nothing, however, is as easy as it seems in the welfare world. Racine, an urban county located south of Milwaukee, was the first "experimental" county. To proceed, the county board had to agree to participate in this project. Since this was the first site, the "big guns" went to meet with the board, Irv Garfinkel and Tom Loftus; even though no real problems were anticipated. The way I heard it, the story went as follows. Word was spreading among the "father's rights" groups that the state was on the verge of toughening up the child support system. Many of these fathers already felt aggrieved by a system they perceived as being stacked against them. Having talked with many of them over the years, I came to realize that their sense of being victims is real. Whether or not they have been treated unfairly in reality is quite another matter though I suspect some have been. Family court is not for the faint of heart.

In any case, the fathers had gathered at a local drinking establishment to get ready for the board meeting. Let us just say that they were highly motivated and lubricated by the time the meeting started. After some agitation, the board decided that it would be highly prudent to table the motion for that night at least. The county sheriff approached Tom and Irv to ask if they would like a police escort out of town. When they responded that such a service would be unnecessary, the sheriff allegedly responded with, "Well, I think it is *very* necessary." I missed that fun night but did chat with a few of these fathers who called IRP to complain about our research. Their anger often bordered on the palpable and could be frightening.

After that stumble, things went much better as final design issues were settled and implemented. Not too long into the "experiment" (really a quasi-experimental design), a problem emerged. Word spread that the new policies were working miracles, child support collections were improving dramatically. Now there was no holding the tidal wave back. Other counties wanted to sign up, including some of our match counties.

What experiment, they cried, when asked to wait until the evaluation had been completed? Who needs that when it is obvious the new policies worked? With Tom Loftus having risen to the position of majority leader in the State Assembly, it was only a matter of time before the percentage standard and wage withholding became statewide policies. Soon, they would be models for change across the country though the percentage standard would never quite survive in its original form.

Remember that conversation with Irv at the IRP receptionist's desk? Already, the child support world was changing. For Irv, however, the real prize was getting the Assured Benefit (AB) into place. He was worried, legitimately so, that the progress being made on the collections side of the ledger would make introducing the AB more problematic. The "savings" attributable to improved child support collections were already being realized. Given that child support collections had already been improved, the AB is likely to be viewed as a pure fiscal outlay.

Still, much progress on the AB concept had been made even though many observers were highly skeptical. First, Wisconsin secured a waiver directly from Congress that enabled us to proceed toward turning the concept into an actual pilot program. We had several years in which to get it off the ground. Some bridges were burned in doing this. The then secretary of the U.S. Department of Health and Human Services was furious that Wisconsin had done an end run around her domain. But we bravely marched on! A great deal of groundwork was done to refine the AB concept; find counties willing to try it, develop procedures and protocols for administering it, and even working on a computerized capability for managing the new program. Tom Loftus was able to secure state legislative authority to proceed on a trial basis.

Moreover, we did go ahead and develop those large data sets we proposed as part of our original vision. We secured access to family court cases throughout the state and even to sealed court cases. Over the years, the IRP team was able to build longitudinal files and to integrate data on cases across programs. These data sets became a powerful analytic tool that fueled a better understanding of family dynamics, the child support system, and relate social programs. It supported many research projects and spawned numerous reform proposals over the years.

Irv, however, kept his eye on his prized Assured Benefit concept; and we did continue to make progress. He was so committed to the idea that he briefly considered running for a State Assembly seat so that he could lobby for the concept from the inside. Sometimes, however, fate intervenes.

In 1986, a pivotal Governor's race took place. Tommy Thompson, longtime Republican member of the State Assembly, ran against Democrat Anthony Earl. Thompson was widely known as Dr. No, since he opposed so many new proposals as minority leader of the state legislature. At the time, the race was a classic left versus right contest though Thompson, by today's Tea Party standards, would now be considered a wild-eyed, big spending liberal and Earl was far from a true Progressive.

Welfare was a big campaign issue. You could feel that the dialogue around welfare was changing almost daily. Two academic books of the era exerted outsized impacts. Larry Mead, a New York University Political Scientist, wrote *Beyond Entitlement.* Charles Murray, ensconced in various conservative think tanks, soon published *Losing Ground.* Mead's book essentially argued that the state should exercise normative control through the welfare system to encourage behaviors deemed appropriate. Murray's work argued that the expansion of the welfare state in the 1960s had, in effect, led to a deterioration of conditions for the very people these programs purported to help.

With Ronald Reagan in the White House, and with the overall cultural and intellectual climate swinging somewhat in a conservative direction, the timing seemed less than optimal for a new public income guarantee initiative. The 1986 Wisconsin gubernatorial election could well decide which way the future reform winds would blow in Wisconsin. Guess what, it did!

CHAPTER 4

THE WELFARE WARS: CRACKS IN THE SAFETY NET

All the forces in the world are not so powerful
as an idea whose time has come.

—*Victor Hugo*

In January 1986, the Aid to Families with Dependent Children (AFDC) caseload in Wisconsin hit 100,000 cases, exactly that number. That would be its high-water mark. It was almost as if some deity had established that figure as the upper-level ceiling. Though a fraction less than half of all cases statewide were minority families, the welfare "problem" increasingly was considered an urban-Black phenomenon. As the caseload climbed during the early years of the '80s, a sense of crisis was attached to AFDC. This would prove a combustible issue just waiting to explode on the political scene. It did just that during the mid-decade Wisconsin gubernatorial race.

Perhaps in anticipation, incumbent Governor Anthony Earl decided to establish a high-level State Expenditure Committee (SEC) to take a comprehensive look at state spending and revenues. It was the periodic exercise that involved a careful identification of budget items where cuts might be made without sacrificing essential services. One issue the committee would focus on was the dreaded welfare magnet concern. Were poor families pouring into Wisconsin to take advantage of the state's generosity? Perhaps that in-migration explained the rapidly rising caseload. For example, while the welfare guarantee in our neighbor to the south (Illinois) was comparable to ours around 1970, by the early 1980s, Wisconsin paid considerably more. For many, Wisconsin had become a welfare magnet irrespective of the existence of any proof for that assertion.

To be honest, many cheeseheads (as Wisconsin natives like to call themselves) do not take kindly to Illinois folk even when they came north as tourists to spread their cash around. They call them FIPs for F%&#ing Illinois People. Surely, they would not look kindly on poor Black migrant families from Chicago who allegedly bring with them crime, drugs, and all manner of social dysfunction. While such fears are undoubtedly exaggerated, perception is everything in welfare debates, the magnet issue being no exception.

Numerous poor families were migrating to Wisconsin from the Delta area of Mississippi and other southern states. In some of those places, welfare guarantees were unconscionably low. If they fell any further, beneficiaries would have to pay the state for the privilege of being destitute. For example, to raise the welfare guarantee in Texas, you had to pass an amendment to the state constitution. You can imagine that did not happen very often. The sixty-four-dollar question remained, what really motivated the interstate relocation of poor families in the first instance. Economic theory, once again, was rather clear. Poor families would try to optimize their utility. That is, they would relocate to a more generous state, all other things being equal.

The last phrase is the kicker. Clearly, there existed some obvious monetary transaction costs associated with residential relocations. It is not unreasonable to assume that a few other factors, some less easily monetized, are in play. Among these might be considered push factors and others would be defined as pull factors. Proximity to family, good schools, familiar cultural features, safe streets, economic opportunities, and so forth might also be brought into the picture. Imperfect knowledge about the comparative merits regarding where you now reside compared to available relocation options make relocation decisions very complex.

In the welfare world, our priors tend to dominate reality. Many tend to take complex issues and oversimplify them. In an article I wrote in the early 1990s titled *Child Poverty: Progress or Paralysis*, I called this very human tendency "perceptual truncation." In this context, welfare recipients are viewed through a limited lens.

They tend to be defined as stick figures making one-dimensional decisions. They are motivated only by relative differences in welfare guarantees across states. Oh, state B pays more than state A? Which way to the Greyhound bus station?

Of course, if this were totally true, all the recipients would have flocked to the highest paying state already, though that state surely would have responded by moderating its generosity to something more comparable to other states. Neither is it likely that the magnet effect plays no part in where poor families choose to live, economic theory could not be that far off base, at least I don't believe that to be the case.

The question has always been, are relocation decisions sufficiently determined by welfare differentials to warrant a public response? After all, many likely policy interventions would undoubtedly incur some costs for those legitimately in need, and not merely the greedy relocators. This issue had captured state officials back in the mid-1970s as Wisconsin became more generous than some of its neighbors. Sensing that this issue might have legs, Bernie Stumbras (of CRN fame in an earlier chapter) insisted that we put some migration-related questions on the new 37-page combined welfare application form back in the 1970s, at a time when we scrupulously tried to excise every superfluous item. His foresight proved beneficial to the study we were about to undertake.

The appointed State Expenditure Committee wanted help with the magnet question. Opinion was divided as to the validity and strength of the phenomenon. And when in doubt, study it some more. This is a candy store counter where the origins of my involvement are a bit fuzzy. I may have been contacted directly by one of the usual suspects in state government, or the call may have come from Paul Voss, a demographer at UW. Paul was on the short side with a receding hairline and a smile that lit up his face. He is just one of those very nice people that do all kinds of volunteer work for good causes. That is, he is a stereotypical Madisonian . . . other Madisonians that is, not me. Doing good might require that I get off the couch. Such folk infuse me with guilt though that still doesn't appear sufficient to move me off my slothful ways.

I do recall going to Sheldon Danziger, IRP director at the time, to ask if he would consider a formal institutional involvement by IRP. I think he sensed the political thicket involved here and backed off quickly. I, on the other hand, would not see the onrushing train if it were three feet in front of me. In the end, his caution probably did not help. When things got messy down the line, IRP was tarnished to some extent since I was such a visible presence in the study . . . guilt by association. I will say one thing about the academy. No one tells you what you can or cannot do. They would even leave a low-life like me alone. I was a true nonentity at the time (still no doctorate at this point though I might have been getting closer at long last). You have a lot of freedom to make all the mistakes you want, and I did just that with gusto. Even later, when I became involved in several kerfuffles with the governor and his people, no one from the university ever said a word to me. If anything, I felt protected even though I had no formal protection. Later, the dean of the School of Human Ecology made noises about offering me a tenured position largely because he thought me vulnerable. All quite remarkable now that I think back on it. It was like a large family of bear protecting a vulnerable cub.

Paul and I, with the help of some graduate students, put together another of those multi-pronged data collection efforts. The data from the state's CRN system was invaluable, particularly with Bernie's prescient insistence that applicants for assistance be asked when they moved to Wisconsin, from where, and whether they had lived in the state earlier in life. We needed a ton more data than that though. We secured that through surveys and interviews designed to tap into the decision-making processes used by low-income families in making relocation decisions. Here I am, putting together another big data set. Why didn't I exploit one of these for a doctoral dissertation? Excellent question! I think the lure of the next policy question always dominated my thinking. Alas, I am the wayward academic.

In any case, here we go again . . . naively asking people what was in their heads. I guess I would never learn. However, I could not escape my concern that making inferences of intent from observed behavior, no matter how reasonable, was inherently subjective. Fortunately, we had access to enough data to ascertain patterns of movement in and out of the state over time. We could tease out whether migration was basically a one and done phenomenon or something more complex. A one and done move would involve a poor family moving from a less generous state to Wisconsin and, once realizing they were in welfare heaven, settle down for good. That, after all, was the common consensus about what was happening.

Let me pause to bring you up to speed on the tenor of the times. The 1986 governor's race was in full fury as we moved to conclude the study. Moreover, the welfare magnet question (and welfare reform more broadly) were big campaign topics, a fact I repeat since it leads to a priceless vignette. Since the magnet topic was so super-hot politically, we were assigned a small advisory group of political actors to oversee the research. I do not recall the membership except that the group included someone from the governor's office and someone from the all-powerful Department of Administration. They were charged with monitoring us to make sure we didn't do too much mischief. While members of the research team could always meet, when we got together with the advisory group, it was deemed an open, public meeting. Those sessions had to be duly posted as such in advance.

So what, you say. Well, idiots that we were, we scheduled a meeting to first discuss results *the* day before the election. Naturally, when we arrived for the meeting the press was there with film crews ready to cover the breaking news. They were waiting for the experts to confirm that hordes of welfare barbarians were pouring over our borders to loot the state's treasury. Hell, this breaking news might sway the election results, which was expected to be close.

There was a moment of panic. We did *not* want to become the lead item on the evening news. Besides, we were far from issuing any summative statement of the research results. After a quick private consult, we decided to start the meeting by covering the most boring methodological issues we could envision. We droned on for a while about sample sizes, statistical error ranges, threats to population representativeness. These were discussed in an excruciatingly boring manner which, for academics, is quite easy to manage. I know I was soon asleep. One by one, the press folded up their cameras and left. One of us followed the last of the press to ensure they had, in fact, left the building. When we were convinced that it was now safe, we opened the discussion to a review of some very preliminary results.

The day before we were to present the findings to the full committee, Paul called me over to his office. All the data had not been analyzed yet though we had a pretty good idea what the story line would be. It went something like this. Yes, we did find evidence that the welfare magnet phenomenon was real. However, the magnitude of the effect was reasonably small, and probably did not rise to the level that warranted any serious response that would further impoverish struggling families. These results were comparable to what other quantitative studies would find in the coming years.

We also found that residential mobility among low-income families was much greater than supposed. Significant numbers moved into and then out of Wisconsin, often going back and forth between states several times. Why? Proximity to families and social networks were important. Some personal crisis would occur, and they might return to their former state, since most were less rooted in one place by career considerations. Clearly, the narrow view that migrant families move in and stay forever was not borne out by the data though, of course, many surely do.

The reasons for relocating were also complex. Strikingly, ease of getting welfare seemed more important than the differential in welfare guarantees. In addition, disadvantaged families tended to move for some of the same push and pull reasons we all do. They were looking for good schools for their kids, safe streets, freedom from gangs and drug peddlers, better economic opportunities, better housing, closer proximity to friends and family who may have relocated earlier. Few, however, mentioned the weather as a salient factor for moving to the badger state, which I thought gave our data some surface credibility. What jumped out at us was that a single, declarative answer as to why people relocate would prove way too simplistic. In a popular measure being floated at the time, migrants would receive the benefits they would have gotten in their former state for some limited period. That initiative seemed unlikely to affect relocation patterns, at least in our opinions, though politicians could claim they were doing something.

Paul asked me what I thought our bottom-line conclusion for the committee should be. I strongly urged that we stay away from any such summative statement. Let us present the data as coherently as we can. Then, let the committee develop a story-line. They are the decisionmakers and we merely are the hired guns. It is their judgment and expertise that counts, not ours. Paul did not buy it, however. "We are the 'experts,'" he argued. "They want our opinion, not just our findings." I remained unconvinced but agreed to go along. He had seniority.

The next day, we provided the committee with a long-winded narrative somewhat along the lines so very briefly outlined above; of course, we had many charts and many numbers just to look expert-like. I found press coverage in the four major papers the next day illuminating. Three concluded that the research proved that Wisconsin was *not* a welfare magnet, and one concluded that we proved it *was* a magnet. I had been hoping for a split vote.

If you think anything was decided by our research efforts, you do not know much about the welfare wars. The Wisconsin Policy Research Institute (WPRI), which at the time had little to do with research and much to do with advancing conservative causes, later hired an economist from Emory University to attack our results. Their hired gun tore into us saying that it was totally stupid to ask people why they moved. They will lie. They will give socially desirable responses, and blah, blah, blah.

Then he went on to "prove" that the welfare magnet "crisis" was costing Wisconsin something like $117 million per year. Yikes, how could I have been so blind? To come up with this figure, he basically assumed that anyone who had lived in another state in the past was a welfare migrant even if they moved into the state a decade before applying for assistance, or even had relocated here as a child with their parents. Apparently, this last group wanted to get an up-front spot in the applicant queue. He also assumed that they stayed on welfare and in Wisconsin forever; assumptions clearly contradicted by our data. The "fall down while laughing your fanny off" part of his analysis, in my mind at least, was an assertion that the state had to hire hordes of new workers to handle the burgeoning welfare-migrant induced caseload growth. The problem was, he never bothered to look at actual caseloads which were falling rapidly during the period of his analysis. Reality is a cruel mistress.

I guess the lesson here is never let a little data get in the way of a good story. Unfortunately, it was such a good story that his conclusions were printed in the *New York Times*. So much for "all the news that's fit to print!" I later heard that this rebuttal of our work was subsequently used in some Public Policy courses as an example of an atrocious, politically motivated hatchet job. Jim Miller, the director of WPRI, laid into me when we met one day, "How could you be so stupid and ignorant not to believe that all these poor (read Black) people are not pouring into Wisconsin for welfare." I think he went on to assert that I must be developmentally disabled.

In a larger sense, the welfare migration controversy is a good example of an inherent challenge in doing policy. When opinions are closely held and are sustained by an emotional component that ties together a coherent world view, conflicting data seldom makes a difference. That is why I am impressed with scholars who do follow the data. Sarah Mclanahan, another IRP affiliate now teaching at Princeton, had raised her children as a divorced mother before marrying Irv Garfinkel. She was convinced that children raised by a single mother could fare just as well as those raised in two-parent homes. Her research, no matter how she ran the numbers, did not support her priors. So, she changed her mind. That story, a scientist who faithfully followed the evidence, was eventually told in a popular magazine. In a world where opinions and beliefs have ossified, it is good (and apparently rare) to see intellectual honesty.

Not long after all this, I wrote a piece for *Focus,* the IRP publication, which is widely read in the policy world. The title was something like *The Wisconsin Welfare Magnet Debate: What is the ordinary member of the tribe to do when the witch doctors disagree?* While I did review the Wisconsin welfare magnet debate, my main purpose for doing the piece was to argue for a more civil dialogue in public policy, one based on reason and evidence and less on ideology and emotion. True, this is a bit like spitting in the wind but Herb Kohl, Wisconsin's senior senator at the time, found it so persuasive (or his staff did) that he had it read into the Congressional Record and strongly urged his colleagues to read it. I did not spend much time hanging around waiting for fan mail.

Is the magnet issue over? No, of course not. That issue taps into primal fears many retain about the "other," in this instance poor Black families, who threaten them in some way. That fear has moved on to newer opportunities, the fear of foreign-born, dark-skinned terrorists being a great example. The introduction of the Affordable Care Act (Obamacare) offers a subtle illustration. Some states have aggressively supported the law and others have not. Some have expanded access to Medicaid while others have refused to do so. This uneven pattern of acceptance and implementation creates situations where the same individual or family cannot get health coverage where they live now but can get it if they move to the neighboring state. Will they move just to get health care coverage? Some might, depending on their situation, many won't. Whenever differentials in coverage across jurisdictions exist, fear of benefits-induced migration will never disappear. To date, though, nothing matches the welfare magnet fears of the 1980s.

Let me continue this tour of the growing welfare wars by browsing in another counter of my candy store. By the mid-1980s, the intrepid legislator from our Welfare Study Committee, Tom Loftus, had risen to be majority leader in the Assembly. As such, he got to call the shots. Undoubtedly, he noticed that the political dialogue around welfare was drifting in a harder, more vitriolic direction. Led by the Reagan revolution, the politics in Washington were less than sympathetic to the poor. As noted, popular books by Mead, Murray, and others were transforming the intellectual climate and casting doubt about the existing welfare state. A more confident and assertive set of conservative think tanks (Heritage, American Enterprise Institute, Cato, etc.) were blasting away at that welfare state and the remnants of the War-On-Poverty with unrelenting attacks. Locally, there were increasing calls for workfare as a solution to the welfare "crisis" with some of these calls coming from Tom's own Democratic Party.

Roughly at the same time I was poking around the welfare magnet issue, Loftus set up a legislative committee to look at AFDC, and to see what could be done to enhance the connection between work and welfare; and to explore any other changes that looked promising. This was nothing like the Welfare Study Committee discussed in the previous chapter. Rather, this committee was comprised of legislators who were directed to come up with specific reform proposals that would be considered by the broader legislative branch. In a very unusual move, though, Tom asked Irv Garfinkel and me to serve as unofficial or nonvoting members of the committee. We were to be expert resources who could keep the debate somewhat evidence focused and rational.

I suspect he feared that once the genie was out of the bottle, anything could happen. The committee might run in directions that Loftus might find reprehensible. Requiring applicants for public assistance to endure a medieval water-test was not out of the question. What is that you ask? The medieval water-test as applied to welfare would go like this: miscreants who dared seek help from the public's largess would be thrown into a body of water. If they floated to the surface, they were deemed to be guilty and hung or, in this case, declared ineligible for help. If they sank and drowned, that would be a sign of their innocence or, in this situation, their worthiness for assistance. Of course, those poor souls would be dead, so cash assistance would be of little comfort to them.

John Antaramian, a Democratic legislator representing the blue-collar city of Kenosha, Wisconsin, was tapped to chair the group. John was rather small of stature but large of heart. He was called the Lebanese flower by some who knew him, capturing both his heritage, and the fact that he was pleasant to be around. He was naturally gregarious, not a bad attribute for a politician. There also was a down-to-earth quality about him as he would always whip his tie off as soon as he got into his office. At the end of the day, he cared about public policy. There was little artifice in him. He basically wanted to do good even if what was good could be very elusive.

I don't think that Irv got into the committee's work as much as I did. He continued to focus on his child support initiatives.

He probably only agreed to do this as a favor to Tom Loftus in the hope that Tom would continue to lobby on behalf of Irv's first love—the Assured Child Support benefit. I, on the other hand, had the attention span of a gnat, and was always looking for the next debacle into which I might sink my teeth.

I was a bit taken by how much the legislators looked to us for guidance. They listened when we brought ideas in for them to consider, unlike my spouse or anyone else who knew me well for that matter. Okay, one more digression here!

I once thought my spouse was beginning to have a hearing problem since she never seemed to hear anything I said. One day, I screwed up my courage and mentioned this to her. Dutifully, she went through all the hoops to get to a hearing specialist who gave her all kinds of tests. At the end, the audiologist asked her why she had come in the first place. When she explained about my concerns he immediately broke into a smile. "Yes, we see this all the time. Your hearing is perfect. You just can't hear anything your husband says. We call this impairment the selective spousal hearing syndrome." True story by the way!

Back to the main narrative! Sometimes a legislator sitting next to me would lean over and ask in a low voice, "How should I vote on this one?" In addition, I searched for models that tried to strengthen the work component of welfare programs. There was nothing earthshaking out there in my estimation, but there were bits and pieces worth looking at. I recall drafting a very detailed model that represented my best thinking (at the time) for accomplishing what I thought the committee might accept. I laid it out in excruciating detail, with lines and circles and triangles and rectangles all signifying an action or decision or programmatic input. It was a nerd's dream of how clients would move through a future welfare office that emphasized work and cash assistance with equal force. I believe I caught several committee members dozing off as I went through it. Funny, I found it quite compelling.

At some point, I realized two things. First, there were few additional resources to make this vision a reality statewide. Contrary to what many people thought at the time, a work-oriented welfare program cost a lot of money. The additional child care costs alone would break the state's piggy bank. Second, locals had to buy into any innovation that altered the basic way they did business. Even I knew that prescribing a top-down model of change was fraught with peril. This would be particularly true if the changes demanded were consequential in character . . . if they required that people really do things differently. When you ask people to alter the core technology of their agency, what it basically does, it is far better to work from the ground up than the heavens down.

In the end, what I really argued for was a "lighthouse" approach. Choose a few sites, work with them closely. Focus more on what you want to accomplish and less on how to accomplish it. Provide lots of help but don't be overly prescriptive. Evaluate and monitor things closely, document what is working and why. Also, be honest about what is not working and why. The purpose here is not to be right but to learn. Be flexible and keep changing. You won't get it right the first time around. Then use these so-called "lighthouses" as exemplar models that others might follow, not slavishly but as a source of inspiration and guidance.

It was not an easy sell at first. Politicians would rather do something big and splashy even if the intervention were shallow and likely to fail. They want to be seen as solving the big problems in a big way. You know, we passed a bill and now all welfare recipients are working. The slow and steady progress of the tortoise appears tepid against the speed and flash of the hare. John Kennedy may have fully appreciated the ancient precept that the journey of a thousand miles starts with the first step, but he was an unusually wise man. Still, my general approach prevailed in the end.

Several things came out of this committee, but the primary product of interest to me was passage of the Work Experience and Jobs Training Program or WEJT (pronounced widget). Five sites were selected to launch experimental efforts to better link welfare with work. They would get additional resources for the task, sufficient resources to have a shot at doing something substantial. I was pleased but cautious. I realized that legislating something and making it work were two different things. If the pilot sites were not provided support and guidance, they could easily founder and lose their way. But hey, Irv was after me to keep pushing the child support agenda; and there was that damn dissertation still hanging over my head. I thought I would keep my head down and just wish them well. It was a nice thought, but once again I was wrong. But I will save that story for later.

Over the course of my work with the committee, I became pretty good friends with John Antaramian who eventually made it to the Joint Finance Committee (JFC). This was an important move for him. Only the more powerful representatives made it to Joint Finance since it dealt with money issues . . . the engine of politics. I recall getting a call from John one day after the committee had done its work. "Tom," he lamented, "I thought I was doing good things with the committee and now everyone is mad at me. What did I do wrong?"

Since I am such a sensitive guy, I laughed. "John, welcome to my world . . . the wonderful world of welfare reform. Personally, I go by one rule. When no one, absolutely no one, agrees with me, then I suspect I am approaching truth. Stay with this topic, and I guarantee you will have a short Christmas list. No one will like you. Hell, not even my wife gives me a card these days!"

Oddly enough, John did stay with it. He pulled me back into the legislative world one more time. He reached out to a Republican, Steve Foti, and a Milwaukee Democrat, Rosemary Potter. It was never totally clear to me what he wanted to accomplish, but I think he had a feeling that there might be some middle road path to welfare reform as opposed to the partisan sniping that was emerging. I did not see any future in this, but I am sympathetic to those trying to breach the barricades in the welfare wars. So, I stayed with it until John left the legislature to become mayor of Kenosha.

Besides, they were a fun group to be with. I recall the first time John introduced me to Representative Potter. I misunderstood something in the conversation and said, "So I understand you are a Republican." "No," she responded indignantly, which I should have guessed since she was way too young and attractive to be a Republican. But I recovered in my own way. "Oh, now I remember what John said. He told me you *think* like a Republican." Then I ducked as she threw her purse at him.

We all went to D.C. I introduced them to the folk I knew at HHS, we met with the Wisconsin Congressional delegation; and we bounced around many ideas. In the end, nothing really happened but I had some more fun. A few years down the road, when he was leaving the legislature to assume the position of mayor of Kenosha, there was a party for him and the other legislators who were retiring. It was held in the Capitol with many lobbyists and press in attendance.

I went to give John my best. It turns out that another of those attacks on the university faculty had been in the press that very day. In fact, the attacks were based on a study that my future colleague, Jennifer Noyes, had just completed as a staff member of the Legislative Audit Bureau. This was many years before I would meet her, of course. Now, oddly enough, she is an associate dean in the very academic institution she once criticized so harshly. Funny how life goes. In any case, her audit fueled the conventional press narrative about faculty being overpaid and spending no time in the classroom teaching.

Being me, I could not leave this alone and asked John why he hadn't mentioned the news article. He suddenly became very animated, and started yelling the words "university professor, university professor!" while pointing in my direction as if he expected the whole room to pounce upon me. As people started to turn and stare, my mind flashed back to my other near-death experiences in life where I faced angry mobs. Let me assure you, even welfare recipients were viewed with far more favor than university faculty among our state representatives at that time. But John really did like me, and the feeling was mutual. That, at least, is the story I am sticking with. In any case, I was sorry to see him go.

Back to the 1986 gubernatorial election! Remember that! It was Tommy Thompson versus Anthony Earl. The welfare issue was a defining issue of the campaign. In the end, Thompson won. Clearly, the state would be taking a new direction. In the aftermath of voting day, no one really knew what that direction would be. Irv realized that his dream of an Assured Child Support benefit had been dealt a blow, but he would not quit. My dream of a robust and collaborative relationship between IRP and the state of Wisconsin would soon diminish, but that was not clear at that moment.

What was certain is the welfare wars were entering a new era. The battles would be more intensely fought. The sides would be more clearly drawn. The fields of conflict would be in Washington and in states across the country as policy devolution became a stronger and stronger call. The outcomes of future skirmishes would be more consequential for all involved. The coming wars, in the end, would change how we treat the poor and the vulnerable in this country.

Yet another counter in my policy candy store started with a call from U.S. Senator Moynihan's office. The senator, at the request of Senator Kohl from Wisconsin, was calling a special hearing on the Wisconsin Learnfare program. Would I be willing to testify? Being the decisive guy that I am, I immediately responded with a firm, "I'll get back to you on that." Learnfare was one of the first of Governor Tommy Thompson's welfare reforms that would catapult him to the forefront of the national debate on what to do with the widely despised AFDC program. The concept was simple. The school attendance of children and youth would be monitored. If attendance did not meet certain standards set by the welfare department, such a failure would be construed as poor parenting which, after all, was the primary job of a welfare mother. Failure to comply would result in a sanction or a lowering of the AFDC benefit until the situation was rectified and the attendance standard was met.

Opponents, mostly of the liberal persuasion, were outraged. Parents would be punished for the actions of ungovernable children. Intra-family power relationships would drift from the adult to the child. Sanctions would make it even harder for these families to cope, and so on. The real concern, in my mind, is that Learnfare would be the first chink in the concept of cash welfare as an entitlement. That might not be bad but only if it were introduced with care and not under the simplistic economic notion that a modest economic penalty, by itself, would work miracles. By this time, I had disabused myself of the view that all manner of ills might be rectified solely with the proper economic incentives. Homo Econimicus existed, of course, but not in the simplified, stick-figure way that economists viewed the world.

Basically, the existing social contract was that if you met income, asset, and family composition requirements, you got a check. In some cases, a work expectation was imposed but the seriousness of such requirements was questionable. This new Thompson innovation would introduce a new behavioral requirement as a condition of getting the full benefit. It would introduce a new "social contract" notion into the relationship between government and clients, one that went beyond the mere constructs of need and an expectation of work effort. You would have to behave properly to get the help you needed, a principle argued forcefully by Larry Mead in his book *Beyond Entitlement*.

In general, people are not all that well versed in history. Most welfare managers at the time thought that AFDC had been created as a full-blown entitlement program in the 1930s. They believed that the reforms now emerging were the first to address the evil consequences of handing out unfettered cash. In fact, what characterized the first three decades of the program were a rather extensive set of behavioral requirements as a condition of receiving help that would make any of the new reformers drool with envy.

For example, there was the "fit home" concept. You had to be a good mother to get help. Your house had to be clean and neat, your children had to attend school on a regular basis, and your moral life had to be beyond reproach. To ensure the last standard, midnight raids were done in many jurisdictions to see if there was a man in the house, and to check on other suspected transgressions such as substance abuse or lack of minimal hygiene. It was only in the 1960s that activist courts and a revitalized federal bureaucracy turned AFDC into a real entitlement. One of my Doctoral Committee members, Law Professor Joel Handler, had written a stinging rebuke of the old system in his acclaimed book *The Deserving Poor*. Joel was a member of my Doctoral committee until he left for a position on the west coast. Before departing, he reemed me out that I was f#$%king up my life by not finishing up my dissertation. That was a common sentiment among my academic colleagues, but he employed more colorful language.

In any case, fast forward a full generation. The entitlement principle was now seen as the way welfare had always been. It was a principle, however, that now was vulnerable to attack by some and as something to be valiantly defended by others. Both sides on the entitlement issue dug in, arguing that their position reflected what the founders of the program wanted. To put it mildly, Learnfare was a hot button issue. Well, just about everything about welfare was a hot button issue by this time. As I often told my students, most of whom probably gagged at yet another of Tom's aphorisms for a better life, one generation's solution is often the next generation's scandal. Hey, I thought that was clever.

Now, I tend to step in horse manure whenever possible. So, I wrote a piece on Learnfare for the IRP publication *Focus* which has remarkably wide circulation in policy as well as academic circles. I suspected I was tiptoeing into a political minefield. So, I tried adding several co-authors to the piece, including names randomly selected from the phone book. I desperately wished to obscure my culpability. But that ruse did not work at all. Anticipating a negative reaction from the other side of State Street, I sent a pre-published draft to the responsible Wisconsin officials. One of them, Silvia Jackson, had overlapped with me in the Social Welfare Doctoral program. Though I had been around the track enough times by then to know better, even I was taken aback by the reaction.

I looked over the changes they wanted made. I think one suggested insertion was that "Learnfare is the most important public innovation since the introduction of Guttenberg's moveable type printing press." That caused me to pause for a moment. Okay, on a more serious note, I have found that politicians prefer that you take firm stands (in their favor of course) and demonstrate unwavering loyalty to them. They want to know if you are for them or against them so that they can categorize you accordingly. They despise the ambiguity too often evidenced by those disingenuous two-handed academic types who are always saying "but on the other hand." President Truman once cried out in despair for a one-armed economist.

They found my "other hand" rather treasonous in this instance and asked for numerous substantive revisions, so many that I was forced to draw a line in the sand so to speak. I politely replied that I had to stand by my convictions, academic freedom and all that. Could it be that I had a backbone? Now, that is hard to believe. I did, however, offer them an opportunity to write a rebuttal piece, an offer which they accepted. I reworked their submission a bit to make it sound better, and we published the two pieces side by side. Thus, the call from Washington!

Upon hanging up the phone, I raced downstairs (well, I took the elevator) to the office of Charles "Chuck" Manski who was IRP director at the time. In truth, I never race anywhere and certainly never use the stairs. Chuck was a brilliant econometrician (most of them seemed brilliant to me) who now is at Northwestern. I admired his academic credentials a lot. He was not, however, the most approachable of men. He could be gruff and dismissive. I must admit, though, he always treated me very well. This might well have been because I was a social work type, and economists didn't expect much from them in the first place. Besides, he liked my writing; he had praised the Learnfare piece with considerable relish.

Now that I think on it, I would get unexpected compliments from some of the more technical economists. Art Goldberger, perhaps the premier econometrician of that era at UW, called one of my pieces brilliant. Tom McCurdy from Stanford and the Hoover Institute introduced me once by saying he always looked for my pieces in *Focus*. Unlike much of his fellow economist's work, he told the audience that he always learned something new from my work. This was undoubtedly an exercise in hyperbole, but nice to hear anyways. The iconic godfather of both IRP and the War-On-Poverty, UW economist Bob Lampman, ran to catch up with me one day as a I walked along the lake path next to the Social Science Building. I had just published one of my first solo pieces in an IRP publication. He waxed enthusiastically about it and encouraged me to keep writing. Unfortunately, that enthusiasm for my expressive talents never seemed to infect my Social Work colleagues.

In any case, I explained the situation to Chuck and concluded with, "I don't think I should go. This can only be bad for the institute. The governor is already suspicious of us, and my big mouth could end all remaining contracts we have with the state." Chuck leaned back and paused. "No," he responded, "you go and testify. You have been asked by a United States senator to share your expertise, (I wondered at that moment if he realized whom he was talking with) and you have a public responsibility to do just that. You testify to what you believe without any reservation, and we will simply deal with any fallout that comes of it." I stumbled out of his office with new respect for the man and the institution that was IRP. This was an example of academic courage, of Galileo standing up to the Catholic Church in defense of his helio-centric vision of our solar system, if only of course he had. I then realized that it would be my fanny at which the governor would aim, not his.

As it turned out, I flew out to D.C. on the same plane as did several Wisconsin officials. The state contingent included the secretary of the department running welfare along with Silvia Jackson, who oversaw the reform efforts; and an ex-Wisconsin legislator who was now a high-level Food Stamp official in the Bush administration. The last one caught me in the aisle and asked if I knew what happened to those who try to stand in the middle of the track when the train is bearing down. "Yup," I responded, "I have a pretty good idea," as visions of my bloody body parts scattered across the tracks floated through my head.

Somehow, I wound up sharing a cab with Silvia into D.C. I doubt it was coincidental since she lost no time before pumping me on what I was going to say the next morning. I responded with some nonsensical redundancy about saying what I was going to say. It sounded stupid even to me. Then she informed me that a representative from the governor's office would be there and, without saying it outright, made it clear there could be dire consequences if I screwed up.

At that moment an obvious truth hit me with full force. It would not be me or any of my colleagues that would suffer if the state contracts were terminated. We would land on our feet somehow though, in truth, I had nowhere to land. It would be the lowly research assistants, the poorly paid data collectors, and other such folk who would lose their source of income. *Better if it were me*, I thought as I checked my expanding waistline. I could surely benefit from missing a few meals.

The hearing room was packed. Apparently, interest in a faraway state reform was surprisingly strong among the movers and shakers of Washington. I was lobbied up to the very last minute. *Really*, I thought, *who cares what I say. My wife surely doesn't while my dog only pays attention to me when he expects to be fed.* I recall one liberal advocate coming up to me. "Well, Tom," she said, "did you bring your balls with you today?" I was tempted to tell her they were permanently attached but I just smiled. Besides, I got the impression she would try to detach them herself if she thought I was about to wuss out. I was on a panel with two evaluators of Learnfare from the University of Wisconsin-Milwaukee (UW-

M). They gave a cautious, but overall critical, statement of how things were going. The fact that UW-M was doing the evaluation, not IRP, is a story I will circle back to in a moment.

Usually I only rely on notes that guide me as I wing my way through talks and public remarks. I like spontaneity and responding to audiences, adjusting on the fly if I detect excess boredom or hostility. I really prepared for this one, however, carefully writing out what I intended to say. Besides, the prepared remarks would be included in the Congressional Record. 1 chose not to focus on the merits of the concept but rather on its design and implementation. Was that a cop-out ... maybe? In truth, though, I did not embrace the hysterical opposition to the effort coming from the liberal community. I had long concluded that Learnfare was a return to the integration of cash assistance and services that had been broken apart in the late 1960s. If done right, it might bring needed help to struggling families and not merely hand them a check. In theory, at least, one might argue that the new social contract would address the causes of destitution ad not merely the symptoms. That possibility would only exist if it were designed and implemented with care.

My favorite Learnfare one-liner (I had a lot of one-liners in my career, a few of them were even worth sharing) was that it could well be the "full employment act for social workers." Mary Ann Cook, one of my favorite bureaucrats as you know by now, thought the line delicious and oft repeated it as did Reuben

Snipper, an official at Health and Human Services with whom I became friendly during my stay in D.C. in the early 1990s.

That vision of the future, as I said, was conditional upon the administrative competence attached to the rollout. I testified that from my perspective, that required fidelity of implementation simply was not happening. I then went through the flaws I saw using a conceptual framework that I later used in teaching social work students the ins and outs of doing practical social policy work. In the absence of more conscientious management, I cautioned, the potential benefits of Learnfare might never be realized. Of course, the anticipated benefits might never materialize if the underlying theory was incorrect, but that is why we should carefully try it out in the first place.

When it was over, Sylvia approached me. "Those comments were very fair, Tom" she said, "we are meeting on the Child Support contract next week, and I think you will be pleased with the outcome." I smiled weakly. The potentially at-risk staff and students would be spared but had I once again sold my soul to Satan to protect them and the institute? I did not think so, but it is a question that has haunted me since. I did check, however, and my balls were still attached.

Back to the Learnfare evaluation as promised! IRP had, in fact, bid on the evaluation contract. This reform, as most did, required waivers of some extant federal regulations. Typically, the feds would demand a rigorous evaluation in such cases since the purpose of waiving the rules back then was to determine if the new approach worked and deserved broader application. The IRP team was strong, being led by the aforementioned Chuck Manski and by Gary Sandefur, a Stanford trained sociologist who would eventually become the Dean of Letters and Sciences at Wisconsin.

While I like to make fun of academics, Gary is an exception. By that I mean he is truly a wonderful human being. He is quiet, humble, unassuming, likes students, and loves to teach. Perhaps his background explains his uniqueness. He is a Native American who was born and raised in a tiny Oklahoma town. He struggled early in life, dropping out of school to work at real, manual labor type jobs. Then he got back on track, earned a doctorate at Stanford, and became an academic star. After a stellar career at Wisconsin, he returned to his home state, accepting the position of provost at Oklahoma State University.

I would have been on the Learnfare program research team. I think my role would involve running for coffee and bringing in the donuts for morning meetings. In any case, one day I got a call from a friend who worked for the state. "Tom," he said, "I just wanted to let you know you won't be getting the Learnfare evaluation contract." I mumbled something about winning some and losing some, but then it hit me . . . the proposal review meeting was not even scheduled for another week. "That is true," he replied, "but they put someone on the review panel with specific instructions to not let you guys win." We had been blackballed by the governor. Had the famous Wisconsin Idea sunk so low?

Now, why would that be? I had never met the man. I suspect that he felt that all academics, particularly the social scientists, were guilty of being Marxists until proven otherwise. Yet, perhaps there was another reason, one based on what looked like evidence. As welfare reform heated up, so did the media calls. While it would become a crescendo in the coming years, already there were numerous calls. While I always tried to be evenhanded, I could not control how I was used by the media. I recall one call from a *New York Times* reporter that was emblematic of so many of these interactions. I could tell from his questions that he was antagonistic toward the reform in question. In reaction, I started off with several positive points about what the governor was trying to do. At the end, though, I had to throw in my concerns as well. Those concerns, of course, were all he used. He had merely waited me out until I said what he wanted to hear.

Another call is a perfect caricature of some of the more outlandish media connections. "Hi Professor Corbett, I am calling about Thompson's latest welfare reform. I can't think of the name at this moment, but are you for it or against it?" I responded that I didn't answer questions like that, but it was not hard to figure out the initiative they were calling about and went on with my usual measured and balanced response. Measured responses tended to piss off most, but certainly not all media types.

Another caller asked about Bridefare, an initiative which I discuss more below. When I finished my (hopefully) balanced response, there was silence on the phone. "Hello," I asked, "are you still there?" Finally, the reporter replied, "Sorry, I was taken aback. You are the first person I have interviewed that did not go ballistic on this topic."

I will admit, the press generally seemed suspicious of Thompson's reforms. Thus, they tended to grab on to my caveats and concerns (many of which were quite real) and not any positive statements I might make. Since any doubt or cautious statements would put you on any politician's enemy list, that is exactly where I landed in the governor's mind, as did the institute. Of course, most affiliates at the institute probably had no idea what Learnfare was (or care), but that subtlety would be lost on the other end of State Street.

One final media vignette before returning to the Learnfare evaluation. The brother of a colleague who was on the faculty of the Public Policy School worked as a reporter for a Milwaukee newspaper. He called from time to time to sound me out. This call was about a recent book purportedly authored by the governor on his reforms. When I mentioned I had not read this literary masterpiece yet, he sent me a copy, which I dutifully perused. "Well," I said, "I give the governor great credit for negotiating the thicket of welfare reform politics. But, in truth, the reform ideas are not new. They are old ideas, many of which were tried in the past, that are simply being resurrected once again." He ignored my compliments on the governor's political skills and focused on my comments about the recycling of old wine in new bottles. In truth, there really wasn't much, if anything, new in the welfare reform debates. Upon seeing the article, I am confident the governor threw a few more darts at my picture that hung on his office wall.

Back to the Learnfare evaluation. As it turned out, we came in second in the review panel's scoring of the Learnfare proposals. When we asked for the scores, it appeared that my informant was spot on. Four of the five reviewers gave us the highest score among the proposals while one gave us something like 35 points out of 100, dropping us into second place. I sincerely believe this was a mistake on the part of the governor. This IRP team would have done a high-quality evaluation that would have been recognized as such nationally. These were true academics. They had no prior agenda or axe to grind though everyone has opinions or priors, as the economists say. They would have gone wherever the evidence took them which, of course, is exactly what most politicians fear. There was some grumbling about challenging the process, but I thought that a very bad idea, probably futile and surely counterproductive though, in retrospect, how much worse could our relationship with the state get?

As it happened, I had an opportunity to chat with one of the two leaders of the UW-M evaluation team one day. I sensed they were qualified to do a good job and had a lot of experience manipulating large education data sets. But I remember thinking after just a few minutes, "Uh-uh, these guys are real liberals. I don't think the governor thought through what he might get when he torpedoed our research proposal." Subsequent events seemed to bear out my initial suspicions. The state and UW-M team eventually got into a very public fight over the course of the evaluation with the feds being brought in to referee. The researchers wound up writing articles asserting political obstruction of their work and threats to their independence.

Eventually, the contract was terminated amidst mutual recriminations. I am not sure we ever learned if the program had impacts though the early data suggested that the sanctions, by themselves, had little effect on school attendance. Again, my argument all along was that you needed stronger support services to go along with the sanctions if any benefits were to be anticipated, so perhaps this is what an unbiased observer might have expected. In fairness to the UW-M team, however, if the data had led the IRP researchers along a similar analytical and interpretive path, the result may have been the same. We would have been vilified by the administration and fired. However, we will never know.

As anticipated, Learnfare was the first breech in the entitlement fortress. Other attacks were to follow one upon the other, too many to document without numbing the average reader into a comatose state. I will briefly mention two, however. First is Bridefare, notice how this also builds on the old workfare label from years back.

Bridefare was the brainchild of Eloise Anderson. Eloise was unusual in some respects. She was a Black conservative and Republican who was very concerned about Black men not stepping up to take their proper role as fathers and husbands. For that concern, she should be commended. Her Bridefare proposal was not that radical when you looked at it closely. It rested on modest financial incentives to motivate young welfare mothers to marry the fathers of their children and vice versa. On the surface, that did not sound outrageous to me. As far as I can recall, there were no shotguns involved. Again, however, the liberal community went ballistic. You would be forcing mothers to marry these worthless fathers. There would be an increase in domestic violence and child abuse. The government has no right to interfere in the private decisions of people, and aren't we forgetting that welfare is an entitlement. You can fill in the rest.

When compared with the moderate character of the changes being proposed, I thought the apocalyptic scenarios being thrown out were a bit hyperbolic. But reason had long been abandoned in the welfare wars. Eloise eventually left to run welfare in California and a stint in a west coast think tank but did return to Wisconsin and now serves as a department secretary in the Scott Walker administration. She was bruised by the reaction to her proposal and, over the years, thanked me several times for my early support.

I do recall one final smile from the Bridefare kerfuffle. One day, I was contacted by the secretary of the Wisconsin welfare department, Gerald Whitburn. He managed to locate me in my social work office, a remarkable feat, since I never spent time there. That prompted my paranoia to kick in as I feared they were tracking me with GPS or something to keep on top of my comings and goings. You can never be too cautious. Of course, there was the day I walked in what everyone called One-West Wilson, a depression-era cement fortress where the top state welfare officials were located. As soon as I entered, all kinds of bells and whistles sounded. I was sure that the next thing I would hear over the loudspeaker system would be the warning "liberal alert; liberal alert; take cover, liberal alert." Then, armed guards would sweep down upon me. But it was just a monthly fire drill, not that I am paranoid or anything.

In any case, he had called to thank me for my kind comments to the press about Bridefare. I assured him that I call them as I see them. Now, he was a rather humorless man, so I tried a little levity to see if I could lighten him up. Using what you should now recognize as one of my tried and true lines once again, I said, "I worry about compliments in this welfare business. I feel I am getting closer to the truth when nobody, absolutely nobody, agrees with what I am saying." I thought I heard a tiny chuckle on the other end of the line as our connection clicked off, but it may have been a groan.

A second initiative worth noting was the "Work, Not Welfare" (WNW) pilot program. This was getting closer to the concept of Welfare Works or W-2 that would be the centerpiece of the Wisconsin reforms. W-2 would not just reform welfare, it would replace welfare with a work program, or so the advance billing claimed. WNW took the goal of bringing the work message up front in the customer's experience and put it on steroids. Now the approach would be work first and then maybe a little welfare if all else fails. Two modest size counties were selected to dry run what would be the precursor to the real thing that was still in the planning stage, one of which was Fond du Lac County.

Fond du Lac was about an hour northeast of Madison. The county director, Ed Schilling, was an MSW from the University of Wisconsin. He said that he had done his policy internship with me (the same practicum experience I was then running in the School of Social Work) many years earlier when I was employed with the state. I had no memory of that but now found him an engaging, thoughtful guy. At the time, I happened to have a wonderful second year MSW and joint Public Policy student (Mary Healy) who wanted to spend some time interning in Fond du Lac. Great! Being a curious sort, I would get to eavesdrop on this new wrinkle in welfare.

As I mentioned, Ed was an interesting guy. Unlike many social workers, he believed that the welfare entitlement hurt, not helped, most recipients. The metaphor that Jason Turner, one of the key architects of W-2, always used was that of a hospital patient. He argued that we treated welfare clients as if they were sick and needed treatment. Most did not, he felt. They were stronger and more capable than liberals thought. What they needed was a strong dose of adult responsibility. If you approached a person as if they were weak and disabled, that is how they would see themselves. If you assumed they were competent and capable, they were more likely to respond that way.

I learned several things from the Fond du Lac director. One day, he told me that doing reform was like rowing upstream. "What do you mean?" I asked.

He leaned back in his chair and then went on:

It is like this, Tom. I have staff that have been doing things a certain way for a long time. You cannot walk in and say the world is now different and expect them to get it right away. Let me give you an example. We come up with a policy question for which there is no answer in the manual. This is not surprising since we are doing brand new things here. But my staff runs in and says, we must call Madison, we don't know what to do in this instance. I scream, no, we don't have to call Madison. We can now use our own judgment and professional expertise to resolve these issues. Oh, they say, I see. Then another issue comes up and they come running in, we must call Madison . . . at which point I start pulling out my hair.

On another occasion he started talking about left and right brain workers. This intrigued me, and I asked him to go on:

I had workers who were great at doing the books. They would put on their eye shades and keep focused on the numbers, making sure that everything added up and that no one was cheating. Now they must look at the clients, ask questions, figure out their problems and their strengths. Their main task now is helping them toward independence. This takes different skills, putting facts together to get a feel for what a person can do, see where family dynamics may be a problem, and use their imagination to fit a customer with a potential employment opportunity. Most of all, they now must work as teams and not as individuals. Where I had mostly left-brain people, those good at doing the books, now I need right-brain folks. These folks are better at seeing the big picture as well as working with others. And you know what, Tom? You can't change a person from one to the other very easily, if at all.

I had these kinds of conversations all the time when I visited agencies and programs over the years. Sure, a lot of them were repetitive or not very interesting. Then again, many of the academic presentations I have endured over the decades put me into a deep comatose state. On the other hand, in the real world I often would come across nuggets of provocative perspicacity that would get me thinking about things. Bottom line, the real world has always been a source of learning for me. I treasure some of the truly remarkable people I met out there, good people just trying to do the best damn job they possibly could. My education would have been woefully incomplete without them.

On another occasion, Ed casually mentioned what was happening as applicants for assistance were being exposed to the Work, Not Welfare rules for the first time. He said it was amazing how many looked at the eligibility worker and said things like, "Hell, if I have to go through all this I might as well keep my day job." Then they would get up and head back out the door. It was a portent of things to come, the old world of welfare as about to crack wide open. That story, though, can wait for the next chapter.

CHAPTER 5

WELFARE WARS: ENDING WELFARE AS WE KNOW IT

The dogmas of the quiet past are inadequate to
the stormy present. The occasion is piled high with
difficulty, and we must rise with the occasion.

—Abraham Lincoln

While Tommy Thompson was moving in the direction of "ending welfare as we know it," another well-known politician had the same idea. When William Jefferson Clinton ran for president in 1992, one of his most popular campaign lines promised to "end welfare as we know it." From the left and the right came similar rhetoric. One question was on the lips of many among both his friends and his detractors . . . what did this mean? An inconvenient question kept popping up . . . tell me once again exactly how you will do this! To wish something is one thing, to do it is another. The devil, as they say, is in the details.

Sometime in late 1992, a memo from the new IRP director, Robert Hauser, came across my desk. It went on about IRP's long-standing relationship with ASPE, the Office of the Assistant Secretary for Planning and Development (ASPE) in the U.S. Department of Health and Human Services (HHS). Federal support for IRP was funneled through ASPE and there was a lot of contact between the two entities. Hauser was asking if any IRP affiliate might want to spend time at ASPE as a way of reinforcing our connection with HHS. My immediate reaction was "go to Washington," no way! I vividly recall crumpling up the memo (I guess we still used paper back then) and throwing it in the wastebasket.

Something happened over the course of the day, however. My mind kept drifting back to Bob's memo. Bill Clinton would be the new president. Welfare reform, along with healthcare reform, would be the big domestic policy issues. Hey, I was getting good at mucking up things in Wisconsin. Why not mess things up on a grander scale? That might be even greater fun. At the end of the day, I recall rooting through the wastebasket to find the memo. I straightened it as best I could and brought it home to discuss with my spouse.

"You want to go to D.C. for a year? Are you serious?" At first, she looked incredulous but when she saw I was being serious for once, a broad smile broke out. "Great, can I help you pack?" Don't you just hate it when your spouse is so eager to get rid of you? In truth, it was not that easy a decision. My wife, Mary Rider, was the deputy director of the Wisconsin court system and could not easily pick up and follow. So, we would face a long commute challenge. Still, I wandered into Bob's office later that week to ask if anyone else had responded to his memo. Nope, the opportunity was wide open. *Oh, goody,* I thought, *guess I am the only moron willing to volunteer for the lion's den.*

Several months later, that damn office phone rang again. It was Ann Segal, a high-level career civil servant from ASPE. Ann is a lovely person, on the short side but with the kind of directed, disciplined personality that inspires confidence. She had a lively mind and very good management skills. She was not a welfare person, coming from a child protection and child care background, but her innate good sense was treasured by all. You would do well to listen when she spoke. She would play an important role in the coming months. "Tom, it is all set up. How soon can you get here?"

The timing, however, wasn't great from my perspective. I had teaching commitments to finish up and my mother was very ill and would soon pass away. I probably could get there in May, early June at the latest, I told her. "Hurry," she urged me, "we are moving ahead on welfare reform and want to get a bill out by late summer." *Damn,* I thought, *I might miss the boat.* A couple of months or so later I recall walking into ASPE hoping that the boat had not already left the harbor. By noon I knew that not only had I not missed the boat, the boat was merely a shell in dry dock. This vessel would not sail for quite a while, if at all. I breathed a sigh of relief. Then I thought, *I wonder what I have gotten myself into?*

When Bill Clinton tapped Donna Shalala, then chancellor of the Madison campus, to head Health and Human Services, she asked a few IRP affiliates over for a briefing before heading to Washington. As we discussed several salient issues, she was surprisingly open about the challenges she faced and her lack of substantive knowledge regarding many of the major issues on the table at that time. We were all confident she would do well, however, perhaps more confident than she was.

Though diminutive in size, Donna Shalala had a powerhouse personality. After all, when she came to Madison, the Athletic Department was in the crapper. In a few short years, Wisconsin was turning out powerhouse football and basketball teams. She knew that was the way to open the wallets of alumni and it worked. Her last words the day of our briefing were that, once in office, she would beef up ASPE which had diminished in size and importance over the years.

ASPE had been created in the 1960s as a long-range planning arm for the HHS Secretaries office. It was also supposed to provide a centralized research and analysis arm to coordinate thinking across the department's broad programmatic responsibilities. In addition, it was supposed to pick up many functions that had been in the old Office of Economic Opportunity (OEO), which President Johnson created as a command center for his War-On-

Poverty (WOP). The WOP was waged from the White House from the time that Johnson made poverty a public issue up to the point where President Nixon turned to other priorities. It was also hoped that ASPE might crosswalk among the diverse program areas within the mega-departments purview, which at the time included education issues, to achieve a modicum of systems integration.

By the late 1970s, ASPE was a power place to be. I happened to be present when Henry Aaron, a Brookings Institute scholar of iconic stature, told David Ellwood, the Harvard scholar heading ASPE early in the early Clinton era, about the relative strengths of ASPE then and now. When he (Henry) had headed the place during President Carter's push for welfare reform, his staff was top-notch and probably could compete with a top university economics department. Henry then told David that the current staff was not up to the job. Gary Burtless, another Brookings scholar of repute who had been at ASPE back in the 70s, nudged Henry and said he was insulting several people in the room. Henry didn't miss a beat and carried on about the dire fate that awaited poor David.

It was true. ASPE was smaller and the staff less accomplished overall. But I found them to be generally competent, disciplined, and hardworking. Besides, David Ellwood and Mary Jo Bane (another Harvard professor who was heading ACF or the Administration for Children and Families) were bringing on board quite a few academics and analytic types. Unlike me, however, most of these other academics had real number-crunching skills.

In any case, we plunged into the work of "ending welfare as we knew it." Cross-agency work groups were setup to be responsible for various substantive issues. Initially, I was asked to head the "make work pay" effort. Basically, this looked at how various welfare-type programs could be massaged to incentivize work properly. This was something that welfare, by definition, did not do. But I also got involved in the program integration work group and did a little work with the child support work group. I was from Wisconsin, after all, the birthplace of the recent child support revolution. I also plugged to have attention paid to the population I called FUBARS (fouled-up beyond all recognition), a term I am embarrassed to say caught on among my new colleagues. My short attention span always pushed me to jump from one issue to another.

The FUBAR issue was critical in my mind, despite my unfortunate choice of labels. The framework for the Clinton initiative presumably emerged from David Ellwood's well-received book titled *Poor Support*. In the book, he argued for a temporary form of cash assistance, shocking only because he was considered a classic liberal. Basically, a client could get up to two years of cash assistance followed by a job. If they couldn't get a real job then a public job would be made available, the details of which were formidable. If they didn't respond to that, things got just a little vague.

Everyone knew that some unknown portion of the welfare population would be a real challenge, having very low skill levels and significant behavioral and mental health barriers. I thought we should jump on that issue, try to get an estimate of the size and composition of the population. Then we could think hard about what to do with them. Simply casting these families off assistance seemed ill-advised and a bit harsh while simply exempting them from any time limit lacked imagination. Interpolating from several different data sources, we came up with a 20 percent estimate which, drum roll please, became the exemption rate that later was built into the bill. I, however, wanted us to think about doing something more proactive with this group than continuing to issue an assistance check. For some reason, that never rose to the top as a priority however. Most feared that getting even employable clients into the labor market would sop up existing resources, leaving nothing for the unemployables.

Over time, I wondered who had come up with the "end of summer" target date to begin with. There were so many moving targets to this effort that simply communicating among stakeholders and coordinating the various tasks became herculean challenges. Ann McCormick had an office next to me. I thought Ann a treasure with her quick Irish smile and a similarly quick mind. Among other things, she was put in charge of keeping the paper work flowing to and from the extended set of people within

ASPE and across all the related agencies and actors that needed to be in the loop. This seemed like half of Washington at some point.

Anyways, it struck me as odd that Ann M. had been assigned this responsibility. She had the second messiest office that I ever had seen in my life. When I peeked in her office, all I could see were piles of paper. I would call out, "Ann, are you there." Then I would wait for a voice to emerge from the other side of a wall of paper. A terrible thought hit me, maybe everything went in and nothing came out. My fear proved groundless, she did have a method to her madness. In case you are wondering, I am not first but third on the list of offices to be condemned by the Board of Health.

In first place was Don Oellerich. Don and I had overlapped in the Social Welfare Doctoral program at Wisconsin though he managed to finish about a decade or so before I did. The betting had been that I would yet be an ABD type (all-but-dissertation) long after I was sitting around drooling in my nursing home rocking chair. After a few years in academia, Don found his niche in government. He was a bright star at ASPE and would become the chief economist at Health and Human Services even though he had no (or very little, at least) formal economics training. As the years rolled on, Don has been credited by everyone who cares as the one person most responsible for saving the university-based poverty research centers.

Don was one of those thin, intense, driven guys. In that sense he was the opposite of me. On the other hand, he was like me in one important sense. He had a very messy office, surely messier than mine, even messier than Ann M's. Since I interpret messiness as a sign of genius, he is up there with Albert Einstein, Sir Isaac Newton, and Aristotle. Still, he knew where everything was. "Don, you got the analysis CBPP did on marginal tax rates?" He would pause, call in a forklift to dig a path to the far reaches of his office, then excavate down three or four feet of paper and reports before pulling out what I needed. My hero!

Though I found the contest for messiest office a welcome diversion, I started worrying about the prospects for reform. It was soon apparent that "ending welfare as we know it" may have been a signature campaign line but it was an in-house powder keg. Fault lines could be seen but generally were kept under wraps, at least for a while. Though generalizations are inevitably faulty, overarching normative positions were easy to detect. The White House representatives involved in the everyday planning, particularly Bruce Reed, took a harder line. There had to be real time limits, for example. The president had promised to "end welfare as we knew it" and that is what we were going to do.

The other main actors generally took softer lines. People from Labor, headed by Robert Reich during this period, tended to be much more liberal in their positions. We could never push people off a cliff . . . something had to be there to catch them like a guaranteed job. Failing that, they would keep getting a check. What kind of position that would be, and what would happen if they failed at the job were continuing sticking points. Ending the welfare discussions was proving as difficult as ending welfare itself.

Not surprisingly, the key actors within HHS came from different camps with David Ellwood, our Harvard-based academic, trying to straddle the fence. His book called for time limits, but he now faced the reality of the intellectual position he had staked out. It is a lot easier to write about an issue than make decisions that affect the lives of real people. I blithely wrote on many sensitive policy issues absent concern since I assumed that, in the end, no one would listen to me. I suspect he had hidden behind the same assumption. Now, however, his emotional response to the reality of a welfare time limit seemingly wavered somewhere between ambivalence and uncertainty.

Mary Jo Bane, another Harvard transplant, was a little harder to read. As someone who ran a program in the real world at one point, I felt she was more cognizant of the challenges associated with moving away from a business-as-usual posture. Wendell Primus was the clear liberal of the HHS leadership group. It struck me that he was desperately trying to hold back a tidal wave of change he saw overturning the safety net about which he retained considerable passion. Still, it was hard for him to be totally open about his preferences since they might well be construed as being disloyal to the top man, Bill Clinton.

Few major policy issues are debated without a range of opinions. Perhaps the range in this instance was a bit broader than most.

Strangely enough, I never heard Donna Shalala's name mentioned at all. Based on her strong presence while chancellor in Madison, I found this puzzling. In my opinion, she was never comfortable with this part of Bill's agenda and preferred to focus on health care. There was another group, composed of cabinet secretaries that occasionally would meet on welfare reform. Their ruminations, however, seemed ethereal to me and had no substantive influence on the planning process as far as I could see.

The real work was done by grunts like me. There were many meetings that started at 8:00 a.m., very early for D.C. The cast of characters would differ from meeting to meeting but David Ellwood, Mary Jo Bane, Wendell Primus, Bruce Reed (representing the White House), Belle Sawhill (a Washington fixture), and various reps from Labor, Treasury, Education, Agriculture, Housing, etc., usually would be in the room. After a hundred or so of these sessions that I managed to attend, I came to realize that we were not getting anywhere.

I started referring to them as the Groundhog Day meetings. This appellation came from the Bill Murray movie of the same name in which Bill lives the same day over and over. That scenario was a bit of a nightmare that I now felt was taking over my own life. In retrospect, what happened is not difficult to infer. The top players with real juice (David, Mary Jo, Wendell, and Bruce) were aware of the ideological divides that separated the main players. I doubt they wanted to display these fissures openly in front of staff.

So, they kept the planning meetings focused on technical details that were hard but less consequential. But without the overall vision, progress was slow and not going in any positive direction as far as I could tell.

As a result, we spent tons of time on issues such as how would we run the clock that calculated the two years that clients were permitted to receive welfare? Under what conditions would it stop, or start, or even start over? I remember one day when we seemed to be arriving at a conclusion on this one issue. Since I had done this welfare migration study, I was well informed of the interstate movement patterns of welfare clients. Reluctantly, I spoke up. "Aaah, now what happens if a client moves across state lines? What happens to the clock? Let us say she sees her clock running out and decides it is time to move from Chicago to be with her sister in Milwaukee, a move that happens more often than you might guess. Does her clock start over? How would the case worker know about her clock status if she came from another state, from Illinois for example? Would they have to call other states to check some states or all?"

I stopped talking as all eyes bore in on me. I had this sudden vision that they were considering placing a note to my chest saying "please feed and give ride to Madison, Wisconsin" before chucking me out the window to the street below. "Okay," David said slowly, "we need a national data base. It can't be that hard, I probably could program one myself." I looked out the window to see if any pigs were flying by.

What was not being dealt with were the fault lines simmering under the surface. They reflected political perspectives on one level and foundational norms on another. If you say you will "end" welfare, you better do so, or Republicans would bitterly attack the president for reneging on such an overt promise. On the normative level, some of the more liberal among our happy family had been defenders of the poor most of their lives. They found biting this bullet of ending cash assistance as an entitlement almost unbearable. Wendell Primus was a perfect example.

Wendell was one of the nicest individuals I have ever come across. He was also one of the most hardworking. A Midwesterner, he brought his heartland work ethic to his Congressional staff jobs on the Democratic side of the aisle. His reputation was that he would out negotiate everyone around the table, enduring long after his opponents dropped to the floor with fatigue. He brought the same passion to this ASPE position as one of Ellwood's deputies. I would get there before him in the mornings, but he would be there in the office until way into the night, at least his emails would continue to arrive timed at midnight and beyond.

There was a frisson of shock throughout ASPE one day as a rumor spread that he would be taking a long weekend with his family. Betting was 10-1 that this would never happen and still no one was taking the bet. His closest staff had to literally push him out the door while he continued to shout instructions to everyone in sight as his wife and family waited downstairs. Wendell had spent his whole life defending the safety net for the poor. Ending it was almost impossible for him. I am sure he worried what might happen if he abandoned his post, and the barbarians from the right stormed the citadel.

There were, of course, many other impediments to progress. Take, for example, the simple issue of paying for reform. We were in a "pay as you go" environment where new fiscal outlays had to be offset by defined budget cuts elsewhere. Guess what, welfare reform cost money. If you were serious about getting people into jobs, there were training costs and child care costs and the costs of those guaranteed public jobs if enough private jobs were not available. The scramble for offsets was furious and futile. Well, someone would suggest we could raise sin taxes on gambling winnings. That idea would last a day until the governors of New Jersey and Nevada and several Native American tribes circled the Humphrey Building where HHS was located. Okay, who has the next idea? That challenge never went away.

There were the usual turf issues. The safety net is spread over several executive agencies and Congressional oversight committees and subcommittees. At a minimum, you had Health and Human Services, Labor, Agriculture (Food Stamps at the time), Housing and Urban Development, Education, Treasury (the EITC), and possibly Commerce, and a few others. I was even sent over to substitute for Ellwood at meetings that included high-level officials from the Defense Department. I can't quite recall the relevance to what we were doing though the meetings were always held in the evenings in the Old Executive Office Building (technically the White House). Even in those days, pre-9/11, it was hard getting into that place . . . like you needed a secret password or such. Late one night, I left the meeting and got lost trying to find the one egress still open. I wandered up to a door labeled "Office of the First Lady." Certainly, I was moments away from being pinned to the ground and being subject to a body cavity search when I finally was able to make my escape.

The point I was getting to, before my inevitable digression, was that too many fingers were playing in the kitchen. The safety net had evolved over decades with little thought to how the parts could possibly work together. By the 1990s, doing comprehensive reform had become a nightmare. You had to get all these agencies, each headed by turf-conscious leaders, to collaborate on a new direction and a new set of rules. Hell, it was almost impossible to get the agencies to agree on definitions for basic things like what defines an assistance unit or how to calculate income and assets. The bottom line was that yes, it was theoretically possible but not bloody likely. It was more likely that the next time I flew back to Madison for a weekend visit home, I would be hopping on a magic carpet for the flight.

Oddly enough, there also were failures of intelligence. I don't mean that the planners were stupid, they were very smart indeed. Besides, they had access to the best and brightest from academia, think tanks, and the top evaluation firms. You could call, and people would come running, many of them at least. A lot of people wanted to be a player in this game. The problem was subtler than that. In some respects, it was the research itself that had led us astray. This is a statement which, coming from an erstwhile member of the academy, amounts to heresy. So, let me explain in some detail.

We had sound research methods to test small to medium-size research questions. The classic experimental design was perfect when you had interventions that were well defined and where subjects (individuals, families, or discrete bureaucratic units) could be randomly allocated to experimental and control groups with relative ease. If done well, this could control for alternate explanatory factors. But when the interventions were large scale and involved, for example, changing the overall culture of a program or interrelated set of programs, researchers could seldom, if ever, control enough of the real-world environment to maintain the rigor that a classical experiment demanded. You could hardly select experimental counties at random and walk in to say, "Okay, you folks are going to upend your whole world in the next six months, are you with us?" Economists hoped that by using large data sets and fancy econometric methods, they could tease out causality and control for those darn alternative explanations of any effects measured.

Robert Moffitt, a respected economist from Johns Hopkins and the head of the NAS expert panel on evaluating welfare reform on which I was to serve, once asked me if I believed the results from the observational studies on the effects of welfare reform favored by quantitative social scientists. "Not really," I responded. He looked crestfallen since his brethren were doing so many of them. "The formal math is fine, I suspect." I went on to explain, "The problems lie elsewhere."

After pausing a moment to collect my thoughts—always an iffy proposition—I continued, "The way I see it you have to make all kinds of simplifying assumptions to make these things work. A state passes a law or regulations saying that they are introducing intervention X. You group that state with others passing what seem to be similar laws and compare them with control states that choose a different route while statistically controlling for hard to observe yet systemic heterogeneity across groups to account for relevant things that might confound the results. You also build in a lag time factor such as it typically takes six months for a state to go from enactment to reality. And then you do some fancy time series analysis. But you never know if the experimental states did what they said they would or did it well or did it in the way they claimed they were or did anything at all. Anyone who has spent time in the real world, like I have, will have large residual doubts. We simply appreciate the messiness of the real world."

He sighed, "Well, Tom, if we can't convince you, then we are in deep trouble." I tried to assure him that my support would always be available for a modest fee.

In 1993-94, what we had were a bunch of small to medium-size experimental studies that convincingly showed that most interventions evidenced small, yet often statistically significant, results. Each of these studies generally looked at individual interventions in comparative isolation. What if you did a Job Club, or exposed clients to a certain training program, or a temporary trial job, and the list goes on. Some were a bit more complex, but none (or none that were examined rigorously) rose to the status of changing welfare in any fundamental way. The results we did have simply were not terribly dramatic nor robust. Welfare use might fall a few percentage points compared to the controls and labor force rise a bit. Earnings could be up by 30 percent but from a very, very low base. Things worked but not by much.

The problem for us was that it *looked* as if the technologies we had at hand would not push that many of the five million or so AFDC adult clients off the rolls into sustainable private sector jobs. So, when you ended welfare as we knew it, you would have to plan for droves of public sector jobs to catch them as we pushed them off the cliff after reaching their time limit on assistance. You could not wish for a different world since OMB (Office of

Management and Budget) or the CBO (Congressional Budget Office) would catch you up. They had access to the same research. Reform was beginning to look way too expensive.

Finally, let me comment on one last impediment. It always struck me that some of the reform leaders were looking for the perfect solution which, as the adage goes, is the enemy of the acceptable solution. Ellwood, as much as I admired him, was at heart an academic. When he got the ASPE job, he told me that this was the position he always coveted. His father had been a policy wonk as well, working on early forms of the Health Maintenance Organization (HMO) concept. Someone mentioned once that David had spent a bit of time at ASPE as a child, looking out over the mall and the U.S. Capitol as his father discussed serious business with the powers that be. Apparently, that is when his desire to sit in the big chair emerged.

Academics are very sensitive to criticism, however. After all, they are supposed to be the experts. They always want to run the data one more time, think through the results with another twist, try to conjure up all possible rejoinders to critics in advance. I always had the impression that he and others were waiting for that one last data run from the Urban Institute or one of the other available think tanks to finally get it all right. But we were doing policy in the real world. There would never be a final, conclusive data run or the perfect, elegant solution.

As the work and the group dialogues and the groundhog-day meetings dragged on, I would ponder these conundrums. This often happened as I boarded the first metro of the morning from Arlington's Courthouse Station into the District. I would get to the Humphrey Building so early that I had to sign in past night security. During the summer months, I would enjoy the first blush of dawn as it framed the Capitol. It could be a beautiful city if you ignored most of the people who inhabited the place. Inspired by this setting, I would screw up my courage to tilt at another windmill by taking a shot at breaking the log jam.

Fairly early on I wrote a memo to David where I laid out my "perfection is the enemy of progress" fears. Of course, it was much longer and detailed than my introduction above. I also think he saw it since his chief palace guard, a woman he brought with him from Harvard, told me how good she thought it was and would make sure David saw it. Of course, that did not mean he ever read it. In any case, nothing happened as far as I could see. I kept thinking about how to get people on the same page at the beginning of the process. There were too many cooks with too many perspectives. We needed some common definitions and maybe a common direction? I think I read something about this in my Planning 101 course.

How about we start by defining welfare? Were Food Stamps welfare? How about the EITC? You knew that many Republicans would so argue . . . maybe a few within our happy family were so inclined. I think I even threw out a starter definition. It went something like this: welfare was a cash assistance transfer to families with little to no assets and income in which we impose marginal tax rates on income and earnings well above what we would dare impose on any other segment of the income distribution. This was not only accurate but eliminated most safety net programs from being considered welfare. Any program, no matter how defensible, once tarnished with the welfare label clearly was at risk of being assigned to some endangered species list. But again, I was ignored.

One weekend in early fall 1993, Ann Segal (I believe) came up with an exercise to see if we were getting anywhere. We knew whose opinions really counted. So, a few key staff sat down and attempted to identify the salient issues and where each key stakeholder stood. We spent the weekend (to avoid onlookers and loose talk) comparing positions where we could and looking for possible points of convergence and compromise. We had these index cards spread out across a large table. I recall looking at the array at one point and exclaiming out loud, "Haven't these people been talking to one another at all?" It was going to be a long fall as we tried to end welfare.

As 1993 ground on, we had another groundhog-day meeting that proved particularly illuminating. For some reason, all the top-level people were elsewhere that day or had to leave early. Still, there was a decent crowd left and many from high up in various participating agencies. As the dialogue slowly ground to a halt, people began to pick up their papers and started moving away from the large table. Then, someone made one last comment about the cliff at the end of the two years of cash assistance. Another participant turned back to the table and said something about not agreeing with that interpretation of "ending welfare." Then others started chiming in, with more than one claiming to really know what Bill had in mind by ending welfare. Now everyone was returning to the table, all thoughts of lunch were abandoned, and a small free-for-all ensued. It struck me that someone should just ask Bill.

Later, I ran into David and mentioned what happened. "Damn," he exhaled with a pained, faraway look in his eyes. In retrospect, I suspect we had a rather civil and polite reform planning process. I recall Eugene (Geno) Smolensky, another former IRP director and by this time dean of the Public Policy School at Berkeley, talking about literally wanting to jump across the table to tear the throat out of his adversaries during the Carter reform days. This seemed out of character since Geno was a laid back, very funny, guy. Though no one seemed on the verge of physical violence this time around, I could see that it was going to be a long winter as we tried to end welfare.

By early in 1994, we were on life support. Most energy was drifting toward the Health Care reform being headed up by the First Lady. Some of us from the welfare side were invited to a secret briefing. There was a lot of secrecy in all this. On the welfare side we sometimes would get a numbered draft of a position paper for a meeting that had to be turned in when the session ended. Still, Jason Deparle of the *New York Times* would have a column on the so-called secret draft two days later. There would be a lot of scurrying around to uncover the source of leaks to no avail. I did see messages from Jason from time to time asking me to call him. I chose to ignore them. After my D.C. days, he and I chatted occasionally about welfare issues, and he acknowledged me in his book on the topic. But I was very careful while in D.C.

One day, Wendell and I attended a briefing on the progress of the health care reform planning group. There were extensive charts and diagrams and all manner of wondrous details on the emerging proposal. I am reasonably smart, but I know I was getting lost. As I left with Wendell, he muttered something about health care proposal being way too complicated and we better not fall into the same trap. I feared, however, that we might. For me, the bottom line of that briefing was that our companion reform effort also was mired in the complexities of change. Perhaps they would have to focus on one or the other, there might not be enough energy to mount two social policy revolutions at the same time.

Then the ax fell with surprising swiftness. Welfare reform planning would cease, all bets were on health care. I was enjoying a relaxed weekend knowing the pressure was now off when I noticed that Senator Moynihan was appearing on one of the Sunday morning political talk shows. He was furious. "We don't have a health care crisis," I believe he shouted as his face reddened, "we have a welfare crisis." While I thought we did have a health care financing crisis, his opinion counted, not mine. When I went to work the next day, welfare was back on the front burner.

I still tried tilting at some windmills. I argued that we abandon any thought of coming up with a national reform. It was taking us too long. When and if we did come up with something, it would look too complicated, too prescriptive, and too inflexible. We risked push back if we came up with a "one size fits all" model. In case no one had noticed, states were already running with reform. They were, as Justice Brandeis once famously noted, the appropriate laboratories of change. States would likely resist the feds now coming in to tell them what to do. Let's come up with a few competing reform alternatives that reflected the major disagreements holding us up. Then, let the states volunteer to try them out. That way the internal disputes might be tested and resolved in the marketplace for new ideas. By this time, Rebecca Maynard had joined me as an ally in this perspective.

Rebecca "Becca" Maynard was a UW trained economist who earned a national reputation as a top researcher and welfare evaluator at Mathematica Policy Research Inc. (Mathematica), one of the top three social welfare evaluation firms. By this time, she had drifted into a faculty position at the University of Pennsylvania and was spending two or three days a week as one of the numerous academic-type advisors to ASPE. Like Jennifer Noyes, she also was blond, very attractive, and smart. And very much like Jennifer, Becca also enjoyed squabbling with me though mostly in good fun. At least I think it was all in good fun. When we later served on the NAS evaluation panel together, we squabbled so often that Bob Goerge from the University of Chicago would scold us with "now, now children, time to behave."

We often agreed on the big issues, however. We approached Wendell Primus to make our plea for a different direction. How about proposing several models from which the states might select an approach they might prefer? The fundamental disagreements separating the planners might be captured in the individual models put out for testing. He listened politely with this wry smile he often had when you just knew he did not agree with you. No, he understood what we were saying, but the administration was committed to national reform.

After a polite passage of time, Becca and I hit him again. This time we pleaded for yet another approach to national reform. Let's not try to write a totally prescriptive law. Our reform proposal could be national in scope, but let's lay out a general road map as opposed to detailing every twist and turn on the journey. You can see by now that I love stupid metaphors. I once again saw that wry grin spread across Wendell's face and immediately knew we were dead in the water. Wendell, for all his goodness and bigness of heart, had been in Washington too long. It seemed to me that he just could not quite come to trust the states. And frankly, I didn't have total confidence in my own ideas. Perhaps Becca and I were getting desperate.

President Clinton soon gave his State of the Union address to Congress. He promised that a bill ending welfare as we know it would be submitted to Congress that spring. I should not have been eating while watching the speech. It took me a while to stop gagging from the food caught in my throat. The next day, I bet everyone within earshot that the date on the Bill would be the last day of spring. In fact, it would turn out to be June 21. Is that still technically spring? In any case, I was certain it would be a long spring as we struggled to end welfare as we knew it.

The reader should realize that, despite all the frustrations it entailed, struggling with reform was great fun. Hey, I had spent two years in rural India in the Peace Corps trying to do agriculture, another topic about which I knew virtually nothing . . . you think I would have learned to avoid taking on impossible tasks. In the end, I learned much from this impossible Washington situation as well, certainly as much as I had benefited from being a pretend farmer in the deserts of India. After all, it is the hard that makes it great, right? And despite the difficulties, the chase for fundamental reform was exhilarating and a superb learning experience. Besides, there were many good laughs and fun times as well.

At one of the groundhog-day meetings, which could be almost as deadly as university faculty meetings with one critical exception. The issues in Washington were much more important. One day, the challenge of teen pregnancy was being discussed. One of the eminent economists in the group suggested we condition future eligibility for Pell Grants on the girl avoiding pregnancy during her teen years. You must remember that economists believe that the whole world can be changed with the correct monetary incentives. We had one regular participant from the Labor Department, Roxie Nicholson. Typically, she was direct in her comments, though they could be softened by her Southern accent. After a moment to consider the matter, she spoke up, "Oh sure, I can see it now. Susie and Jim are going at it hot and heavy in the back seat and suddenly Susie is going to shout, 'Stop! Stop! I will lose my Pell Grant.'" After the laughter died down, we moved on.

One time I was running around like a crazy man going in three directions at once. I saw one of the young female presidential interns. These PIs, as they were known, were competitively selected from the top public policy schools to serve a couple of years in D.C. while they learned their craft. I shoved a big document in her hands and pleaded with her to make some copies while I dashed off in another direction. I really didn't notice her gender and would have asked the coat rack in the corner if I thought it would have done any good. But, of course, she gave me great grief for several weeks about this—the male superior asking the female subordinate to do grunt work.

I liked the PIs and most of them were quite talented. I would help them sharpen their writing and test them on their critical thinking skills by getting them to see the unintended consequences to decisions that looked good to them at first blush. I suspect that they looked upon me as an older, somewhat avuncular figure that ought to be excused for his lapses in political correctness. One day, my offended gal called me a *snag*. I considered that either her final insult to me as punishment for my earlier transgression, or a great compliment. I was not sure which. It sounded like the latter. Maybe the S stood for sexy or stud. But it stood for sensitive as in sensitive new-age guy. Not as good as I had hoped but it could have been worse. I did get the last laugh. One day, I had a camera with me and asked her to pose for a picture. As she smiled in my direction I added, "One more thing, could you lift your skirt a little higher." The paper weight she threw in my direction only missed my head by an inch.

They got their revenge though. Mary, my wife, came to D.C. many a weekend. When she finally visited my office at ASPE during a longer stay, they sprung a little surprise. As I was showing Mary around, I thought I noticed furtive figures darting in and out of my office. When we finally walked into my sanctuary, we both started laughing. There were pictures of scantily clad women hanging on the walls and on my desk. I think there was a big mug saying, "world's greatest lover." And there was a woman's stocking coming out of one of my desk drawers. In fact, one of the gifts they gave me as I headed back to Madison was a big mug that said, "Tom's fan club." It had pictures of several (female) staffers on it.

One day, Ann McCormick came running up to me late in the day. "Glad I caught you. Would you like to go to New Jersey?"

"Why Ann," I responded, "this is so sudden, and we are both married. And besides, I have been there before. It is not so great."

After a groan, she went on with the business at hand. Apparently, the New Jersey governor was dedicating a new something or other involving welfare reform, and he was promised a representative from the Clinton administration. None of the real representatives, however, could go so the real power brokers nominated me. Ann promised me that all I had to do was stand there like a dummy. *Perfect*, I thought, *I am just the man for that job.*

On the train the next morning, I thought to myself, *I bet Ann lied to me. She looks so innocent but . . .* So, I worked up a few notes as I desperately tried to recall what the reform might be—they were all starting to sound the same to me. Fortunately, as promised, there was someone at the Philly station with a sign for Jim Corbett. *Close enough,* I thought. As he drove me over to Camden, I asked for an agenda. Sure enough, Clinton representative, Jim Corbett, was scheduled to speak right after the governor. I knew it, Ann had lied!

That was okay, by then I had been flying around the country giving talks on where the administration was going without really saying anything. My friend John Karl Scholz, now dean of the College of Letters and Sciences at U.W., had spent two stints in D.C, the last one as deputy assistant secretary for Tax Analysis in the Clinton administration where he worked under the brilliant and controversial Larry Summers. Karl, as he is known, was simply flabbergasted that I could go off and speak for the administration without my remarks being politically and substantively vetted. Either the ASPE brass trusted me, or they hoped that some angry mob would mortally attack me, thus sparing them from the ordeal of listening to my stupid ideas any longer. After considering the two possible explanations, Karl went with the second option.

Anyways, what surprised me was the barrage of media questions when I finished. "Well, what did you think of what the New Jersey governor was doing?" "Did it fit with President Clinton's vision of reform?" "Why did the president support this initiative?" "And just what are you going to do with all the poor welfare people in Camden when they can't get jobs and you throw them off the rolls?" Now that was a good one, there were no jobs in Camden. After I blah, blahed for a while, it ended.

I saw the light at the end of the tunnel which, unfortunately, was on the other side of the room. A gauntlet was positioned between me and freedom, composed mostly of favor seekers who, to my amusement, thought I was someone important. This barrier to freedom was buttressed by a gaggle of reporters who, despite my eloquence, were not yet quite convinced that New Jersey was showing the way for the nation on welfare reform. One young man slowed me up. "I have the solution for how to reach all the young, lost black men on our streets," he said. When I asked what that might be, he pushed a business card in my hand and beamed, "Rap music." I mumbled something about getting in touch and pushed on.

Another time, Wendell came into my office just before noon. "Tom, can you fill in for me. I am supposed to give a talk to an audience over at Social Security." I assured him that would be no problem as I looked around for my calendar to mark the time and date. "The car is running downstairs," he responded. I noticed that he once again had that same wry grin I had seen many a time. I had winged a lot of lectures and talks but this kind of request sounded more important. I often organized my talks on plane rides to various venues, but the car ride to SSA was not nearly as long. My recollection is that the expected speech was on the administration's vision for welfare reform. I had been giving creative speeches on that topic for some time now.

Many of my talks that year were to various audiences with some stake in the reform effort. I think I was supposed to pave the way for the reality of what was coming, and to intuit where future resistance might lie. Thus, my forays into the real world were both a marketing and intelligence-gathering efforts. On several of these, Mark Greenberg, representing the Center for Law and Social Policy, had also been invited.

Mark was a Harvard Law educated advocate for the poor. He was not a shouter though. He was low-keyed and very analytical. He knew the federal regulations inside and out and was constantly sought after as a consultant by states. He always spoke in slow, measured terms; and often made me feel guilty that I was not as nice a person as he, nor as substantively informed; and certainly not as smart. After a career on the outside, he finally joined the federal government in the Obama administration. More recently, he joined the Migration Policy Institute here he worked on issues at the intersection of migrants and human services.

Mark and I got into a ritual. I would give the administration's spiel, or what I thought was the spiel. It must have been okay since no one ever yelled at me upon my return to D.C. nor was I ever physically attacked by the audience, though ominous rumblings were occasionally heard. Then Mark would get up and say something like, "Now I have known Tom for many years and he is a very nice guy, 'but' beware of some of the things he is saying here today." Then he would gently, in the most moderate and measured terms, explain how I had gotten in bed with Satan himself. When I was on some panel, I remember Wendell also commenting that he thought I was the most conservative member of this group. I recall thinking at the time, what the—! Someone should email my home state governor, Tommy Thompson, with this news. He is convinced that I am a left-wing terrorist nut case. Go figure!

On the other hand, there were a few uplifting moments! Not many, of course, but one stands out! I had written a piece for *Focus* called *Child Poverty: Progress or Paralysis*. It came out in the spring of 1993, just before I left for D.C. Over the next decade,

I would come to appreciate what an impact that piece had, quite remarkable really. But for me, at the time, it had been published and then soon forgotten. I seldom looked back. I was the same with tests in school. Other students would gather to go over how others had answered the questions. I only wanted to walk away. It was a done deal.

My first inkling that my fifteen minutes of fame was about to break hit me like a two-by-four one day. Several of us working on the reform effort gathered to make a special presentation to a bunch of D.C. based movers and shakers. This was an audience of welfare specialists and various power brokers and I knew that the higher ups were quite nervous that this should go well, including folks from the White House Domestic Policy Council. As we waited to enter the meeting site, someone said that the room was abuzz because they wanted to meet this guy named Tom Corbett who had written this amazing article. What, this must be a joke!

I guess not. It turned out I was a minor celebrity. A few weeks later I got a call from the GAO, now the General Accountability Office. They had called UW to see if this Tom Corbett could come to speak to them about this *Focus* piece and were delighted to find me in D.C. I was a little disappointed that this chat would overlap with the ASPE summer picnic. We surely needed some down time. I promised the other staff that I just needed to run over to GAO for a quick chat and would soon catch up with them for the fun and games. When I got to GAO, the receptionist said, "Oh, you are our speaker for the afternoon." That didn't sound good. Then I walked into this large room that was filled with many, many people. This really didn't look good. I never made it to the picnic.

The talk was much longer than planned and I, as I often did, improvised on the spot. The Q&A went on for a long time and then some people wanted to chat in a small group. About a decade later, I stopped by GAO to visit a former student who now worked there. One of her supervisors stopped by her office and introduced herself. She had been at that talk in 1993. She told me that they used my piece for several years when Congressional requests came in for background information on welfare. They thought it a most balanced and insightful piece. Go figure!

One day, a call for me was received at ASPE from a Sargent Schriver. My immediate reaction is that it was a call from either the D.C. or Arlington police. I had already been identified as a scofflaw by the Arlington city fathers for not paying a wheel tax while temporarily renting an apartment in their fair city. Apparently, you could not park on their streets without forking over some money for this tax. I thought they had caught me up in another such transgression. But the call was from *the* Sargent Schriver, Kennedy's brother-in-law and launcher of both the WOP and the Peace Corps. Since I referenced his anti-poverty efforts in this article, I suspected he wanted to praise me or call me a schmuck for getting it all wrong. But I'll never know since we never did connect.

The bill came out. It was long, complicated, and prescriptive, much as I feared would happen. As I mentioned earlier, a fair amount of my rhetoric had survived. That sad fact, however, was not going to save this sinking ship as it finally limped out of the harbor. After a committee hearing or two, Congress began to obsess about the fall elections. It was 1994 and Newt Gingrich and the Republicans were about to storm the barricades. Clinton's effort to end welfare as we knew it was dead. Others would be better situated to say whether my contributions to Clinton's proposal were meaningful in any way. I can say with confidence, however, that I left a lot of laughter behind. I did try to lighten the place up. It goes without saying that Washington is a place that desperately needs more laughter.

One fine day in June 1994, I packed up my Honda hatchback with my parting gifts and the best wishes of a staff I had come to appreciate so much before heading back to Madison. There was a bit of drama in those last days. There was some talk about my staying at ASPE. Despite the frustrations, I did enjoy the experience greatly. In retrospect, I probably never seriously entertained that possibility though my wife and I did look at housing in the area. In any case, it would have been a bigger mistake than the one I made in accepting the tenure track faculty position that had been ginned up during my Washington stay, another "back-forty" idea I discuss in more detail in a later chapter. Playing in my candy store from the sanctuary of the academy proved infinitely preferable to wandering about in the ideological jungle that Washington was becoming.

Back in Wisconsin, I would get to watch Tommy Thompson end welfare as we knew it up close and personal. In fact, Wendell kept saying to me and others at IRP, "You keep an eye on what the governor is doing, try to assess what is going on." Fortunately for the intrepid readers of my tale, this part of the narrative is much shorter than my Washington adventures. We at IRP would be watching from the outside as Governor Thompson put together the Wisconsin Works or W-2 program. It is not as if we did not try to help. We tried very hard to get involved but with little success.

Upon my return, I found I was associate director of IRP. Again, I can't recall how this happened. It just seemed to happen, along with this half-time clinical assistant professor position in Social Work. The rationale for the faculty position apparently came from the higher-ups in the U.W. celestial bureaucratic body. The faculty position appeared to solidify my ongoing teaching role. Not that long after my return, Barbara "Bobbi" Wolfe, the new director, invited all the head people putting W-2 together to a summit meeting on the top floor of Van Hise Hall. This included J. Jean Rogers, Jason Turner, Shannon Christian, and several other top officials including the secretary of the Welfare Bureaucracy, Gerald Whitburn.

The setting was where the board of regents for the whole U.W. system met . . . a site that offered spectacular views of Madison, the beautiful lakes that surround the city, and the bucolic countryside beyond. We brought in a powerhouse lineup of academic stars to describe their expertise and what they had to offer. We ended with an offer to help in any way we could and gave them our phone numbers. Our offer was met with dead silence. No one called. Did the governor hate us (me) that much?

I knew that we had fumbled the ball during one unfortunate IRP sponsored event. J. Jean Rogers was a top state official at that time and a very close confidant of the governor. We invited her to be on a panel to be held during the annual IRP Summer Workshop. This venue brought to Madison many high-tech poverty researchers from around the country where they fought over methodological approaches employed in their respective research papers. It was nerd heaven. But we always had one policy event to lighten the mood. This year it was a discussion of W-2 which already had captured national attention. I could see the horse manure right in front of me but, as usual, plunged ahead anyways.

Jean described the vision and principles of W-2 in somewhat general terms since it was still being planned. I moderated the session and could see that tension was rising between the governor's confidant and Bob Haveman who also was on the panel. They were making side comments to one another. During the Q&A session, some particularly sharp questions came from the audience, particularly Robert Moffitt and Peter Gottschalk. By the end, I sensed that Jean was furious. Most likely, she thought she had been set up and by me since her invitation came from yours truly. Of course, she never saw how badly these guys and gals treated each other during their verbal brawls over picayune methodological disputes. This was just business as usual in the cutthroat world of the academy. She, however, did not know that. IRP was now deeper in the crapper, and I spent the evening wiping a lot of it off my shoes.

I guess I never understood just how deep the muck was until I was invited to an event at the Joyce Foundation in Chicago. They had been supporting my work, and I had a good relationship with some officials there. My favorite project officer, Unmi Song, called to ask if Tommy Thompson might come to speak at the dinner before their annual board meeting. I said sure, he was already unofficially running for president and probably wanted any exposure he could get. "But don't ask me to contact him," I added, "I guarantee you, I am not on his Christmas list." "No problem," she said as she invited me to the festivities. I never refuse requests from people who give me money, so I went but with some trepidation. Yes, I can be bought and for surprisingly little money.

The panelists that night included the governor (who thought I was a left-wing terrorist), Mark Greenberg (the liberal advocate who followed me around when I was in D.C. telling folks I had gone over to the dark side), and the mayor of Milwaukee (a Democrat who did not know me from Adam, but whose primary aide was someone I had worked with in the past).

As I was working the room before the event, the president of the foundation came up to me and whispered that the governor had arrived. Before I could say anything, she grabbed my arm and pulled me toward him. As soon as he recognized me, he got red in the face and started in, "Why are you always attacking me?" and added a few more *bon mots* before ending up with something about me "getting on his train." Somehow, I did not get the impression that he was asking for my company on his next cross-country vacation.

I was saved for the moment when a Joyce board member, and law school professor at UW, saw what was happening and intervened to save me from further attack. The governor was quite vexed at my presence, and I feared he might stroke-out on the spot, his face was quite red. The brave intervention of the board member from UW proved only a temporary reprieve. After the dinner and talks, there was a Q&A session in which one member of the audience asked the governor what the foundation could do to help him with his work on welfare reform. He literally jumped up to the microphone. "I am glad you asked that. You can start by not giving money to these institutes that go around attacking me. I have brought in the best minds and we will reform welfare. Give me the money and I will make better use of it." He started to sit down and then jumped back up, "And these comments are directed to Tom Corbett out there," as he waived a menacing arm in my general direction.

I guess it really, really, really bothered him that I was there. It certainly gave me a better sense of his deep animus toward me and the institute. As he later swept out of the room, still obviously upset, he caught my eye and clearly mouthed the words "call me." Now there was an invitation I could refuse. And all this time I thought I was a hell of a nice guy. Go figure!

I hate to say this, but people at my table were giggling throughout his tantrum. I suspect his actions were considered juvenile, if not outright childish. I can understand that politicians might see enemies everywhere. Perhaps he even thought the foundation was out to embarrass him, and that I was part of the scheme. Still, it escapes me how my presence could do that. I had never, not once, actively lobbied against any of his welfare proposals and even helped when I agreed with the direction he was taking things. In any case, his reaction was not the sort of thing done among the genteel world of philanthropic do-gooders. At one point I felt a presence at my shoulder. It was the foundation president. She leaned over and whispered in my ear, "Tom, in our eyes your stock has just gone up."

Several years later, I coincidently happened to be visiting the foundation in Chicago on that president's last day. She was leaving to assume the head position of a well-known national charity called Second Harvest. I was ushered into her office to extend my best wishes, and she brought up that incident saying she had used it during her interview for her new and far more public position.

I was curious how she used the story but there were too many of her staff around. Not wanting to disrupt the ceremony, I made a graceful exit. It yet remains a matter of curiosity to me.

Evidence that I would not soon be on the governor's Christmas gift list kept coming. During one of my endless trips back to D.C., a National Governors Association staff person mentioned that my name came up as a perfect resource person for a project they were launching. Her colleagues readily agreed. She was about to pick up the phone and then remembered that Thompson had recently become the titular head of the association. She suddenly had visions of him blowing his top and put the phone back down.

On another occasion, Bobbi Wolfe and I were chatting with the secretary of the Wisconsin Labor Department, whom Bobbi knew socially. Her department would play a major role in launching W-2. Again, we offered our assistance, thinking this might be a way to get involved. She would love our help, she admitted, but mentioned that we were in trouble over there, nodding in the direction of the Capitol. A favorite vignette of mine involves my spouse. She came home one day to say she had been introduced to the governor by her boss, the director of the Wisconsin state court system. She held the position of one of his two deputies. First, the governor flamboyantly kissed her hand before moving his kisses up her arm (that was her story at least and very believable). Second, her boss told her afterward that he was desperately relieved that she had kept her maiden name and that Tommy had no idea she was married to that dastardly Corbett guy. Chances for a judicial pay raise would have been shot that year for sure, he weakly joked.

The irony was that I, at least, saw a lot of positive things in W-2, which was considered an unmitigated disaster amongst the liberal community. Yes, it did end the entitlement to welfare. It ended welfare as we know it far more completely than anything Clinton could have produced given the normative tensions within his party. Sure, some people would run afoul of the new expectations and we must remain cognizant of their suffering. And I was under no illusion that the jobs most recipients could expect would lift them out of poverty. But as I argued to anyone who would listen, neither would the old AFDC program, which already was facing a "race to a zero-dollar welfare guarantee" given the fears of welfare-induced migration and a general distaste for handing out unfettered cash. Besides, I always thought we could do a better job than we had previously done of integrating low-income women into the labor market.

I always thought the governor deserved credit for two things. While the ideas he pushed were not all that original, virtually every reform idea had been thought up or tried at some time in the past, he proved remarkably successful in making them a reality. Most of his predecessors had failed at that. And second, he invested quite a lot or resources in those welfare clients who played by the rules. He freely confessed that welfare reform would cost money, at least in the intermediate term. Moreover, he backed that belief in many ways.

He greatly expanded child care availability, access to health care for those getting jobs that did not provide it, and job preparation opportunities. He nominally supported the "make work pay" ideal that Clinton and Ellwood championed. After some wavering, the Thompson people committed to Food Stamps and the state EITC as necessary work supports and income supplements.

While he got the notion that work should be feasible and that it should pay, the governor was prepared to pull the plug if a client was not willing to play by the rules. He bought into the notion that motherhood was not a disability that warranted automatic eligibility for income supports. In important ways, the feminist revolution had chipped away at that premise starting in the 1950s. Women, including young mothers, began to enter the labor force, a trickle at first that later became a torrent. Work for all women, including mothers, had become the expectation, not a societal anomaly.

The Thompson team deserves a lot of credit for pulling it off, getting W-2 enacted. I must say that doing reform at the state level is easier than in Washington. It is always hard no matter where it is done, make no mistake about that. Washington, however, is a town built around the notion of inertia. Any idea, even the most innocuous, will be met by highly organized and disciplined opposition. You want to honor apple pie and motherhood. Forget about it. The Cherry Pie Institute and various father groups would be all over you within forty-five minutes with a well-funded and sophisticated oppositional campaign. While similar things happen at the state level, the counter weights to any proposal are not so numerous or as powerful though well-funded backers of business interests have been in the ascendancy in recent decades.

In retrospect, I suppose the governor did me another favor in addition to putting me in the good graces of the Joyce Foundation. What If his people had called us to help them with W-2? Where would I have found the time? I was stretched beyond belief including faking at being a halftime tenure track assistant clinical professor of Social Work. One small vignette captured my desperate situation during this period. I received a call from someone in the bowels of the UW bureaucracy. The woman on the other end of the line went on about some issue in a research project. Not only could I not understand the issue, but I had no recognition of the project at all. "How can that be," she responded to my protests of ignorance, "you are listed as the principle investigator." *Then we are in trouble,* I thought.

We still managed to do a lot with W-2. I had many friends in the bureaucracy who did not share the governor's dark opinion of me or the institute. I conversed with them a lot and sometimes would arrange for secret information drops straight out of the height of the cold war. "Tom," the would-be traitor would say, "I am calling from a pay phone. I will walk down State Street wearing a red hairpiece and a fake beard that runs down to my navel. I will be carrying the latest draft of the W-2 plan in a plain vanilla envelope.

You walk up State Street carrying a similar envelope containing blank pages, so the two packages look identical. When you see me, our code will be 'the irises are blooming in Copenhagen' if all is okay. Then pretend to bump into me and we will both drop our packages. In the confusion, we can exchange them and continue walking in opposite directions." Okay, it was never quite that clandestine, but the state people involved were very nervous about secretly working with us. One state employee was seen walking into the Capitol at the end of the work day and grilled the next day about her intentions. Was she clandestinely meeting with Democratic lawmakers? It so happened that her condo was located on the other side of the square and this was her usual route home in cold weather. Paranoia was everywhere.

What we did with such illicitly obtained information was innocent enough. Since there was a lot of interest in what Wisconsin was cooking up, we published several dispassionate explanations of the plan in *Focus*. We even had a conference and published a book on how to evaluate a complex reform such as W-2. Jennifer Noyes, who was put in charge of W-2, later regretted that IRP's evaluation plan was not used to assess the program early on. However, political emotions ran high at that point and such a collaboration was impossible. In reality, we were academics, not advocates. Our primary mission was to understand and evaluate the reform, not push any ideological or partisan agenda, at least as a research institute. Individual academics, of course, were always free to follow the dictates of their opinions but most of my colleagues, as I, were dispassionate observers in the policy arena, not daily partisan nor ideological combatants.

Since I also had occasion to travel around the state talking to welfare officials, employers, and other real people I got a good feel for what was happening on the ground. One vignette has become a talking point for me over the years. It came up during a discussion with the welfare manager in La Crosse County, a medium-size county that borders with Minnesota. The numbers may not be exact (though close, I believe), but the story line is pretty much as she told me:

> Here is what we experienced in our county. Before W-2 we had about 1,400 AFDC cases. Even before we launched the program, the caseload began to decline as news about the new program spread. When we sat down with the state to negotiate the block grant structure under which W-2 would operate, we had maybe 800 to 850 cases left. Madison and we agreed that 400, maybe a little more would be a good estimate for the post W-2 caseload. When the smoke cleared, we had 60 cases left. I was not in favor of W-2. I was really concerned that people were suffering out there. So, I sent social workers out to the homeless shelters, the soup kitchens, to look under the bridges. We even went over to Minnesota to see if they

had drifted over the border. We found some, but most had just disappeared. It was amazing.

Howard Rolston, head of evaluation for the Administration for Children and Families at HHS, called one day. "What is happening in Wisconsin?" he asked in amazement, "these caseload declines are unbelievable." He did not say this, but he almost sounded as if he thought they were being faked somehow. Now, Howard is a big supporter of random assignment experiments, which I also defend as the gold standard for evaluating many research questions. What I wanted to say that day, but am not sure I did, is the following:

Most of the welfare reform we have seen over the last decade has been tinkering around the edges. We added something here, took away something there. And when we assessed impacts, we found some effects, but they were seldom, if ever, earthshaking. What you are seeing here is what happens when you change everything at once, when you transform the underlying culture of a program. We had no evidence on what would happen if you did that, thus we are shocked by the results. This story is not over, however. It has only just begun. One thing is certain, however. The face of social assistance has been dramatically altered, and we better start thinking about what we need to do to understand what is happening.

I have skipped over a lot of things that happened during this period, a few of which will be picked up in future chapters. One trip among the many stands out and deserves a quick mention here. I got a call from the Unitarian-Universalist (UU) headquarters in Boston. They are a liberal church with a strong social justice emphasis. They asked if I would come to Boston since welfare reform was such a big topic there. Where wasn't it in those days?

"You want an advocate," I protested. "I can give you the names of some wonderful people." But he stressed they wanted me and that they knew I was not an advocate. I was not totally convinced but I went. I figured with my track record I would be in enough trouble with St. Peter when my time came so maybe this would put a point or two on my side of the celestial score card. Later, it hit me that the UUs don't believe in any specific creed, so I was never sure my getting involved with them would help in that regard. Given my record in the spiritual department, I was probably beyond hope.

The day turned out to be like a political campaign. It started with a visit to the State House. I expected about a half-dozen sleepy legislative aides sitting around a table gulping down their breakfast. I walked into a large hall with a standing room only audience with many real legislators in attendance. As I gasped, my host whispered that they were voting on a welfare reform bill later in the day. *Nice time to tell me,* I recall thinking at that moment! Then there were a series of public talks where I was not always quite sure whom I was addressing. After these talks, it was off to lengthy interviews with the editorial boards of the major newspapers.

That evening we went to the studios of WHA, the Boston Public Television station, to film two episodes of a current events show. The format was unique. The panel was carefully chosen to represent opinions that ranged from the ideological left to the right on whatever the topic was for that evening. That night, it would be welfare reform of course. There was no moderator. You just started talking and the three cameras captured the dialogue. I easily fell into the role of peacemaker with my "on the one hand" and "the other hand" style.

I was appalled when I later saw a video of the shows. The dialogue was mildly entertaining though I hate shows with drummed up controversy. What really disturbed me was the camera situated at my back which, to my horror, captured all too well my balding head. It is amazing how infrequently you get to see back there. Darn, I could no longer deny the reality of a creeping hair follicle disaster. Creeping? Hell, my hair was in full retreat. There really are some truths that ought to be kept hidden.

As I dragged my tired body back to the hotel late that evening, I concluded that I should have charged them twice my usual fee. But then I figured that two times nothing is still nothing so what the hell. The epiphany from the day, and the purpose of my telling the story, is the following. In your own home base, you are just another guy they have heard all too often. But when you fly into another state, you suddenly become a brilliant expert again. Good for the ego!

Outside of Wisconsin, in fact, my reputation never suffered such slings and arrows as it did within the Badger State. To the outside world, I was viewed as a straight shooter. Of course, Ron Haskins, *the* former Republican welfare expert among the Congressional staff and now a Brooking Institute scholar, would always give me grief. He would call me a running dog of the left, and I would return the favor by labeling him a running dog of the right. But we respected one another and enjoyed each other's barbs. When he sought me out for lunch at a conference once, I asked why he would choose to eat with such a well-known leftist. His response was that he knew he would not be bored. When he would call, or when we ran into each other, he would inevitably ask how those Communists were doing at Moscow-On-The-Lake. By that he meant the University of Wisconsin, or was it only IRP?

One day, Ron, Mark Greenberg, and I were on a panel at the University of Chicago and were to speak in just that order. Ron started his talk as follows:

> *When Susan (Mayer) set this panel up, she told me that she put the handsomest, smartest, and most articulate speaker first. Then there would be a tiny drop off between the first speaker and the second (Mark). And then, there would be a huge, unbelievable drop off between the second and the third (meaning me).*

As Susan (a well-known University of Chicago scholar) tried frantically to signal me she had not said this, I just laughed. It was typical of the banter Ron and I exchanged, but it did hit me that many in the audience who didn't know either of us well could well be confused. On another occasion, Mark Greenberg once told the assembled audience that the best thing about the conference we were attending was that Tom Corbett did not introduce him. I found this kind of banter a relief. We all were part of a close-knit fraternity. With all the seriousness and angst surrounding welfare and poverty issues, we needed an occasional good laugh.

At the turn of the century, when Washington swung back to the Republican side, Wade Horn was waiting to be confirmed as head of the Administration for Children and Families (ACF) in Health and Human Services. He was a quite well-known conservative on marriage and family issues, and not a favorite of the left. I personally found him thoughtful and approachable. Howard Rolston, who headed the research and analysis arm of ACF, called one day in a small panic. His national evaluation conference was coming up (where representatives from all fifty states would gather to hear all the latest research on human services worth hearing). It turns out that Wade would not be confirmed by Congress in time. No confirmation, no Wade! "Could I fill in?" Howard asked. "Sure," I responded. I was always willing to help a friend. It struck me that if I could fill in for a conservative icon, I probably was not seen as Satan's playmate by everyone. Now that I ponder this, I wonder if Governor Thompson had been confirmed as Secretary Thompson of H.H.S. by this time. If he had, Howard had taken a large risk in tapping me for this public role.

One awkward moment occurred after Thompson clearly had been confirmed. An H.H.S. official I did not know called one day to ask if I would help with some splashy event they were putting on in Washington. This was not an unusual request at all for me, and I was happy to keep federal officials happy. After all, we survived in large part on federal dollars. Whatever the topic was is now lost to memory. I also promised to secure the services of a senior welfare administrator from Iowa since I knew they were doing something relevant to the topic, whatever it was. In any case, the H.H.S. official was most grateful and then she gushed with bubbly enthusiasm, "Oh, I can't wait to tell the secretary that you have agreed to help us out, with you being from Wisconsin and all."

My brain froze for a moment and then the call was over. Tell the secretary, tell Tommy Thompson! Oh, the poor woman . . . this image of Thompson exploding with rage when she told him flashed before me. He did have a temper. Should I call her back? I could just see her next assignment. She would be on her knees cleaning every toilet bowl in the Humphrey Building, where Health and Human Services is located, with only a toothbrush as a cleaning tool. In the end, I let it go, hoping for the best. When I did meet her, I could see no visible scars, so I assume the secretary was never informed of her innocent faux pas.

The cold war between IRP and the state of Wisconsin slowly softened over time as well. I did take advantage of a couple of easy opportunities to communicate to the governor that I was not just another knee-jerk leftist, at least not then. Rather, I was a thoughtful leftist who considered his opinions carefully and would separate myself from any orthodoxy that struck me as ill-advised or unsupportable. Well, I flattered myself that I was such a guy.

On one occasion, I recall being interviewed by National Public Radio along with the Thompson (from separate locations), when he was yet governor. I took the opportunity to agree with him on several points he made. In the puff piece in *USA Today* where I was named the national "welfare expert," I also praised the governor's actions in areas where we agreed. And he (his staff at least) could see that we did not use IRP's national presence to bash W-2 but merely to inform people what was being tried.

One day, I got a call that the governor wanted to meet with me and my colleague, Michael Wiseman. I quickly perused some catalogues to see how much bulletproof vests cost. The day of the meeting they called again to say the governor had an emergency meeting in D.C., but we should come anyways to meet with the several top officials including a couple of department secretaries. Mike decided that if the governor was absent, it was not worth his time. So, I conned IRP affiliate John Witte, a political scientist and rumored Republican, to accompany me. I wanted a witness in case the rumors of a secret torture chamber where liberals were taken to be waterboarded were, indeed, true.

I quickly relaxed as I sensed that the purpose of the meeting was not malevolent but rather designed to tease out whether the IRP crowd was going to cause trouble as W-2 made its way toward legislative approval. Trouble! I laughed internally. Who in the world listens to a bunch of eggheads? Besides, IRP doesn't take any positions. Like all university entities, it is a loose collection of very independent academic entrepreneurs primarily concerned with which office they would get and whether their parking space was preferential. In any case, academics could not be told what to believe or do, at least within reason. That was what academic freedom was all about. I mean, you couldn't root for the Ohio State Buckeyes or be a Chicago Bears fan, now really! Seriously, I had about as much influence over what my colleagues did, or politicians believed, as I had over my wife . . . by that I mean absolutely none.

As I pondered whether to take a sip of the drink I had been offered, and thus risk death by poisoning, an aide interrupted our discussion to ask if I could briefly step into the adjoining room. The governor had called from Washington to speak to me. *Oh, this can't be good*, I thought. "Tom," I could hear his familiar voice booming on the other end of the line, "are they treating you well out there?" I wanted to say something about being suspicious of this drink they handed me but instead said that all was fine. We went through a few more pleasantries as I wondered what this was all about. Then he ended with, "Now you call my appointment secretary and set something up. We have to have lunch when I get back."

What was that about? I thought. Clearly, he was buttering me up to defuse any mischief I might be entertaining. I did call his appointment secretary. I had to at least presume the man was serious. The secretary, however, sounded totally incredulous that a total lowlife like me could entertain the notion that the governor would waste any amount of time on such an absolute nobody. She and others probably had a good laugh on that one after I hung up. I did stammer something about it being his idea but all I got was a "sure, we'll call you, don't call us" response. Guess what, the call never came.

One day in the future, Bobbi Wolfe and I did get invited to the governor's mansion for lunch. Unfortunately, this was along with sixty or so other invitees to hear the governor talk about W-2. The occasion was a visit from British dignitaries who were interested in Wisconsin's reforms and in stopping by the Poverty Institute. Thus, we believe the governor felt obligated to invite us. Bobbi recalls that Thompson stopped by our table, as he did all the tables. Her recollection is that his comments to us were not overtly hostile but neither did they convey any warmth. Our presence apparently was tolerated at best. In any case, it was not a heart-to-heart talk to thaw the State-IRP cold war but at least he did not yell at me.

What I most recall from that day was his description of how he came up with his central ideas for W-2. He talked about inviting small numbers of Milwaukee welfare mothers to the governor's mansion for lunch. He would ask them what help they needed to get into the workforce and become independent from welfare. He ticked off what he had heard—child care, continued access to health care, transportation help, and some skills training. He then pointed out how W-2 was designed to fill those needs. I thought, *Good for him.* Asking the customer is a wonderful way to think through what changes are needed. But I was also discomforted. I suspect it would never occur to him, or most policymakers for that matter, to look to the academy for advice or help. Most of my colleagues could have ticked off the same list of impediments along with reports and analyses about what to do. The distance between the State Capitol and the university is about a mile as the crow flies. In terms of psychic distance, the gap can appear insurmountable at times. There is a cultural gap that needs to be bridged, one that I address later in this book.

W-2 ended welfare as we knew it in Wisconsin. What had been a cash income support system became a work-focused initiative with a small, residual cash assistance program for those obviously unfit for the workforce. Not long after W-2 went into effect, many smaller counties had a handful of cases left at most. Quite a few of the smallest ones no longer had a single case.

Passage of the Personal Responsibility and Work Opportunity Act (PRWORA), which Bill Clinton signed in 1996, appeared to end welfare as we knew it across the nation. Welfare for struggling families with children was turned from an entitlement to cash assistance into a fixed amount of money to be spent largely on getting (mostly) mothers into the labor market. Some remained on cash assistance but in much smaller numbers than before. After all the dust had cleared, the national TANF caseload was probably 40 percent of what the old AFDC caseload had been, not as big a decline as in Wisconsin but still eye-opening. Welfare, or at least the old AFDC program, had been ended as we knew it.

It also was the end of an era but not the end of the debate. In fact, as we will see later, it was just the beginning of a fascinating dialogue about where to go next. That is the great thing about being a policy wonk, you never work yourself out of a job.

CHAPTER 6

SEARCHING FOR
THE HOLY GRAIL

Changing the culture means changing how we do business.
Changing how we do business means changing how we
organize within Human Service agencies and how we
interact with the community and how we interact with
our clients. It means partnerships. It means collaborations.
It means relationships that didn't exist before.
—Joel Rabb (Ohio welfare official)

My phone rang one day, probably in 1987. Of course, it now occurs to me that my life would have been a lot simpler had I not answered so many phone calls. When it rings at home I seldom jump to answer it. This irritates my long-suffering wife who gives me "the look." "What?" I would respond (to the "look"), "it will either be for you or a call for me that I don't want in the first place." Somehow, though, I felt duty-bound to answer calls to my office phone.

I wondered at times, "Do I have a job description?" More importantly, "Does it actually say I have to answer the phone?" Perhaps I am not obliged to pick up the receiver. Ignoring that irritating ring would have simplified my life immensely, particularly at the university. Surely, then, I would not have been distracted by so many nonacademic seductions like saving the world. Inevitably, though, I would answer the damn phone. It is that brooding responsibility thing we who were raised Catholic do so well—the omnipresent detritus of guilt. Plus, phone-ignoring is probably another venial sin. Just about everything is a sin.

This caller was Jim Kennedy from Kenosha County in Southeast Wisconsin. I cannot recall where I first met Jim, but he had struck me as a nice guy, so maybe this call would be okay. "Tom," he starts, "we are dying here." Well, that grabbed my attention. Perhaps I would never save the world, but I would give saving Jim a shot, him being such a nice guy and all.

"Gee, Jim, shouldn't you be calling the paramedics instead of me?" He ignored me, as I find that most people do, and continued with a description of their plight. Kenosha was one of the five pilot counties that had been selected as WEJT pilots, an initiative with which I had been intimately involved in developing while working with the Wisconsin legislature. Many concerns I had when this reform was launched were coming to pass. The pilot counties were given broad guidelines and some resources. They were then told to go forth and do the Lord's work. That is, they were charged with getting those welfare slugs into jobs. Regarding how to do this, they were left pretty much to their own devices other than collaborate with the local Private Industry Councils, the presumed labor market experts. Apparently, no one had given them my detailed plan for getting recipients into jobs that I had shared with the legislative committee.

Jim went on to explain that they were welfare experts, not workforce people. They were trying, as instructed, to work with their peers from the Private Industry Council (PIC), the system with nominal responsibility back then to get those with labor market challenges into the work world. But it didn't seem to be working. "Could you help us?" Jim pleaded. Whenever I get that kind of request, I am tempted to respond with a hearty, "Me? Are you smoking those funny cigarettes?" But I assured Jim I could find people who could help and would set up a meeting to chat further. I could not permit the concept I had worked to birth in the legislature die a stillborn death.

Fortunately, at the time, IRP had two visiting scholars with the interest and skills to do the job. One was Larry Mead, the author of *Beyond Entitlement*, a conservative call for diminishing the entitlement character of welfare by introducing proactive initiatives to motivate socially approved behaviors. The other was Michael Wiseman, a labor economist from the University of California-Berkeley who had studied workforce development programs. The final member of the Kenosha team would be the same Bernie Stumbras you met in earlier chapters.

At the time, Bernie was out stationed at IRP from his home state agency on an intergovernmental transfer arrangement. I do not know if this is what he wanted or if it was a form of bureaucratic exile. Bernie was smart and a visionary. He had a low-key manner about him with a soft, whispery voice. But he could be very stubborn when he thought he was right, as some talented people tend to be. I would not be surprised if he confronted the new powers that be who came with the Thompson gubernatorial team and had been banned to IRP as a form of punishment. In fact, numerous state employees sought me out over those years looking for a similar kind of refuge at IRP. Morale in public service was plummeting.

Now that I reflect on it, this was quite a team. Larry Mead is a classic patrician, Harvard educated and an avid sailor who loved competing at a very high level in that sport. He tended to speak carefully and in measured terms. His thoughts were typically expressed in flowery language, almost as if he were reading from one of his published papers. Like virtually everyone who spent time in my candy store, Larry was very smart. And yet, he could be rigid in his thinking with his world view set and impervious to any change of views. Oddly, I found him quite insecure for a man who had already achieved so much acclaim. Now, I was the one who could lay claim to any legitimate insecurity in this group. Yet,

I seldom let my lack of talent or skills get in my way of bustling my way through new policy china shops. Such hubris is a gift or, much more likely, a form of delusion.

As mentioned above, Michael Wiseman filled out our little team. He is hard to describe, having a mercurial quality about him. He would be funny and insightful one day, then acerbic and withdrawn the next. But you wanted to grab onto the nuggets that flowed during the good times because few were better at spawning ideas and seeing things that mere mortals do not. Like Larry, he also could express himself in luxurious language that employed ingenious metaphors to make his points. Woe it be to any agency into which this group of misfits parachuted.

Our Kenosha counterparts were a good match, however. There were three main players. Jim Kennedy was the quiet guy with an ever-present smile. He was on the nerdy side, preferring to be crunching numbers and analyzing stuff than doing anything else. George Leuterman headed the welfare side of things for the county. He was a strong, smart, manager type who exuded the kind of can-do confidence you want in an executive. E. Clarke Earle was the overall county director. He was a man of large, sometimes conflicting, qualities. He was brash, brilliant, uncompromising, and passionate. You did not want to stand between him and his goals. He also could be profane and very funny. We all wished we had written down some of his better lines, though we would have to delete a whole lot of profanity. We often referred to his better asides as "the sayings of Chairman Earle!"

We spent a lot of time in Kenosha over the next couple of years. At first it was pro bono, who could resist a good challenge? Eventually the state kicked in to support our continued work as the project evolved into something exciting. The core of the problem was this: the welfare agency was in the business of handing out benefits. Their focus was on making sure that only eligible people got those benefits and in the right amount. It was a part auditing and part cop responsibility. You were always looking out for fraud, abuse, and waste. What welfare people did not do is get into the lives of their clients to try to learn their strengths and weaknesses, their motivations and limitations, their aspirations, and any obstacles to those dreams. Those were more professional tasks better left to others located in traditional social service agencies.

The Private Industry Council (PIC), on the other hand, tried to get people into the workforce. Yes, their nominal focus was on populations that might face impediments to full participation in the labor market due to obsolete skills, age, minor physical impairments, diminished cognitive or mental capacities, or insufficient zeal. Their underlying focus was on getting as many successful placements as they could. To do that, they needed to curry positive relationships with local employers, which meant delivering desirable job seekers . . . those who were motivated, presentable, possessed necessary soft skills, and who could be trained to do the work. Thus, they were sensitive to the risks associated with pushing applicants who might fail and possibly undermine future relations with employers. In short, they did not want to push "losers" onto their key stakeholders.

An institutional cultural disconnect existed. One system wanted to place so-called hard-to-serve clients. The other system wanted to place likely-to-succeed clients. One set of antennae focused on the welfare client while the other set was much more attuned to the firms hiring the client. One system spent more time doing auditing and monitoring functions while the other was involved in more counseling and rehabilitative tasks. Larry first termed this disconnect as a problem between competing 'institutional philosophies.' I later termed it as a problem across conflicting institutional cultures. Whatever it is called, neither side understood the other very well and when communications break down, suspicion and blame are sure to follow.

Whatever the term used, the breakdown between the welfare and workforce development systems was complete when we got involved. Kennedy and Leuterman made somewhat moderate complaints saying that they would refer clients they thought were job ready to the PIC and never received any feedback after that. Their referrals simply disappeared into the other system as if it were a black hole. E. Clarke Earl, as was his wont, summarized the problem directly and succinctly. "Those f---ing b----rds lied to us." I suspect most of you can do the translation.

The relationship between the welfare and PIC systems was probably beyond life support. Almost instinctively, we started a process of turning the Kenosha folk into workforce-type people. If you cannot outsource the labor-market attachment responsibility, then build in in-house. Our little team split up and did different tasks. What I recall most vividly was spending hours with Leuterman, Kennedy, and assorted other county officials locked in a room with a blackboard. We started on a process that had no name at the time. Now, I would call it the "line of sight" or "visioning" process.

At the time, I had no set methodology for what we were about to do. But when in doubt, wing it. After all, they thought we knew what we were doing. I recall asking a few initial questions and then built on their responses. What do you want to accomplish? You want more clients in the workforce, is that right? Well, what is it about the current way you do business now that would possibly help achieve that goal? Not sure? Then let us start at the beginning. What is the beginning you ask? Good question! Let me take a sip from my soda while I come up with an answer to that one.

Making it up as I went along, I recall saying something like "Let us envision what a young woman might say to herself when she thinks about your agency." She probably says something like, "I need money and that is where they give out money." Is that what you want her to first think about? No! Would you rather have her think about getting help finding a job and later think about money?

But why would she possibly think that, or at least in that order? What message are you, through the design of your programs and agency, sending out to this young mother, to all young mothers? What do you *signal* to her and the broader population of potential applicants about your mission and purpose?

Then we kept moving through each step in the hypothetical life trajectory of a client or customer. A couple of discussion starter questions mutated into an ongoing analytical process. What are they thinking when they come through the front door of your agency? What does she see first? What might she do first? Who talks with her first? What does this person say and do? Are any decisions made at this point? What are they? Then what happens next and next and next? At some point we hit upon a key insight. The critical issue of work never comes up until way late in the sequence of events that the client experiences. It becomes an afterthought, a mere inconvenience and not something central to the agency's purpose or mission.

Okay, then, what happens when the work question does come up? You say that the client may get a letter telling her to make an appointment with another agency. Consequences are mentioned for noncompliance but who knows if they are believed. The client may or may not actually contact this other agency. If they do not, the welfare agency may or may not be notified of the transgression. Even when your agency is notified, a lot of time has passed already. When notified, your people probably do little more than send another letter. It is like spanking the pup a week after they pooped on the rug and just as effective.

As our chalk diagram of circles and triangles and rectangles and lines spread across the board, the institutional life of a welfare client became clearer. Suddenly, or not so suddenly, we all could see the big picture. When all was said and done, it was all too clear the work message had no immediacy. It was, at best, a mild administrative irritant. When we tried looking at case files, we could see a huge "leakage" problem. Clients who were supposed to go from point A to B, from the welfare worker to someone who would help them get a job, too often never got to point B. In too many cases, it was hard to figure out what was happening.

No wonder that few were getting into the labor market or, if they were, no one knew about it. When the agency began to look at its system from the customer's perspective, the problems were obvious. The work message was delivered too late in the process, as we just saw. When it was raised, it simply looked like another speed bump to be hurdled by the client. There were too many transaction costs (calls to make, trips to make, appointments to schedule) just to minimally comply with what was being asked of the client. Finally, feedback mechanisms to monitor client progress were inadequate to nonexistent. They were simply getting lost somewhere out there amidst a byzantine, administrative labyrinth.

I am reminded of a study we did in Dane County (where Madison is located) a few years hence. By this time Mary Ann

Cook, the woman who initially dragged me into the welfare wars, now held a top county-level position. She was worried. The county could demonstrate very few work placements despite spending a lot of money for that purpose. I recall a conversation that went something like the following: "Mary Ann, this is Dane County. The unemployment rate is less than 2 percent. I cannot walk a couple of blocks without seeing a dozen help wanted signs. Even if you manacled your clients to their beds and forbade them to look for jobs upon pain of death, more of them would have gotten hired than you are claiming. Believe me, many are finding work, you just don't know it. And if you don't know about it, you can't get credit for it."

What was happening was not hard to figure out. Clients would be sent to another agency across town to obtain employment help. When they got a job, probably before reaching this other agency, no one reported this fact back to the initiating caseworker. Often, the client just seemed to disappear from the agencies' purview. No one systemically followed up to see what had happened. This was a fundamental communication failure among agencies poorly linked together in a very imperfect system. With this simple insight, Mary Ann and crew would be off and running to create an integrated welfare-work agency of its own.

A few years down the road, I walked into Dane County's new integrated work center, which also housed the former welfare functions. I asked Mary Ann to help me with a video I was developing for a project at the time. I started to explain that I wanted to capture the culture change from the old isolated welfare system to the new way low-income women with children are treated when they walk through the door of a full-service agency. I thought this would require some discussing and perhaps a script. But within seconds Mary Ann stopped me and said, "I know exactly what you want."

She called over a frontline worker who had been with the agency for a while and gave a brief description of my vision, perhaps discovery as Hollywood's next hot director was not far off. The woman sat down at a desk with another worker to play the client. The camera crew went to work. We filmed the old welfare culture in black and white, and the new culture in color. Our "actors" hit it perfectly with virtually no prompting. The old culture was all about collecting information, cutting off the client whenever they asked for help with problems, and stressing fraud and fear. The new culture was inviting, probing for what the customer needed, and talking about how this integrated agency could help the whole family to a better future. Even I was stunned at the sharp contrast and how well the staff could capture and portray the transformation that had taken place.

But I have digressed far afield yet again. What to do with the Kenosha Gang when all this programmatic change yet seemed a futuristic dream? With the problems identified, solutions slowly emerged. If the work message is communicated too late, move it to the front of the customer's experience. If transaction costs are too high and client "leakage" is a big problem, collocate essential services so that everything is available in the same physical location. If feedback is too episodic or faulty, make sure you bring workers who must communicate about the same case into physical proximity with one another. In principle, all this sounds reasonable and simplistic. It was simply common sense after the fact. However, it was revolutionary at the time. Common sense only becomes common in hindsight.

Years earlier, in the infancy of my career, I recall watching my colleagues at Wisconsin's state-level super-agency that was created to facilitate better communications across programs at a top management level. I would listen to staff drawn from the welfare side of the ledger as they talked about those from the services side . . . those social work types had soft opinions about the client populations, thus not recognizing reality. Likewise, the service-oriented staff viewed their welfare counterparts as being too hard and distrustful of these struggling families, of not appreciating what they were up against. At the time, I was too raw to put the meaning of these asides into any larger context. Now, however, the snide comments I had overheard were beginning to make more sense.

Each side had been acculturated differently. At the beginning of their careers, they may have self-selected into a career trajectory based on internal hardwiring, professional preparation, or simple circumstances. On the last factor, I recall chatting with a county director one day. He related how he started out in his career. When he first was hired, his boss told him that he would be processing welfare applications. The man in charge waived off protestations from the new hire that he knew nothing about welfare, that he wanted to be a social worker. "Not important that you know nothing about the program," the director told him, "you look mean and ugly, and that is exactly what I want an applicant for welfare to see first—a mean and ugly look! Maybe then they will just go away."

Once an individual is propelled on a professional trajectory, it is likely they probably will be surrounded by like-minded people. They would be rewarded for thinking in certain ways, viewing clients more and more as their peers do, absorbing simplifying perceptions that made a complex world less confusing (e. g., most or all clients are like this), and adopting tactics that others assure them are tried and true. When suddenly they are thrown in with other officials who do not speak the same language or share the same presumptions about the world, there is a tendency to become further isolated in a cultural cocoon most familiar to you as if you were warding off an invasive virus.

My long-time colleague, Jennifer Noyes, who was tasked by Governor Thompson to manage the merged welfare and workforce development people at the state level many years later, called it the "plop" factor. You can plop folks from one institutional culture into a mega-agency dominated by another culture, but you cannot necessarily make them swim together. This is particularly true if you throw them in the same pool naked, without any preparation for what it will take to get along. Most focus on not drowning one another, or perhaps on drowning the other person intentionally, as everyone frantically sloshes around trying to avoid contact with those from the other side while seeking the upper hand in any emerging competitive confrontations.

Back to Kenosha for a moment! The longer they struggled with key challenges like getting the work message to the very front of the application process, the more they realized that small changes would be insufficient. When you added in all the transaction costs and leakage problems embedded in the existing system, the more they recognized that profound changes were needed. They were not likely to achieve their vision through incremental change. They needed something truly transformative!

They pretty much threw out the old organizational structure and built something new from the bottom up. I am not sure I recall an aha moment, but by the time we had finished our blackboard "line of sight" exercise, merely tinkering with the status quo was viewed as totally insufficient, bordering on the ridiculous. Our intrepid band from Kenosha then started to create a brand new one-stop shop that would fully integrate all welfare and essential job placement functions. Again, while this was rather commonplace by the late 1990s, it was revolutionary in the 1980s.

Once they got the vision right, I am not sure how much they needed from us. One day I recall asking the Kenosha team what they were getting from our hanging around all the time. I believe it was Jim Kennedy who responded with, "We just need someone to tell us we are not crazy." I paused before responding, "Well, let me be the first to say you are totally out of your mind, but for heaven's sake, don't let anyone stop you." And they didn't! I recall being in meetings where Earl confronted less than eager future partners. It was not always a pretty sight, but he got it done. He did what change agents do, blustered, cajoled, threatened, and charmed. Most importantly, he never lost sight of the prize. I think our role was to clean up the blood spatter after the sessions were over.

At one point, they needed additional state resources to keep moving. When they sent the budget in, it was returned with the request to cut it back some. They waited awhile and sent a larger budget back saying their re-review indicated additional costs. No, no, the state said, we need a smaller budget, go back and do it over. But our intrepid heroes came up with an even larger budget the third time, thanking the state for requiring them to take a closer look. Otherwise, they might have missed some essential costs in their haste to meet the previous state deadline. The state caved at this point, a wise choice.

One of my favorite contributions was to come up with a front-end diagnostic tool. We would triage clients into four levels as they came into the system. The applicants at the highest level were the pass-throughs. The assumption was that they would need minimal attention since they were considered job ready, probably requiring no more than access to job networking help. The second level did need some attention but were in pretty good shape. Perhaps they needed a course or two, some intensive help with job-seeking skills and interviewing techniques. Still we might expect them to be on their way in three months, a year at most.

Then we got to the serious groups. The third group we called system dependent. They had more severe impediments to employment. Here we were talking about serious issues such as substance abuse, legal problems, and cognitive challenges. They required more intensive help, perhaps even some structured work experience activity, before transitioning into the labor market. In addition, family problems might require multiservice interventions, which would require coordinated agency interventions. Still, with help, there was an expectation that they could make the transition to work though not likely in the short-term.

The final group, the FUBARS were, in our scheme, fouled up beyond all recognition. This was the group I wanted to focus on while in D.C., but no one else appeared interested. Of course, Director Earle always preferred the more descriptive obscenity to be substituted for word "fouled." According to the director, such folk typically responded only to the potted plants situated in the corner of the room during the application process. Efforts typically were made to shift these clients to a federal disability program.

This reminds me of a program that existed in neighboring Michigan during this time. Their governor was in a competition with Thompson to be the top dog in the world of welfare reform. Their initiative was called something like the zero-cases initiative where every case would be transitioned into the labor market. I was visiting a local agency there and the director told me they were within a case or two of meeting their objective. "You will have no more cases," I asked incredulously since this was a distressed county. "Oh no", he replied, "we will have succeeded with all our employable cases." Of course, that is always the catch, figuring out who is employable.

Back to Kenosha. We developed individualized bureaucratic pathways that the client would travel, based upon the initial diagnosis. The scheme was used for many years though some felt that this initial triage was not terribly predictive of subsequent progress. Clients that looked like basket cases upon arrival at the agency might rebound quickly without much help. Others who looked like pass-throughs might reveal hidden impediments with time. Later, when Governor Thompson launched his famous W-2 welfare replacement program, they used the exact same schema. I was disappointed that he never called to thank me for my contribution. Perhaps he couldn't find my telephone number.

One of my favorite, though embarrassing, moments came when a group of legislators were touring the state holding hearings on WEJT and other welfare issues. My friend John Antaramian was leading this merry band in an era when legislators were still known to talk across party lines. Mike Wiseman and I were to speak but E. Clarke Earle was scheduled to address the group just before us. Earle launched into this peroration telling the legislators that they should give the Institute for Research on Poverty two million dollars to evaluate the one-stops that were emerging (read Kenosha County) and help spread the innovation elsewhere. As he went on and on, I slumped further and further into my chair.

When Earle finished, it was my turn to speak. John smiled at me as I slid into the speaker's chair while, at the same time, hastily applying a disguise over my face. He remarked that my fees had gone up considerably since I had consulted with his committee for free. "Well," I stammered, "you know the old saying . . . you get what you pay for." Apparently, the legislature did not think I was worth two million dollars. Go figure!

When the Kenosha one-stop opened around 1990, it soon became the talk of the welfare world. Representatives from all over the nation and foreign countries with advanced welfare states came to see what they were doing and how they were doing it. They won national awards and recognition. But I noticed something right away. Not many who came to observe were able to rush home and duplicate the model. No matter how much they loved what they saw, replication proved damn hard. That was an insight I stuffed into my back pocket.

Around 1990, my damn phone rang again. This time it was from someone named Neil Zank, the executive director of the Council on Employment Relations. The Council was an advisory group that had been established to advise presidents on selected labor market and workforce issues. The president at the time was George H.W. Bush. Apparently, no one had told Neil that I was considered a left-wing terrorist in some Republican circles. Thus uninformed, he invited me to participate in a series of sessions the commission was organizing that would be dedicated to achieving better collaboration among programs for low-income and vulnerable populations. Now, where had I heard that theme before? Perhaps it was because I was beginning to sense that replicating the Kenosha model might be more difficult than I had imagined. Perhaps it was because I was stunned that a high-level Republican appointee was inviting me anywhere. But I agreed to go without much hesitation. Once again, I was glad I did.

There were three major sessions, each with a distinct target audience and focus. The session held in Washington D.C. concentrated on collaboration at the federal level. I must note that I had another one of those ego-inflating moments where people sought me out at the break to say nice things about my insights, and to pump me for more information. In retrospect, this must have been a new crowd for me, more conservative, a group that had not heard me endless times before. This is a good thing to remember: keep changing the cast of characters around you if you want to stay interesting. While you will be spouting the same old crap, they might not have heard it a dozen times before.

The second meeting was in San Antonio and zeroed in on collaboration at the state level, while the third session was held in San Diego and dealt with local collaborative efforts. I wish they had done these in the reverse order because the message from each level was unique and clear. Going from local to federal would have been made even more apparent where the opportunities for substantive change lie. That message could then have been taken to Washington. Those were the people who needed to hear this message.

The local-level crowd that convened in San Diego were unambiguously positive about collaboration. Yes, integrated program structures are where we must go, since our current way of delivering benefits and services to troubled families makes no sense whatsoever. The overall service system needs to be redone in a way that permits providers to deliver help that is coherent and rational. That way, customers might be able to make sense of the programs designed to assist them, and the services provided could be more efficiently delivered.

The San Antonio session (state-level stakeholders) was supportive of program integration but more cautious. There were a lot of yes-but comments. Yes, we should move in that direction, but there are some real problems and impediments to doing so. They pointed out what they considered federal impediments and some local forms of resistance. In some cases, they felt impotent to change the way business was done despite seeing the need for such change. Still, this group was supportive overall. It just had a few residual concerns.

At the federal level, the mood was basically "are you kidding?" Oh, most paid lip service to the concept of greater collaboration, but a lot of attention was paid to the things that made substantive collaboration a nonstarter. It might cost money. It would require a realignment of turf across the entrenched executive agencies. And the Congressional Committee structure was simply beyond being touched by the hand of reason or the hand of God. There, program oversight and budget responsibilities had been divided up by the same British diplomat who drew the Mid-East national boundaries sometime after World War I. That map put together conflicting religious and ethnic groups that hated one another with a passion while separating like-minded groups from one another. But all the Washington attendees did like the food that was provided.

Throughout this process I had grown to rather like Neal Zank. In truth, I liked most folk who wandered through my candy store. He was a dead ringer for John Sununu who had been governor of New Hampshire and was serving as Bush the elder's chief of staff at that time. They could have been identical twins. Neil still had not been told that I was the enemy, so he asked me to write a chapter for the book that came out of their conferences. Neither the book nor the final report submitted to the president had much effect, as far as I could see. Still, I had no hesitation about at least writing a book chapter. After all, I had learned a lesson that would stay with me as I plunged deeper into this issue. Service integration had the best chance of success at the local level.

Still, circumstances demanded that I tilt at the federal windmill one more time. Though I remained skeptical, this next effort at least gave me the title of this chapter . . . that human services integration is the holy grail of public policy. You can keep searching but the odds of success are rather long . . . Powerball lottery long. I was also coming to the realization that this issue was going to become a rather long counter in my policy candy store, one laden with both sweet and sour goodies.

The issue of human services integration cropped up during the year I spent in D.C. messing with Clinton's reform proposal. One of my responsibilities was to work on ways we could achieve better coordination and efficiencies among programs, particularly cash and cash-like income support programs. I wonder how I got such assignments. Do I look as if I enjoy pain? No matter, my integration work group looked at where some broader synergies across a set of nominally-related systems might be exploited.

Administrations may have changed with Clinton replacing Bush (the elder) as president, but overall Washington remained the same. You can change the fish in the pond, but the water remains murky. We looked at ways in which the rules, definitions, and administrative protocols across systems might be synchronized to minimize conflict and inefficiencies. While individual executive agency officials paid lip service to the problem and gave tepid support for seeking a solution, it was impossible to generate any sense of urgency to make the necessary changes.

The same barriers were raised again and again. There really was a rationale behind their unique program definition or protocol or rule and, by default, their rationale was better than that of the other guys. Or the costs of change would be prohibitive. Or maybe it was the other program that ought to accommodate them, since they were doing God's work while they had no idea what those other folks were doing. Or it would have to go back to a Congressional Committee for approval and, of course, that was impossible. And if all else failed to be persuasive, God would strike them dead if they changed anything.

While some action would be forthcoming if the president knocked heads across the executive agencies, the goal of administrative efficiency was a back-burner issue compared to the flame-bright controversies surrounding "ending welfare as we know it," or the conflagrations that inevitably popped up in the Middle-East. Though this topic had a separate section in the language of the Bill submitted to Congress, I thought the language lacked sufficient fire and zeal to accomplish anything. Besides, the bill proposing Bill's reform vision, as we know from the prior chapter, died a quick death.

The program integration section laid out the rationale for collaboration, gave examples of what might be done, and called for mechanisms through which future progress might be made. The language reminded me of the pious statements in my Catholic catechism as a young man; nice to live one's life that way, but rather impossible to inform behavior in the real world, at least for weak people like me. It seemed we were pushing too many tough decisions down the road, hoping that the bureaucracy might be seized by a paroxysm of reason and rationality. It was probably all we could do.

I am proud of one thing, I think. I must admit that some of my rhetoric made it into the final version of the bill. Nothing, however, topped my introduction to the program coordination section where I called this vision the "holy grail of public policy, ever sought but seldom achieved." Now, I had no reservation about using such colorful language. I knew that early drafts would go through several layers of review, both for substantive accuracy and political acceptability. I assumed that this language would be excised or changed as being too flowery. This holy grail language survived, however, to my surprise and delight.

When I left ASPE to return to the university in June 1994, they had a nice party for me. It was rather special, in fact. I am guessing they were afraid that I would change my mind and stay. It might be harder to do that after a nice going-away party. One of the many gifts I received was a simulated goblet covered in golden tin foil to represent the holy grail. I was moved to tears and henceforth became attached to this metaphor to designate any effort to enhance collaboration across programs or agencies.

Like one of those teen horror movie sagas where the monster is killed time and time again only to be resurrected to dissect just a few more coeds, the service integration agenda would not die. The next resurrection, for me at least, took place within the discussions of the WELPAN Network. WELPAN is a topic I discuss in the next chapter and will save the detail for then. In brief, this Midwest network (there were related groups in other regions) was a group of senior state welfare officials from seven states located in the Great Lakes section of the country. I organized the group right around the time that national welfare reform passed. It subsequently met on a quarterly basis for over a decade, during which the welfare reform drama played out. The dialogue among this group was like having a front row seat in welfare wars.

In any case, the participating state officials bonded over time. After all, whether they shared a common perspective or not, they faced similar challenges. As they became comfortable, they began to push the envelope of change. In part this reflected a unique aspect of the network. The venue gave them a chance to get away from day-to-day responsibilities. It gave them an opportunity to think, to expand their vision, to create a vision in concert with their peers. They realized, maybe with small nudges from me and some of the resource people we brought in, that reform demanded that they think beyond their own programs. Upon reflection, they did not need much nudging at all. They had long been aware of these issues.

These welfare officials realized all too well that they were no longer in the check-issuing business. They were now in the people-changing business. At a minimum, that required a more professional, less automated approach to their clients. They intuitively knew that simple solutions would not suffice given the knotty problems that many vulnerable families encountered. Most likely, real solutions would demand that they identify and adopt multifaceted service strategies that cut across several service systems simultaneously.

Members of the network divided up substantive policy areas among themselves to explore this notion of collaboration in detail. For example, how would they better integrate workforce programs and welfare, child welfare and welfare, housing and welfare? Each of their separate working papers was discussed among the group members. From these discussions, there emerged a greater appreciation for how central to future reform was a systemic rethinking of the way they functioned. It was time to rebuild things from the ground up. In 1999, they tentatively broached the integration topic by publishing a piece on how the different cultures of the new Temporary Assistance for Needy Families program (TANF) and the Food Stamp program (now SNAP) worked against one another at the operational level. The cultures in these two programs clashed rather violently.

Then, they went on offense, shifting from critiques of what was to a visualization of what might be. Over the next several years, the WELPAN network published two major papers—*The New Face of Welfare* in 2000 and *Recreating Social Assistance: How to use Waiver Authority to Eliminate Program Silos* in 2002. The first work laid out the transformative changes that they thought welfare was undergoing. It had moved from a bureaucratic function, where complex but routine tasks were repetitively carried out, to a vision that could only be achieved through coordinated multiservice interventions delivered over time. Everything was different in this new world, even if most people didn't see it.

This second WELPAN paper argued that states ought to be given additional flexibility to create that new world of social assistance. In a narrow sense, it was an argument in favor of the Super Waiver provision that President George W. Bush had inserted into the TANF reauthorization proposal. This provision would permit broad waivers of federal regulations across several executive agencies at the same time. Mechanisms would be set up to move requested waivers along, theoretically removing the bureaucratic sclerosis that impeded innovation. This would sweep aside the kinds of barriers that thwarted the kinds of integration agendas articulated in the Employment Commission report and the Clinton welfare reform effort. More importantly, it would locate the center of gravity for integration among the states and local communities, where innovation was more likely to occur.

Alas, as with all welfare proposals of the 1990s, the Super Waiver proposal met with a severe backlash from liberals. The essence of the counter argument went as follows. The federal government is the final protector of the poor. If we take away those protections and let states do what they wish, the poor will be left vulnerable to the whims of state and local jurisdictions. Liberals kept reminding anyone who would listen about what happened to many poor people before the courts and the federal government took an activist role in the 1960s. African-American families almost never received benefits in many Southern states, irrespective of eligibility. The states argued that things had changed but reservations on that score remained.

Defenders of the Super Waiver argued that times had changed. In addition, defenders would point out that states were brimming with new ideas for attacking poverty. The federal government could never muster such motivation and purpose. It was time to let the states loose to become the laboratories of democracy that many envisioned they could be and that Justice Brandeis had touted perhaps a century earlier.

One last WELPAN vignette on the Super Waiver issue deserves mention. The typical WELPAN meeting would be in Chicago though we circulated around participating state capitols from time to time. During the height of the waiver dialogue, we decided to have a meeting in Washington. The WELPAN members were unanimous in their support of this additional flexibility and dismissed arguments that increased state flexibility would be used to disadvantage poor families. Of course, these were states with reputations for generally good government. Nevertheless, these state officials wanted to bring their arguments for more flexibility directly to the lion's den.

During an earlier meeting, Joel Rabb (from Ohio) mused that, "We (the states) needed a more liberal waiver authority, not necessarily to overcome federal impediments to innovation, but rather to overcome resistance within our own states. Too often, my colleagues from other state agencies would tell me that they would love to work with us, but federal rules prevented it. Now, I would be able to look them in the eye and say that there is no reason for not moving ahead. Now we can get a waiver of those stupid rules."

Anyways, we arranged for a meeting in D.C. where the group met with Congressional staff, with key movers and shakers, and with executive agency officials. There were some moments of drama. A key Democratic Hill staffer said no way would the Democrats agree to the waiver provision. That precipitated a spirited push back from the WELPAN members. Though a majority of the WELPAN members probably were Democrats or leaned toward liberal positions, they argued back forcefully in a unified voice. They needed the flexibility to design and deliver better, more coherent services to their clients.

Of course, the WELPAN arguments were to no avail. When ideological lines are set, not even acts of God can move them. What we witnessed was a mini-lesson in the creeping partisan paralysis that consumes Washington to this day. The anger among network members was palpable. They felt disrespected, that they were not worthy of trust. Most were long-time civil servants who had worked diligently on behalf of the people they served. Now, they were implicitly being told that the federal government was there to protect the public from their evil ways. I could see the steam rising from their ears. On that note, it is time to shift away from WELPAN, but I assure you we will return to their endeavors again. Stay with me as I take the thread of this narrative in a slightly different direction, though I do stay with the Super Waiver debate.

I first introduced Jennifer Noyes way back in the preface. She was Governor Tommy Thompson's policy advisor and welfare chief, who endured stories of my life on that interminable travel debacle from Madison to D.C. Though she barely survived my forced companionship on that first trip, she kept coming back for more. Funny, during my dating days, women inevitably fled after one evening with me. In any case, we became good colleagues and even friends though my socialist ways and never-ending witticisms often put her good will toward me to the test. Eventually, I convinced her to join us at the institute where eventually she held my old position as associate director. Recently, she assumed a position as an associate dean in the College of Letters and Sciences.

When Jennifer walks into the room, people notice; men do, at least. She is tall, blond, with classically cut facial features and a pert nose. When we first travelled together, she always complained about being picked out of the airport queue for the random special screening they did in those days. Why always her, she groused. "Hey," I responded, "some bored security guy sees a tall stunning blond in line followed by an old, slightly overweight, balding schmuck. What do you think he is going to say? 'Hey, I'm picking the fat old guy to spend the next few minutes of my boring life with.' I don't think so!"

Beyond that, Jennifer was whip smart, quick of speech, and had an encyclopedic knowledge of federal-state programs. She had been valedictorian of everything in school and often was the smartest person in the room, unless I also was in that room. Now, I always had a penchant for hanging with the smartest gals I could find, like Carol Simon from my college days whom I introduced while reviewing my near-death experiences. As I recall, Carol was ranked first academically at my alma mater (it damn well was not me), got her advanced degree from Harvard, and became a college dean later in her academic career.

I sat down one day and realized that all my high school and college girlfriends (the serious ones, at least) went on for doctorates. My long-suffering spouse has a law degree. What I could never figure out is why these extremely smart women hung out with the likes of me. As far as I can tell, any academic success I enjoyed is attributable to charm, wit, and a heavy dose of Irish blarney. Apparently, it is true that there really is no accounting for taste. But Jennifer has put up with me as a professional colleague over the years, and we did form a very good working relationship.

Her only fault, besides having an abominable sense of judgment in selecting professional colleagues, was that she is a Republican. Normally I would feel the need to disinfect myself after any extended interaction with a member of said species. But I concluded long ago that Jennifer is not really a Republican, though she heartily disagrees with me on that point. In my view, she cares too much about good public policy, and about people, to be considered a member of the dark side. Recently, she has confessed to me that she finds positions staked out by today's Republican party quite objectionable. On the other hand, whenever we shake hands she always whips out those disinfecting wipes to thoroughly cleanse her own hands. I wonder why? I should ask her about that.

One of our first collaborations, ironically, was on the topic of collaboration, more specifically the Super Waiver debate. While I had been touching on the integration agenda for over a decade, I now took it on with focus and more energy. It probably helped that I now had a smart collaborator with whom to work on the knotty challenge of collaboration.

For me, at least, the Super Waiver issue was an awkward starting point for this renewed effort. I am not unsympathetic to liberal concerns about eroding federal protections of vulnerable populations. The political appetite for providing help to the poor and struggling is not evenly distributed across states. Furthermore, when benefits and services evidence distributional abnormalities across jurisdictions, the specter of welfare-induced migration will push more generous states to cut back on benefits, or at least to seriously think about it. In short, local control may spur innovation and advancement, or it may spawn an inexorable race to the bottom. In advance, it may not be possible to predict which will prevail. Such are the difficult choices faced by policy wonks.

Earlier, I explained the origins of the phrase the "holy grail of public policy." Service integration certainly meets the definition of a "wicked" policy problem. By way of review for other old-timers like me with short memories, a wicked policy challenge is one where our ends are not well defined, contention exists around supporting theory, the means for achieving ends are a matter of debate, evidence upon which to decide outstanding questions does not exist or is ambiguous, and normative or partisan contention renders productive communication very difficult. These are the fun issues, though they do lead to premature baldness, insomnia, and hypertension . . . all of which afflict me.

Not surprisingly, we have been pursuing this "grail'" for a long time without resolving the challenge. The struggle for a coherent, rational, and individualized service system goes back to at least the post-Civil War period. Rising industrialization, urbanization, and immigration from southern and eastern European countries (plus the dreaded Irish) led to extreme poverty and social exclusion in urban areas. A deficiency of resources attributable to the individual was defined as pauperism, a term one no longer hears. Paupers were those individuals whose deficient character and moral flaws led to a life of turpitude and indolence. Drunkenness, sloth, and aggressiveness were viewed as the prevailing disposition of the worst of these, usually my Celtic ancestors. This might explain a lot about me except for latent aggression, which my dominant trait of abject cowardice does not permit me to display.

Except for Civil War pensions, all public aid was local and often the concern of private charities. These charities abounded with little coordination or supervision. In response, two reform movements swept the Eastern seaboard at least. The Scientific Charity movement tried to professionalize the work of volunteers who went into the homes of the destitute, ultimately leading to the first School of Social Work at Columbia University in 1898. The Charity Organization Society movement, on the other hand, attempted to rationalize the provision of assistance by improving the level of communication and coordination across local providers of help. The fear was that some were abusing the system while the neediest could fall through the cracks. I made the mistake of serving on a social policy panel at Columbia's centennial anniversary in 1998. That was fine, but they subsequently assumed I was an alumnus and, for years, kept dunning me for contributions. I think their pleas for money only ceased when they wrongly assumed I had passed on to my heavenly reward.

Periodically, over the coming decades, there were efforts to better coordinate services and charities, particularly the raising of money, through community chests and the emergence of the United Way. With the advent of the New Deal in the 1930s, however, public aid initiatives proliferated in an alphabet soup of new programs and agencies. By the 1960s, there were further calls for redesigning assistance programs along more rational lines. The Model Cities program was part of the WOP. It was an attempt to coordinate a host of services at the community level. Block Grants were introduced to combine funding streams, thereby reducing separate federal funding and regulatory silos. But the Block Grants were viewed by many as a transparent way to reduce overall federal support and became controversial.

From the 1960s on, the federal government tried to stimulate collaboration across the different programs serving similar populations. Sometimes the feds focused on related income transfer systems, other times on related service programs. They pushed states to create super agencies like the one I was first hired into as a young state policy wonk. These centralized bureaucracies did not always (perhaps never) resulted in much coordination where it mattered, at the operational level; but they seemed like good ideas at the time. The feds also developed pilot program initiatives that supported collaborative efforts at the state-local level as a way of inspiring others to follow suit. But the anticipated spread of the new model programs never happened as expected. The feds continued to push and prod with only small, and too often temporary, successes.

When Jennifer and I realized that a liberal and a conservative could work with one another (assuming I obeyed her every command), we earnestly dove into the Super Waiver controversy. Of course, blind obedience comes easily to me since I had been married forever. I likely jumped into this debate in response to arguments from the WELPAN network and she probably more from a general conviction about the preference of local control over policy decisions. No matter, we found one another to be on the same team.

As we looked around, we hit upon one insight. There was a lot of service integration and programmatic collaboration taking place around the country. It was happening all the time and in many different service contexts. Most were spontaneously generated efforts borne out of the desperation to do a better job of serving families. Yet, too many of these efforts were struggling to thrive, and too many did not survive over the long haul. They were bucking many headwinds such as counterproductive federal and/or state regulations and funding streams, bureaucratic inertia, union or civil service inflexibility, and many other such impediments. Somewhat to our surprise, we noticed that some places were making it work quite well despite the presumed impediments. It occurred to us that there might be fewer insurmountable barriers to breaking down the silos between programs and agencies than was thought. Perhaps the conventional wisdom needed a deeper look.

With support from the Annie E. Casey Foundation and later the Joyce Foundation, the two of us embarked on an effort to first try to diffuse the animus surrounding the Super Waiver proposal and then seek to find out more about what makes local innovations work or not work. The first effort probably was doomed from the start, but we immersed ourselves in it with the old "what the hell" attitude that all good policy wonks must possess. A bit of insanity is quite necessary to tackle some of these issues. We set up several meetings in D.C. with many of the key actors to facilitate a rational discussion of that issue. Yes, I was still naïve, even optimistic, despite having been around the track many, many times.

A few days before one of these meetings, I received a call from Robert Greenstein, the head of the Center for Budget and Policy Priorities (CBPP) in D.C. I had met him on several occasions and was always impressed with his command of facts and his personal gravitas. Though he often came across as if he had just consulted with God, I knew he was not always right . . . none of us are. It was just that he always seemed to be right. He was a force majeure in Washington and could stare down the toughest insiders. I saw him come close to intimidating David Ellwood during my Washington stay, not an easy thing to do given David's sound ego. I broke out in a cold sweat just realizing that he had tracked me down in Madison.

He gave me the "what are you thinking?" routine that was followed by the "I know you mean well, Tom (you total doofus), but don't you realize you have fallen into the arms of Satan" speech. In the end, we agreed to disagree.

Jennifer and I also spoke at several forums on the matter. I recall one put on by the National Governor's Association. Jennifer and I were on a panel with assorted welfare experts. At some point, a paper was distributed to everyone. It was a statement denouncing the Super Waiver provision as the worst policy idea since the Dred Scott decision that affirmed the constitutionality of slavery. It was signed by every liberal and left of center group and individual that I could imagine.

So, I am sitting there thinking, have I really fallen into the arms of Satan? But no, I concluded perhaps in a moment of self-delusion, too much of what goes for policy debate is really scripted beforehand. Once handed their lines, the actors carry out their assigned roles without thought or imagination. In the policy arena, there is nothing more deadening than seeing the same play, and hearing the identical lines, for the thirty-third time. Sometimes you simply must walk your own walk. You might walk right into the quicksand, but hey, you did it on your own.

On that note, I remember another time when I spoke before a Wisconsin legislative committee on some issue regarding the famous Wisconsin Works (W-2) program. It was before I started working closely with Jennifer, but we knew each other and she and

Jennifer Alexander (the secretary of the State Welfare Department at the time) were in the audience. I had briefed legislative committees many times in the past but this, it would turn out, would be my last trip up there.

As I sat waiting my turn, I listened to the speakers who preceded me. I was appalled, though I had been through this drill numerous times before. Perhaps I was simply getting grumpy in my old age. Each speaker struck me as coming straight out of central casting, saying exactly what you would expect, given the organization they represented. There were no surprises and no new information, just rehashed scripts from years past. I remember thinking, how do the legislators do it? How do they listen to verbiage that is so predictable? Had I endured this with any regularity, they would soon notice my lifeless body slowly swinging from a nearby rafter. It was almost as bad as being in a faculty meeting.

I can no longer recall much of what I said that day. However, I do recall pointing out that W-2 could not be faulted for not ending poverty in Wisconsin. The program it replaced, the AFDC welfare program, did a miserable job in that regard as well. Welfare, by its structure, is not an anti-poverty strategy, at least as poverty is conventionally measured, which strikingly ignores noncash benefits. Any assistance provided tends to replace and not supplement earnings and the guarantees (the amount given absent other income) must be kept rather low to avoid an uprising from the general populace. On finishing, committee members mentioned how refreshing it was for a speaker to provide objective evidence and a balanced point of view. I did sympathize with them if they had to rely on me for that! I was tempted to mention that the former governor saw me as the Devil incarnate who surely could trace his genealogy directly back to Karl Marx.

Back now to the main story! Jennifer and I spent most of our time working with what we called "lighthouse sites." We selected places that seemed to be doing exemplary work on program or systems collaboration and then did site visits. We engaged in what I now call *institutional ethnographic* analysis, which is not an official line of inquiry. Still, I find that those words roll off the tongue. Put plainly, we used our experience and smarts to get inside these organizations to figure out what is going on. Now, if I had been halfway smart as a young man, I would have pimped this term as a new methodology through which we might unravel the deep secrets of institutional dysfunction and make them whole again. I could have done those 2:00 AM infomercials alongside the guys hawking Ginza knives, and made millions, okay hundreds, of dollars as an expert on such matters. There could have been book and CD to sell, along with the movie rights. If not that, perhaps I could have palmed it off on my Social Work colleagues to save my tragic excuse for an academic career. Seriously, though, good intentions flounder on the shoals of institutional dysfunction all the time. We need to develop the diagnostic and theoretical tools to better manage the doing of extant policies as opposed to the creating of new policies.

Our collaborative work on these issues stretched over a decade and could fill a book on its own. In fact, we have published several articles in *Focus* and written several reports. We also developed a manuscript ready to go on the topic, but I was never sure that the world was ready for it. Rather, I excised significant portions of that work to include in another book of mine titled *The Boat Captain's Conundrum.* Absent the handful of readers of this present blockbuster running out to get a copy, I will just give a thumbnail sketch here. You can wait for the movie to get the full story.

We organized a group called SINNET, the Service Integration Network. It included people like Susan Golonka, Courtney Smith, Jim Dimas, Mark Ragan, and James Fong among others. All had been doing work in this area; we compared notes to brainstorm about how to advance the integration agenda. We spent much time comparing our experiences and understanding of the underlying issues before convening several venues to explore key issues with stakeholders and those doing integration in the real world.

Susan Golonka and Courtney Smith also pulled us into the work of NGA (National Governors Association). This trade organization periodically polls governors regarding what issues are high on their interest list. The issue of cross-systems integration, as it came to be called by NGA, typically made its way to the top of these interest lists year after year. They convened an "academy" where a small number of states are selected to participate in workshops designed to facilitate the planning and execution of model programs. Top officials were invited to a kickoff session. They then go back home to start their projects and subsequently gather together once again to share lessons learned and for motivational booster shots. Jennifer and I served as staff for the sessions.

I recall sitting on the initial planning sessions for Wisconsin and Pennsylvania. In the Wisconsin session, the secretaries for the State's Labor Department and Services Department were struggling to get the discussion off the ground. It was too abstract, more like a cheering session to do good things rather than a substantive discussion. I gently suggested that they focus on some actual target populations and specific issues that both organizations served. What might they accomplish if they worked together on these real families and actual problems rather than in isolation? One of them jumped up with data on the number of child welfare cases which fell under the purview of both departments but from distinct therapeutic perspectives. Soon, they were off and running. Dealing in the concrete is a better path to progress than abstract discussions of intent.

Wisconsin later launched a series of six pilot projects in counties around the state. We assisted as much as time allowed, writing a report for the state on what was going right and what was going wrong. As with so many other similar projects, the people at the top were smart and motivated. But they were also overextended.

Doing service integration requires a lot of hands on attention and that was not forthcoming. I recall that we asked for a meeting with the top people in both departments and it took months to arrange. When you are engaged in systems change, oversight must be continuous; and a clear vision and message from the top must be reinforced repeatedly.

Jennifer then worked with the Center for Law and Social Policy to identify any federal impediments to doing integration at the state level. This was a shotgun marriage of the left and right perspectives, but it worked well. Their joint work explored whether the presumed federal impediments observed at the state level were as important as people said. Were these presumed barriers overblown? In either case, what might be done about them?

I, on the other hand, started to work with Barbara Blum, a grand old lady who had run human services in New York State, had been the CEO of the prestigious Manpower Development Research Corporation (MDRC), and had headed the Foundation on Child Development (FCD). She and I began to look at how we could better evaluate and learn from the extensive experimentation on service integration that was going on around us. We were convinced that existing methods were inadequate for the task and convened the best and brightest from academia and the evaluation firms to explore the question. The assembled expertise was able to document why existing evaluation methods fell short, but never really came up with an answer to the shortcomings. Alan Werner from ABT Associates and Sandra Danziger from the University of Michigan worked hard on a proposal to systematically explore methods suitable for these complex questions, but funding never materialized. Besides, I was approaching the stage in life where another major initiative did not have great appeal. The question remains, how do we rigorously evaluate interventions so broad in scope that they transform the very culture in which the services are delivered?

Jennifer and I also convened several workshops in which we brought together some of our pilot sites, our "lighthouses." At these sessions, we vetted what they were doing, what was going right, what was going wrong, and what might help them advance the integration agenda. One was a joint SINNET/WELPAN meeting held in St. Paul Minnesota in 2003. The synergy and connection between the lighthouse sites and the top state welfare officials was great to observe. There seemed to be such great promise and hope for the future in that room. As someone who contributed nothing to the world through his own efforts, it was wonderful to bring together those making actual contributions.

We found such sessions stimulating, as did the participants. Too often, they were out there struggling to overcome so many obstacles in seeming isolation. They felt alone and often frustrated. I recall we met with top state officials in Utah, a state that was quite active in doing systems integration work. I asked at the beginning of the session how they were doing. After a pause, one of them said, "We are exhausted." In truth, they looked rather spent. As they began to discuss what they were involved in, however, their animation and spirit returned. If nothing else, these sessions were welcome therapy to them. I wished we had obtained sufficient resources to do more of them.

The greatest fun was going out to the lighthouse sites around the country and Canada. I won't bore you with a list of names that won't mean much to the average reader. Let us just say we made many site visits either singly or together. Poor Jennifer, she got to hear about the rest of my fascinating life. How she maintained her sanity is yet a matter of wonder. Sometimes we went as learners, sometimes as consultants. The role did not matter, we learned much from those doing the work. The reality is that the real experts are the ones working in the trenches. It was from their sweat and inspiration and effort that we drew some wonderful insights and lessons.

I do recall one visit to a local office in the state of Oregon. They had developed a team approach to dealing with difficult family situations. The members of the team tapped into several types of expertise—mental health, child protection, substance abuse, family dynamics, income support, workforce development, and so forth. The lead worker, or case manager, would be selected according to the primary issue that needed to be addressed though all members of the family would be incorporated into a comprehensive treatment plan.

It all sounded ideal, and I became a bit suspicious that we were getting the county's public relations pitch. I probed whether they all worked together as well as they claimed. After a moment's pause, a young man spoke up, "It was hard for me at first. I admit that. I had been in the Marines earlier in my career. I was used to always following orders, obeying the rules set out in a manual. When I started here, I was lost. I went to my supervisor and asked for the manual, I needed to know the rules I was to obey. My supervisor looked at me, paused, and then reached inside his desk for a book. But it wasn't a manual. It was a self-help work that laid out the seven habits of highly effective people. Eventually I got it. There would be no hard and fast rules. We were to use our professional judgment and work as a team to do the best we could. I had to learn what the others could do and how I could fit in. It took me a while, but now I am totally convinced that this is the best way to work with these families."

From dozens of such insightful moments, we learned that doing integration is both simple and hard. Most people approach the task as a conventional planning effort. They spend enormous amounts of time on organizational charts, on innovative automated case management tools, on new training protocols and procedures manuals. They change forms and they change buildings and they change the places where people sit and do their work. Such innovations often are fine. Sometimes they are essential to what you are trying to achieve. In the end, however, they may not be enough. The heart and soul of doing integration lies elsewhere, and the secret is finding where that elsewhere is.

While the details of doing integration are many and exhaustive, the essentials are few and fundamental. First, know what the problem is you want to fix. Second, identify what population needs attention. Third, articulate what you want to achieve at the end of the day and make sure you focus on customer changes, not bureaucratic changes (the latter are only interim markers toward what you really want to see). Fourth, figure out what it is you do now that doesn't get you there. Fifth, think through, very carefully, what you need to do to get from where you are now to where you want to be. Sixth, walk in the customers' shoes . . . envision how the new system would look from their perspective. Seventh, be honest! Why in God's name would what you are proposing result in the realization of the changes you are seeking (i.e., what is your theory of change)? Eighth, think through what resources and structural changes are needed to facilitate the new customer experience in your reformed system. Ninth, think hard about what kind of people you need for the new system, the ones you have now might not fit. And tenth, how will you know you are on the right path, what markers will you pay attention to as a signal that you have transformed the customers' experience in a way that just might possibly create the outcomes you seek?

These points may seem like common sense. In many respects, they are. And yet, there are pitfalls all along the way. The reality of effecting change demands that we get outside of the business as usual framework that dominates conventional thinking. Even simple nostrums strain our abilities. For example, we repeatedly talk about the necessity of adopting a customer perspective in thinking through what is wrong with the current system and what might be required in an alternative one. What happens first, what happens second, what happens third, and how will a customer react at each stage. Sounds simple but doing this well, and in a constructive manner, takes considerable talent and sensitivity. This process is the line of sight exercise I fell into out of desperate necessity way back in Kenosha County. Most managers and planners are too top down in their perspectives. They prematurely pronounce what is best, but do not work with those in the trenches to figure it out and get the necessary buy-in.

By coincidence, Jennifer and I ran into the same Wisconsin county welfare manager who told me the story of the unbelievable caseload decline associated with the implementation of Wisconsin Works. Now, we were there monitoring their efforts at service integration. The county director painted a very eloquent and compelling picture of the vision he had for merging services to provide families with comprehensive, coherent, and effective help. It was quite moving, though I did notice that the welfare manager just sat there with her arms crossed not saying a word. Then she blurted out, "This is the first I have heard of this." The director kept talking and she again interrupted, "This is all news to me." Though embarrassing, the real lesson lies elsewhere. It is good to have a vision, but it is much better if everyone shares it.

The biggest challenge faced by policy entrepreneurs seeking to integrate service systems involves the recognition of that cross-cultural friction can play havoc with the best of plans. Every agency and program functions within an existing culture, one that is often shaped by their core technology or their fundamental purpose. Workers bring professional biases in with them through prior training and a good deal of selection goes into matching the backgrounds and dispositions of prospective employees with the program's dominant culture. Once on the job, the employee also internalizes a whole set of context-specific biases and norms that become part of their identity and which further shape their behavioral tendencies. They adopt a common language, a common attitude toward their customers, common frames of reference and language, and a common appreciation of what their institutional purpose is along with who is important in their external environment. The acculturation process is typically so seamless that the individual is unaware it is happening.

When two agencies are brought together, the cultures of each may clash, sometimes violently and sometimes subtly. It is here, in what we call the "under the waterline" arena where so many sharks lurk that result in good intentions going astray. There are steps that can be taken, but first one needs to recognize the character of the challenge. Getting at these "under the waterline" impediments is not always easy, but this is exactly where the customer's perspective can be very helpful. The problem is particularly acute when you are trying to merge programs drawn from radically different core technologies. As suggested above, the core technology is what an agency does as its primary business. For example, a traditional benefits-issuing system like SNAP employs complex but routine tasks to do its business. A more conventional service agency dealing with family crisis, for example, will employ more professional models in working with customers, often relying upon the expertise of frontline workers to make critical decisions. Workers drawn from these two institutional traditions are likely to evidence distinct norms, operating assumptions, and behavioral patterns. They see their roles in different ways, view their clients according to their own fashion, and express themselves quite uniquely.

Sometimes it is not until you get staff and workers drawn from different institutional cultures together that the conflicts are manifest. Jennifer and I once met up for a series of meetings with officials in Michigan from the (then) welfare side and the workforce side of things (we flew in from different sites and thus had little time to prepare). Since the get-together was called by the welfare side of things, the workforce people were immediately suspicious that we were their hired guns brought in to somehow help people on the other side intrude on their turf. Eventually, though, we began to focus on substantive issues and real-life case issues. Gradually, we could visibly see officials on both sides begin to see how collaboration could be a good thing. Of course, with my big mouth, I did almost foment a rebellion among several counties against state leadership which required the top person to intervene. But the welfare and workforce people had bonded together for the first time, at least while we were involved.

We had a similar experience in Indiana. We met with officials from the welfare and workforce development side of things. As the meeting began, the dialogue almost immediately broke down into mutual accusations and recriminations. If there were failures and problems, it was because the morons from the other agency did not get it. For a while, Jennifer and I thought a food fight would break out. My first instinct was to direct all the hostility toward Jennifer, but it occurred to me that she might beat me up if I did that. Somehow, once again, we managed to redirect the hostility that was brought into the room toward discussing hypothetical case situations that they faced daily. Over time, you could see animosities diminish and attitudes evolve as they struggled with more practical ways for helping families they served in common. By the end of the day, they were virtually locked arm-in-arm while singing *We Shall Overcome*. Get people to focus on substantive problems to be solved, and a constructive dialogue can replace silly disputes about turf.

Okay, the change was not that dramatic, nor is getting discussions on track easily done; but our Indiana experience was repeated elsewhere to varying degrees. Unfortunately, we never had a chance to carry out the full experiment in the Hoosier State. The new governor, Mitch Daniels, decided to privatize the administration of the welfare functions and signed a multiyear contract with IBM. Talk about culture clash. Within a short time, the feds got involved as the issuance of benefits fell way short of acceptable standards. The feds threatened the state with huge penalties. The experiment ultimately collapsed, and the contract had to be terminated despite the governor's very public support and backing. Guess what, business models are not always suited for public purposes. Duh!

Based on a long litany of such real-world experiences, Jennifer and I wrote a few articles on the topic as I noted earlier. People still come across these and call us asking for help. They tell us that no one else gets it like we do. This culture thing is what they are struggling with and they need a lot of help dealing with these real, but obtuse, issues. In two trips to Toronto, Canada, I saw the same issues and challenges as we had observed in the States. One of my last real-life vignettes occurred in Washington State not long before I effectively retired. It was a university-sponsored gathering to discuss how academics could work better with state officials. At an informal evening session, I was chatting with a top Washington State official who brought up how difficult it was to advance service integration. I started to respond with an overview of some of the cultural friction issues we had seen in so many sites. As I talked, her eyes widened. "That's it," she exclaimed with excitement. "That is exactly where we are failing."

One last lesson for now! Officials at higher levels of the bureaucracy, whether at the local, state, or federal levels, need to adopt a new management style. They need to be less top-down and prescriptive in perspective. Japanese officials and entrepreneurs listened to management guru W. Edwards Deming after World War II while American industrial leaders ignored his advice about quality circles and learning from the bottom up. That has been a hard lesson for managers in this country to learn since it involves letting go of complete control. Giving up even the appearance of power is a courageous act.

The integration agenda can spread if we change attitudes and cultural predispositions at the top. Top officials must experience operations at the ground level. They must encourage boundary-spanning (communicating across agency lines), risk-taking, and lateral (innovative) thinking. They must encourage experimentation and then provide support for venues where the innovators can learn from one another and subsequently become guides to others who are prepared to take similar risks. Ultimately, they must trust those closest to the customers.

In retirement, I belong to a group of retirees from academia and government who still hope to contribute to public policy. I went on a small rant at one meeting where I moaned and groaned about some mistakes I thought were being made in Wisconsin's efforts to advance the integration agenda. One of the other members at that time, the retired dean of the University of Wisconsin's Business School, looked at me and said, "Tom, you have just summarized all the best thinking to come out of business schools over the last decade." See, I thought, who needs to be educated to make sense.

The integration agenda will not go away. So many providers rediscover the need for a more coherent and individualized service system because the advantages remain obvious. I sometimes feel that locals trying to do integration are a bit like alcoholics, a topic I know something about. Too many of them are out there struggling to bring some sense to the way they help clients. But they feel alone and misunderstood. They believe that they are confronting challenges and problems that absolutely no one else has dealt with in the past. The reality is that their take on things is dead wrong. Many others have struggled and still are struggling with the same issues every day. We need to articulate an infrastructure to bring them together . . . an AA for those bitten with the integration bug. The addicted need the counsel of others suffering from the same affliction.

Ultimately the notion of institutional culture, so critical to doing service integration, is also critical in so many other arenas. I turn to it again in the next chapter where I talk about bridging the gap between knowledge producers and knowledge consumers—the academy and the real world. Now, when talking about cultural conflict, it doesn't get any better than this.

CHAPTER 7

A FAILURE TO
COMMUNICATE

A mind, once stretched by an idea, never regains its original state.
—Oliver Wendell Holmes

There is a famous line in the iconic movie "Hud" where the grizzled old prison guard says to the Paul Newman character, "What we have here is a failure to communicate." This chapter is about one more rather long counter in my candy store, the one that tackles yet another wicked problem . . . what I call the "failure to communicate" challenge. It concentrates on the failure of those who are supposed to be producing knowledge to bring what they discover to those who might best use it.

I will start this story in 1993, back in ASPE, when we yet used those yellow pads to note missed calls. Yes, this chapter also starts with a call out of the blue. I looked at the name of the caller . . . it said Unmi Song. Well, I knew a Miri Song but not an Unmi. Miri had been a student of mine at UW and interned with me at

IRP where she helped with the now famous article called *Child Poverty: Progress or Paralysis* that everyone seemed to love. Perhaps the receptionist had misinterpreted the first name.

Miri's contribution had been to encourage me to publish the thing in the first place. One of my (many, many) faults is that I would develop interesting thoughts in my talks and, if I liked them, reuse them so frequently that I assumed everyone in the Western world had heard them, perhaps more than once. Miri convinced me that the central ideas in this piece would be new and exciting to many others. Despite my public talks, there were legions of folk out there thirsting for my inspirational insights. "No way," I would argue. "Way," she would respond. She wore me down and proved correct.

The short story on this piece is my use of a cute metaphor to capture the welfare population. In pursuing reform, I argued that the heterogeneity within the target population was of paramount importance. All recipients were not alike. Hold the presses, right! Ah, it is never the insight itself, but how one uses it that is the key. Think of these families as falling into layers, as you would find in an onion. Each layer represents a different type of family that is confronting distinct issues and, most critically, which then requires a tailored service strategy. On the outer skin were the issues easiest to address, and the more difficult challenges were located closer to the core. This was not unlike the four tiers I developed in Kenosha that the W-2 planners later stole, which is where I suspect my thinking on this matter likely originated.

The clever part in my argument was to assert that all sides in the welfare wars were right and all sides were wrong. People tended to look only at selected layers of the onion. They would see the problems and solutions associated with that layer while assuming they were looking at the whole onion. This is what I called the "truncated perception" problem. It is analogous to the "tunnel vision" we see in many professions. If a spouse is murdered, it must be the husband. By the time detectives have spent two years trying to convict the poor sap, who was innocent all along, the real miscreant is long gone. Back to welfare, the consequent screaming at one another inevitably leads to the paralysis we were seeing everywhere. The 'softs' in the welfare wars see recipients as victims of a cruel economic and social system. The 'hards' see beneficiaries as morally lax and lazy exploiters of the public's generosity. It is hard to have a civil dialogue when the starting positions are so far apart. The tragedy is that both capture part of reality. Starting from that premise, I developed a matrix that laid out reform proposals by selected welfare icons from across the political spectrum and tried to show how their ideas fit within a comprehensive approach to reform and thus complemented, not competed, with one another.

From the reaction I was seeing, my basic pitch was selling in both in Peoria and in Washington. For years after, strangers, upon being introduced to me, would say, "Oh, yeah, you are the onion man. I used to keep that article next to the commode." I always took this to mean that they wanted easy access to it, not that it as suitable as toilet paper. Such accolades, if that is what they were, afforded me with a few easy retorts, "oh, yeah, the onion piece, tears come to my eyes every time I think of it." After a while it got a bit tiring, and I altered my response. "You think I am that "onion" guy? No, no, I am not him. Didn't you hear? He died, from an overdose of garlic. Tragic . . . really!"

Most of my better thoughts, and I did have some, emerged while giving a talk somewhere. The onion metaphor is no exception. I was registering at a hotel in Vermont where a roundtable discussion was to take place the next day. The organizers had invited all the big players in the state and a few outside "experts" to get everyone focused on where to go with welfare and poverty in the future. It would include both state welfare insiders as well as public power figures such as top judges and legislators who brought very little expertise to the welfare topic.

A key organizer of the event caught me as I was registering and said, "Tom, can you do the lead off comments in the morning, kind of frame the issues for the group?" As usual, I agreed. *This could be a tough task,* I thought, *given the diversity of the audience.* I figured I would need some simple, overarching framework to structure a complex and conflict-prone issue such as what to do about welfare. Hence the origin of the onion! "It seemed to work very well." I said to myself, *Tom, you really are a clever devil.* Excessive talking to oneself is yet another sign of serious problems.

Getting back to the call! Since the person I thought was calling, Miri, had convinced me that not everyone in the Western world had heard of the onion analogy, I owed her a debt. Maybe she was in town, and I could take her to lunch. She had been an unusual Social Work grad student in that she had done her undergraduate work at Harvard. I doubt she could see her future in counseling distressed couples, so she drifted toward policy as possibly being a bit more intellectually challenging. She did her advanced placement in my practicum policy class and her internship at IRP under my supervision. I was never sure whether that was legal, but my personal policy was never to ask. I cannot recall where she had gone next but years later, after her Ph.D., she was considered for a position in Sociology at UW before ending up in England at the University of York.

As I started to call back, I realized that it was a Chicago number (probably no lunch then), and then a voice on the other end of the line that did not sound right. After a few awkward moments where I probably said, "How the hell are you?" To be followed up with "Who the hell are you?" I realized I was talking to someone who gives out money. It was a bumpy start to a relationship that would support a good part of my efforts to bridge the chasm that existed between the academy and the policy world. Perhaps I should also have labeled this counter in my policy candy store the holy grail of not constantly embarrassing oneself or some such thing.

I had always been a bit chagrined by the failure to communicate between two worlds of importance to me . . . those that thought of themselves as creators of knowledge and those who saw their roles as turning abstract notions into something real and functional. I spent my professional life wandering back and forth between these worlds, so the character of their mutual interaction remained of keen interest to me. I recall a moment way back in my state job days when a consultant had been hired (by the feds, I think) to help various states spruce up their QC operations. The fellow assigned to Wisconsin was perfect for academia . . . a total technical nerd with few people skills.

The final verbal report to top state officials was almost too painful to endure. They could not understand him, and he had trouble figuring out what they wanted to hear or at least what they needed to hear. Perhaps he had larger problems. He offered me a job with his company and, as I noted earlier, he offered to hire my wife sight-unseen when I mentioned she did not want to give up her job. I persisted in my refusal despite the sweetened offer. He obviously was not a good judge of talent.

As I made my transition to the academy with Irv Piliavin's welfare error project, I could see that Irv was having trouble selling his proposal to the state folk that counted. He could talk research but not policy. The state officials, on the other hand, didn't believe an egghead could contribute anything of value to their work and only saw his project as a potential pain in the rear. I was clueless about research at the time, probably still am. I could, however, effortlessly translate between Irv and the division brass. At the meeting to give the final okay to state support of the project, there remained significant opposition. At one point, I thought the tone was going negative and that my stay at the university would be about four weeks and not, as it turned out, four decades. I might be wrong, but there probably was more than a 50 percent chance that they would have turned Irv down had I not been at the table.

There are so many vignettes over the years that drove home this disconnect between knowledge producers and consumers. I recall one national conference that had been put together early in the welfare reform period by the American Public Human Services Association (APHSA), which had been APWA or the American Public Welfare Association. Apparently, welfare had become such a discredited concept that they no longer wanted to tarnish their brand by including that tainted word in their title.

They had convened what they called the welfare CEOs (heads of welfare agencies) from numerous states to meet and dialogue with representatives from the top evaluation firms and think tanks (these included MDRC, ABT, Mathematica Inc., Urban Institute, IRP). For the first couple of days the evaluation firms chatted about their ongoing projects and hinted strongly about the superb services they might provide to the attending states. The final session was to focus on the research questions of interest to the CEOs at the gathering. I was stunned when I realized that only three researchers remained for this last session . . . Alan Werner, a gentleman from Mathematica whose name I forget, and yours truly and I barely count as a researcher. Didn't the others think the real world had anything remotely interesting to say? Could not they see that this was a fantastic opportunity to see future research possibilities? What is going on here?

Later, I recall one of Howard Rolston's first national evaluation conferences. Yes, this is the same conference series where I gave the plenary address instead of Wade Horn, but that would occur down the road a bit. This was a maiden voyage for the concept. Howard therefore put together an advisory committee that included Barbara Blum and myself, among others. He wanted independent feedback on how it went and how it might be improved. The maiden voyage was structured as a typical conference format where the "experts" from the big evaluation firms along with a few academics presented their wisdom to the assembled masses. It was lecture style followed with a few minutes for Q&A at the end of each session.

It went like this. The first session ended in deafening silence . . . no questions. I suspected that no state person wanted to risk asking a stupid technical question in front of all their peers. On the other hand, I had a long career of asking stupid questions and had no self-respect left, so I started the ball rolling. The same happened in the next two sessions. Then, after the fourth panel, the whole audience turned to me when it was time for Q&A. They were probably drooling with anticipation at my next asinine query.

The substance was great, but the format needed work. Barbara and I later explained to Howard that he needed to find a way to generate more of a two-way communication dynamic at the conference. The passive, lecture-type format, we thought, diminished real learning and prevented state participants from seeing how the new knowledge might translate to their situation. It would not be easy, but it was worth a try. Howard did modify the format in future years. And I put that experience in my cognitive filing place.

I doubt that Unmi Song and I talked about such matters in that first call. In fact, I have no recollection of the substance of the conversation or how she came across my name. My guess, someone who did not like her suggested she call me. In any case, we must have made promises that we would stay in touch when I got back to Madison. We did, in fact, continue to chat. We also made plans to overlap on a trip to the Twin Cities after I was settled back in Madison. I was there on some child support evaluation project in which IRP was involved, one of my numerous projects the details of which are now all but lost to my memory. It may not seem like it, but you are only getting the highlights on this tour.

She was travelling there to seek out new project possibilities for the Joyce Foundation. I was always taken with her proactive style. She did not wait for ideas to be brought to her. She sought them out by actively engaging the real world. It was apparent to me, though, that she had not enjoyed a great deal of prior experience with bureaucrats or what they did, so I was able to smooth the conversations at some points. As I have often said, I am very nice to people who give out money. In any case, this serendipitous common trip gave us an opportunity to share ideas in a relaxed manner over dinner and as we walked around looking at the Christmas lights in downtown St. Paul.

I have often kicked myself for never asking her how she came across my name in the first place. I doubt she came across it in *USA Today*. Someone probably said, "Hey, get in touch with Corbett if you want to help the downtrodden. The way his career is going, he is about a year away from Food Stamps himself." Still, as with so many cold calls I have received, it had an outsized impact on future events. Opportunities and projects just kept falling out of the sky into my lap. I am a fortunate man, indeed.

Either at the end of 1995 or early in 1996, I made a formal proposal to the Joyce Foundation for a regional learning network. This was not the first of my silly ideas they supported but certainly the most significant. The network came to be known as WELPAN or the Welfare Peer Assistance Network. The primary notion behind the concept was that the states were now the experts. They were running ahead of the national government in innovation and experimentation. What we needed now was a way to stimulate their exciting work and provide a venue though which they could help one another.

Yes, research and expertise were necessary, but the actual transfer of knowledge had to be more of a give-and-take, more intimate and two-way as opposed to unidirectional. The audience needed to participate in the exchange to fully vet what the information might mean to them and not remain passive absorbers of divine truth. Not surprisingly, the seven states that would comprise the network coincided with the states on which the foundation focused—Illinois, Indiana, Iowa, Michigan, Minnesota, Ohio, and Wisconsin.

As best I can recall, the inspiration for WELPAN did *not* come out of any talk I had given. It emerged from a workshop I convened during my ASPE days. I was struck by how little the people in Washington were aware of the exciting things going on in the states. Perhaps if an innovation was being evaluated by MDRC or one of the other big firms, they would see a report but that was too far removed from seeing a new idea up close and personal.

So, I came up with the notion of "Bringing the Real World to Washington." I dug up some unused money in the ASPE budget and invited three or four exemplar (lighthouse) sites to talk about what they were doing and why it was exciting. For the first session I brought in the gang from Kenosha, officials from Riverside California (a site that was making national waves at the time), and representatives from a Pennsylvania-based teen-pregnancy focused program that Becca Maynard favored. There probably was a fourth site but that one escapes my failing memory.

The serendipity, or foresight, associated with the event occurred just before it was to take place. I looked at the room. There was a table up front with chairs set out in typical audience style. I suddenly grabbed a passerby to help me rearrange everything. We strung two or three tables together in the middle and placed all the "audience" chairs around the periphery.

With this physical format the participants would talk among themselves and not to the audience. All these years later, I am not sure why I thought this important at that moment.

As soon as the session started, however, I recognized a different tone to the event. The participants slipped into a dialogue, not speeches. They bounced off one another as they saw common challenges and exchanged solutions. It was as if the feds were not in the room. They truly began to teach one another and learn from one another. Toward the end, of course, there was a Q&A so that the flow could go from the central table to the periphery; but a different and exciting dynamic had been established. There was less defensiveness and more honesty since they quickly understood that they all were in the same boat and faced similar mountains to climb. There was less competition to look better than the other program. When it was over they were hugging one another and exchanging contact information. I surely stuck that experience in my cognitive file for future use.

Later, after returning to Madison, I had occasion to organize an event in D.C. The topic was the development and use of social indicators. Briefly, social indicators are measures that tap the well-being of a community, whether neighborhood or county or state or nation. The tricky part involves interpreting what the measures mean and thinking through how to use the information for policy or management purposes. I was heavily involved in the topic at the time, as discussed in the next chapter, and thus the rationale for this event. Again, the participants were largely drawn from localities and states that were doing (using) social indicators as inputs to the policy process. The larger audience encompassed federal officials, think-tank representatives, and academic types interested in either the development of social indicators or their use.

Through the good graces of Deborah Phillips, we held the session at the institutional home of the National Academy of Sciences. Deborah was doing some work there at the time. As it turns out, she is everything I am not—smart, attractive, and nice. In any case, I was glad she was willing to help. I must have thought that this august venue would somehow lend an air of importance to the event. Or perhaps I hoped that some of the wisdom that had accumulated in this venerable site over the years would rub off on me somehow. That surely did not happen, but I did luck out again. As with the ASPE event, I tried setting it up so that the locals would chat mostly among themselves while the others primarily listened, at least at first.

I saw some of the same dynamics I noticed at the ASPE event. Lightning had struck twice, my suspicion that the approach led to a more dynamic dialogue was reinforced. More importantly, Unmi Song was there. She had grown up in the D.C. area but did her academic work at the University of Chicago where she focused on business and economics. After a stint doing mergers and acquisitions in the private sector, she drifted toward the philanthropic community. Unmi was of Korean descent. She was quite attractive with luxurious black hair (I focus on hair because I have so little left) and an incisive mind. Like with Deborah, we were opposites. Unmi was focused, goal oriented, and disciplined . . . I, not so much.

She ran the foundation's employment section and found a way to support some of my hare-brained welfare ideas under that umbrella. I really enjoyed her a lot, but I am totally sure I drove her beyond the point of distraction with my careless ways and incessant jokes . . . there was no off switch. She did not suffer fools lightly, so why she put up with me for so long is beyond explanation. In her defense, she did fire me on numerous occasions. I can still see her in my mind now saying, "Corbett, you're fired," just like Donald Trump used to do on TV before he rose to a position from which we all would like to see him fired. Then I would respond with a "thank god" and "oh, by the way, I will call you about the next meeting in a week or so." At that, she would roll her eyes.

The first grant she had sent my way supported Mike Wiseman and I as we wrote a few papers to try to bring some reason and balance to the welfare debates which were descending further into vitriolic name calling, if that were even possible. The proposal was well written if I say so myself. It must have been since Unmi called to say that it was such a pleasure to read a well-reasoned and written proposal, so unlike much of which she had to endure. The underlying concept, however, sucked. Another report or paper by some academics was like dumping a thimble of water into the Atlantic. It doesn't make much of a wave. Dissatisfied with that project, I dragged out those vague concepts that had been floating around my head since the ASPE and NAS sessions I described above. This regional network idea was born.

I conned Theodora Ooms into joining me in this venture. Theo was a matriarch on the Washington scene. She had spent much of her professional life trying to bring rigorous research and rationality to the Washington policy process as it affected families, children, and marriage. She will always be remembered as the godmother of the Family Impact Seminars which I discuss further below. In addition, she helped Bobbi Wolfe and I organize some IRP events for Congressional staffers in D.C. on issues we thought critical to debates about the social safety net in the 1990s. One of these was on the Block Grant approach to funding programs, a strategy regaining considerable traction at that time.

Unmi was so moved by this WELPAN concept she gave us enough money to finance maybe two meetings if we kept them small, if we hitchhiked to the Chicago offices of the Joyce Foundation (who gave us free meeting space), and if we brought our own bag lunches. Clearly, this was a trial run. What I recall best about the start-up was trying to convince Wisconsin and Minnesota to participate. I sucked up what little courage I possess and had a face-to-face with J. Jean Rogers, who still seemed to dislike me rather intensely. Dislike a sweet, harmless guy like me, go figure! In truth, it was not so much a dislike as a visible rage.

Her tone was so frosty I began wishing I had bought one of those bulletproof vests our soldiers use in the Middle East. However, I turned on my best Irish charm which, it sadly turns out, is surprisingly useless. When it became clear that I was not leaving until she agreed to join us, Jean reluctantly relented. Good thing for her since I was just on the verge of using my secret weapon— telling her my life story.

Then I called Minnesota. I got to someone named Ann Sessoms who was destined to become one of my favorite members, and who stayed with the network until its demise. In fact, I still hear from her on occasion, though usually just so she can remind me what a sad sack I am. On that first call, she appeared as reluctant as J. Jean. Finally, after a few protests about how busy she was, she came out with her real reservation. "Listen, I am not going to another meeting and listen to the Wisconsin people tell us how great they are. And I certainly don't want W-2 crammed down my throat." I assured her that would not happen, but I had absolutely no idea how to prevent it. Many of the Wisconsin people did think they rather walked on water. That, of course, is silly since I walk on water all the time and have never run across one of them out there.

It turned out that Ann was quite nice, funny and extremely knowledgeable about the programs and policies. She also could be no nonsense and direct and quickly became an ally of Unmi in the hopeless task of keeping me in my place, or at least in giving it a try. Ann would give me the "look" when I got out of line with my so-called wit. Unmi would follow up by whacking me upside the head or, when I was having a very good day, by firing me.

In August of 1996, one person from each participating state except for Ohio (which sent two) gathered in the Joyce Foundation conference room. Given my prescience, admittedly a wondrous gift, national welfare reform had just passed. AFDC would be replaced by TANF, the Temporary Assistance to Needy Families program. In short, a new era of social assistance was breaking forth. The question on that day of the first meeting was whether WELPAN would be around for only the conception of the new era or would it be around for the entire birthing process?

Eventually two other offshoots of WELPAN would take root. There was a west coast version called WESTPAN. With my assistance, it was launched by Barry Van Lare, a long-time Washington fixture who served as a kind of ubiquitous consultant and guru to states on welfare and related human services programs. I remember Barry and I were on the phone with a representative from the Packard Foundation who was considering supporting the west coast venture. Despite my assurances that state officials really, really prized these meetings, she could not quite see how they differed from any other workshops and conferences that states attended. She would almost be convinced and then back away. After several ebbs and flows, the sick feeling of being in a faculty meeting (or maybe one of the old Washington groundhog-day meetings) overwhelmed me and I sort of snapped. "Oh, screw it," those were my exact words I believe, " . . . I can scrounge up money for the first meeting. Let's just do one and see if it makes sense to proceed further." Representatives from Alaska, Arizona, California, Hawaii, Idaho, Nevada, Oregon, and Washington attended. They loved it as much as the Midwest states and Packard kicked in, at least for several years.

Somewhat later, I was contacted by Dick Nathan who headed the Rockefeller Institute of Government at the State University of New York (SUNY) in Albany. Dick had taught at Princeton for years and had earlier served in the Nixon administration. He seemed an intellectual by breeding but a man who also wanted to leave a distinct imprint on public policy. He was assisted by Tom Gais, a quiet and thoughtful man. Tom and I only shared a first name, our temperaments were quite distinct. For one thing, Gais always thought before he spoke. I, on the other hand, typically spoke first and thought afterward, if at all.

They wanted to set in motion a series of WELPAN-type meetings among four southern states (Arkansas, Louisiana, Mississippi, and perhaps Missouri). Dick had some contacts down there and saw a dire need to help them out. Governments in the deep-south, he opined, were not as well developed as in other sections of the country. They needed all the help they could get. I could not agree more and signed on to help.

Now, I had traveled throughout most of the country in my avocation as a wandering policy wonk. Yet, I had never gotten into the real Dixie. Arriving the evening before the first meeting, I wandered around the State Capitol building of Mississippi in Jackson. When I saw people working on the Capitol lawn, my initial thought was that they had put their maintenance crews in very striking uniforms. Then it hit me that they were wearing the classic horizontal pin stripe prison garb of a chain gang. Why waste taxpayer's money when you have forced labor available.

We did get a nice tour of the governor's mansion. Southerners can be gracious, that is for sure. The meetings were held in the State Capitol building itself at the good graces of a former governor, William Winters, who was a friend of Dick's. I casually chatted with the former chief executive for a while. He shared with me his near-death experiences as governor such as the time he tried to excise the stars and bars of the confederacy from the state flag. I was going to tell him mine at the hands of angry social workers but refrained, not wanting to one-up him. I wondered which group might be more rabid . . . racist rednecks being asked to hide their heritage, or social workers being asked to do paperwork. My money is on the social workers.

At one point he pointed out a marble statue and asked if I knew who it represented. I had noticed it earlier and said something about this man being one of the more rabid racists ever to serve in the U.S. Senate, Senator Theodore G. Bilbo. His racist rhetoric became more extreme over time, reaching such a pitch in the 1946 election that a Senate investigation was initiated to examine his conduct. He then told me a story:

> When I was governor it bothered me that we honored this man by having his replica situated right in the middle of the State Capitol, directly under the rotunda. So, one Friday afternoon, I instructed the maintenance people to move him to a less conspicuous location. I came in Monday morning and, by God, he was back under the rotunda again. I tried again, and the same thing happened. People give things up very hard down here.

When Tom Gais sent me a draft of the agenda for the first meeting, I knew they had missed the essence of the WELPAN experience. Dick and he had scheduled too many agenda items into the sessions. This would almost guarantee that the experts (Dick,

Gais, other SUNY staff, even yours truly) would talk to the state members. There would not be enough time for them to dialogue among themselves or interact meaningful with the resource people present. Thus, they would fail to develop a sense of ownership over the process or the bonds essential to a real network.

When I talked with Tom at length he understood my concerns, but the agenda was out already. We fortunately were able to basically ignore it as the meeting unfolded and, guess what? These deep-south states also hungered for more. Absent a formal name at the start, we very informally referred to this group as BUBBAPAN.

Now we had three sample points which all showed a similar result. State officials loved this format. It proved so popular that the head of APHSA asked for a meeting during one of my frequent trips to D.C. By way of a preface, when Theo and I were first doing WELPAN, a top staff member from APHSA wanted to chat with us. We had a telephone conference. It was clear that the organization, or at least this official, was very upset about what we were planning to do. Theo tried to be accommodating and argue that we were not invading their turf, that we respected what they did. I was bemused. How would this little network of seven states (at the time) threaten this large and well-established trade organization? Perhaps I underestimated Washington's capacity for self-interest and paranoia? In the end, Theo and I did not diminish the APHSA representative's hostility one whit, and we simply agreed to disagree.

When I now met with the head man, he was very amiable. "We struggle a bit getting states to our meetings, economic times are tough and travel budgets are being cut back. They seem to love WELPAN. What is the secret?" Of course, one secret is that we paid for the members' travel expenses, which helped immensely. They did love the meetings, though, that was undeniable.

There were other reasons for the network's popularity as well. By this time, I had heard WELPAN members informally discussing which national meetings they would attend or not. Often, they decided to skip certain meetings or only reluctantly attend because they thought it more a requirement than a learning opportunity. This was particularly true of federal meetings where nonattendance might be a form of mutiny. Occasionally, I would ask about their reluctance. Responses varied, of course, but ran along somewhat similar lines. They sometimes felt as if they were being treated as half-literate children who were being scolded or being told to eat their spinach because it was good for them. They felt that those lecturing them often had little appreciation of the complexities they faced daily.

I explained to the APHSA head what I thought were WELPAN's core elements. The network belonged to the members. We might suggest topics and outside resources, but they had the ultimate say on everything. And the members did exercise control, even to the point of barring federal officials stationed in Chicago from attending at least parts of their meetings. In a sense, they were considered the experts, not the academics, or the think-tank types, or the high public officials we brought in. We gave them plenty of time to dialogue among themselves, to bond, and to really vet either the research put on their plate or the issues they were confronting as welfare reform rolled out. It was a cook's tour and the APHSE head listened respectfully. Whether he acted on it, I have no idea.

At one point, Barry Van Lare, Tom Gais (on behalf of Dick Nathan), and I tried to jointly approach foundations for more support to spread the WELPAN concept across the country. After all, the dramatic character of welfare reform would take years to work itself out. In the meantime, the states were experimenting with all kinds of new ideas and concepts. Welfare was being transformed from a limited form of income support into what might be considered an exciting opportunity to create a more comprehensive system of social assistance. States would need to help one another if the potential was to come to pass. At one point I spoke to an affinity group of foundations who banded together around their common interest in helping poor families. It all seemed so obvious to us, but perhaps not so obvious to them.

The philanthropic community responded to our combined entreaties with depressing indifference and misunderstanding. There was a lot of "now tell us again how your meetings differ from other meetings." The most common response was "we would love to give you money for a meeting on topic X. That falls into our priorities, but what if your members are not interested in topic X?" Or we got the "I am sure the network is bang-on, but we don't support infrastructure, only substance . . . this is not exactly bricks and mortar, but it sounds like infrastructure to us." And there was always the variant of "We need to see results. We are a results-oriented foundation. Can you promise that new laws attributable to our investment will be forthcoming?"

To be honest, I could not. What members told us time and again is that they left sessions energized and full of ideas. They would communicate these back home, sometimes following up with phone calls to their fellow members or contact through a LISTSERVE we set up. What came out of the other end of this broiling process might be results not easily traced directly back to the meetings, but change did happen; and the network did play some part in many of these changes. The neat kind of causality we were being asked to provide was not a measurable certainty. You were influencing the decision-making process and that had to remain the expected reward.

I remember being at some meeting (they tend to collapse into one continuous session in my memory) where Helen Neuborne was present. Helen was from the Ford Foundation. Like most foundation-types, I found her knowledgeable and accomplished. At one point in this gathering, I slipped out of my witty, nice guy persona (really, I could be like that), and went on a bit of a rant about the myopia and narrowness of philanthropic world. I am not sure what got me started, but I did rather forget that Helen was there. I can yet recall the sheepish grin on her face when I noticed her presence. I started to stammer a quick apology, but she quickly cut me off. "You are absolutely right, Tom, but that is the way it is I am afraid."

No one ever came forward to fund BUBBAPAN and it dissolved after several meetings. WESTPAN went on for two or three years and was taking off just as WELPAN had. What I found remarkable in our Western franchise is that a tiny, very conservative state like Idaho still had things in common with a huge, more liberal state like California. I had wondered about that at the start. The west coast network also gave me a few memories, a chance to visit Las Vegas (which I doubt I would have visited if not for work), and a memorable half trip to Seattle.

A WESTPAN meeting was scheduled to start in Seattle on the afternoon of September 11, 2001. I decided to fly out that morning since the time zone changes would give me ample opportunity to get there on time. One of my favorite former students, Rachel (Weber) Frisk, who by then worked at the GAO, was to attend as well. She was working on a big welfare study at the time and was scheduled to share some of her findings. Barry Van Lare would also be flying out from Washington.

I had been through about five awful trips in a row (with delayed and cancelled flights), so was pleased that I made it to Minneapolis. It looked like clear sailing from there. Then I noticed a pool of people watching a TV monitor with great interest. It quickly went downhill from there. The full extent of the 9/11 disaster all unfolded in slow motion. For a while I still thought I could get to Seattle, though late for sure. When the enormity of the disaster became clear, I made a dash for the rental car place. Fortunately, I had used it before and knew where it was located since hordes of others would soon follow me. Barry Van Lare had flown out the night before and was stuck in Seattle for a week. Like me, Rachel was scheduled to fly out the morning of the eleventh. Later, she told me about being swept out of National Airport into streets of panicky people as smoke drifted over from the nearby Pentagon, which had just been hit. She said it was all too surreal. It was!

WELPAN did last for well over a decade. Theo had moved on to other concerns after a couple of years. Eventually, Jennifer Noyes joined me as co-coordinator of the network. That certainly gave it ideological balance, though both of us were very careful not to let our biases intrude too much. The Network eventually ended sometime after Unmi moved on to become head of another Chicago Foundation that focused on the arts or some such thing. Jennifer Phillips, who had moved to Joyce from the Mott Foundation, picked it up for a while until she too left for other pursuits.

During its life course, WELPAN was, as I often say, a front row seat to the reality and possibility of welfare reform. The group first met, as I mentioned, literally days after the enactment of TANF.

As of the first session, we barely had enough money for one more. People came, but with the caveat that they were unusually busy. National welfare reform was upon them. Maybe they could spare a single day to see what this was all about. Ann Sessoms did not like Wisconsin, perhaps a sentiment shared by others. J. Jean Rogers, who was the only state attendee I knew when the meeting started, did not like me, to put it mildly. I thought our prospects less than bright as we kicked off our first meeting.

At the end of the day, the topic of a next meeting came up, which would be the last unless Unmi coughed-up more dough. Everyone whipped out their calendars. They struggled to find a common date that would work . . . they were busy folk after all. I still recall the representative from Indiana saying, "This has been so great. I would be willing to come back on a Saturday if that works for the others." I leaned back in my chair and mused, *What the frack just happened here?*

Ann, who didn't want to come in the first place stayed a member to the end. Some several years after its demise, she noted that she still found some WELPAN products useful to her job (she is now retired). J. Jean Rogers left her position as head of W-2 early in the WELPAN timeline (to be replaced by Jennifer Noyes as the Wisconsin representative). J. Jean took a position with Vocational Rehabilitation in the north part of Wisconsin. She surprised me by asking if she could still attend the WELPAN sessions, even though her new job took away the rationale for doing so. I can attest to the fact that her loyalty to the network had little to do with any growing affection for me, though her negative animus had abated. Really, who could stay mad at such a charming Irishman?

Unmi graciously gave us the resources to support a robust WELPAN concept. Now, we could expand the membership. States could send two, even three people, to the sessions. We could now bring resource people to meetings to share their knowledge and help to stimulate thoughtful dialogues. We strived to keep it small enough so that everyone could sit around the same table. We developed the concept through trial and error. In the beginning, though, we toyed with going in a different direction.

I thought it might be a good idea to more formally wed WELPAN to academia, to seek a marriage of sorts between knowledge producers and consumers. It turns out that there was a Big Ten consortium that facilitated (I was told) communications across researchers at the member universities. I spoke to the University of Wisconsin people involved in this and they appeared interested. When I broached the idea to the WELPAN members, I hit a brick wall. One member put it this way: "Too many academics sit on the outside criticizing us for what we are, or are not, doing. They do so without trying to know the realities we face." They did not need that kind of second-guessing from a group they saw as generally naïve and at the same time arrogant. They were interested in what some academics had to say, but they would do the choosing of which ones they wanted to hear.

That kind of negative perception toward academics cropped up from time to time. Once we did survey where they would prefer to get their information and had a subsequent discussion on the results. Academic research was way down the list. It was viewed as inaccessible, irrelevant, and dated. Again, people in the academy were looked upon as removed from reality. They tended not to keep abreast of rapidly changing conditions and realities. They did not fully appreciate the complexity of the world in which public officials operated.

Statistical significance is fine, and most WELPAN members got it, but there was such a thing as substantive significance as well. If you have a big enough sample size, you can find associations among a lot of things. The magnitude of the difference may not be great enough, however, to offset all the other potential costs associated with change. Such a calculation needs a critical and experienced eye to competently assess. Most academics do not have the experience to make those judgments. That, however, does not inhibit them from criticizing public officials for ignoring the evidence. Of course, good evidence is ignored all the time . . . no one is completely in the right here.

The mechanics of WELPAN were simple enough. Each meeting typically started with what we called the state round-up. Each state would bring the others up to date on what was happening, what issues had cropped up, new wrinkles they were confronting, pretty much anything that struck their fancy. That session was *always* off limits to outsiders other than the IRP facilitators and any Joyce folk that wanted to stop in. Anyone around the table was able to chime in with comments or questions. If we needed to stay on a specific topic longer than expected, we would do so within reason since the agenda was viewed as malleable. At times, these sessions turned into quasi-therapy sessions as the stresses of those days got to people who cared very much about what they were doing. After a time, members knew they were among friends who were going through the same things, whether they were Republicans or Democrats, conservative or liberal. Over time, a bond formed among the members with new additions to the group quickly being integrated into the network's culture. On more than one occasion, tears flowed in the room, often after another of my attempts to be witty.

In the afternoon, we usually brought in resource people. These could be academics, folks from think-tanks or evaluation firms, top federal officials, or program people who were running interesting innovations. Sometimes we mixed and matched, sometimes we looked at several innovations in a single meeting. No matter what, the choice of topics and resource people were up to the members. We might make suggestions, but they had the final word. The morning of the second day often was spent vetting the issues raised on the first day. This gave everyone plenty of time to absorb what they had learned and to think through how it might be of use for them. As the meeting came to an end, we discussed potential topics for future meetings.

We had special meetings. Some were held in various state capitals, where that state would demonstrate ideas and concepts they were trying out. These show-and-tell sessions often involved field trips to actual pilot and program sites. We had Washington meetings. We had meetings that tied into larger conferences. We had meetings where we brought in officials from other systems like child support and workforce development. There was a rhythm to what we did but it was not cast in stone. If there was an opportunity to learn by doing something different, or the possibility of having an impact by reaching out in creative ways, we did it. Sometimes we stretched things a bit far, and Unmi would fire me again; but I was getting used to that. In the end, the woman was very forgiving.

By far it was the substance that I found to be most interesting. And after all, it was all about me. The first thematic issue the group focused on was the identification of what contemporary welfare reform was all about. Here was a chance to think through the purposes or ends of what they were trying to achieve. After all, you cannot know what you want to do unless you can describe where you want to be. The subsequent dialogue was long and serious.

The members came from different places both politically and ideologically. One moment was especially memorable. "No one has mentioned poverty." I pointed out, "After all, I am from the Institute for Research on Poverty. You guys are killing me here."

After Unmi chimed in that my demise "sounded like a good plan to her," Joel Rabb from Ohio spoke up. Joel, like Ann, remained with the group for the duration. We became good friends over time. He could be loquacious but spoke in gentle terms. He obviously cared about his work and the people he served. It wasn't until after his retirement that I realized the depth of his goodness. He is involved in humanitarian projects that take him to Texas and Southeast Asia, two under developed areas that needed a lot of help. Apparently, this was a family trait; his brother, a minister, was killed in Haiti while helping the suffering of that country after a horrific natural disaster. Joel's primary flaws were remaining a diehard Buckeye fan and having a disposition for taking potshots at Wisconsin athletic teams.

Joel said something like the following to support leaving eliminating poverty off the goals of welfare reform. He offered a rationale in his usual measured way with a slight Texas accent from his youth that could still be heard:

I don't think we should focus on poverty and I will tell you why. When we were administering the AFDC program everyone blamed us for not doing enough to reduce poverty. Well, that program was not designed to eliminate poverty, but we got the blame anyways. If we now say that reducing poverty through TANF is our goal, we will simply be setting ourselves up for failure. It will take far more than what we have control over to make a dent in poverty. I want us to attack poverty as much as the next guy, but we do not have the tools yet.

The list of reform purposes covered many domains and specific measures. At some point we decided to formalize our thinking in a report. I won't summarize substance here. Interested readers can go to the IRP web site to see this and other WELPAN products. The ends laid out encompassed a rather broad range of individual and family behaviors and circumstances. These WELPAN deliberations suggested to all of us that no longer thought of welfare, or its replacement, as an income maintenance program. We were beginning to think of TANF and other related systems as vehicles through which to strengthen families and communities. It was an ambitious agenda they were setting out but one that generated excitement among them.

Next, they decided that they wanted to go public with their conclusions. However, no one knew what kind of approval needed to be secured so that the final document could be published as an official WELPAN document. It took a while to finalize our product and give everyone an opportunity to vet it back in their home states before it was released in the late 1990s. As home states came to trust WELPAN the release of future reports seemed easier.

It was not clear at the time, but the character of this first product set up future discussions quite well. In terms of overarching themes, WELPAN would move on to an extensive dialogue about the transformative nature of services being provided through

TANF. This dialogue would incorporate a clear rationale on why the silos between TANF and other service systems had to be broken down so that related service strategies could be merged. Occasionally, I would hear people say in various meetings around the country, "Well, as WELPAN has noted . . ." or see someone pull out and reference a WELPAN report. On occasion, one of my federal friends would ask what WELPAN thought on some issue. The little Midwest network was gaining traction.

Now, not all meetings were lofty discussions of macro-issues and strategies. There were plenty of discussions about details. How should states deal with a specific federal requirement? Was drug testing of recipients a good idea? And so on. Of course, I would waste time with my wit, which usually elicited the "look" from Ann, a whack upside the head from Unmi, and a sly chuckle from Joel and others.

Humor was critical, as was keeping a non-partisan and non-ideological approach to running the network. In the later years, Jennifer and I were co-facilitators. She was conservative, and I bordered on being a socialist. She was a Republican, while I liked to think of myself as independent but usually voted Democratic. Yet, I doubt if either of us betrayed our leanings and biases. I recall one day when a member from Iowa said the following. "Tom is the perfect facilitator for us since he doesn't know anything." While true, what I think she was trying to say is that I did not try to push any agenda on them. In a world where they were surrounded by people with strong leanings, Jennifer and I apparently proved refreshing. Besides, she was organized, unlike me, which Unmi and the members found refreshing.

When the issues were highly technical, we let them school each other. But when we were discussing issues on a more macro-level, I often would take a more active role. I would listen to what they were saying. Then I would do what I do best. I would lean back and muse something like the following, "Here is what I think you are saying." Then I would launch into a (hopefully) short monologue trying to weave the discussion into a thematic whole. I would stop, pause until their blank expressions cleared and/or the laughter died down, and wait for feedback upon which we would further refine the thread of thought that had emerged. Mostly, this process would go back and forth as we worked toward a new synthesis of what TANF meant and where reform was going.

Pushing the group along was a persistent fear shared by all. When TANF was enacted, a block grant was created for providing states with the resources to carry out the program. This replaced the sum-sufficient funding mechanism (you received what was necessary to operate the program) that was in effect since the start of the program in the 1930s. The amount of the grant was based on AFDC caseloads as they existed in a given base year, 1994. When TANF came in the caseloads dropped dramatically in most states, some more than others. Still, almost all had a short-term windfall since the amount of the grant was based on a much larger caseload than they now served. This gave them resources with which to try out new ideas and approaches.

Two fears stalked the WELPAN discussions. First, the excess money would somehow be siphoned off for other purposes. Second, key politicians and others would forget about welfare as an issue. They could easily see politicians saying, "Oh, we dealt with that last year so let's move on." For the WELPAN group, they saw the struggle as just beginning.

There was a sense that the clock was ticking, prompting members to identify a single priority on which to focus. We had better reconceptualize what public assistance was all about or the TANF block grant would wither away in the face of inflation. Worse, it might be cut as caseloads continued to fall. This bleak prospect seemed inevitable even though the needs of those families they wanted to serve were, on average, more complex than in the past and thus require increasingly expensive interventions. They also wanted to reach out to non-traditional populations (at-risk youth) to intervene in a way that problems could be prevented before they became irreversible.

Having laid out some ambitious program purposes in the first report, the group expanded its thinking about a transformed approach to social assistance in several subsequent reports all of which are available at the IRP web site. In addition to the reports, we also developed a set of videos that captured some of our thinking on film. We typically called what we saw as emerging reform possibilities the "New Face of Welfare."

At one point, we tried exploiting newer distance-learning technologies to reach officials at the county level. Kara Mikulich, a newly hired project officer at the Joyce Foundation, provided us with support to launch this concept. Kara got her undergraduate degree at Holy Cross College, where I would have gone if fate had not pushed me in a different direction. She then obtained her law degree at Stanford. Kara was a lovely person with a high tolerance for pain. She, unlike Unmi, forgave me all my sins and never fired me, not once. I always told Unmi that Kara was the nice program officer from Joyce.

In this project, Judy Bartfelt and I put together elaborate telecasts to reach locals who were sitting in studios throughout the Midwest and beyond. Judy was an IRP affiliate who had also earned her doctorate in Social Welfare at UW. The broadcasts were a mixture of prerecorded videos, live panel presentations, and Q&A sessions. The questions could come in via phone or fax, and the panelists would answer. Clearly, these events were very labor intensive. The quality was excellent, but we knew that to continue would absorb too much time and energy which I knew I did not have. Thus, this experiment did not last long. Besides, you could not generate the intimacy and creativity that existed within the WELPAN setting.

WELPAN helped bridge the communication gap between the knowledge producers and policymakers by bringing researchers and analytic types into an intimate setting where a true dialogue could take place. The resource people invited were often known to be good communicators and there was plenty of time to digest what they had to say. More to the point, the members could probe and ask questions to figure out if the substance of the research was applicable to their idiosyncratic situation. Even better, they could vet the material with their peers to further explore whether an idea was worth pursuing or how it might be modified to accommodate local circumstances.

Most of all, WELPAN gave the members a chance to think. Policymakers don't have much time for thinking through what they are about. Neither do academics strangely enough. When we had European academics spending time at IRP they would ask me when we all sat around talking about ideas. Excuse me, I would respond with a chuckle, sit around talking about ideas! Sorry, you must have this place confused with a university, everyone is too busy here to think about stuff. It is worse in the real policy world where continuous meetings and immediate responses to crises consume all available time for each day. More than once I heard a member say, "I finally get a chance to lean back and think about things when I get on the plane to come to these meetings."

While Theodora Ooms helped with the birthing process of Peer Assistance Network concept, her real fame was as the godmother of another model designed to facilitate communication between researchers and policymakers. As far back as the 1970s, she was most concerned that families were being overlooked in the policy-making process. We did economic impact analyses and environmental analyses, but new policies and programs were launched with little thought as to how they would affect families. Why not do something about that?

She developed a model called the Family Impact Seminars (FIS). At first, the model was used with the Washington congressional audience in mind. A topic would be chosen, speakers carefully selected, and brief talks would be made to the audience with a follow up Q&A session along with carefully prepared briefing reports. The speakers were selected if they were good communicators and were prepped to be as non-partisan as feasible. I had the good fortune to attend a couple of her Washington seminars and, after we got to know one another, Theo appointed me to her national advisory board.

Theo could only reach congressional staff members, not the legislators themselves. Still, staff members in Washington are critical to the policy process. Besides, her hidden agenda was to help those influencing policy to think about families in more critical ways. Don't just look at the surface of a policy or program. Think deeper to assess the subtle, perhaps unintended, consequences as these innovations impacted families. She was trying to get people to approach policy in a different way, in a less narrow and provincial way. She wanted them to look at policies as they rippled through society.

By the early 1990s Theo could see that the locus of policy making was drifting toward the states. She decided to work on developing an FIS capability at that level. For some reason, she really wanted IRP involved in Wisconsin. Though IRP's reputation on the national stage was stellar, we were tainted in Wisconsin, which is obvious if you had stayed awake while reading the prior chapters. But I went out to the training that Theo gave to potential state FIS coordinators, including a bright young new faculty member at UW named Karen Bogenschneider.

Karen is in perpetual overdrive. She goes at 110 percent all the time. She is a perfectionist in all she does, which is quite a lot. I get tired just watching her. In most ways, we are total opposites. I recall when she came into the university television studios just before we were going to do one of our distance learning programs. I was lounging there in my usual relaxed posture as she bounced up saying, "How can you be so calm, I would be a wreck right now." I explained to her I have done all I can, it will now be what it will now be. I offered such profound or profoundly stupid utterances with annoying regularity. Despite our differences, we have co-authored a book together as well as several articles. In addition, I have been a close consultant in her work with the Family Impact Seminars.

I am not going through the entire history of the seminars. Originally, Karen and I were to run the Wisconsin seminars as a team. However, it turns out that my main contribution over the years has been to provide her with an endless supply of email jokes. She apparently has kept a running file of them for future use, or perhaps to blackmail me which wrongly assumes I am capable of shame. In those early days, she also kept reminding me that we had to be non-partisan. I would reply that I get it and five minutes later she would remind me again. I suspect she feared my reputation as a left-wing terrorist was true. Perhaps she thought I would unfurl a communist banner and begin singing leftist songs like *The International* or *Solidarity Forever* during an FIS seminar.

She did take a chance and let me help a little with the first one, and to speak at a couple of others. I do recall the first one vividly. The model back then was much shorter than it is now with the seminar finishing by noon. It so happens that I was scheduled to speak at a Wisconsin legislative hearing that very afternoon. I won't even try to recall what the topic at the legislature was that day, probably something to do with welfare. However, I recall a Republican legislator on the panel I was about to address asking for some time to make a few comments before the proceedings were to start. She launched into a highly laudatory set of comments about this Family Impact Seminar event she attended that morning and suggested to her colleagues that they would be well advised to attend in the future. I thought, *Damn, I think this is another winner.*

Karen also uses a video snippet of me as part of her outreach campaign to others, particularly when seeking more money.

Whenever I have been present she tells the audience that they must pay special attention to the next video bit since the expert shown demands a payment for each time it is used. This gets the audience's attention as they wonder who this egomaniacal character might possibly be. Of course, the egomaniacal character is me! It gets a good laugh, so I don't mind. But I am still waiting for those damn payments.

Over the years, I have been amazed at Karen's energy and focus. She is one of the most organized persons I know and pays extraordinary attention to detail. I have wandered through life making it up as I go. She is the consummate planner. The FIS concept would not be what it is today if it were not for her dedication. Theo saw this as well. After launching the state-level FIS projects in several states she turned the whole thing over to Karen who created the Policy Institute for Family Impact Seminars (PINFIS) which is now known as the Family Impact Network. This entity would be a platform for extending the FIS concept to additional states.

When I was in a position as a manager of IRP, I helped in any way I could. I saw FIS as a potentially important part of the institute's outreach mission. Over time, the number of participating states reached about half of all states. She ran this network while running the Wisconsin state seminars and earning a named professorship in the School of Human Ecology. She is also recognized as a leading expert of family policy, having written a classic textbook and being asked to speak worldwide on the topic.

A typical Wisconsin FIS day looks as follows: it starts well before the actual seminar day when Karen works with an advisory group comprised of state legislators from both parties and a few other key state informants. As a group, they select a topic for the next seminar . . . a topic they know will be on the front burner that year. Karen then scours for experts who have researched the issue employing accepted scientific methods. She then vets them carefully to determine that they do not have a partisan reputation and that they can deliver their message in an objective manner. Working with them, she develops a briefing report that summarizes the information they will deliver. If needed, she will prep them on how best to communicate with policymakers. Unfortunately, many in the academy do not have a clue about how to do this.

On the day of the seminar, there will be relatively brief presentations followed by Q&A. The audience at this point includes legislators, legislative aids, executive agency officials, interested stakeholders, and academics. The press is *not* invited so that legislators and all participants can feel comfortable. This is followed up with a lunch for interested legislators only. Then there are break-out sessions for each speaker where the topic can be explored more fully. Depending on interest, one-on-one meetings are set up with the governor or his staff as well as top executive officials, if warranted. Finally, video and audio recordings are available for legislators who could not attend or would want to relive the experience.

The sessions are remarkably well attended by legislators who give them extremely high marks for objectivity, scientific rigor, relevance, and usefulness. In short, a remarkable number of legislators love and overtly endorse the seminars. In fact, they rate them higher than other sources of input except for their constituents whom, after all, they work for. Why all this positive feedback, you might ask?

Here is my best guess. Politicians are surrounded by people with agendas, people who seem to want to help, but are peddling one thing or another. True, sometimes a legislator likes what is being peddled but that is not always the case. They spend their days embroiled in a highly partisan cauldron where talking with people on the other side of the aisle is now tantamount to treason. They simply cannot escape this environment where highly scripted positions and beliefs are a daily fare. For them, access to quality, objective input is very hard to come by. Yet, the more serious among them know that policy choices not backed up by good evidence can easily be bad investments.

The seminars are a breath of fresh air. Participants are exposed to rigorous information imparted in an objective fashion. They get to listen to experts who know how to talk to them, who are not trying to make them feel stupid or put them down. They even get to indirectly interact with the enemy (members of the opposite political party) in a safe venue. This gives them a chance to see the concerns and interests of their day-to-day opponents.

Best of all, they get to see the university in a new light. Here is something the eggheads are doing that, incredible as it sounds, might be useful. Typically, they see the university as a remote and alien world filled with elitist, entitled academics. They hold such views only because the typical university is an isolated island largely inhabited by elitist and entitled prima donnas. Sitting in these FIS sessions, I am sure that many a legislator has glanced toward the heavens fully expecting the sky to be full of flying pigs. Really, the university is doing something useful! How could that have happened. On the other hand, many of my egghead colleagues view legislators as barely qualifying as *homo sapiens* since, in their eyes, politicians fall short on the sapiens (or wisdom) dimension.

I am yet friends with Terry Wilkom, whom I introduced earlier when talking about the 1970s era Wisconsin welfare study group. He was a powerful Democratic politician in the early 1970s. For a while in retirement we had Florida winter homes not far from one another. Terry was an eclectic and thoughtful man who spent time in both government and the private sector, at one point working closely with computer genius Seymore Cray. Periodically, we would chat about the old days including how things have changed in the legislature. Yes, there was partisanship back then. In public, on the legislative floor, the two parties would attack one another. But then they would dine and drink together in the evening where they often worked out deals to keep government moving. That is no longer the case. Real communication across the partisan and ideological divide is rare indeed in the current climate. The FIS is a treasured exception.

I did drift away from any day-to-day involvement in the seminars. However, I remained close to the concept, and how Karen helped develop it over the years. I served on her various advisory committees and Boards, as I had for Theodora earlier. In addition, Karen would email and call me often, sometimes a lot. Once she focused on an issue, she was a tenacious bulldog.

Working with Karen could be taxing. The worst issues involved deciding what something should be called, deciding on a title. Sounds simple but not when Karen is involved. Every detail is given extraordinary thought and helping her label something is a kiss of death request from my perspective. First, she sends me a list with several possibilities. I would select one and give her my reasons for my choice. So far so good! Then I would get a longer list back. In some cases, my first pick is gone! *Hmmm, what happened to my initial choice?* I would think. I might make another selection or even tweak one of those now on the list. Then another list would appear. This one is even longer and with none of my prior selections to be seen.

At this point desperation sets in. Now I start sending messages that Tom Corbett is seriously ill, perhaps even about to expire. But now another even longer list of options appears. "No, really," I would reply, "Tom Corbett expired last night, really sad but true." Perhaps I have used this ploy once too often, since she never believes me anymore for some reason. So, yet another list inevitably arrives in my email box. At this point, I hang myself, or at least try. The damn rope inevitably breaks . . . I really need to go on a diet.

My favorite Karen story, however, involves the time she introduced me as I was about to give a talk. I no longer recall the topic, but it was a Wisconsin audience of mostly family extension agents whom I believe had some connection with the university. In any case, the overwhelming majority were women. It started off all right. She had gone through my CV and counted all the talks I had given. She was impressed. I was stunned. The number was impressive by anyone's standards. Suddenly I felt tired. It was a partial list after all since who could recall them all? I stopped listing them after that. Anyways, Karen loved the onion piece that I bragged about earlier at some length. For this introduction, and loving props that illustrated her point, she had brought along some fake onions that she wanted to use. That was okay. Then she tried to say something about how I carried them around all the time in my pants pocket. Uh-uh!

It was at that point that things went downhill. She began to describe a bulge in my pocket that somehow came out as if I was, indeed, quite a very well-endowed male. If you knew Karen, you would know she was clueless. She is very innocent and sweet. By now, though, the audience was howling though I could tell she had no clue as to why. Nothing I was to say would top that introduction, but I was pleased when several women later pressed their telephone numbers into my hand. Karen finally got it later in the day when a male colleague of hers gently explained how he would have been fired on the spot if he had made the same remarks. Since then I have asked Karen to write "for a great time, call Tom at . . ." in various women's rest rooms but she flatly refuses.

I saw FIS as a natural complement to the Peer Assistance Network concept. FIS had a different target audience, state legislators. WELPAN focused on state executive agency folk. Of course, there were differences in structure and protocols. Yet, there were many similarities as well.

Both efforts turned "ownership" over to their target audience. Karen is guided by a legislative advisory committee . . . the agenda of the WELPAN group was determined by the members. Both provided members with a safe venue. Karen has done her best to keep the press away. In WELPAN, we had a strict policy of what was said in the room stayed in the room, unless everyone agreed to make something public. Parts of meetings were off-limits to outsiders when sensitive topics were being discussed. Both stress an objective approach to the deliberations, striving for education, not advocacy. If either target audience even smelled an agenda, these experiments in communication would have ended quickly. Both worked to bring rigorous, objective analytic work to the target audiences. I suspect the WELPAN audience was a bit more knowledgeable about available research and could often select their resource people while Karen expended more energy in searching for and then screening potential FIS presenters. In the end, both of us suggested resource folks we trusted and who were considered good communicators.

My feeling was that both the WELPAN and FIS audiences prized the "honest broker." Both are bombarded with information all the time. Much of that input is biased in one way or another. Decisionmakers do not have time to sort through the blistering maze of material, nor sort out which document or report is worth reading and which is not. FIS does the sorting and recomposing of the messages in a way accessible to the intended audience. The legislators and their staff are exposed to the policy nuggets without having to wade through reams of methodological detritus. Most importantly, they got the material in several formats, so they could both digest it and vet it with their peers. For example, research summaries and policy recommendations are made available in audio formats so that legislators can listen as they ride to and from the state capitol and their home districts.

WELPAN did the same thing. It gave members an opportunity to be exposed to information in a safe environment. Typically, they were not hustled with obvious agendas and, if they were, there was ample opportunity to sort things out. They had the luxury to absorb and vet any input with their peers and with the so-called experts themselves. There was plenty of time for give and take.

The policy relevance of a new idea could be examined in detail with consideration of local variations in context and settings being discussed. Perceived problems that might inhibit serious consideration could be addressed adequately.

Both FIS and WELPAN-type initiatives performed one remarkable service. Both made rigorous information accessible to policy audiences. This was not always academic work, but it generally was work that would pass scientific muster. The question remains, why do we even need special strategies for accomplishing this end? Why don't members of the academy do a better job of bringing their work and insights to those who might use their knowledge in practical ways?

Karen and I write about this failure in our book, *Evidence Based Policymaking: Lessons from policy-minded researchers and research-minded policymakers.* You are more than welcome to peruse this 300-plus page work for the full story on how the academy has failed the policy world (see resources at end for more detail). We need the royalties. We have also written several articles that build on our underlying theory.

The bottom line is that there is a fundamental disconnect across the cultures of these two worlds. Each person absorbs core assumptions about one's professional role, preconceptions about how the world works, signals for how to behave, and guidelines for how to treat others. I see the differences in many places. I would look at journal articles written for policy-minded outlets.

Over time, they increasingly became more sophisticated in terms of technique and methods which is fine. However, many of these would end with a section on policy implications that borders on the laughable. You can just imagine the author or authors struggling mightily to get the methods and analysis straight and then dashing off something about the meaning of their results for the real world in a few minutes before hitting the send button to the journal editors.

I personally would love going back and forth between conferences in the real world and conferences in the academy, simply to experience the contrast in styles. In the real world, presenters would use a power point with clear, concise statements that summarizes the findings succinctly and carefully draws out the application of those findings. There would be a discussion about methods but only enough to convince the listener that the numbers were not generated from a crystal ball or on the back of an envelope. Most importantly, speakers would talk with sufficient clarity to be understood, almost as if communication were an important element of their presentation. How delightful.

Perhaps it has changed now but, in the past, this would be my experience when attending the IRP Summer Workshops for the high-tech researchers. Not all that long ago, the speakers would still be throwing up transparencies with columns of coefficients representing various data runs while talking at breakneck speed as if one breath would allow a critic in the audience to pounce on some real or imagined error. They seldom got to the application part of their talk as fights would break out over how one or more equations had been specified. Demonstrating their technical *bonafides* seemed far more important than what the research results were or how they might be applied. I could never escape the sense that the search for truth played a secondary role to engaging in technical one-upmanship.

I am engaging in hyperbole with the above example, and not all academic conferences were remotely like this, but there is some truth here. If you are in the policy world, which can be distinguished from the political world, you prize certain things. You want input that is clear, concise, and available before the end of time. The input should be based or rigorous methods, but these methods are only a means to an end, not the end itself. You want declarative sentences that communicate something clearly. You want to know how the information might be used. And you want honesty where necessary caveats are acknowledged without reservation.

If, on the other hand, you are in the knowledge-producing world, methods are what count, the message is secondary. Interactions are often based on a one-upmanship designed to demonstrate who the sharpest pencil in the pencil box or the brightest bulb on the marquee might be. Obfuscation, or leaving the audience puzzled, is too often seen as a virtue and not a vice. Time, of course, is not much of a concern since the pursuit of truth is timeless.

If you followed a young man or woman who stayed in the academy all through their professional training and landed in a research university at the end of the road, what would you find? Most likely you would find someone who had few clues about how to talk with a policy person. Moreover, they would see few reasons why they should bother. You would have a person who would, if given a choice between curing cancer and publishing a peer-reviewed article in some obscure journal, would chose the latter in a heartbeat. You would get a person who, if given the choice between spending an afternoon talking with officials about the applicability of their findings or spending that afternoon running just a few more estimates that will not substantively change the outcomes of their research, will chose the second option without a moment's hesitation. You will find someone who is further and further self-contained within their own small, theoretical world and see absolutely no problem with their isolation or with the character of the larger institutional norms that shape their world view.

I watched what happened at IRP over the decades. When I first got there, faculty from the economics department played a big role in the institution. Now, I cannot think of one full-time economics faculty member who plays an instrumental role in the workings of the institute. The engaged affiliates located on the campus are associated with Social Work, the Public Policy School, and other more applied disciplines. When Karen looked around for a faculty successor as head of PINFIS, particularly as she headed toward retirement, she came up empty. One likely successor seemed to be on board until that potential successor asked one day if talking a lot with legislators was a requirement for the position. It is, of course, and she immediately lost interest.

When I was at ASPE, the people looking for evidence would seldom turn to the academy. This was still true even though the reform effort was run by Harvard-based academics. Instead, they would turn to the evaluation firms and think-tanks that now dot the D.C. landscape. What if they did call an academic? Here is what they would have heard: "Well, that is a good question. I just might have a graduate student who could look at it next semester. Or if I get some support, we can have a response to you in three years." "Three years," my ASPE colleague would think, "but I was hoping for some feedback by EOBD (end of business day) tomorrow afternoon." Again, hyperbole to make a point!

The policy world moves in real time, the academic world operates in a timeless world where the pursuit of truth obeys no clock. My ASPE colleagues probably wanted a best, well considered guess but that is not what you are trained to do in the academy. Science does not operate that way. It is not that one world is right and the other is wrong, they are simply different.

I could labor on about certain blind spots on the policy side of the ledger. They also have cultural blinders that make them poor communicators to academics whom they often avoid based on assumptions that are not always accurate. But perhaps I should bring this chapter to a close. Besides, it is more fun to pick on my peers in the academy. They really offer themselves as easy targets for a bit of good natured ridicule.

PINFIS (now called the Family Impact Institute) has been transferred to Purdue University along with the foundation resources that sustain it. Karen never found a faculty member to take over her role nor did she ever get real support from the administration at UW until they were lobbied hard by some powerful people on Karen's national board. The university finally is stepping up to support the Wisconsin seminars. It took a while, and some head-bashing, but they did get (I think) that this helps improve the campus's image on the other end of State Street. As noted, Karen has a national advisory board that includes current and former top power players in Wisconsin (and elsewhere). They were literally shocked at the university's initial indifference to the fate of the Wisconsin seminars as was I. I thought the university missed a huge opportunity to support a worthwhile program that could help its tattered image in the legislature.

Karen and I started our book on evidence-based policy making with one of my favorite vignettes. It was the lunch break at some conference, again, which one has long faded from memory. Larry Aber, an excellent researcher into early childhood issues who was then at Columbia, asked my second favorite Republican Ron Haskins what role research played in policy making in Washington at least. "Five percent," Ron replied, "maybe 10 percent at the most. I will tell you what counts in Washington. It is values and power." The researchers at the table were a bit crestfallen. Several years later, Haskins wrote that the role research played in policy decisions at the federal level had fallen to 1 percent. Apparently, things are getting worse. The researchers that were at the lunch table would now be suicidal given his reassessment of the value of their contributions to the public good.

From my perspective, Ron is right. As a member of the academy, you cannot assume you can walk in and bowl over policymakers with your intellect and your evidence. You need to walk in their shoes for a while, see how they view the world. You must feel, just a bit, the pressures and influences and rewards that shape their environment. Learn to speak their language, if you will. You can reach policymakers. It is not a hopeless endeavor. Hell, I did it and I don't have many friends, other than the ones I rent from 'Friends-R-US.' It just takes a bit of effort and, of course, you must care about their world and what they do.

I spent a lot of time in the real world. Did I get bruised from time to time? You bet, but I also learned a lot. The real world remains one of the treasured corners of my candy store and a source of so much of what I have learned. Some of the candy found in each counter in my store came directly from dipping my toes into the shark-infested waters of the real-world. Of course, I always kept my eyes out for those sharks. They will jump up and bit you in the behind.

CHAPTER 8

TO SEE THINGS, YOU HAVE TO GO OUT AND LOOK

The trouble with the world is that the stupid are

cocksure and the intelligent are full of doubt.

—*Bertrand Russell*

The title of this chapter is quite recognizable as one of Yogi Berra's famous malapropisms. Of course, I might have said something just as stupid myself. He was born so much earlier than I, however. It is most likely, therefore, that he said it first.

In a loose way, this is a chapter about epistemology or about how we know things. That is a rather odd subject for someone who still cannot figure out the duration of the boat captain's lunch break, a classic high school algebra torture. You must remember those classic exercises employed to destroy teen minds. They went something like this: the river is flowing one way at a given rate while his craft is moving the opposite way at another known speed while a buffeting wind is diagonally impeding the craft at x mph.

Given all this, how long does the captain take to finish his lunch? That is how all these puzzles looked to me. I was so clueless in the face of this high school plot to destroy my sanity that I titled a recent book of mine *The Boat Captain's Conundrum*. By now, you should be sick of hearing about my abject failure at basic high school algebra. Clearly, I am a bit obsessed by this deficit in my talent repertoire though, oddly enough, this affliction has never kept me from discoursing on weighty issues.

Moving on, this is a drama in four acts. The first covers my involvement in the social indicators movement that flared anew in the early 1990s. The second act touches upon my participation in a frontal attack on the official poverty measure, a task that obviously needs to be done and yet remains just beyond our reach. The third discusses my participation on the National Academy of Sciences expert panel of research methods for evaluating welfare reform. Yes, even the slowest of us can rise to lofty heights. The final act describes my more general assault on what I saw as the deficiencies of our research methods given the rapidly changing landscape of social assistance at the turn of the century.

As I noted earlier, it is difficult to pinpoint when and how I started constructing some of the counters in my candy store. I believe I started on this counter with a phone call from Robert Haveman one fine morning. He asked, "What do you know about social indicators, Tom?" I told him I knew nothing and hoped that would be the end of it. "I'm going to have someone drop some stuff off for you to look at, okay?" The words "what about the word nothing did you not understand, Bob?" were on the tip of my tongue when he hung up.

This is where I always make a mistake. I can never quite get past my people pleasing weakness. So, I resigned myself to looking at whatever he had for me to peruse. Within minutes I heard a thud outside my door. This scheme obviously had been well planned. When a sigh of resignation, I looked to discover a box containing an assortment of reports and documents, the accomplice in Bob's plan clearly felt spasms of guilt and had already escaped from my view. Upon cursory review, I discovered that each publication employed an assortment of social indicators to assess the condition of various jurisdictions, large and small. It looked interesting but so what! My deeper suspicion was that Bob simply was cleaning out his office.

Soon enough, the box of free reports was followed up by a suggestion from Bob that I solicit a planning grant to initiate a project for generating a status report on Wisconsin's children. Obviously, no one else at the university wanted to do this. At such times, I would wonder why I never even got a chance to draw a short straw and thereby escape such missions that others clearly were avoiding. My only understanding of what a "status report" might look like came from this pile of reports Bob had someone dump in front of my door. Some of these documents dated back to the 70s, the 1870s that is, though many had seductive covers printed in glossy colors. Still, it started to look a bit intriguing to me. Even then, I did not have much of a life. Besides, I had begun to realize that big things can start with small beginnings.

As I pondered the task, I considered that we had been living through a demographic earthquake. The number of children in single-parent homes had risen from about 8 percent in 1960 to over 25 percent in the early 1990s. Births to unmarried women had increased from 5 percent to about 30 percent over the same period. Some 70 percent of teen births were to unmarried mothers, up from 15 percent in 1960. The foster care population was exploding, jumping by some 60 percent in the several years after 1985.

People were looking around in alarm. Is our civilized world lurching toward chaos and the abyss? Probably not, but perhaps we ought to be looking more closely at what was happening just in case. After all, you could get updates on what the equity markets were doing all day long. My smart phone (the irony of my having a smart phone is not lost on me) has me in touch with stock quotes from around the world on a real-time basis. If that is the case, why don't we collect at least rough data routinely on our children whom we widely advertise as our most precious resource? So, I started down the road on a modest quest . . . to see if we (me?) should do a status report on Wisconsin's children.

Within a year, I forged a collaborative effort between IRP and the Wisconsin Council on Children and Families (WCCF) to secure small amounts of financial support from several Wisconsin foundations and from the University itself, no small victory getting the tight-fisted university to kick in. I recall that Tom Loftus, our intrepid child support champion in the Wisconsin legislature, had by now become part of this scheme. He recently had lost a bid to be governor against Tommy Thompson and was now unemployed.

The two of us hit many funding possibilities. I recall a visit to a friend of his who was running for U.S. Senate in the Democratic Party primary race. This candidate was running for the seat that Russ Feingold ultimately was to win. The odd thing is that I wound up doing two morning long briefings for Russ and his top campaign staff. These briefings took place rather early in his campaign when no one was giving Russ a chance. Though blazing smart, being a Rhodes scholar, he had little money and was thought of as a Madison liberal, a quality that did not always play well outstate. In truth, it never played well outstate.

It turns out that I was the only egg head willing to put in some time with him when his prospects looked so bleak. After he won, we would periodically run into each other on the Friday night Midwest Express flights back to Madison...a popular method for getting home among those who spent half their lives in D.C. He would hail me as his welfare guy, occasionally sitting next to me on the flight. I recall one flight where we discussed how the welfare reform wars were playing out. We both agreed that reform was not yet the unmitigated disaster it would eventually become. I found it unusually rewarding to discuss policy with a politician who is smart and cares. Russ tried to recapture his Senate seat, which he lost during the 2010 debacle for the Democrats. I saw him at a campaign event in 2016, another disastrous year for Democratic candidates, as he tried to wrest his old seat from an unreconstructed Tea Party advocate but unfortunately failed. He yet fondly recalled those long-ago briefings of mine that took place during far better times.

Anyways, this other candidate was on the phone that day during Russ's successful run for the seat, calling potential campaign donors. He tried to take a break to chat with Loftus, but his handler was clearly annoyed and kept pushing him to get back to the calls. There is no break from the 24/7 grind of raising campaign money, not even to help poor children. This is another reason I could never have run for public office even though the man who was to become the majority leader in the Wisconsin Assembly seriously asked me to run for political office when I was a young man. He was serious! Shockingly, my political suitor was a smart, educated man who sported an MA from the Kennedy School of Public Policy at Harvard. He should have known better. What the hell was he thinking?

I could never do that no matter who asked. You need to prostitute yourself on a continuing basis to raise money. If I beg for money it will be for a good reason, like a big yacht for me or something equally egregious. The bigger reason for my reluctance to run is that you had to be nice to people, or so I thought at the time. I don't like people. The biggest reason is my awful personality. I could never put up with all the whiners that want everything but never want to pay any taxes. I am sure I would be jailed for whacking some idiot upside the head when they cheesed me off while making totally stupid points.

We also visited Senator Herb Kohl, a multimillionaire businessman and, until his retirement, a popular senator from Wisconsin. Despite his wealth and very public persona, he had to be just about the most reserved and shy man you could imagine. Trying to engage him in small talk was painful as Loftus and I worked our way around to the topic of whether one of the Kohl family foundations might kick in a few bucks for our worthy cause. We handed him a written summary of the plans to monitor how Wisconsin's kids were doing. He crumpled our inspiring plans up in his hands before beating a hasty retreat to his inner office.

I mentioned this to a colleague back at IRP whose husband worked for Herb for a while. She laughed. "You should have asked him about the Milwaukee Bucks," she told me. At the time, Herb was an owner of the professional basketball team in Milwaukee, and apparently that is the one topic he could become animated about. Despite his severe shyness, I thought he was a very good senator.

In short order, we put a funding package together. The WISKIDS initiative was launched as a joint venture by the IRP and the Wisconsin Council on Children and Families (WCCF), a Madison-based advocacy organization for children. Over the next several years, this initiative produced several products—brief bulletins on selected topics, special reports such as a detailed look at schoolchildren in Madison, and the statewide KIDS COUNT report that is perhaps the signature product of the Casey Foundation.

Perhaps the best outcome was that we lured Tom Kaplan back to Wisconsin and to IRP. Tom had been a highly respected state worker who found it increasingly difficult to work in the Wisconsin bureaucracy as the institutional culture changed from a program focus to a more political focus. He had found refuge teaching at a small Pennsylvania college when I called him to see if he would return to help us with WISKIDS. I am not sure I finished the call when I heard a click on the line. He was racing to catch a flight back to Madison. Apparently, teaching kids at some backwater college was not a dream come true. He later took over as associate director of IRP when I stepped down.

Virtually from day one of the WISKIDS effort, I sensed that the state of the art with respect to indicators of child well-being was quite primitive. Those doing this work were aware that the existing data sources were insufficient for the task at hand, as were the extant approaches for using those data. Eventually, I concluded that IRP should initiate a more concerted effort to address the larger set of technical and substantive issues related to producing and using these indicators. After several of the annual publications, it was clear that WCCF could produce the WISKIDS report without our help, perhaps better in fact. Either that or they thought I cost too much and decided that a monkey could do the job just as well. The smart money is on the monkey theory. Besides, I always lose interest as anything becomes a more-or-less routine task. I could never stand boredom.

I was more attracted to the broader challenges of improving the use of social indicators. The frustrations and constraints of producing a status-of-children report are several. You are always walking a fine line between description and advocacy. Every step in the process, the selection of indicators, mode of presentation, choice of baseline or comparison data, is partly subjective and thus vulnerable to second guessing. Just think how controversial the assessment of school performance has become. Critics rant about the impossibility of really getting at the value-added component of a school or group of teachers. How do you really account for uneven starting positions and overwhelming contextual impediments or advantages? You can always statistically control for some things, but do you get them all? Now, apply those same doubts and concerns to measures of how well communities or states are doing.

While some purveyors of indicators have a transparent advocacy agenda, others strive to dispassionately portray the condition of children. The latter, despite their proclivities toward objectivity, recognize that their choices about data selection and presentation may well shape subsequent interpretations in unintended ways. In short, I could not help but notice that there were few accepted standards for choosing and displaying data in this emerging field of social indicators.

The temptation to slip from the goal of informing society about social conditions to influencing current policy debates is ever present. For example, data often were arrayed in scorecard fashion—ordinal rankings of states or counties from best to worst. The implication was that jurisdictions at the bottom were losers. They should do more or at least do something different. When viewed more closely, the real meaning of such rankings is less clear. Are the favorably ranked jurisdictions working harder at protecting their kids or do they simply have fewer problems to address in the first place? Culpability, it turns out, is a slippery notion. Making such determinations demand a more rigorous analysis than the mere publication of available data typically provide.

The inevitable desire to assign meaning to descriptive data leads us to inappropriately assign blame or praise in some evaluative sense. If births to unmarried teens increase, then it must be the failure of (pick one or more) the schools, the federal government, Democrats or Republicans or Independents, television, working mothers and permissive fathers, or good old "rock and roll." Looking at temporal trends and casually assigning causality is very seductive but extremely hazardous. We all know that correlation is not causation yet most of us forget this simple fact when data trends comport with our theoretical or normative priors.

In addition, available social indicators, at the time, tended to rely on what was available. Thus, indicators tended to cluster in certain domains of child well-being that often covaried with one another. Other important areas were underrepresented or ignored all together. Still other measures were confounded with supply versus demand problems. If kids in foster care went up, is it because more kids were in trouble (a bad thing) or more foster care slots suddenly appeared (perhaps a good thing)? Similar issues arise when reports of child abuse and neglect trended upward in an exponential fashion as they had in the not too distant past. Was society going to hell in a hand basket (bad) or were teachers and nurses and neighbors being more attentive to the well-being of children within their purview and taking actions to protect them (good). The number of people incarcerated in America increased from 300,000 to some 2.3 million over several decades. We now have one-quarter of all prisoners world-wide with only 5 percent of the population. What happened? Has society broken down, was it our get tough on crime approach that included harsh and mandatory sentences, perhaps a way of controlling urban minorities, or merely a growing demand for paying customers as we transitioned toward private, for-profit prisons. Take your pick.

I pondered such mysteries at the time, and many more, largely because I had such a boring life and policy mysteries always amuse me. Perhaps I ponder them because the answers, if I were to stumble on any, might do a bit of good down the road as well. That, however, might be taking a rose-colored view of things. All this struck me as another adventure and I started looking around for more allies, particularly since I was not conversant in the technical data issues surrounding the collection of indicators. Robert Hauser, then director of IRP and a superb scholar and researcher, was an enthusiastic supporter of this idea.

Bob Hauser and I visited Nicholas Zill in 1992. Nick then headed Child Trends, a respected research organization in D.C. We discussed the issues we believed needed addressing and reached an agreement that the time was right to push the social indicator agenda. Ah yes, another windmill at which to tilt my flagging policy lance! It turns out that the next year, by the summer of 1993, I was at ASPE attacking that other windmill . . . welfare reform. It was a good year for futile gestures. My location in D.C. was convenient for pulling together a team to push the indicator agenda. A planning team of IRP affiliates, staff from ASPE, and scholars from Child Trends (Kris Moore by then had replaced Nick Zill as CEO) put together a plan. I just love plans though typically I am less eager about carrying them out.

Anyways, I helped lay out three national conferences to be held over the next three years. I always jumped at the chance to organize such fun activities since I knew I was not important enough to get invited on my own. The first would bring together a small number of important individuals in what would amount to a planning workshop on indicators of children's well-being. The second would be a more ambitious and in-depth effort to bring together the best expertise available to focus on the issues identified in the planning workshop. The final session would be action-oriented, concentrating on legislative and resource issues necessary to translate the desire for a comprehensive set of indicators into reality.

The band of co-conspirators had grown. Added to the mix were experts such as Jeffrey Evans from the Center for Population Research, Deborah Phillips, director of the Board on Children and Families at the National Academy of Sciences, William O'Hare, associate director of the Kids Count project at the Casey foundation, and the ubiquitous Wendell Primus. We drew a host of top scholars from many disciplines and perspective to systemically examine how a comprehensive array of indicators might be put together while dealing with numerous technical and logistical impediments. It was a herculean task, but the scholars went at it with gusto. The work produced some two hundred measures covering many distinct domains. It was a scholar's delight and a number cruncher's nirvana. It is one thing to come up with a measure in the abstract, quite another to use it in the real world.

I think that the surrounding policy environment added urgency to the agenda. There was a lot of talk about further devolution of social policy to the states, particularly after 1994 when Republicans took over the House of Representatives. If that were to come about, the classic ways in which program oversight was exercised would be eviscerated. Narrow, categorical programs for helping the poor were very visible. You pretty much knew how many child care slots there were or how many kids got a certain vaccination.

When dozens of distinct programs are lumped together into broad funding streams with substantial control being given over to states and even local authorities, the picture can cloud over immediately. Planning flexibility and fungible dollars could be a force for extreme good or unmitigated evil. How would the good people in Washington know what was happening to vulnerable kids and why? A comprehensive set of social indicators collected in reasonably efficient fashion and used to monitor population health and well-being would be a great start toward ensuring program accountability, detect positive or negative trends, and serve the "canary in the mine shaft" function. This last function can be thought of as an early warning mechanism that problems were emerging, and some proactive actions were possibly required.

I began collaborating with people like Kris Moore and Brett Brown from Child Trends, the late Bill Prosser (ASPE) and Matt Stagner (now at Mathematica) and others. With support from the PEW Trust, we went to work. I recall working with Kris and Brett on one paper where I laid out a conceptual framework for thinking about the use of indicators. I wanted to communicate a simple but often overlooked reality that a number is just a number until you put it in context. Kris, for one, loved the framework I came up with and used it often over the next few years.

Take one measure, any measure. The meaning is not resident in the number itself but in how it is used. I laid out an ordinal scale of sorts. You could use a piece of data for *descriptive* purposes. For that limited use, not a great deal of attention or focus might be required. But let us say you use it for *monitoring* purposes. Then you might think about taking some action if, let us say, a time series suggests an adverse trend in these data. In that case, you might want to take more care in both the quality of these data and in subsequent interpretation. Say, however, you kick the same measure up to the *accountability* level of use. Now you are intending to use that measure in specific ways to reward or punish based on which way the data go when compared to some established standard or against the comparative performance of others. Now, collection and interpretation issues are paramount, and much care must be given to these factors. It can be very easy to game indicators when the stakes get this high. Some have discussed both the lure of this use and the attendant difficulties as the *metric fixation*. Finally, you might use a measure to make *causal* inferences. While people do this all the time, this is a hazardous venture to be done only with extreme care. You must be able to account for all other explanations for any observed trend, a scientific demand which is not easily satisfied.

On a more practical level, I and others kept pushing the broader indicator agenda. In December of 1995, we brought together over fifty members of state and federal agencies and others concerned with the well-being of children. In 1996, I lent some assistance to a twelve-state project on state-level child outcomes that was launched largely under the aegis of the Administration of Children and Families (ACF). The goal of this effort was to continue the momentum that was building and to work toward a consistent terminology, toward a consensus set of child outcomes, and toward agreed upon measurement tools for assessing how children were doing as policy devolved toward the states.

When I became acting director of IRP, I noticed that our prior work to generate all these excellent measures with a host of scholars had never been formally published as a book which we had intended to do all along. So, I beat the drums and got Bob Hauser, Bill Prosser, and Brett Brown to edit a comprehensive work titled *Indicators of Child Well-Being*, the compendium of social measures for our generation. I anointed Betty Evanson, our indefatigable editor at IRP, to set the ball in motion. Since I was running this show from behind the scenes I should have attached my name this final product but that was not my thing. For one thing, I was already pursuing other policy windmills. For another, self-promotion is not my style. In ways I discuss later, these decisions cost me professionally. Still, I did write the preface for the volume.

All this activity and dialogue possibly had some effect at the highest levels of government. On April 21, 1997, President Clinton issued an executive order, "Protection of Children from

Environmental Health Risks and Safety Risks." Among other things, the order established a four-year, cabinet level task force to recommend federal strategies for children's environmental health and safety; and to prepare a biennial report on research, data, and other information that would enhance the government's ability to respond to risks to children. The order also required that the Office of Management and Budget convene an interagency federal forum on child and family statistics. Its purpose is to produce an annual report on the most important indicators of child well-being in the United States. The last time I looked the report was still being produced.

I want to make one thing clear. I had little or nothing to do to do with the executive order. But in the policy world, things often work in circuitous ways. You nudge and prod and nibble around the edges, and suddenly something happens. Maybe you had something to do with it, maybe not. You never know! When in doubt, I like to take credit. As I often note, when I went to India in 1967 as a Peace Corps volunteer, the country was importing grains to feed its people. When I left two years later, it was a grain exporter. I like to take credit for the turnaround. Numbers don't lie after all. Okay, thy don't lie when you like them.

Now let us switch to Act 2 in our drama which also starts with a phone call. I was contacted by Mike Laracy, who was with the Annie E. Casey Foundation, and by Jennifer Phillips, who was with the Mott Foundation at the time. Included in this four-way conversation was Gary Burtless of the Brookings Institution. As best I can recall, Mike and Jennifer were interested in finding ways to make poverty a front-burner issue again. This was the 90s and everyone was focused on dependency. Could we help them out? Sounded good to me! I am in the poverty business. I never worried that we would end poverty, but the specter of people not caring any more about the issue was another matter entirely.

Somehow, Gary and I turned that original concern into a project to update the poverty measure itself. In my eyes, this was a natural extension of the indicator work I had been doing. After all, how many times have we all used the old bromide "you get what you measure?" The official measure sucked. Everyone knew it. It could be that improving the measure was what Mike and Jennifer wanted all along, but I don't recall that being the case. Unmi Song (Joyce Foundation) probably would be firing me again, probably on a weekly basis, but Mike and Jennifer were quite accepting of my tendency to wander off script.

Our official measure of poverty went back to the onset of Johnson's WOP. The generals of that war needed to define the enemy. The task fell to a mid-level bureaucrat in the Social Security administration named Molly Orshansky. She took an old study which estimated that food represented one-third of a poor families' budget. Then she grabbed a more recent estimate of the cost of a minimal basket of food necessary to keep a family of four going. She multiplied that figure by three and there you had it . . .

a poverty measure for the ages. All you needed was an equivalency scale to adjust for different family sizes and a way to update it over time like changes in the Consumer Price Index (CPI). *Voila!* Her statistical child probably represented fifteen minutes of work on her part.

Of course, our conference call took place some three decades later. Much had changed by then while the only big changes to the official poverty lines were minor technical adjustments. Now, however, food represented about one-seventh of a typical family's budget and considerably less than a third of even the poorest families' expenditures. Moreover, we now had many more in-kind transfer programs whose resources were not even counted as income in calculating the official poverty rate. And what about cost-of-living differentials! You mean we used the same poverty line in New York City as we did Mayberry, North Carolina? Even my dog, Rascal, knows that is nonsensical and he still poops on the rug.

I mean, really, how hard would it be to update the damn thing and at least use a halfway decent measure to assess something so vital to society? The answer is that it would be very hard indeed. Ideological and partisan conflict now was making everything virtually impossible. But that did not mean we would not bang our heads against the wall for a while trying to get around the paralysis that had crept into my craft. Insanity, according to Einstein (or maybe Freud or was it Aristotle?) is doing the same thing repeatedly and getting the same rotten result. Uh-uh, I do believe I resemble that remark!

It goes without saying that we were not the first to see a problem here. A National Academy panel had been formed in the early 1990s which published a reasoned report on the topic in 1995. The problem, as we saw it, was that reports get published all the time and then nothing happens. It gets some press coverage and then some desultory comments pro and con before disappearing in the wake of another scandal involving the Kardashian sisters. Gary and I decided to establish a venue for those most interested in advancing a better, updated measure and to get some smart people working toward that end. We hoped to keep the momentum toward change gong.

When the project started, I had recalled seeing Gary at conferences and workshops over the years but did not know him all that well. He struck me, even upon these cursory interactions, as an extremely smart guy. I sometimes wondered how I got to work with these brilliant guys and gals, the ones who everyone in school would point to and say, "That one will be president someday or maybe find a cure for cancer." I think the same kids pointed at me to say, "That schmuck will be doing twenty to life for being too stupid to breathe." Come to think of it, though he could not have been that bright, he really liked the wage bill study I had done years before, at least according to Sheldon Danziger.

Anyways, I noticed a pattern when we would chat on the phone. He would start off monosyllabic, as if my call had interrupted some deep thought or analysis that had him on the brink of a creative breakthrough. I was always tempted to stop and tell him I would call back later, when he could focus better. But then he would start to respond. Soon, we were going back and forth at breakneck speed deciding on future strategies or what needed to be done. And then, suddenly, he would say something like "gotta go now," and the conversation would be over just as I was about to go on to my next point.

I was flying out to Washington the day that the edition of *USA Today* came out naming me the national poverty expert. Notice how I have woven this very unimpressive accolade into the narrative in several places. I picked up a copy at the airport and brought it to a meeting I had scheduled with Gary and Wendell Primus. I showed them the story, assuming they were more the *Washington Post* or *New York Times* sorts and likely had missed this breaking news story with film at eleven. I would characterize both men as being on the serious side, but this piece of news left them doubled over in laughter. I don't believe the New York Times picked up on this earth-shattering event. Go figure!

The litany of problems identified by the NAS panel and others went something like this. Among other things, the official measure:

> *Excludes in-kind benefits, such as food stamps and housing assistance, when counting family income.*

Ignores the cost of earning income, including child care costs, when calculating the net income available to families with working members.

Disregards regional variation in the cost of living, especially the cost of housing, in determining a family's consumption needs.

Ignores direct tax payments, such as payroll and income taxes, when measuring family income.

Ignores differences in health insurance coverage in determining family income, and medical care needs in determining family consumption needs.

Moreover, the official measure has never been updated to account for the changing consumption patterns of U.S. households. I noted earlier that expenditures for food accounted for about one-third of family income in the 1950s (as Orshansky had estimated in her back of the envelope calculation) but they now account for as little as one seventh of such outlays. While subjective estimates of a reasonable poverty threshold (based on polling data) were very close to the line Orshansky drew up in the early 1960s, Americans now deemed the line much too low according to representative survey data tapping their subjective impression of how much it took for various prototypical families to get by at a minimal level.

Several essential remedies were clearly required. We needed to change the measure of income, alter the poverty threshold, and update the survey used to determine the percentage and distribution of the poor. As we moved forward on these tasks, and others, we brought in all the heavy hitters involved in the poverty measure debate. This included Bobbi Wolfe (IRP director), Dan Weinberg (U.S. Census Bureau), Bill Hoagland (U.S. Senate Budget Committee), Katherine Willman (Office of Management and Budget), David Betson (University of Notre Dame), Allan Scherm (Mathematica Inc.), Cynthia Taeuber and Charles Alexander (both from the Census Bureau), Tony McCann and David McMillen (House staff members), and Ron Haskins just to name a few. We held workshops, commissioned technical work, and held larger conferences. The most frantic period of effort was over the 1998 calendar year.

We generally attacked the problem on two levels. First, there were numerous details to be worked out. I never heard so much discussion of Out-Of-Pocket Medical Expenses or OOPME in my life or how variations in housing costs might be used for calculating differences in living costs across increasingly smaller jurisdictional areas. Good old Molly developed the original measure in an afternoon. Our brain trust was struggling mightily in a miasma of technical conundrums. For a big picture guy like I pretended to be, this was a level of minutia that had me nodding off at times.

The political battle was the second line of attack. We were not naïve though perhaps just a smidge overly optimistic. We had all been around the track several times and knew this was not an easy sell. Therefore, we moved ahead very cautiously. We agreed that any new measure would only be used for statistical purposes. That is, any new threshold would not be used to allocate funds or determine eligibility for program benefits. Just think if the poverty thresholds were raised and suddenly millions of additional people suddenly became eligible for government help. Second, we would try to massage the details of any new measure so that the number of poor would approximate the number found under the old measure in some reference year, say 1992. This was a major concession but would provide some continuity to the numbers in the short term but then allow them to vary in the future.

But even these accommodations would not be enough. I recall a presentation by a very smart analyst from the Bureau of Labor Statistics. He pointed out that under a likely new set of poverty measure thresholds the distribution of poverty across the country would change dramatically even if the aggregate number for the whole country were the same as under the old measure. Basically, the number of poor on the east and west coasts would increase while the number in the middle would fall. You could argue that this new-fangled measure was only for statistical purposes, but would you be believed? Governors on the coasts would soon scream that they were now at risk of being screwed in terms of federal support since they now had more poor people but might not get enough federal help to deal with them. Those in the middle would scream about some liberal plot to shift federal resources to the heathens living near the two oceans and deprive them of the necessary resources to help their own destitute families. We would only please the number crunchers.

I can vividly recall a discussion I had with Ron Haskins on the issue. Ron, though a Republican, is a very thoughtful guy who loves evidence and approaches issues in a quite reasonable way. You might sense that I find the term "thoughtful Republican" an oxymoron. That is only because it is. In any case, he stonewalled me when I talked with him on the poverty measure issue. He would not budge. In fact, he would not even banter with me as he typically did, never calling me a Communist once during our conversation. I strongly suspected he knew he was responding politically rather than rationally and this bothered him deeply. It bothered me as well.

Another time I was attending the IRP Sumer Workshop. It was lunch time and I left the wonderful eighth floor conference room overlooking Lake Mendota with Tom McCurdy. Tom was a high-tech economist who also loved doing policy and often worked with the state of California from his Stanford faculty position. He was also quite conservative, but we got along famously. As we exited the room, I brought up the need to change the poverty measure. Tom pushed back. I held my ground and our voices elevated. He is a big man, even bigger than I am, and we groused back and forth until I noticed the other researchers taking a wide path around us. I knew Tom's bluster for what it was. It was simply the way he devastated his colleagues in the dismal science who made a methodological or econometric error in their work. He was never meek but, down deep, he remained a decent guy with a big heart. It was just his style. Still, I was afraid that some who did not know him as well as I feared he might floor me with a right cross to the jaw. People did get vexed on these issues.

As a last gesture, Gary Burtless, Barbara Wolfe, Wendell Primus, and I drafted a public statement setting out a reasonable set of principles for improving the official poverty measure. The principles we enunciated were developed and voted on at a conference we had convened in Madison. The attendees included many of the key stakeholders in the poverty measure debate. Unfortunately, we ran into a meeting space problem and used a conference hall located in the university hospital located on campus. While that was convenient for those who, by now, were sick to death of the topic, the real downside was that they had to eat food from the hospital cafeteria. Good thing medical help was so close.

We circulated our statement of principles among key academics and government officials around the country. The number who signed on represented a who's who of poverty researchers, political aficionados, and statistical measurement icons. Their prestigious reputations made the document a significant one indeed. Even years later, I remember getting contacted by Becky Blank, sometime before she became chancellor of the U.W. Madison campus, asking for a copy for some purpose or another. It is not that typical to get such a wide consensus from so many top people on any controversial policy question.

Did everyone jump on the bandwagon? No, not really. The official poverty measure is still with us and remains the standard for most policy and resource allocation purposes. At the same time, experts are now agreed on a set of alternative measures that are in wide use. They are routinely published by government agencies and are the preferred measures for analytic and scholarly uses. Some in the press are also cognizant of the new measures often using them in more serious pieces on the topic.

The poverty measure debate is emblematic of the paralysis that has consumed Washington. If people associated with one side of the normative and ideological debate suggest a change, the other side feels compelled to oppose it. It does not matter how reasonable the suggested change might be or how obvious is the need for change. There must be some political advantage somewhere even if it were not apparent. Obamacare was a concept first developed at the conservative American Enterprise Institute and implemented in Massachusetts by the governor who later would be the Republican candidate for president. When a Democratic president embraced it, suddenly it was evil incarnate spawned in Lucifer's lair. The political paralysis was never more apparent than after 2008 and Obama'a election. Republicans in Congress entered a pact to stonewall anything the new President did even if it would clearly benefit the country. Seizing power back took precedent over everything else.

In our earlier poverty measure debate it was never clear who would win and who would lose overall. A higher poverty threshold would lead to greater number of the poor, advantage liberals. Including excluded sources of income in the calculation of resources would result in lower poverty numbers, advantage conservatives. Of course, including in kind benefits in the calculation of resources might show a sharper drop in poverty from pre-transfer estimates to post-transfer estimates. This could advantage either side depending on how one views the world. Liberals might argue that the safety net works and should be further expanded. Conservatives might argue that the safety net works so well now that no further expansion is needed, maybe now we could even cut the net back a bit to give another tax break to the Koch brothers. As that old song says, the beat goes on.

Did we fail? This is hard to say. In doing policy, particularly those involving wicked social issues, there are few hard and fast victories. Failure can be equally elusive. Even debacles that appear definitive and irreversible don't always last. Still, I suspect we did have a substantive impact over the long haul.

I recall one large conference on the poverty measure topic that we scheduled to be at IRP, not in D.C. Washington insiders from Census and Labor Statistics and other such technical agencies arrived the night before and joined us for dinner at a local restaurant. At one point, I apologized for dragging them all out to Mad City (Madison's unofficial nickname), suggesting that they all could have gathered in D.C. with greater ease. One of them responded, "No, we couldn't. The truth is that it is not easy for us to meet in Washington. We would have to get permission from people higher up if there was a hint that policy decisions were being discussed. Then, all kinds of turf and politics would intrude. But we can get permission to attend an IRP sponsored meeting. That is safe. People assume we are merely discussing technical matters that no one cares about except us nerds, and that is seen as appropriate. This is a godsend for us." I spent enough time in D.C. to know better, but their plight never quite occurred to me before. I suspect my year there was a special time when the urgency of welfare reform overrode traditional turf concerns, at least for a while.

Again, we had prodded and pushed and nudged and got people together to exchange ideas and thereby motivate further progress. In the end, the world did move a little and that is a good thing. If we played a small role, so much the better! I do know that Mike Laracy gave a talk at IRP a while back. I was not there but colleagues told me that he mentioned that one of his first grants at the Casey Foundation was to IRP and Tom Corbett on the poverty measure issue. That gave me solace. He apparently did not see our work as a waste of the foundation's money to be deep sixed in the archive of pitiful foundation grants.

The third act in this drama involves my participation on an expert panel created to look at how we should evaluate national welfare reform. The panel, the resources for which were provided by ASPE, was created under the auspices of the National Academy of Sciences in 1998. Apparently, ASPE officials agreed that welfare reform was altering public assistance in such dramatic ways that new and creative thinking was required when we tried to assess what was happening.

Connie Citro from the NAS staff called and asked if I would be willing to serve. I did not even have to say, "I will call you back." Make no mistake, I was sure she meant to call some other Tom Corbett, but this promised to be fun, so I immediately took advantage of her error. I had been ruminating over these matters for some time during that period and this would give me an opportunity to muck things up on a larger scale, perhaps even bringing some prestigious co-conspirators into my nefarious web. And who knows, perhaps some of my tinkering on these evaluation questions described below had led to the creation of the panel in the first place. In any case, I dove right in not even bothering to see if there was water at the bottom of the pool.

The connection between science and the federal government, as represented by the National Academy of Sciences, goes back to the Civil War period. As iron clad vessels began to replace the traditional wooden ships, the ship captains discovered that their compasses were rather useless. It might strike you that this is not a good situation when people are shooting at you. The newly installed metal sides apparently impeded the compass needle from accurately seeking out the magnetic north pole. This surely would be a variable I would have to consider in estimating the length of the captain's lunch break, my old algebra nemesis. In any case, Abraham Lincoln asked some leading scientists to figure out what to do about this dilemma, and they did. The president was happy. The union boat captains were happy. The confederacy, however, was not so pleased.

The full title of our group was the "Panel on Data and Methods for Measuring the Effects of Changes in Social Welfare Programs." It was to be chaired by Robert Moffitt (Johns Hopkins) and staffed by Michele Ver Ploeg (NAS). The other members were John Adams (Rand), John Czajka (Mathematica Policy Research, Inc.), Kathryn Edin (then from Northwestern), Irwin Garfinkel (Columbia), Robert Goerge (U. of Chicago), Eric Hanushek (Hoover Institute and Stanford), V. Joseph Hotz (UCLA), Richard Kulka (Research Triangle Institute), Rebecca Maynard (U. of Pennsylvania), Susanne Randolph (U. of Maryland), and

Werner Schink (former head of welfare research for the state of California).

NAS panels are selected for balance in terms of politics, perspective, and approach to the subject matter. I could sense the rationale behind some of these selections. Adams, Kulka, and Goerge were big data guys. Edin was an ethnographer. Maynard and Czajka were program evaluators. Moffitt, Garfinkel, and Hotz were skilled economists with considerable program and policy knowledge. Hanushek came out of education and was considered an excellent analytical guy with conservative credentials, and so forth. I suspect I was selected for comic relief.

We were vetted carefully and had to fill out exhaustive questionnaires. Most of the details now escape me but I do recall queries about the sources of research support and current and prior professional affiliations. I recall thinking that I hope they don't chat with Tommy Thompson. If they had, my tenure on the panel would be short-lived indeed. In addition, no one apparently thought to mention that I undoubtedly had a file deep in an FBI vault somewhere due to my anti-war activities during my college days. Nor did anyone think to check with my high school algebra teacher. I recall writing on one algebra test the words *veni, vidi, flunki*. This was Latin for I came, I saw, I flunked, which paraphrased Caesar's summation upon his conquest of Gaul. The teacher of the class scrawled a one-word response across my exam paper: almost.

I was also told they wanted people who would be able to get along with one another. You spend a lot of time together, dealing with tough issues from varying perspectives. Arrogant loners or rank egotists could cause no end of problems. Eliminating academics with those negative attributes immediately pares down the list of available candidates enormously. No wonder I made the cut, getting along with people must have been my strength. I did get along with people, other than my governor, of course. Besides, I had no ego left by this point in my life. I had nothing to be arrogant about. That had to be the reason I was selected.

In any case, there was a real need for the panel. Cash welfare had been transformed by the passage of PRWORA (Personal Responsibility and Work Opportunity Reconciliation Act) in 1996. The legislation had several parts, but clearly the most important was turning cash welfare from an entitlement into a block grant. The big picture is this. States would now get to make the big decisions on how to run their programs. They would have a fixed amount of federal dollars to help families and children previously served by the Aid to Families with Dependent Children program. Obviously, all that freedom brings with it a certain amount of uncertainty.

Even before PRWORA, cash welfare was dissolving before our eyes. I wrote a piece for *Focus* in the mid-1990s that showed the growth of federally granted waivers over the previous decade or so. At the beginning of the period examined, only a few states had secured permission to change existing federal rules and regulations.

Moreover, the changes granted were limited in scope. By the time of national reform some 80 percent of all states had secured at least one waiver and a few, like Wisconsin's W-2, were turning welfare upside down through multiple waivers. I am reminded of the same-sex marriage issue in recent times. What had seemed like an impregnable wall against recognition of these marriages, once broken, suddenly permitted a torrent of change.

Today, it may be difficult to recall the angst brought about by the 1996 law. Obviously many rejoiced either for ideological reasons or a belief that TANF might possibly help these families better than the former cash welfare program. But many advocates for the poor were crushed, with some verging on hysteria. There were estimates of a million or more children suddenly being thrown into destitution. In Congress, some opponents such as Senator Moynihan painted apocalyptic visions of mothers and infants huddled by grates for warmth on winter nights. Dickensian visions of the worst catastrophes imaginable were featured in the press and other popular publications.

Foundations threw money at anyone who would document the impending disaster in some convincing or compelling way. Many so-called leavers studies were done where those exiting welfare were tracked for a while. Most indicated some hardship but nothing in the way of apocalyptic doom anticipated by some. Neither did these studies provide support for miraculous increases in work or family stability among low-income families with children. It was all rather ho-hum. Of course, we knew less about those who might have sought aid under the old regime but never bothered to apply under the new rules.

I did not join the chorus of doomsayers though I had concerns of course. The evidence from Wisconsin, which was ahead of the curve, left me somewhat sanguine about the consequences of wider reform. Besides, I had long been saying that AFDC was disappearing whether reform happened or not. To repeat my standard joke about welfare from my D.C. days, "We had better reform it before it disappears." AFDC did nothing to provide recipients with anything close to an acceptable living standard, never mind lift families out of poverty. The program had been the object of such loathing in its last years that most did not mourn its passing for long. Many, however, did worry about what would happen in its absence if you see the distinction.

In any case, our role was to be scientists. As such, we were not to be sidetracked by trivial concerns like, for example, real people. I am being facetious here but only to a point. Our deliberations could not be influenced by any prior normative agendas we might hold as individuals and they were not in any obvious way. There is, however, a built-in bias into any deliberations within what I call the academy, as with any other group. Every group has a culture that shapes attitudes and behaviors.

The assembled group was very smart indeed. They were, however, for the most parts, eggheads or (as my good friend Karl

Scholz often calls his econometrician colleagues) propeller-heads. They spent most of their time working with equations and data and talking to other propeller-heads who were equally fascinated with equations and data. Even Werner Schink, the genial evaluator from California state government, was ensconced in the safe cocoon of Sacramento. Okay, Kathy Edin did talk to poor women on occasion; and Becca Maynard had been out in the real world from time to time, but she was now mostly in the academy. As the deliberations went on, I was struck by one uncomfortable fact. My very smart colleagues knew little about the real world or the rapid changes taking place there.

Why is this important? Well, a key to doing research is getting the question right. If you fail at that, you cannot later be bailed out by fancy methods or whiz bang econometric tricks, at least not in most cases. I had been spending a lot of time in welfare and human service agencies throughout my career and would continue to do so until I hung up my policy shingle. A lot of that hands-on work in the later years was due to WELPAN along with my fascination with service integration. In truth, many of my projects had gotten me out into the world where I could see things up front and personal.

Whatever the reasons, I was talking to a lot of officials and workers who were doing reform daily. I was seeing what they were talking about, how they were seeing the world, what visions and goals were driving them on. I also went into what we called "lighthouse" sites to film what was happening both for WELPAN and a related Distance Learning project. This little sideline turned out to be serendipitous indeed. Why? When the panel started its deliberations, they still saw TANF essentially as a cash assistance program. Of course, they could see the federal changes in the law, the new freedoms given states, a new funding formula. But the real impact on what localities might do with newly acquired discretion had not fully revealed itself yet. Caseloads were falling but the dynamics at the operational level behind these trends were poorly understood. The videos would fill in that informational gap.

I was beginning to get some data at this time through WELPAN that would show just how transformative reform was in some places. Some 72 percent of AFDC dollars in the seven Midwest states had been going for cash assistance in the old welfare era. That proportion had fallen to less than one-third of expenditures in the post-reform era. In Wisconsin, it fell to something like 12 percent. The biggest expenditure item was now child care. In addition, significant sums were going for training and various human services to strengthen and stabilize families, ends long neglected in the cash-transfer era. The transformation shocked even the members of WELPAN who had their staffs put the numbers together. It was part of a thought I had that we could track the meaning of reform by "following the money."

As I said, I had been thinking about these issues even before I was asked to be on the panel, thinking of related activities that might even have inspired the creation of the panel. I had started working with Barbara Blum (and with Bobbi Wolfe and others) on thinking through what changes would be needed within the evaluation community to accommodate the realities of a changing welfare world. The reform movement was emblematic of the change but perhaps the transformation went beyond PRWORA. Perhaps we were on the edge of a new era of social assistance. I will get back to that thought in a moment.

Would my fellow panel members believe me if I said they were missing the boat, that the welfare world had changed beyond what the academy had observed? Probably not! I have an honest face but still. I had a plan, though. Have I said I love plans before now? If I could get the panel to view some of these interviews I had taped during my numerous site visits, perhaps they would get a glimpse of the larger picture of what I believed was happening out there. Perhaps they would believe those doing reform even if they thought I was full of bull-hockey.

"Hey, guys," I suggested, "want to see some movies? No, they are G-rated, sorry to disappoint you Becca." I did take some expected grief about who would bring the popcorn, and whether there would be a cartoon along with the main feature and so forth. Despite the ribbing and perhaps skepticism, I did show the videos at the next meeting. I looked around, they were watching. Eric Hanushek told me later he learned more from the videos than from anything else on the panel. And I do believe the tone of the dialogue changed after that. Frankly, I am certain it did.

The eventual report issued by the panel was titled *Evaluating Welfare Reform in an Era of Transition: A Report of the National Research Council.* The report was long and technical, a real snoozer as most such reports are. But the main points were on the mark as I saw them. Very simply put, it argued that we had to broaden the populations of interest to virtually all the low-income population with children. Beyond the leavers who were getting a lot of attention, we needed more focus on families yet receiving benefits and those not on assistance because they were diverted, rejected, or discouraged from applying. Families with special needs—physical and mental—constitute the core of the hard to serve population and deserve special attention. These are the FUBARS I worried about while at ASPE.

The report also called for an expansion of the outcomes of interest. The motivation here is that different stakeholders (national or state legislators, administrative officials, specific interest groups drawn from distinct segments on the ideological spectrum, and so forth) will focus on different ends for welfare reform: increasing work and self-sufficiency, reducing out-of-wedlock births, promoting marriage and family stability, improving the general well-being of families and children, and spurring programmatic innovation by giving locals more control. The report then went on to enumerate several domains within which specific dependent variables were described.

Finally, the report identified several categories of research questions. At the broadest level were a set of issues reflecting the well-being of the low-income population at large and for subpopulations of interest. This fit very well with my general fascination with social indicators. Second, there were a set of policy and programmatic questions new to welfare evaluations. Unlike the era of a federally dominated cash-transfer system, we now had a proliferation of new approaches across the country. We needed studies of the wide variation in strategies and approaches that were emerging at the local level. We also needed to examine the changes in programs and approaches outside of the formal TANF system since reform had stimulated a lot of innovative cross-systems thinking. It was no longer just about welfare anymore in these new one-stop mega agencies being developed.

Finally, we needed to fully explore and explicate a comprehensive list of research issues and match them up with appropriate methods. Up to this time, welfare evaluations had predominantly stressed random assignment experiments, the gold standard for doing impact evaluations. This had been true to the virtual exclusion of other methods.

Now, however, we were expanding the scope of interesting questions and thus had to carefully consider whether other analytical approaches might prove more appropriate to the nature and character of the underlying concern or contextual circumstances. Sometimes, for example, you are interested in assessing the effects of a bundle of changes including altering the culture of program agencies. In such cases, traditional experimental methods are likely to prove inadequate or infeasible. You need to drift toward time-series modeling and comparison-group designs using carefully constructed comparison group populations composed of ineligible populations. In extreme cases, monitoring the use of social indicators or administrative proxies (benchmarks) for the real outcomes of interest might be the best we can do. This is hard to do well but necessary until we come up with more rigorous methods at some future point.

The report also spent a lot of time examining national and sub-national data sets and exploring what would be required to develop an adequate data infrastructure to monitor the well-being of those populations we cared about. This became increasingly important as we devolved responsibility for their care to officials located closer to where help was delivered . . . the local community. One passage tapped my concerns quite well, where reform was characterized as a "moving target" which is "still evolving."

> . . . . *states, having largely accomplished their caseload reduction goals, are now turning their attention to the provision of services to poor families, in general, and to women and families who are not receiving welfare. The provision of work supports, such as child care, as well as*

services meant to address other problems and barriers women experience in attempting to reach self-sufficiency, are widely discussed. Welfare reform is a continuing, dynamic process as states gradually confront new problems and face new challenges. The energy in this evolution is an indication of a system that is constantly trying to improve itself, which is clearly desirable, but it makes the problem of evaluation quite difficult.

All in all, I thought the tone of the report responsive to the concerns I had raised throughout. I had pushed the notion that reform was spinning off in ways that were creating dramatically new forms and strategies for helping not only traditional welfare clients, but new populations not previously served by traditional cash assistance programs.

The videos I had shown the panel contained many interviews of local and state officials talking about this brave new world reformers wanted to create. Given this refreshing sense of freedom at the state and local level, the rush to innovate with great imagination and commitment could be seen, spurred on through mechanisms such as WELPAN. It was a perfect world for me if only I had created this new academic niche called institutional ethnography. More on that inspirational concept in just a bit. Ah well, we get too old smart.

There is one thing you can count on with any welfare issue, even the boring or technical ones. Someone will be mad at you. The

Manpower Demonstration and Research Corporation (MDRC) probably was the premier evaluation firm of welfare innovation. They were totally committed to the classic experimental design and viewed some of the report's findings with alarm. Howard Rolston, the chief proponent of experiments within Health and Human Services, also was concerned about the tone of the committee's work. He was sitting next to me at some meeting one day when a comment must have reminded him of the expert panel's report. He suddenly gave me a whack on the arm. "Ouch," I responded, "what was that for?" he responded with something like, "That is for influencing the committee so much." I protested that I was one small voice among many, but to no avail. Apparently, some folks had an exaggerated sense of my influence in the world.

Being a member of a NAS panel is not exactly a lucrative undertaking considering that serving on one can get you whacked on the arm. Your only reward for providing this service is doing something for the public good which most members are certainly willing to do. Still, they feed you well and they do throw in a few other perks into the pot, like an emergency travel number. At one meeting, a hurricane was moving along the Atlantic Coast brushing alongside D.C. All day I watched the winds and rain increase and kept calling the emergency travel number they gave me. "No, Dr. Corbett, your flight back to Madison is okay," said a cheerful voice on the other end of the line. I protested that I could see the trees bending at a ninety-degree angle outside my window, but the cheerful voice insisted that all was okay.

Of course, when I get to National Airport, it is a ghost town. The few people there looked at me as if I were a total lunatic, a common enough error. "There is a damn hurricane out there, what the hell are you doing here?" said the bemused person behind the ticket counter. So, now I figure that there is not a hotel room within fifty miles and call the emergency number I was given. "Dear caller, we are sorry to inform you that we are flooded out temporarily," said a soothing voice on the other end of the line that sounded eerily like that cheerful voice which had recently assured me that all was okay. But there was yet another number at the end of this long message informing me of their woes. Fortunately, the voice that answered this call was still above water level and eventually did manage to get me a room for the night. I still had questions about this so-called perk, but all had ended well in the end.

Another night our deliberations were done for the day and a group of us left the NAS headquarters near the D.C. mall. We were heading off to an upscale restaurant located near Dupont Circle. Now, I mentioned earlier that Becca Maynard and I did squabble a bit, mostly in fun. Well, all in fun, really. The only person I know who really hated me was Governor Thompson. Becca and I knew the town best and told the group to follow us. Then Becca immediately turned one direction and I the other. "The restaurant is not that way," I said. "Yes, it is!" she responded. So, we wound up standing in the middle of the street arguing while this group of smart people waited for us to decide which way was up. After she and I wagered twenty dollars on which of us knew the correct way, I managed to convince everyone to follow me. How I prevailed is a wondrous event since I never, ever win arguments with those of the female persuasion. Now that I think on it, I don't believe she ever paid off the bet. Maybe I should give her a call?

There is a fourth act to this drama which both preceded and succeeded the expert's panel deliberation. Even before national welfare reform, Bobbi Wolfe and I started looking at how the changing character of welfare might challenge the evaluation community. This last act began picking up speed in 1995 when devolution began to look like a runaway train and welfare was already being decentralized through an aggressive policy of granting waivers to the states of various federal rules and regulations. Just about any state with some crackpot idea could get permission to try it out.

I casually started tracking major studies and research initiatives out there, mostly to keep atop the lay of the land. I sensed that the research community was feeling some angst about their neat welfare world falling apart. After all, a lot of evaluation money was being thrown around. At some point, Bobbi and I concluded that we should bring leading evaluators together for a chat, not always the easiest thing to do since many were competing with one another for resources. It is a little like getting Verizon, Sprint, and

AT&T to cooperate freely with one another. However, I knew by this time that people would come even if only to make sure that they missed nothing which might advantage the other guy.

So, in February of 1996, IRP and the National Center for Children and Poverty (NCCP) organized a rather large national conference in D.C. on the future of research and evaluation in anticipation of the anticipated transfer of responsibility for welfare policies and programs to the states and even local communities. The conference was financially supported by ASPE and the Foundation for Child Development (FCD) which Barbara Blum headed at the time. It was in putting together the conference that I first met Barbara, a relationship I would treasure until she retired from public life.

The mood at the conference, which brought together many of the premier academic and evaluation firm researchers in the country, was palpably pessimistic. Many felt that the glory days of welfare evaluation and research were about over as the locus of policy split into fifty or more separate fiefdoms. Of course, dire predictions don't always come true, even when made by very smart people. For one thing, only cash assistance would be turned into a block grant later that year. The remainder of the social safety net went relatively untouched. And second, the philanthropic community would pour some one hundred million dollars into finding out what might happen if radical reform became reality while the federal government would spend millions more. Besides, the better talent within the research community always comes up with more research questions, even if they are not always on the mark.

This gathering generated a lot of useful conversations about emerging research and evaluation challenges. It may well have contributed to ASPE supporting the formation of the NAS panel a year or two later. More people began to think hard about the uncertainties in detailing the character of new program and policy interventions (particularly those that cut across traditional silos or program lines). Researchers became more cognizant of a need to identify additional outcomes of interest now that they were exploding beyond the usual suspects (poverty reduction, work, and independence) and to be more careful in determining the correct unit of analysis for each study. On this last issue, one could see going from individual to family to multi-generational entities to the community and who knows where else.

One spin-off from the dialogue initiated at the 1996 IRP gathering involved bringing together foundation officials for a presentation and discussion. Bobbi Wolfe and I put the event together with the help of Eric Wanner who headed the Russell Sage Foundation at the time. My memory is that Larry Aber, then at Columbia University, was involved as well. He had to be since I clearly recall meeting him at his office prior to the larger session. At that main session, we provided an overview of changes we saw occurring in the nation's safety net along with our perspective on the challenges such changes posed for the evaluation community at large. It was a kind of big strategic planning meeting designed to get interested members of the philanthropic world on the right track. What made this gathering memorable for me was that it was held at the World Trade Center which, just several years in the future, would only be a memory.

Another outcome from the large 1996 gathering of the research community clan was to identify a subgroup that really thought we needed to focus on what we called process or implementation analysis. Barbara Blum and I pulled that group back together the next year and collaborated with them through conference calls and workshops. All this effort and thought culminated in the publication of an edited work titled *Policy into Action: Implementation Research and Welfare Reform* that finally came out in 2003. It was put out by the Urban Institute and was edited by Mary Clare Lennon, an associate of Barbara Blum located at Columbia University, and myself. Other contributors included Demetra Nightingale and Pamela Holcomb (Urban Institute), Irene Lurie (SUNY-Albany), Lawrence Mead (NYU), Evelyn Brodkyn (U. of Chicago), Kathryn Edin (Northwestern at the time), Catherine Born (U. of Maryland), Robert Goerge (Chapin Hall, U. of Chicago), Tom Kaplan (U. of Wisconsin), and Rebecca Maynard (U. of Pennsylvania). In addition, two practitioners added contributions, Joel Rabb from the Ohio and Don Winstead formerly from Florida but working at Health and Human Services in Washington at the time.

The volume was a leap forward in discussing what it would take to unravel the dynamic complexity of evolving welfare systems through advanced implementation evaluation methods. The genie was clearly out of the bottle by this time and would not be stuffed back in. The question was . . . what did this genie look like?

There was a straightforward rationale for focusing on implementation analysis. We knew there was a lot of talk about what states and localities were saying they wanted to do. This goes back to the old AFDC waiver days when it seemed every governor was stepping before the cameras announcing the he or she would be ending welfare as we knew it. A key question always lurked in the background . . . did they do what they had said they were going to do? Was the character of their actual interventions anywhere close to the rhetorical posturing? Did the fidelity of their implementation approximate their initial vision to any degree? Our volume on assessing the implementation of new ideas was a step toward seeking methods for answering such questions.

As I said before, too many times perhaps, I wish I had developed this new area of study called institutional ethnography. I know that someone will now tell me that they have been teaching this for years at St. Mary's of the Celestial Swamp College. You can even get a Masters in the field. But no one in the poverty arena called themselves one of these that I recall at least. And few of the top poverty researchers I knew spent much time in real agencies talking to real officials. Yes, Evelyn Brodkyn, Irene Lurie, Larry Mead, Michael Wiseman, and Sandra Danziger (and colleagues) did spend time in the real world and I am sure a few other academics along the way. Most implementation investigations were being done to support an impact analysis and were not considered to be serious contributions. I am confident those really interested in getting inside organizations to look beyond the surface did so in disguise and always worried that their colleagues would view such an activity as this with great suspicion. Why is this alleged academic not doing real academic work? What in God's name are they doing out looking at real agencies and talking with real people?

I remember a chat with Jason Deparle once. Many of you will recall that Jason was THE *New York Times* reporter doing welfare and social safety net articles in the 1990s. He was writing a book on several women affected by W-2 at the time. At some point in our conversation, I suggested he might someday want to write a book about how the welfare bureaucracies were changing and speculate what the future might hold. I could tell the topic held no interest for him. People would want to read about other people, especially if suffering were involved, not about what they assumed would be bloodless bureaucracies.

On another occasion, the head of the British Bureau of Pensions and other things was visiting Wisconsin both to see the Wisconsin-Works program and to stop by the Institute. He would have been like the equivalent of the Secretary of Health and Human Services or the head of Social Security in the States. After his talk at an evening session at IRP, I asked what about the Wisconsin reforms had impressed him the most. He did not mention the falling caseloads or the new work requirements or the services to strengthen families or any of the other changes most observers might choose to cite. What he talked about was the physical layout of the new welfare offices in Wisconsin. He was taken by the fact that they did not look like traditional welfare offices at all. They literally invited people inside with their warm and professional ambiance. I found it fascinating that this is the message he took away from Wisconsin. Of course, perhaps he was being nice to a known liberal audience and did not wish to reveal all the ideas for slashing the dole back in Britain he was taking away.

At the same time, his observation uncovered a deeper insight. When cash welfare transitioned into a work program, perhaps it was permissible to spruce up the physical layout. You wanted people to come in the door and get their life on the so-called right path. Society sanctioned those programs designed to make people independent. On the other hand, they despised hose programs that appeared to abet dependency. When you get program purposes right, a lot of other things fall into place including the layout of your physical plant.

The bottom line is that I did spend a lot of time in agencies talking to people who design, manage, and work in these systems. I suspect it really is true that you should go out and look at stuff if you want to see anything, if you want to get beyond a surface understanding. Yogi Berra was smarter than we thought. I learned as much putzing around in the real world as I did sitting in the research presentations at IRP or in the many academic conferences I attended. You learn different things in each setting but they all have value.

I could see the foundations of welfare and social assistance shifting as most of my colleagues were yet grappling with yesterday's theoretical and management questions. I sensed that many of my peers were doing 'rear view' mirror research, focusing on the past rather than what might be coming up just around the next corner. My "rearview mirror" analogy was a term Barbara Blum loved and would often use herself. I could turn a phrase.

I tried to express what I was seeing in articles, book chapters, *Focus* pieces, and WELPAN reports throughout the late 1990s and the early years of this century. At the risk of boring readers to tears, I will summarize some of the things I saw as briefly as possible. There were several macro trends going on during this period, three of which I mention here are found in the Lennon-Corbett work *Policy into Action*:

Redirection. The redirection theme involves the transformation of public assistance for poor families with children from a system of cash support based on economic need to one aimed at fostering individual and community change. The goals attached to the new concept of support have multiplied over time. At the local level, they may include communities coming together to improve parenting, family formation, family functioning, and decision making with respect to fertility and sexual activity. Some proponents of reform also anticipate that the redirection of welfare policy will help heal dysfunctional communities, restore public confidence in social assistance programs, and eventually result in better transitions into adult roles by poor and disadvantaged children.

Reinvention. The reinvention theme embraces the transformation of public management from a focus on inputs and protocols for action (tightly allocated resources for specified purposes and explicitly spelled out procedures for which tasks should be done and how) to outputs (how well program goals are met). Proponents of the new focus argue that greater freedom for managers to structure the processes by which they shape and deliver services will enhance program efficiency and responsiveness. The reinvention theme also emphasizes accountability for results and working within market forces. Some went so far as to challenge the presumption of a public- sector monopoly on the provision of assistance. The challenge to the evaluation community associated with this trend is to develop social indicators to continuously assess the situation at discrete levels and put in place an appropriate data infrastructure to support this evaluation work.

Reallocation. The reallocation theme encompasses the shifting of program and policy authority from higher levels of government to levels closer to the problems being addressed, not only from the federal level to the states but also from states to localities. The new flexibility afforded to lower levels of authority, proponents suggest, substantially increases both cost effectiveness and the responsiveness of programs to actual needs. This theme is reflected in a sense of professionalism on the front lines of service agencies where workers now exercise considerable discretion.

These themes were producing a visible shift from a bureaucratic, centralized income transfer system to a professional mode better suited to changing complex behaviors. Nice words, but what do they really mean? The more I looked and talked and watched as people did their work, the more I saw the following. Program purposes were transitioning from income support to job placement to providing help to sustain and strengthen the person's place in the labor force to focusing on family and community support. After all, as many officials told me, you cannot separate the link between strong families and good workers. Each reinforces the other.

These emerging, elastic, dynamic organizational forms that were bubbling up just after the turn of the century were pregnant with possibilities. They represented a shift in the underlying paradigm of what we knew as welfare. The WELPAN network summarized their thinking about this transformative period as follows:

Traditional welfare programs focused on the provision of specific benefits or services such as issuing a welfare check. Emerging perspectives now push us in the direction of thinking about 'preventing' counterproductive behaviors and achieving positive outcomes.

Old ways of thinking typically focused on a case . . . often the adult in the household. Emerging strategies now have us considering entire families and the environments in which they work and live.

Old ways of thinking considered the situation today of for this month. This is what we call a "point-in-time" perspective. New ways of thinking consider issues and challenges over time and across generations. We call this a "point-in-process" perspective.

Old ways of approaching social assistance depended on autonomous workers in very isolated agencies carrying out a limited set of tasks using bureaucratic methods. New ways see collaborative workers operating in networks of service systems, employing professional models of intervention.

Old welfare strategies tended to respond after problems became severe enough to warrant public attention. Now, some programs try to anticipate and prevent individual, family, and community dysfunction.

Old ways of thinking offered band-aids for specific problems. Newer strategies work toward comprehensive solutions that cut across traditional program and service technology boundaries.

As we moved further into the 21st century, I recall thinking how many of my candy counters were spilling over into one another. The work on social indicators and implementation methods, on the "holy grail" of service integration, and on WELPAN's *New Face of Welfare* were merging into a foaming, churning froth of change. All that was most exciting! And yet, it also seemed time to think about closing my candy store to more business or at least cutting back on the hours it would be open. How could that be? A decade ago, it all seemed so promising. It was fun to watch dedicated public servants buck against inertia and fear of the unknown to try new things and to envision the improbable. Now, I was beginning to sense something else.

I would sometimes muse that I had been there when they had put the nail in the coffin of the old individualized AFDC grant structure which had so much discretion built into the rules. We (some of us) thought it scandalous at the time when workers nosed into the client's personal lives no matter the justification. We would end all that through flat grants, through new rules that did not permit any discretion, and though an automated case management system that wrested much control over the program from agency workers.

Now, some three decades later, I was working with agencies throughout the mid-west and beyond to turn the welfare entitlement back into a people-changing system. Maybe that old aphorism is true after all . . . the more things change the more they stay the same. There was a wisp of despair in the air that the sense of change and innovation in the air could not be sustained indefinitely. Perhaps if we had all been a bit younger!

Charles Murray had an article which was originally written for the *Wall Street Journal* republished in *Focus* not that many years ago. It called for a replacement of the panoply of welfare programs, as he called them, with a demogrant or basic income guarantee. It was a throwback to the Negative Income Tax schemes of the early 1970s. I was struck again by the circular nature of doing policy. I was taken by just how intractable wicked social problems are and how they defy permanent solutions. They keep coming back to us again and again like one of those fiends that terrorize sorority houses in horror movies. Just when you thought the monster finally dead, back it would pop to terrorize you just a bit more. It would be easy to get jaundiced and cynical and a tad paranoid.

I will admit that even during the heady days of planning for a "new face of welfare," there was the realization that darker days were ahead. As late as 2002, I was still optimistic. Then IRP Director Karl Scholz asked me to prepare the introductory essay for a major special edition of Focus where we asked our most iconic affiliates to prepare articles on various poverty issues. I titled my seminal essay *The New Face of Welfare: From income assistance to social assistance.* In this 2002 piece, I tried to lay out the future of reform and the outlines of a new age for helping our vulnerable citizens. Even as the words were yet drying on the page, it felt like a paean to an era soon to be lost.

Already, though, people and politicians were forgetting about welfare as an issue. Poverty was being lost in concerns about terrorism and the continued drift of the nation toward the political right. The money would dry up. Attention and concern would move on to something or other that appeared more exciting or controversial. Finally, those most excited about the possibility of change would leave or retire or simply grow old. And all of this pessimistic scenario did come to pass, at least in part. WELPAN ended in 2007.

Was there any sense of disappointment in the end? Not really! For one thing, the social policy world I would leave behind was not the one I inherited at the start of the journey. Like the many students who passed through my courses, I suspect I left behind many small and not so small contributions. And even if I didn't, hell, I got to work in just about the best candy store around. Of course, everything in the policy world is not cotton candy and games. Let me take a moment or two to explore the dark side in the next chapter.

CHAPTER 9

DARKNESS AND LIGHT?

The modern conservative engages in one of man's
oldest exercises in moral philosophy; that is, the search
for a superior moral justification for selfishness.

—John Kenneth Galbreath

Hiraeth is an old Welsh word. It means a yearning for a world that
you believe once existed and is now lost, but in truth probably
never existed. Such is the human condition . . . pining for some
utopian dream while enduring what can better be described as a
dystopian reality. Then again, our present situation cannot predict
what is around the corner with any certainty. Progress is not linear,
nor do socio-economic conditions inexorably get better over time,
at least in any obvious way. In terms of public policy, we seem to
have hit a rough patch.

Progress toward an opportunity society stalled in the 1980s
and has been on the defensive since. It is enough to tax one's faith
that all will turn out well. The inescapable truth is that doing

policy is not just an intellectual endeavor. It is also an emotional journey. We would like to believe that only the prefrontal lobes are involved. Alas, the deeper reaches of our brains involving our emotional apparati intrude all the time as we explore in these next two chapters. Sometimes, that emotional element can be a definite drag.

Looking back over my long life, it becomes clear that I have endured several normative and emotional life cycles, often tied to wild swings in the apparent condition of the world around me. As a kid, I was entombed in a dominant Catholic, working class, ethnic culture. It was a black and white world, governed by layers upon layers of stereotypes and prejudices. As such, it was a very conservative place to be even though everyone around me was a Democrat, at least in a nominal sense. We had to fight the Communists and WASPs and other sorts of evildoers. We had to be suspicious of all whom we did not see in the true church on Sunday and even those not seen in the ethnically defined true Catholic Church. Everyone who was not part of our ethnic, religious, and racial tribe was certainly suspect. We seemingly had a rather endless supply of suspects to fear and hate. Paranoia was everywhere.

Fortunately, I managed to escape my cultural prison. By age twenty, I was the leader of the leftist group on my college campus, fighting what I considered an ill-considered war in Southeast Asia and an unconscionable racial apartheid system in the South.

While a college student, I tried to help vulnerable kids in a poor neighborhood as part of the War-on-Poverty program launched by President Johnson along with working the eleven-to-seven shift emptying bed pans and performing other menial tasks in a large, urban hospital. I had become a hopeless idealist and do-gooder looking for small ways to save the world. And then it would be off to India as a Peace Corps volunteer, two years in the Rajasthan desert trying my hand as an agricultural guru. Okay, not all my adventures were well considered.

In *Confessions of a Clueless Rebel*, I recount these early experiences and the transformations in me they generated. Instincts for seeking the common good for a larger community were always there for me. Even where obvious societal flaws existed, and many did, I had this primitive feeling that things would get better. Now, the truth is I am by disposition a jaundiced fellow for the most part, I now look back at my moments of early optimism with bemusement. Not long ago, I took note of the Brexit controversy in England. Will that country leave the European Union as it voted to do? Will Scotland and Northern Island break apart from the United Kingdom? Will that great collaborative experiment known as the European Union, born in the unspeakable horrors of the Second World War, fracture and fall apart? I thought the ties that bind across the pond would only get stronger. Even as a rather young kid, growing up in a narrow and provincial culture, I saw great merit in moving toward a one world government. I even joined some group called the World Federalists which, in hindsight, probably was a Communist front organization. This basic instinct for cooperation and community is likely hardwired within me.

Eventually, I emerged into my professional life. I was saddened to realize that one could not put off adulthood forever. Rather than passion and commitment, reason and evidence dominated my approach to issues. Rather than overthrowing a corrupt or misguided system, I became more concerned about making our system work better. Reform over protest; Synergy over division. I kept looking for ways to bring disparate points into a sensible whole. There just had to be some way to bridge competing ideologies and normative positions, to get people to work together and not repeat futile arguments ad-nausea. By inclination, I was a man of compromise and the middle ground, searching for ways to make marginal progress in what I saw to be the issues that would elude any quick fix.

As I type these thoughts, I am drawn once again to my days teaching the policy arts to second year Social Work master's students. This was at a time far removed from the halcyon days of the War-on-Poverty where caring for the disadvantaged and vulnerable was an explicit national purpose and "what does it do for the poor" a litmus test for good policy. Our new mantra, as many wits have pointed out, had become a war on the poor, the new litmus test is "what does it do for the filthy rich." Today, with Republicans controlling the major branches of national government, there is a systemic and almost frantic push to unravel what remains of the American safety net, the basics of which were erected from the 1930s through the early 1970s. Ayn Rand had replaced Mother Teresa as the spiritual icon to be worshiped.

The political strategy employed to fracture our prior social compact, which had been premised on the understanding that we all bear some responsibility for one another, has deep roots. Deficits explode as huge tax breaks are enacted that are skewed toward the wealthiest citizens. Promises that lost revenues will be recovered by some fanciful economic boom are pure poppycock. The nominal rationale for this giveaway is that the economy needs stimulation. Deficit spending, either through increased outlays and/or reduced taxation are traditional ways to prime the pump. Typically, though, this is done when the economy is slack and demand lagging. At those times, increased public spending would seem the preferred strategy, if stimulus in fact was needed, which it is not. Increasing the demand for goods and services, a bottoms-up approach, is the most direct way to stimulate spending as rising income and wealth inequality dampens consumer spending among the many falling behind. Reducing taxes is less effective though conforms nicely to the discredited supply side theoretical framework preferred by Republicans. Give the rich more, they will take care of us. How can one claim such with a straight face?

What could possibly be the rational for reducing taxes in an expanding economy, particularly for the wealthiest Americans?

Unemployment is low, and the labor force is experiencing one of its longest growth spurts in history. GDP growth is modest but steady, and wages are beginning to respond to the healthy economy created over the Obama years. There is no need for a stimulus except for obsequious greed. In fact, the challenge facing America is not a sluggish economy but extreme and growing inequality along with a starved public infrastructure. The tax cuts imposed would only exacerbate this situation. For mainstream economists, there are profound concerns related to extreme wealth and income inequality. Can you maintain a healthy economy when the mass of people can no longer afford the basics? Can you ever respond appropriately to problems when your ideology prevents you from increasing public spending to sustain necessary levels of demand? The last time we saw inequality like this was before the crashes of 1929 and 2008. But why worry!

For wealthy Republicans, the benefits of tax cuts are obvious. Sure, they might be uncomfortable for a moment or two when it is pointed out that they are violating the traditional tenet of the Republican fiscal prudence. The GOP was once the party of fiscal sobriety and balanced budgets, at least until the Democrats seized that role about a half century ago. At least, however, GOP rhetoric had always been in the right place.

Starting in 1980, if not earlier, fiscal insanity and trillion-dollar deficit explosions became good public policy. They changed for two fundamental reasons. First, the right needed to reward the uberwealthy who financed the political machine that kept them in power. Second, exploding deficits gave them an excuse to go after public spending on the nonwealthy. Nothing irks the super-rich more than benefits going to those who are not of their select tribe, even if withholding assistance results in human suffering and even amenable deaths. In past decades, Republicans would offer rationales for treating the less fortunate in such a callous manner. Now, they appear to feel that is no longer necessary. A generation or two of endless promotion of basic shibboleths such as government is always the problem and individuals can spend money more wisely than the public sector has transformed the underlying ideological framework for thinking about things. The emotional basis for our sense of political identity has been altered in a fundamental way.

Traditionally, going after the poor has always been easy in America. The average American has always been uneasy helping the down and out, a disposition likely derived from our deeply-rooted tribal divisions. The built-in heterogeneity of our society serves to sustain the "us" versus "them" divisions that corrode the nation's fabric. It has been too easy to see them as different and unworthy, the price we pay for a society that has been distinguished by ethnic and racial diversity. The real money, however, can be found in those more universal entitlements such as Medicare and Social Security. If you are going to be successful in redistributing massive amounts of money to the top of the income pyramid, you need a pretty good cover story as you attack the more broadly popular entitlements. Otherwise, old people with pitch forks will storm your political barricades. Even if you are not moved by the plight of starving children, a survival instinct kicks in for Americans whose own interests are threatened. You must protect your own tribe at all costs. It remains to be seen whether our exponentially growing debt, fueled by recent tax cuts, is a good enough cover for further redistributional policies from the less well off to the economic elite. It is the 'we are broke' so we must cut your social security argument. It might still work, but the recent Bernie Sanders boom introduces some doubt.

Of course, it is possible just to be honest. You could tell voters that we consciously created a massive, multi-trillion-dollar deficit through unneeded and ill-advised tax giveaways. You can tell voters that most of this policy largess went to the politician's uberwealthy friends . . . the very people who have seen their share of the economic pie expand from about 10 percent of the total to almost one-quarter in recent decades. Of course, you could try arguing that the need for this giveaway is obvious. Wealthy political patrons expect a return on their political donations to self-serving Political Action Committees (PACs), which now can run into the hundreds of millions by some of the larger donors. They are not making such donations out of any interest in good public policy. Besides, there is a moral justification. Think how the lives of the wealthy are improved by being able to purchase that fifth Renoir for their guest bathroom without thinking about the cost.

On the surface, our public postures appear cruelly selfish and indifferent to any minimal sense of real morality, how could this have happened? How did we go from a period in the 1960s where new policies were judged by "what they did for the poor" to the new mantra of "what does a policy do for the rich?" Perhaps it is only by chance that our politics are so toxic, that our policies now seem so skewed toward those who need public help the least. No, that did not happen by accident. It is the result of a planned, well-funded, and superbly executed strategic initiative that goes back for half a century or more. Remember this. In 1962, about 80 percent of Americans believed that government could be counted on to do the right thing most of the time. Today, only 20 percent agree with that sentiment in some polls. That kind of tectonic shift in public attitudes does not happen absent some guiding agent.

A well-funded and broad based informational campaign, really a misinformation campaign, has been carried out through a host of interest groups, think tanks, and specialized media outlets. Social media further abets the balkanization and tribalization of American beliefs and politics. Institutions such as the courts (i.e., the Federalist Society) and higher education (i.e., the Leadership Institute) are under attack by those zealous to find liberal tendencies that undermine the natural order everywhere. The death knells for sanity probably came with ending of the Fairness Doctrine during the Reagan era and the Citizens United ruling earlier in this century. These decisions guaranteed that unlimited money could be poured into the political process and that no checks would prevent torrents of unceasing propaganda from swaying a majority from sensibly voting for their self-interests or for causes that extend beyond their own selfish purposes.

Now, some of the poorest counties in America vote overwhelmingly for leaders who want nothing more than to eviscerate what remains of the safety net on which they depend so much. The generation of unreasoned fear and the creation of easy scapegoats works as well today as it did for Goebbels during the 1930s. Substitute illegals or brown-skinned terrorists for Jews or Gypsies or Slavs and you have an instant recipe for controlling 30 to 40 percent of the electorate. With a little voter suppression and gerrymandering, staying in power is within reach no matter how repulsive the proposed agenda.

Some in the mainstream academy continue to struggle to preserve rationality and evidence despite the prevailing political headwinds. As mentioned earlier, Karen Bogenschneider has been working with state legislators for many years in her efforts to bring research to these political figures through the Family Impact Seminar (FIS) model. More recently, she has been interviewing current legislators and longer-term political observers to get inside the mindset of key policymakers. Her assessment is that most politicians are well meaning and hardworking folk. All things being equal, they would prefer to base their decisions upon good evidence, at least for those decisions outside the ideological hot button items. For knowledge producers, the key is to bring rigorous evidence to this key audience in an effective, non-agenda driven ways. In effect, academics need to get outside of their normal culture and become familiar with the world of policymakers. Few do, unfortunately, and honest brokers are difficult to find for most legislators.

That is not the only difficulty at present. Ideological and normative controls are more effective in the current environment. Members of each political party are expected to toe the line for a set agenda, often articulated by outside organizations such as ALEC or the NRA or the Club for Growth or the Leadership Institute or the Federalist Society or one of the many other special interest with enormous clout and chests full of money. Independence and evidence-driven decisions are left to the few areas where special interests simply do not care. The result is that the traditional policy arts, at least those taught in policy schools seem less relevant today. We see less debate among experts touting studies to firm up an evidence-based point and more use of research to defend priors or exercise pure power.

Effort and strategy alone, however, probably cannot sustain a substantive transformation in the underlying political premises or foundational belief sets. You need a saleable theory that strikes a chord at some sub-rational level. In the mid-1990s, Keynesian principles dominated with Republican Richard Nixon famously proclaiming that we are "all Keynesians now." That theory made total sense for the times. The Great Depression and the World War II had left a residue of faith in the potential for government to do good. Conservatives lambasted Roosevelt as a "traitor to his class," but realized the popularity of his programs. The 'right' had lost the battle over core belief systems.

On the defensive, they had to turn that new foundational faith in a proactive government around. For the wealthy, too many average voters now embraced the heresy that government had an essential role in diminishing the abrasive consequences of free markets. People accepted the principal that the public sector should afford all people at least a shot at a decent life. For many traditionalists, that seemed utterly contrary to the notion of a people free from government intrusion and a philosophy that markets alone ensure a fair distribution of resources and opportunities. A natural law was being violated. In the eyes of the elite, a new moral philosophy was needed.

Fortunately, for those opposed to large and intrusive government, there is a long history of economic and philosophic thought to buttress their views of good government meaning less to almost no government. Early thinkers such as Adam Smith and Frederick Bastiot laid out the principles of free trade and open markets. These principles shaped the thinking of this country's founding fathers. The iconic phrase in one of our famous foundational documents was first written as ". . . pursuing life, liberty, and property," not happiness. One revolutionary father, John Adams, is quoted as saying, "Property is surely a right of mankind as real as liberty."

In the first half of the 1800s, Carl Menger developed the Austrian School that pushed conservative economic and political principles and gave the free market and minimalist government hawks a semblance of academic legitimacy. Later in that century, Herbert Spencer translated Darwin's biological evolutionary theory into a social framework. It was here that survival of the fittest notion came into common usage. Integrated with Calvinist principles, the new perspective offered a powerful rationale to justify extreme selfishness. Those who were the most capable rose to the top of the social pyramid. They had the skills and motivation to succeed. Those who did not deserved little sympathy or support. Their plight was God and nature's way of assigning them to their just position in life. To help them would contravene the laws of nature and do more harm than good.

A whole number of thinkers and would-be philosophers struggled to keep the conservative vision alive even as broader circumstances brought the virtues of free markets into question. Frederick Hayek, Ludwig Von Mises, Murray Rothman, and Milton Friedman pounded away at the advantages of economic and personal freedom amidst so many seeking collective security during the economic collapses that occurred with predictable regularity. The great, worldwide depression of the 1930s presented a societal calamity that the old conservative bromides could not easily sweep away. Many were ready for a new explanation of the world and Keynesian theory was offered as an alternative to economic orthodoxy.

Naturally, many of the economic elite had desperately opposed the New Deal and the subsequent expansion of the federal government through Johnson's Great Society. Roosevelt was despised among many of the wealthy, a traitor to his class. That was not surprising. What was surprising is how many poor whites also embraced conservative concepts or were amenable to the coming ideological counter revolution. The great African-American thinker, W.E.B. Dubois, wrote in the 1930s that many southern whites preferred a psychological wage to any increased monetary compensation. They would support anyone who permitted them to feel superior to those below them on the racial hierarchy scale, at least as seen in their eyes. That latent racial animus would burst open as a political and voting reality as economic conditions gradually improved. Some argue today that the Trump phenomenon has not been driven by economic anxiety, which is real enough, but by racial anxiety, which is undeniable. The basic anxiety associated with a blind fear of losing ones' preeminent social position in society as demographics evolve toward a racially diverse nation remains the 900-pound gorilla in the room. Anglo-Saxon dominance is under siege.

Arguably, the philosophical pushback by the right might be traced back to the 1950s, a period when conservative thought clearly was on the defensive and a liberal explosion was just on the horizon. James Buchanan, stung by the recent Brown versus the Board of Education Supreme Court ruling desegregating public schools, founded the Virginia School of Political Economy; a bit like the Chicago school of economic thought but more extreme. Gathering like-minded scholars, they began bringing forward economic principles that had fallen into disrepute.

The founding principles of this school or movement, were traditional. Government should keep its hands off the economy. Only the market should reward effort and distribute goods. Whatever distribution of income and wealth occurs is efficient and fair. Any efforts to remedy inequality will be artificial, inefficient, and morally bankrupt. Any services beyond those deemed essential (e.g., defense, policing, a sound currency, and contract dispute resolution) and the taxes necessary to support them are unnecessary and an inexcusable penalty on the winners in society. Progressive tax schemes are the height of confiscatory evil since they penalize those responsible for creating economic prosperity in the first instance. Their bedrock premise was that there is a natural order to things and proactive government upsets that order leading to the morally bankrupt misappropriating resources from the true guardians of society's well-being.

Of course, when they started the school, the safety net was only partially developed but was expanding inexorably. The top marginal tax rates, however, were in the 90 percent range, a holdover from the war years where the national debt exceeded the aggregate worth of the economy. Certainly, such extreme progressivity provided an opportunity to make easy points about heavy-handed taxation. It was not unreasonable to argue that these high tax rates might dampen America's competitiveness. This was probable likely to happen once the rest of the world got back on its feet after the war and America no longer was producing half of the world's economic output as it did when other economies were in tatters. Think of Korea in the early 1950s, during that horrific conflict. It was a backward, autocratic, and desperately poor country. Today, it is a democracy and an economic powerhouse that competes with us in many economic sectors.

The explosion of domestic spending in the 1960s and early 1970s further stirred the waters leading to a political backlash. Despite the Barry Goldwater debacle in 1964, the core conservative believers never lost heart. Then, the civil rights legislation of the mid-1960s broke the historical partisan anomaly where liberals and conservatives could be found in each party. The Republicans eventually purged their liberal wing while the Democrats lost the deep South. Within a generation, the parties had realigned along ideological fault lines. Almost two decades after the Virginia School began to resurrect conservative political ideas, Lewis Powell, future Supreme Court justice, wrote a memo to the U.S. Chamber of Commerce in 1973 that decried the loss of competitiveness in the economy that could only be restored by a return to bedrock conservative economic principles. More to the point, he laid out a basic strategy which, with generous support from the economic elite, paved the way to a sustained, comprehensive playbook to turn the country in a different direction.

Forty-plus years later, the ideological revolution seems complete, though Washington has yet to be turned into the ghost town for which many on the right pine. Starting with Ronald Reagan, the new mantra of lower taxes and limited government (except for defense) gained steam. Though there were bumps along the way, this new mantra became the default position of American politics, its dominant position assured by the marriage of economic theory with the social agenda of evangelical conservatism in the late 1970s. From that point on, liberalism was on the defensive, some might say life support.

For a policy wonk like myself, the current situation is more than bleak. It is hard to imagine a more depressing world. Programs are being savaged without any concern as to consequences for vulnerable populations. Policy is driven almost entirely by ideology and a frantic search for dollars to finance the never-ending desire to cut taxes on the wealthy further. To the Virginia School and the earlier moral philosophers, tax progressivity is a mortal sin. Ideally, fairness meant taking the same amount from each person to fund essential public needs and no more. There, moral sense is simple. Taxing the wealthy excessively, or at all, penalizes success, upsets the moral order, and introduces impediments to the free flow of capital and entrepreneurial energies. In some instances, they have argued with apparent success that some rich ought to pay proportionally less than the average citizen. Thus, the lower tax rate on deferred dividends, a primary source of income for super wealthy hedge fund managers. Warren Buffet has criticized the fact that his secretary pays proportionally more in taxes than he does. While such principles might have appeared extreme a few decades ago, they take on an aura of essential spiritual precepts in our current era.

Consider the following for just a moment. The tools that poverty scholars are immersed in as students and rewarded for as members of the academy now appear less relevant, at least in the political arena. Ideology dominates evidence. Republicans now turn to ALEC (the American Legislative Exchange Council) for their legislation, not to experts. The council was founded in 1973 by Paul Weyrich and other conservative leaders to counter the increasing control on daily life imposed by various regulatory agencies like the Environmental Protection Agency (EPA). At the beginning of the twentieth century, the academic warriors carrying forth the spirit of the Wisconsin Idea wrested control of law-making from corporate interests, at least in part. In the later part of the twentieth century and the beginning of the twenty-first, legislative control slipped back to corporate interests with ALEC leading the way. That was not by accident nor through inattention by the way.

Given this horrendous reality, what would I say to prospective policy students today, at least those who would bring science, evidence, and an abiding interest in the public good into the application of their trade? What would I say to those wanting to follow my path into the policy arena? Could I tell them that doing policy is a worthwhile way to spend your life with a straight face? Could I talk about the challenges and joys of struggling with society's most compelling problems with any enthusiasm knowing that entrenched norms and political rigidities appear to dominate reason and compassion? Where will these young policy aspirants apply their academic skills or express their normative instincts? Ah yes, we are back to the concerns that motivated the writing of this book in the first instance.

In my humble opinion, not enough members of the academy are pushing the boundaries of programmatic and institutional change. Not enough are trying to better understand the psychology and sociology of beliefs and actions. Yes, I can think of several scholars from research universities who focused on the institutional and normative dimensions related to poverty and welfare policies. However, the majority ply their academic trade in the usual ways . . . examining narrowly constrained technical issues from afar by using secondary data sets manipulated by advanced econometric techniques. There work never extends beyond the reaches of their frontal lobes, their rational part of the brain. Relatively few immerse themselves in the raw complexities of the real world or look at how public decisions are really made. Those that do are not always very effective.

The reasons for this are not difficult to infer. For one thing, focusing on any deeper understanding of institutional, political, and ideological realities can be quite labor intensive. Professionally speaking, this can be counterproductive for committed members of the academy where cranking out a continuous and endless series of articles is the one and only key to success. For another, it involves too much interaction with real people as they go about doing the public's business. That means getting outside their own comfortable cultural cocoon . . . yuck! For still another, it is reasonably certain that you will wind up in some obscure backwater of the academic world. And finally, we really don't have an academic sub-discipline that trains scholars to understand institutions from the inside nor how pure policy is prostituted by the human dimension, at least not in the same way some scholars are trained to study families or communities in an intimate way.

Below I argue that the academy (scholars, researchers, evaluators and the like) can do more to help policy entrepreneurs develop cutting-edge models of human services. Academics might be able to do more if we can tweak the ways they are trained to do their craft and to carry out their professional responsibilities.

Perhaps we can even shift the basis for allocating rewards and honors within the academy. In this regard, I fear, I may be sinking into a quagmire of delusional thinking. Let me be as clear as I can at this point. I am not talking about any revolution or any 'storm the barricades' moment. I am talking about some modest tweaking for those members of the academy who focus on public issues and social problems. This would include students of public policy, social workers, sociologists, wayward economists and political scientists, public management types, and the like. Many students self-select into such fields driven by a desire to have an impact on the real world.

I think we need to broaden the perspective of policy scientists by developing a new academic sub-discipline which I term institutional ethnography, a concept I mentioned earlier, perhaps too often. This focus would embrace the broader dimensions of doing policy to include the cultural, normative, and political dimensions of the policy arena. Policy debates no longer focus on technical matters but larger contextual issues. In the future, we will need to look at people more fully, not just as the stick figures that populate models reducing complex humans to homo-econimicus caricatures. The term institutional ethnography remains useful since, in my mind, it is closely related to the ethnographic skills brought to bear on families and communities and thus enjoys a rough sort of familiarity to a subset of scholars. Even better, it is so ambiguous that we can make it whatever we want.

Developing a practice oriented sub-discipline that uses a broad brush that might embrace institutional and ideological realities will not be easy. Do we have a theoretical basis for training future academics to be more interested and skilled in working with public officials who run human service systems or the interest groups that frame public discourse? Perhaps poverty research needs to focus as much on how decisionmakers arrive at decisions as opposed to what decisions they make? When the Institute for Research on Poverty was created in the 1960s, academics from the discipline of psychology were part of the original team. They were long gone by the time I became involved in the mid-1970s.

Even if we do sell the academy on the need to look at how they do their business, would this new set of skills and aptitudes constitute an innovative disciplinary focus or is it covered within existing advanced programs? Would such a new focus gain traction in research universities that prefer the creation of new knowledge over the introduction of extant knowledge to solve problems? Would such a focus appear overly applied to top faculty members ensconced in the traditional disciplines? There are many stories of doctoral students being directed away from applied evaluation topics for their dissertations simply because such topics strike their mentors as being too real world in character. That is what paid-for researchers who work in evaluation firms do, not what scholars do, or so the prevailing prejudice goes.

Thus, my ideas for a new scholarly focus are introduced cautiously, knowing that they might be bucking-up against the prevailing winds in the academy. And yet, it is true that there are respected members of the academy who do ethnographic work and surely there are those who study organizational theory. Many academics also give much time and energy to public policy issues and making the world a better place. A few even feel comfortable interacting with policymakers and administrators and agenda-shapers, engaging in such tasks with both ease and skill. Yet, most members of the academy generally do not seem comfortable with such vague intellectual tasks or with the people interested in such topics, particularly at top research universities. It is a little like Garrison Keillor's observation about men and monogamy. Yes, they do go together on occasion, but it is a little like seeing a grizzly bear motor down a forest path on a 10-speed racing bike. You simply are amazed at the sight.

Thus, I argue that policy is more than incentives and economics. What I propose would be a new blend of the conceptual and the practical arts where theory and practice are fused in complementary ways, where intellect and reason are brought into a more harmonious balance. If people with such blended attributes and perspectives exist out there in the academy, few are included among mainstream poverty researchers and there surely there are not enough of them. Such work, however, has never gained a firm footing and certainly little favor at least in that portion of the academic world that touches upon the topics of interest to us . . . poverty and welfare policies. In my day, I cannot recall any of my academic colleagues getting up at a conference and saying...that sucks, unless they were referring to a misspecified econometric equation. We need more outrage and emotion today. That is my story and I am sticking to it.

Why don't we train policy scholars to better understand deeper institutional settings, unexamined political realities, or the way normative positions are established and reinforced. Such topics are relevant. Policy cannot be separated from some understanding of the rudiments of organizational theory or human behavior where you are exposed to the cultural forces that shape our institutional and community lives. At best, scholars are exposed to the obvious dimensions of reality. They study the structural dimensions of institutions such as span of control, vertical differentiation, the permeability of organizational boundaries, environmental influences and boundary (or horizon) spanning. You can learn about different ways of organizing tasks within organization, by function or by purpose or by geographical area of responsibility. You might even be exposed to more advanced concepts such as matrix-management forms or the easily observable elements of the political economy. The human element is covered if at all, usually by paying a cursory homage to the informal networks that lurk behind the more formal skeletal outlines depicted in the organization charts. Knowing that informal networks exist does not tell you much about how they function, however.

Organizational theory and practice, it turns out, has changed over the decades. One can trace the evolution of organizational thinking from the early days when rigid conceptual forms were imposed upon bureaucracies as a sign of progress. According to Weberian dogma, good government was carried out by functionaries who performed their duties in a robotic fashion, without bias or favor as the saying goes. This was viewed as an advancement over the cronyism and abusive discretion that ruled earlier forms of public service where merit had little place in the choice of personnel and favoritism played a disproportionate role. As the modern notion of bureaucratic uniformity and impartiality emerged, variation from the prescribed rules and protocols were viewed with increasing disfavor.

It was not long before theorists realized that the formal attributes of organizations left much to be desired as pathways to any real understanding of what public agencies (or private bureaucracies for that matter) were all about. More attention began to be paid to informal networks within bureaucracies and political spheres, nontraditional communication patterns, the spontaneous emergence of power centers, and the breaking down of formal structures and institutional boundaries. We came to appreciate that formal structure and the eco-skeletons defined by organizational charts captured far less of what mattered in organizations than we originally thought. Rational constructs and organizational forms were replaced with shifting new patterns that dissolved into notions of "garbage can" can theories defying easy categorization. People and relationships, with all the messiness that implies, were increasingly important.

In the real world, cause and effect are mediated through complex and opaque administrative and all-to-human mechanisms that do not operate in any transparent way. They function outside our casual purview and can only be seen if one has the skills and craft to peer inside to unravel the complex working of modern institutions and the political environments in which they operate. We often talked about the "black box" of policy making, how new rules and programs were implemented. This black box focuses more on how rules and regulations come into being in the first instance. You craft new rules at the top of an administrative pyramid and hope that what comes out at the bottom resembles original intent. Sometimes it does, sometimes it doesn't.

My great fear is that the world might well be evolving faster than those ensconced in the academy realize. If that happens, they will be imposing research questions and methods that are not appropriate for the new bureaucratic and political forms, nor the policies that are emerging on the ground. If true, it is easy to ask the wrong questions and arrive at answers that appear irrelevant or wrong to the very audience you are trying (or should be trying) to inform. Remaining in touch with the real world and keeping abreast of evolving realities is not easy. In fact, it is damn hard. But it is damn essential. The first task of any research effort is to get the question right.

Let us look at your ordinary ethnographer. For a moment, imagine the challenges faced by such a scholar working with poor families. They cannot waltz in and establish an immediate sense of trust and cooperation. No, it takes time to build up a rapport and to establish a relationship. The researcher probably must be tested on an intimate level several times before the subject will feel comfortable revealing information that is considered sensitive and private. The researcher must also work to communicate effectively which undoubtedly demands that they first embrace local vocabulary and rhythms of communication patterns. Nothing can be rushed, and the researcher must be careful not to impose their own understandings onto their subjects. Clearly there are rules for doing this work, but there is also a craft involved. Not everyone can do it or at least do it well.

Any researcher wanting to understand the institutional and human dimensions through which policies are mediated must make a similar investment. They need to understand their topic from a broader perspective. They must get to know how these systems work on an intimate level, one that goes beyond the surface and into the deeper realms of institutional culture. You must learn a new language and set of listening skills. You must be sensitized to seeing things within the bureaucratic environment that other, less sensitive observers, might well miss. In effect, we need to embrace a new craft.

As Karen Bogenscheider and I discuss in our book, *Evidence-Based Research*, the cultural gap between the worlds of knowledge-producers and knowledge-consumers is so vast because, in part at least, neither can speak the language of the other. Neither appreciates each other's world. Neither fully understands how members on the other side look at things. Appreciation starts with some level of understanding of underlying cultures. If you cannot talk with one another, the prospects of developing a working relationship diminish rapidly. Yet, both groups are so comfortable within their own worlds that they cannot see what separates them.

I have pounded at the following point many times and in many ways . . . every profession has its own culture. The academy—where researchers are trained, and future professors are socialized—has a very distinct set of norms and values. Theoretical work is preferred to practical or applied studies. Empirical or observational studies employing high tech estimating techniques are highly valued as are rigorous experimental designs that advance our theoretical understanding of the world. Applied work, program evaluations, management studies are all viewed as marginal activities that seldom rise to levels worthy of attention and reward within the academy. Even confirmatory research of high quality can be ignored in tenure and promotion decisions.

As implied earlier, members of the academy who study poverty and related topics often operate as if institutions and politics do not matter. Policies are treated as if they function in a *deus ex machina* manner where a program is launched and somehow works its magic, or does not, irrespective of the structural arrangements through which the policies are actualized. Economic incentives are seen to weave their magic somehow independent of a world where humans can distort or misapply policy signals and program information. Economists were legitimately surprised when the Earned Income Tax Credit and various wage bill subsidies went undersubscribed for so long. They had embraced a notion of economic man as a utility maximizing being that would behave rationally under most, if not all, circumstances. Naivete can exist even among the smartest of us.

It should not come as a shock that real people are not as rational as the utility-maximizing stick figures used in a good deal of economic analysis. Real people make *satisficing* decisions based on faulty reasoning, partial information, and misleading input. People in bureaucracies and in the political arenas are no different. You cannot walk in and impose a new way of doing business simply because it is rational or theoretically persuasive or well-meaning. You must account for the cultural idiosyncrasies, embedded values, and sometimes irrational emotions that real people carry with them. You must account for all those critical cultural nuances that play havoc with rational intent. Hell, Freud became a household name for revealing the existence of the irrational id in contrast to the more rational super ego. We all talk easily about market failures that impeded efficient economic performance and study these shortcomings well. Administrative and management failures are also critical but less well appreciated and studied. Managerial pronouncements made absent a full understanding of the environmental milieu within which a program operates can well be an exercise in futility.

I still recall a classic case study from my early days as a doctoral student. Management gurus introduced performance-based incentives into a public jobs placement agency. Workers were to be rewarded by improving their success rate in placing job seekers in actual jobs. Agency effectiveness had to improve, the incentives were clear as was the theory supporting the new policies. In the real world, however, job placements plummeted. A little digging revealed why. Informal cooperative arrangements among workers disappeared as they hoarded hot employer prospects for their own clients. A collaborative working environment became a narcissistic, hypercompetitive one. So much for good ideas. But unless you had the skills to get inside and figure things out, what happened might have remained a mystery.

The subtleties of organizational life can be messy and even inscrutable for those fully trained and socialized within the traditional academic culture. Scholars often prefer a world where noise can be assumed away and the causal paths between independent and dependent measures operate as if by magic. I can recall many talks where the academic starts by saying something like the following: "Imagine the following highly simplified or stylized world so that my math can work." The scenario he or she then paints is replete with pictures of this idealized world populated by our stylized stick figures and dominated by very simple interpersonal interactions. I am glad that the math can work for them but that does not help real policymakers who do not have the luxury of operating in clean and rational and highly stylized environments.

I have argued at some length that some academics ought to be prepared specifically for careers that focus on the more nuanced dimensions of institutional and political life. My bottom line is this. We hope that future researchers will be more prepared than we were when working with agencies and bureaucracies and, critically, people from cultures other than their own. If we want scholars with the flexibility and courage to cross-walk between cultures, we need to train them differently. Perhaps then they won't be in the position of sitting in a room full of expectant officials who ask them, someone they considered an expert, how to turn a welfare agency into a work program. Making it up on the fly is not necessarily the best way to go. I can tell you that from personal experience. Okay, I managed to fool people, but I was born with an excess supply of blarney... an Irish gift.

Perhaps this chapter can be summed up in one suggestion . . . we need more inquisitive generalists.

CHAPTER 10

VALUES AND OTHER INCONVENIENCES

You must become the change you want to see.

—Mahatma Gandhi

In this chapter, I continue my rant for bringing more balance to the policy arts. We who spend our lives in the academy, or in any intellectual pursuit, fancy that we live our lives grounded in reason and cognition. In the end, that may simply be an illusion. We also are creatures of the beliefs and feelings that reside deep within us. We simply hide our inner moral and emotional compasses behind more elegant and seemingly logical verbal or quantitative edifices. Even the most elevated jurists are not bound by an abstract set of laws, at least not when it counts. They make controversial rulings based on personal norms and prior experiences and then, only then, weave elaborate cognitive constructs in support of their fundamental sentiments. It is called "post-decisionism." If the law were something solid, existing out there, we would not have so many 5-4 decisions.

My phone rang one day in early 2009. Nancy Simuel was on the other end of the call. 1 had seen Nancy only once since 1969, when a group of young men and women packed up to return to the U.S. after two years as Peace Corps volunteers in India. That one prior meeting occurred during a talk I gave in Milwaukee, the purpose and audience now long forgotten. After finishing, a Black woman walked up to me. She looked vaguely familiar, but I could not quite place the face. This was a weakness of mine as someone in the policy arena. I could never remember names and even faces. Good thing I never ran for public office. She asked if I was the same Tom Corbett who had served in the Peace Corps in India in the 1960s. "Nancy!" I shouted. We hugged and spent few minutes catching up.

Now she was calling to tell me about a reunion of our Peace Corps group that was being planned for later in the year on the west coast. I had never attended any reunion before, but this one was not to be missed. As I said in the preface, that gathering of the India-44 volunteers triggered emotions and memories that prompted many of us to search for who we were, what we were thinking back when we were so young and foolish, and what we had become in the subsequent years.

Sam Rankin, another fellow PC Volunteer, once asked a question that got me thinking. What was it that got each of us on that plane to India in 1967? Though Peace Corps was larger in the 1960s than it is now, only a fraction of the country's youth applied, fewer were selected; and many of those who started out did not finish their tours. For the India-44 group, we had close to a hundred trainees on day one in 1966. However, only about one-quarter of that total were packing up to return home in 1969 after finishing two-years of service in what was considered one of Peace Corp's more difficult stations.

It is not as if we changed the world or altered India's prospects. The stark fact is that we enjoyed most of the benefits from our volunteer experience with the host country getting comparatively little in return. I must confess, just in case you missed this fact, India was a grain importing country when we arrived in the blistering heat of summer 1967. When we left in that same blistering heat two years later, India was a grain exporting nation. I will let the reader draw whatever inference they wish from this fact. I admonish you not to be confused by those who argue that the extensive drought that ended during our tenure there had anything to do with this reversal of fortunes.

If I was to become a pretend academic later in my professional career, as you will see in the next chapter, I was surely an imposter as an agricultural expert in rural India. I am now certain that India and Peace Corps were my training ground for faking it later in life, what could explain not being chucked out of the academy in the first six months. As we trotted off to save the world, we were nothing more than a bunch of city boys given a bit of technical training and dropped into the middle of the Rajasthan desert. Not the best of ideas America has ever had but at least India did not sever diplomatic ties with the U.S. due to our incompetence.

I do recall a basketball game, however, when things might have turned ugly. A group of us volunteers competed against a team from a local Indian military installation, or maybe it was the police. Whatever they were, they were big and tough. We had beaten the boys from the local university a couple of times already, so they brought in these ringers. I still recall driving to the basket several times and repeatedly getting punched in the stomach with no foul ever being called. Now that game almost did turn into a riot though the crowd of locals watching the event appeared to very much enjoy our physical mauling. Despite all, the Indian Embassy had a nice evening for all former volunteers to India during Peace Corp's fiftieth anniversary in 2011.

More than one poor farmer asked me if they should try these new varieties of high-yield seed (part of the green revolution that emerged in the1960s). I would grab a handful of dirt from his field, grind it in my hand, examine it, and throw it in the air with a great flourish. Then I would turn to the farmer and with an expression of total confidence while exclaiming, "Yes!" In truth, I had no idea what I was doing, a sense of general bafflement I brought forward with me into my subsequent professional endeavors as a policy wonk. Still, I cannot think of any better preparation for my career. In some fundamental ways, we all wing it through life.

Most of my early life experiences, all detailed in *Confessions of a Clueless Rebel*, contributed much to my later policy and even academic ventures. I worked in a hospital on the graveyard shift, worked with disadvantaged kids in a War-On-Poverty community action program, and spent countless hours on the political issues of the 1960s when I probably should have been studying for my classes. But, in hindsight, none of these activities were wasted. They broadened the set of experiences I would bring to the policy table and even sharpened my analytical skills. The top colleges look for experiences outside of the classroom in their prospective candidates. We probably need the same breadth of experiences in those seeking to embrace the policy arts.

In the 1960s and early 1970s, a simplistic idea took hold. Some very smart people thought that we were entering a new era where data and evidence would replace ideology and values in the making of public policy. We had new mathematical and statistical tools along with larger and more comprehensive data sets. Surely, emerging technologies would permit rational analysis to replace ideology and prejudice in doing the public's business. This certainly sounded like a reasonably idea. Then again, so did the notion that the earth was flat in medieval times. If you sailed too far out into the ocean you would surely fall off the edge. That conclusion also made great sense at the time, just look about you. Why all the ocean's water had not already fallen over the edge, though, might have caught me up for a moment.

Taken to the extreme, it appeared to some that quantitative analysis would dominate future policy work. All we would need is great data sets and whiz-bang estimation techniques and utopia would be ours. Serious people talked about the 'end of ideology." Such hubris seems humorous now, along with other 1960-era prognoses that we would exhaust existing supplies of fossil fuels in 35 years and that the biggest social problem for the next generation would be an excess of personal leisure. Beware of sure-fire prognostications. They have an annoying habit of turning out to be wrong.

It is a good thing I listened to my heart rather than the predictions of the wise men of my youth. As idealistic kids, we went off to India because, after all, it seemed like the right thing to do. It made sense in terms of our normative positions. The values we had somehow embraced motivated our choices back then, as did Kennedy's inspiring words about sacrifice. Such fundamental factors as basic values yet play a dominant role in policy making and in how we approach social problems. They fully inform our decisions about what is a just or fair society. Perhaps that is why technical sophistication alone is not enough to address the "wicked" social problems we face. Despite pretenses to the contrary, we are not fully rational beings. Homo-econimicus has its uses but is not infallible.

You can quantitatively assess traffic flows to devise better stop light patterns during rush hour. Perhaps only a few will be mad at you for the changes subsequently made. You can quantitatively estimate labor supply responses to various income guarantees and benefit reduction rates. I guarantee that some people will be mad at you no matter how reasonable and evidence-based your policy suggestions might be on that issue. But when the policy questions tackle larger questions involving the good society, like what role government should play in equalizing economic outcomes, things really get dicey. In the big questions, reason and data play even a smaller role next to feelings and beliefs and values and prejudices.

If David Ellwood's tenure at ASPE was personally disappointing to him, as I suspect it was, that was likely due to his surprise at how little reason and evidence meant in Washington. The halls of power in Washington march to a different tune than the halls of scholarship at Harvard. I still can hear John Antaramian, the Wisconsin Assembly representative who chaired the welfare reform committee with which I worked, as he uttered the following despondent words, "Tom, I thought I was doing some good with the committee and now everyone is mad at me." Can you imagine how more shocking it is for an academic, used to arguments over evidence, to face irrational attacks based on ideology and partisanship. A word to the wise, don't become a policy wonk if you want to have a lot of Facebook friends, or enjoy rational dialogue. You want reason and logic, focus on closed-system activities like chess.

As I pounded away *ad nauseum* in the prior chapter, policy is dominated by norms and beliefs these days. Oddly enough, as our analytical tools become more sophisticated, our political discourse seemingly becomes more primitive. More than other advanced countries, Americans are much more likely to disbelieve in evolution (40 percent), believe in angels (65 percent), and argue that the world is 6000 years old. Elected politicians argue, publicly, that climate change is not an issue since God will resolve the issue should he decide it is worth His time. These same politicians, a few at least, pray for an apocalyptic conflict between Iran and Israel since that apparently is a necessary step toward the second coming of Christ as prophesized somewhere in the Bible which, they will argue, supersedes the Constitution as a guide to the principles of proper governance of this nation. It is very difficult to argue with such logic. It is one thing to find a few deranged elected officials shouting obvious nonsense but more alarming that such beliefs are found here in greater numbers than the remainder of the civilized world.

This fact raises a question, one I have revisited many times over the years. It might rank up there with the top two or three questions to be faced in life. From where do our fundamental beliefs and feelings arise? How do we get to be who we are? Are basic beliefs and values hardwired? Are they all learned? Is it nature or nurture or some combination of both factors that determine what we believe and how we feel about things? All these are important queries since they determine the cultural milieu and conceptual frameworks that shape how we see both our policy world and ourselves as policy actors.

When I have had a dispute with one of my favorite Republicans . . . a Ron Haskins or a Tom McCurdy or a Jennifer Noyes . . . our differences have nothing to do with their being less intelligent than I or that I have a better command of the evidence or that I am more astute at using facts. These people probably are better informed and quicker of mind than I can ever hope to be. I must admit, though, a lot of conservatives I have run across really do strike me as dumber than dirt but not these nor many others like them.

The point is that differing perspectives do not always reflect a failure of reason. If that is the case, then we must look elsewhere, perhaps to differing value systems for at least part of the answer. Moreover, we need to think about the etiology of these value systems for just a moment, even if a final answer is likely to elude us. The older I get, the more I sense that our core, individual sentiments are hardwired. We bring them forward into life. Since this is not a text book, I simply will share a few observations based on a lifetime of thinking about such matters. Let me start with a compelling vignette or two.

A former neighbor of mine had married an Air Force pilot and was living near Jackson, Mississippi in the early 1960s. She had a black maid, as did all white housewives of that era. One day, she heard a commotion and realized that the neighbor kids were throwing stones at this maid as the poor woman hung out the laundry in the backyard. My acquaintance scolded the kids and sent them off home. Her phone rang a few minutes later. The mother of one of the kids started yelling at her about harassing her children. When my friend responded with how rude the children had been to her domestic help, the enraged mother ended with a kind of warning, "Down here, a nigger is just a nigger." Apparently, throwing rocks at black maids was good sport in the South in the early 1960s. My friend talked back, asserting that there was no excuse for such behavior.

Later that day, someone from the sheriff's office knocked on her door. His message was simple. "Up north, where you come from, you may have different ways of looking at things; but when you are living here you have to abide by local ways. Here, a nigger is just a nigger." She had been warned. And if she still hadn't gotten the message, just to make sure, someone rode past her house that night and fired a shotgun blast through the front window. As I listened to her story I recall wondering. What if those kids, their mother, the sheriff's deputy, and the nighttime rider had been raised elsewhere, with a different culture? How would they have turned out?

Decades later, she remained a liberal and an active Democrat. Her brother, who grew up in the same home environment in Ohio where the family was raised, is quite conservative and a lifelong

Republican. The mother of both also had been a lifelong Republican until her eighties. Then she became fed up with the right-wing direction her party had taken and became a Democrat. Still, she initially had trouble accepting Obama as a presidential candidate because of his color. She could not easily shake the stubborn prejudices of her youth and decades of reinforced thinking about race. I did not challenge her beliefs. I merely expressed my own feelings in a quiet way. I recall her listening to me intently as I talked about how much I admired the man, Obama. She did not respond at the time. When I next saw her several months later, when we returned to Florida for the winter just before the election, she had become an avid supporter of Obama. She had held a fund raiser in her home the week before. I look at such families and wonder, why the different life trajectories? In one family we have one liberal, one conservative, and a mother who bucked lifelong habits to switch ideologies and shed long held beliefs.

I had a friend growing up named Ron. I spent a lot of time with him and his family. We played all the usual sports together, and I spent much time at his house. Yet we argued quite a lot as he tended to reflect the conservative attitudes of his parents on race and other social matters. I loved his parents. They were good and kind people who merely reflected the very same grounded beliefs I found in my own family and most others of my cultural milieu in that generation. I drifted off the reservation by rejecting the consensus world view of my culture very early in life, something that puzzles me to this day. Ron did not.

We reconnected many years later as adults when his father passed away and later spent time together when I was in Washington working on the Clinton welfare bill. At that same time, he was at the Pentagon for a brief stint as a Lieutenant Colonel in the Army Reserves. During several rounds of golf at the War College in D.C. where I dinged several cars belonging to the military brass with my errant golf shots, I got to know him again, now as an adult. His whole belief system had changed 180 degrees. Now, he was quite liberal on virtually all matters including views on race, economics, and on war and peace. This last set of views I thought surprising for someone who had risen so high in the military. By the early 1990s, he was more of a peacenik than I. It was as if his true values had been waiting to emerge until after he got away from the influences of his early home life.

I know I absorbed much of my local culture as a young kid. Still, early on I could feel a struggle within as I drifted toward a more liberal perspective, long before Ron made a similar journey. As I put my Peace Corps reflections together, and talked to other volunteers, it became evident how early on I deviated from the norms of my community. As mentioned earlier, nothing in my early years suggested anything special. I showed no intellectual promise. At the same time neither did I display any early signs of being a budding serial killer. I was so very average.

As I became old enough to ponder things, however, I began to evidence streaks of independent thinking. By my early teens, I was arguing that the Supreme Court was correct in desegregating schools even though I doubt anyone in my environment shared my enthusiasm. I still can see my family shaking their heads. "What the hell is wrong with him?" While sitting in a Catholic high school, I kept fighting (within my head at least) with my religion instructors even as I convinced myself to enter a seminary to study for the priesthood. For example, I could never quite accept the church's birth control arguments or the belief that a merciful God would not embrace alternative paths to spiritual truth. I really rebelled at the concept that nonbelievers in Catholicism were automatically doomed to hell, or maybe it was limbo back then, if they found spiritual comfort in another religious tradition. I mean, really, some child in Mongolia is not going to see God because he wasn't smart enough to be born in a Catholic family in Worcester. Excuse me!

I am not sure I was totally aware of this at the time, but I searched continually for ways to make small contributions to the larger good while continuing the struggle to accommodate religious conviction with the application of logical thought. Consistent with that personal struggle, I entered the Maryknoll Seminary after high school, an order that did foreign missionary work. My going in that direction was, in retrospect, an ill-disguised way of trying to help others I saw as less fortunate than myself. Eventually, I figured out that I was far less interested in saving souls than I was in helping what I considered oppressed people find a way forward.

It helped me that a few Maryknoll members of that era were into the Liberation Theology side of the Catholic spectrum, where Christ's teachings reflected Socialist, even Communist, tendencies. Back then, people still remembered Dorothy Day's Catholic Worker movement. You also had the Berrigan Brothers and Father Groppi who were Catholic priests at the forefront of fights for peace and justice. I simply had trouble with that belief in a personal God thing, otherwise self-sacrifice for a larger purpose made sense to me. Many other young Catholics of my era, however, went in a very different direction . . . joining the FBI or CIA or Military Intelligence to fight America's and God's enemies. They found my beliefs despicable, dangerous to the point of bordering on treason. I found their beliefs totally inconsistent with the sense of Christ's teachings as I absorbed them in my childhood. One faith but starkly different visions of what was right!

In college I sought work as an orderly in a hospital on the eleven-to-seven shift before heading off to classes. The night shift in an urban hospital can be taxing. There never was enough staff, sometimes only a senior student nurse, an aide, and myself ran the whole floor. Dealing with the sick and the dying offered many rewards but also many moments of drama and high emotion. You never forget stumbling on a patient's final moments and taking their pulse as you helplessly watch their life ebb away. I could have found easier work, but this permitted me to help others as I made enough money to keep body and soul together as I made my way through school.

My other college-period job was working with kids in a community action program that was operating in a distressed neighborhood. My boss in this program was a social worker. Over a couple of beers one day, he told me that I would make a great social worker and should seriously consider it as a career. I instinctively felt that was not right, don't you have to like people to be one of those. Still, I considered the MSW program at Boston University for a bit. When you don't have a plan for life, though, the smallest of matters can redirect the angle of your life trajectory. I still recall chatting with a very attractive coed, telling her I was considering going on for an MSW. She gave me this "you are way too smart for that kind of career" look. I believe that specific ambition faded from view immediately after that. Yes, I could easily be swayed by a pretty face.

During those chaotic sixties and seventies, there was always a struggle between emotion and reason. At Clark University, my undergraduate institution, I can recall learning about how the U.S. had conspired in the overthrow of governments of which it did not approve while supporting governments that were barbaric and oppressive. We did so simply because these barbaric regimes endorsed our national interests. It was irrelevant that they tortured and murdered their own people. I remember burning with shame and outrage as I became aware of my country's recent history while in college. In the previous decade, we casually conspired to overthrow elected regimes in Guatemala and Iran when they threatened the interests of fortune 500 companies. If we are no different than the other side, where in heaven's name is our moral authenticity?

After a near-death experience in my first anti-war march, I drifted further into leftist politics. I helped form something called the Student Action Committee (SAC) the acronym being a play on the title for the Strategic Air Command (also SAC) which flew bombers 24/7 so we could always retaliate when the Russkies attacked as they surely would. We were just so clever in those days. I even joined the Students for a Democratic Society (S.D.S.) though this was before the organization went into a death spiral of nihilistic self-absorption and violence. At the point I joined, there were a lot of very smart folk involved. Many struck me as blazing quick in their analysis of events and issues. I loved the intellectual sparring that went on. But there were signs of problems just ahead where endless debates over who was truly a leftist and which ideological position was the purest replaced reasoned argument about right and wrong. I am reminded of the Alt-Right extremists of today. It was only a matter of time before some could only prove their credentials, or their ideological purity, by turning to violence. I would remain an acolyte of Martin Luther King and Mahatma Gandhi. That was whom I was.

One humorous vignette as a would-be leftist occurred during my selective service medical exam. It is a revealing story. Okay, probably not, but it is a fun story. After Peace Corps I was in Milwaukee. I received a notice to report for my draft physical which I dutifully obeyed. At some point we all took a paper and pencil exam. There was an academic section which I breezed through followed by a kind of mechanical arts section where you did things like figure out which of the tools on the right was most like the tool pictured on the left. I had no idea what was going on in this part of the exercise and just made wild guesses. Perhaps intelligence is context specific after all.

The real fun was at the end of this mechanical arts exercise clearly designed to humiliate me and deflate any remaining sense of intellectual superiority. First, they asked if you had ever belonged to any of the organizations they listed on page Q. Most of the listed organizations looked like they had become extinct sometime during the Spanish Civil War period of the 1930s. I recall the Abraham Lincoln Brigade being listed. This group referred to those Americans among the 30,000 international volunteers who signed up to fight for the Spanish Republic against Franco and the Fascists. They were defending the elected government while Hitler was backing the military-led right-wing insurgents. I knew everyone in the room that day was too young for most of these groups (who developed such a silly list?).

The kicker was the open-ended question at the end. It asked if you belonged to any organization that advocated terrible things against the United States. Now I saw that other guys were causing trouble during the whole procedure while I politely went through my paces. Here, though, I did raise my hand. "Does S.D.S. qualify under question Q?" I asked, feigning innocence. "You bet your ass it does, buddy," a large, rather grumpy-looking sergeant replied. So, I answered yes and put down S.D.S. in the space provided. At the end of the process, when all before me were handing in their paperwork and exiting out the door, the final official between me and freedom looked at my name and then at me with what I interpreted as utter contempt. "You report to the third floor!" he barked. Uh-uh, this did not sound good but obediently I did so.

I sat quietly until three men arrived and ushered me into a room. I think they said they were from one or more intelligence agencies, interesting that we need so many of them. They started grilling me on all kind of things even including sexual partners. What was with that? Perhaps they were looking for Soviet female agents who seduce innocent young men like myself, then trading sexual favors for state secrets as if I would have any of those. I recall thinking that I would have to check into that at the time, perhaps I could make up some state secrets to trade. I answered some of their silly questions for a while, rather a long while in fact. During all this fun, I kept wondering why I did not see any of the real troublemakers from earlier in the day. This was obviously the equivalent of the principal's office to which the hardcore delinquents had been banished for suitable punishment.

At some point, I must have gotten bored. When they asked, "Well, you Commie Pinko, will you fight any, and all, enemies of the United States?" I leaned back and considered the question for a moment before responding along the following lines, "Now, would you first define enemy for me." The interrogator's eyes narrowed. I could tell he had concluded I was a Commie rat who needed to be squished like an annoying bug. It went on like this for quite a while, they would ask something, and I would have fun by running them in circles. Soon they were making veiled threats about dropping guys like me behind enemy lines in Vietnam. It was hard to take them seriously no matter how hostile they tried to look. As it turned out, I did turn twenty-six before my turn to be drafted came up though it was a close-run thing. If I had not made it, I would have been faced with a real moral dilemma. Would I have gone to Canada, to jail, or what? That would have been a real test as to whether I had any moral spine at all.

My wife once mentioned hearing at a conference that the ideological spectrum is not a straight line but rather a horseshoe. Both ends are closer to one another than to the middle. Each end may have very different substantive beliefs but those situated at the extremes look at the world in similar ways. There is a right and wrong, a black and white answer to all questions. Moreover, there are all kinds of things to be feared out there in the world, evil is everywhere and omnipresent. They typically see a small tribe of people who really have the right answers, who see the true way. Since life is this dangerous place with plots and enemies everywhere, one must always be vigilant and prepared to defend truth and justice, at least as they see it.

From my early anger at what I thought was a rather indefensible war in Vietnam and glacial progress toward social justice at home, I gradually moved to a different place. I became more intrigued by the intricacies of policy questions rather than the easy, often emotional, answers that were typically offered up. My rational side began to dominate my passionate side. The more I immersed myself in social problems such as welfare and poverty and family integrity the more I realized that good intentions and the bright clarity offered by one's values were not sufficient to finding satisfying solutions. It surely was not the case that values ceased to be important. I saw they were important indeed. It was merely the case that defining what is right or wrong is not always as simple as advertised. In fact, evidence cannot easily resolve normative ambiguity.

Welfare, defined broadly, was a case in point. Who held a better claim to being more compassionate? Would it be those who would extend income assistance to the poor without any substantive behavioral expectation in return or would it be those who would demand something back in return for the provision of help? Many of the severest critics of welfare were those closest to the poor themselves. They saw the two sides of the issue, what might happen in the absence of help and what might happen when help was given in the wrong way. The separation of cash from social services in the late 1960s was a rational decision at the time on both normative and efficiency grounds. I certainly bought into it. Yet, as with any policy decision that is easy to make in the moment, the true consequences are manifest only with the passage of time and in so many unexpected ways. Later, I concluded I had been hasty in my decision.

I recall the surprise Wendell Primus experienced when, during the planning for Clinton's welfare reform proposal, he tried to exempt those recipients with a physical disability from facing a work expectation as a condition for receiving cash assistance. It was the classic liberal thing to do. But the advocates for the disability community were generally outraged and yelled at him. They wanted to be treated like all others. They wanted to be viewed as responsible adults and as full partners in society. True, they may need some assistance, but they did not want that help in the form of a simple hand out. They did not want to be treated as lesser citizens.

I have never forgotten a long-ago article I read written by a New York Supreme Court Justice. He recalled growing up in the 1930s. It was the depression era, and he and his young college friends flirted with Socialism, even Communism. He argued that this was not a bad thing at all. It was the times that forced them to question all the assumptions with which they had been raised as children. They used this very challenging period to rethink everything they thought they knew and believed. In doing so, however, they were required to develop a foundational philosophy and world view that was theirs, not something handed to them. They did not put principles for living on like a suit off the rack. Rather, they were woven piece by piece in the cauldron of both large events and intense debate. He felt strongly that having gone through such a process made him and his childhood friends become more independent thinkers. In any case, they all went on to productive lives as adults.

My early years had been a kind of roiling, volatile, provocative, stimulating course in what life was all about. All that turmoil in the early years proved great preparation for a policy career. I developed an instinctive feel that getting to the truth would never be easy. Doing policy was fun because the best issues are very wicked. In truth, technical problems can be extremely complex, but most are solvable. I suspect there is an answer to that age-old question of how long it takes for the boat captain to eat his lunch when the river is going downstream at Y miles an hour and the boat was chugging upstream at Z miles an hour. I will never figure it out though. For those who command its mysteries, mathematics can answer so many questions that I find mind-bending . . . the speed and trajectory of a craft necessary to hit a moving celestial object located some three-billion miles away (as the New Horizons project did in a fly-by mission to take close-up pictures of the planet Pluto) or estimate the temperature of some distant sun in a faraway galaxy.

It is when we bring the human element into the picture that things get dicey. Some policy questions are beyond science. For example, questions about abortion likely will remain beyond the ability of science to resolve. It is fundamentally a question of values and belief. Others can nominally be answered by science but are not easily resolved! While 97 percent of scientists can agree that humans are contributing to global warming, that will not dissuade a substantial number of Americans from deciding that all these scientists are full of crap. Others will resist paying for necessary solutions to a planet that is heating up since the earth will burn to a crisp only after they are gone. Why bother, then? Within this volatile mixture of values and evidence and self-interest, our capacity to solve societal problems is taxed to the limit.

Science does a great job of providing input into our policy debates but a lousy job of providing final and irrevocable answers to or wicked social problems. Science can estimate the effects on labor supply or marriage probability or even fertility decisions associated with various income-guarantees and benefit-reduction rates (the rate at which benefits are lowered for each dollar earned). It can give us good data on welfare-induced migration or whether wage bill subsidies work. Such estimates, however, are seldom definitive. It cannot, however, resolve fundamental political or ideological disputes about which way to go when foundational norms are involved. One person's "that is not so bad" is another person's "that is unacceptable." It is such disputes that make some social policy questions so contentious and ultimately irritating!

While normative disputes disrupt political agreements even when social science provides reasonably clear results, this is far from the case in many situations. In fact, science can often add to our confusion. I recall attending a research presentation one day at IRP. The topic had something to do with crowd-out effects of the provision of a publicly provided health care option. Basically, what proportion of employer-provided health coverage plans would disappear if a public option were introduced, an unintended consequence that many would find unappealing? The presenter ran through a bunch of econometric studies that employed alternative assumptions and specified the equations in different ways. The results ranged from a crowd out effect of zero (no loss of private plans) to something like 75 percent where a large majority of private plans would disappear. I remember thinking how the average policy maker would respond. Thanks for nothing! The typical politician probably would grab the result that comported with his or her priors and run with it. The uncertainties attached to some social science results can further abet normative contention.

I used to be a little annoyed when I first started attending seminars and brown bags at IRP. Someone would ask a nontechnical question and be shot down with a quick "that is a normative concern of no consequence to us." The discussion would return to some technical question to the relief of most in the room. Over time I realized why this happened. The normative questions were not resolvable or at least not easily so. I suspect that is why so many in the academy are loath to enter the policy fray. It takes a peculiar type of masochist to expose themselves to the slings and arrows of the real world where clean answers are difficult to find, and many times rejected. I guess I was just born to be that kind of masochist. Still, I was always sensitive enough to caution my students that the real world is highly over rated and to be avoided at all costs if alternatives are available.

While values are inseparable from policy, neither can we do policy absent other personal attributes like curiosity and risk-taking. I recall a young woman my wife hired many years ago. My wife and she stayed in touch for decades. On the surface, this woman had everything going for her. She earned a Ph.D. a law degree and was sufficiently sophisticated as a computer systems person to work for the Chicago Board of Trade doing systems work. She was attractive, quick witted, very personable, and easy to be around. Moreover, she could communicate well orally and with the written word. If you took all the separate parts of her, she had more to contribute to any endeavor, including the doing of public policy, than I could ever hope to do. And yet, she remained in rather low-level positions through her professional life, always staying in jobs where others would tell her what to do. Both my spouse and I were baffled by this.

Something was missing in her, a vital spark. Yes, you need at least a few of the technical skills to be a policy wonk (though I obviate the necessity of that requirement to a large degree). You also need the soft skills I discuss in chapter one. And it might be a good thing to have a decent set of norms and values as discussed above. Beyond those things, however, you need that indefinable spark. You need to want to tilt at those hopeless windmills. You need to want to make a difference. You need to be able to take chances and suffer defeat, many defeats. You need to have an abiding curiosity about how the world works. We are talking more than science here.

When we do find students with the "right stuff," we need to do much more to prepare them for the trench warfare of doing policy. Was it Bismarck who said that watching policy being made was akin to the making of sausage . . . not a pretty sight? When preparing for my Peace Corps service in India, we received as much training in the culture we were to experience as we did in the substantive area in which we were supposed to contribute. Perhaps that is something to think about as we educate the next generation of knowledge producers. They need to be prepared just as diligently for the softer skills they will need and the professional cultural challenges they will face as they do for the technical skills to be mastered.

The academy provides virtually no preparation for teaching at the university level for those pursuing doctorates, except for those who support themselves with teaching assistantships, which really is on-the-job training. Amazingly, the academy provides even less training in what it means to contribute to the policy making process or how to do it, even for those doing relevant research. By that I mean the academy does precious little to acquaint students with the institutional cultures in which policymakers function and the vernacular ordinarily employed by them. Producing highly technical work that satisfies the academy will not suffice if one ever wants to cross the divide into the real world. Wishing does not make it so . . . you must work at it.

In the end, I loved the "wicked" social problems that others found so vexing. I loved working with other passionate and smart people as they struggled to find some way forward amidst the fog of policy wars. That the issues were so hard, and the slogging forward so impossible at times, made it even more worthwhile. It might have been futile but it sure was fun. It really is the hard that makes it great.

Technically, I have entered my eighth decade. That is, I am fast approaching my dotage. In my head, this fact once again permits me to vent to my values and emotions, much as I did as an irresponsible college student. I read the *New York Times* and I find myself once again roiling with emotions not felt since the 1960s. I am deeply troubled that we have concentrations of income and wealth not seen since just before the great crash of the 1920s. The Gini coefficient, a measure of inequality used by economists, now shows income and wealth disparities in America close to those found in Banana Republics that we used to laugh at not long ago.

A tiny fraction at the top of the distribution, 0.1 percent control 23.5 percent of all the wealth in the U.S., while the top 1 percent commands at least 35 percent. On the other hand, half of all Americans have negative net assets. Yet, too many of those at the top of the income distribution see fit to spend their fortunes turning the policy levers further in their favor. I sit back and stare with wonder. Is there no end to such avarice and greed?

When I look to the future I see many problems ahead. Then again, we have always seen problems ahead. Still, let me end this chapter with some thoughts I shared in 2013 with an audience of college level faculty who teach courses on poverty and public policy across the country (the complete talk can be found in the 2013-14 Winter edition of *Focus*):

When I look to the future what I find troubling is that our easy strategies for dealing with declining economic opportunities (stagnating incomes for most families along with growing inequality) appear exhausted. We have already delayed marriage, had fewer children, thrown our spouses and partners into the labor market, saved less and borrowed more (using household equity as personal ATMs), and added more advanced credentials after our names. And our children often delay establishing their own households (good luck in kicking them out of the nest). And still, economic outcomes grow more equal.

And yet, so little outrage. When new policies are posed, not enough ask, "What does it do for the poor or those falling further behind in an increasingly bitter Darwinian struggle for success?" So, let us ask again, have we lost the War on Poverty? On a superficial level, yes! But let us think of the question in a different way. Think of the trends over the past several decades that would be expected to exacerbate poverty and increase the economic struggles for so many.

Demographic changes—particularly the rise on single-parent households raising children.

Globalization—where firms seek to lower labor costs by outsourcing higher-paying jobs overseas.

Technology-driven changes, automation, and computerization—where tasks formerly done by humans are now done by digital technology and robotics (can robot-driven trucks be far off?).

Immigration—rising in the mid-1960s, we saw the proportion of foreign born jump from 5 percent to 23 percent, many (though surely not all) of whom are low-skilled individuals.

Deunionization—unionized workers in the private sector fell from about one-third of the workforce in the 1950s to about 7 percent in recent years.

A fractal economy—even within specific sectors of the economy, compensation has grown wildly unequal even in the face of modest differences in talent and contribution. A typical CEO's remuneration went from 27 times the average worker's pay in 1973 to 262 times the average in 2008.

Macro-policy changes—aggregate federal taxes and benefits reduced inequality by 23 percent in 1979 but by only 17 percent in 2007.

When you consider these trends and others that might be cited, maybe we did better than many of us had thought in at least moderating the adverse effects of an increasingly hostile world for the less-well off. Still, so much remains to be done.

I remember asking a colleague many years ago why he thought the United States had such an impoverished safety net for the disadvantaged. He gave only a one-word answer: heterogeneity. Over the years I came to appreciate his terse response. We are too tribal and have no common identity. It is too easy to say, and to believe, that the less successful are "them" and not "us." They did it to themselves. We are not all in this together. It is instructive to note that Americans are much more likely (by some 30 percentage points) than out European counterparts to respond positively to questions that assign success to personal factors as opposed to luck or social environments or family fortunes.

Let me finish by returning one more time to the Wisconsin Idea. Key to the idea is that one generation helps the next . . . passes on the torch so to speak. Each of us has a responsibility to pass on to the next generation an understanding of and a passion for an issue, poverty, and a population, the poor, that too often go unnoticed these days. If we do not, who will?

In sum, the poverty warriors of my generation probably did do a better job than we ever imagined. At the same time, the problems before us loom larger than ever. As resources concentrate at the top, the remainder of society could well descend into some version of a Dickensian horror, a Darwinian struggle of epic proportions. Democracy itself may be in danger as a wealthy oligarchy struggles to maintain privilege and power. I hope I am wrong and am comforted by the belief that most doomsday prophecies seldom come to pass. But you never know, you just never know.

What I do know, or at least strongly suspect, is that poverty research in the future must extend beyond the narrow confines of technical questions. The usual methods and conventional investigatory strategies will not plumb the deeper psychological and sociological terrains where belief systems are formed and sustained. Think about the following for a moment. The country becomes absorbed in the death of one child and the capture of the responsible miscreant. We were glued to our televisions during the Boston Marathon bombing where three people lost their lives. The whole city was locked down until the perpetrators were apprehended. There was widespread outrage.

We have tens of thousands of amenable deaths each year due to an expensive, inefficient health care system, totally bizarre gun laws, and unacceptable levels of inequality and child poverty. Yes, some protest, particularly the mass shootings in our schools, but little gets done. The future of poverty research needs a broader net, more imagination, and a healthy dose of old fashion moral passion. We need a new generation of policy wonks that care and carry within themselves a fire born of anger. There is, however, some good news. The good news for future policy wonks is that my generation left so much work for you to do. Simply consider the vast numbers of working class folk out who have seen their incomes stagnate for so long while watching their opportunities evaporate in the face of automation, globalization, and the loss of supports such as deteriorating educational opportunities and declining union strength. They face a future of opioid addiction and the allure of snake oil salesmen like Donald Trump.

You can thank me later.

CHAPTER 11

A WAYWARD ACADEMIC OR THE CULTURAL DISCONNECT

Too much sanity may be madness—and the maddest
of all is to see life as it is and not as it should be.

—*Miguel de Cervantes*

This chapter overviews the sorry story of my misfortune as a wayward academic. Not everything in my career was wine and roses. In exploring this tragedy, I tap into some dark and myopic corners of the academy's culture as well as my own many personal failings. I start this story by pointing out that one topic defined my final years as a policy wonk and wayward academic. It was the concept of professional and institutional culture writ broadly. I focused on institutional culture as an explanation for why separate programs are difficult to integrate into seamless service systems in several other works, chief among them *The Boat Captain's Conundrum*. I also focused on the concept of professional culture and the disconnect between the academy and the policy world in *Evidence-Based Policymaking*, authored by Karen Bogenschneider and myself. Most of all, I do what I do best in this chapter. I whine a lot. I have two undeniable talents, napping and whining. I am waiting for them to be made official Olympic sports.

Culture, in brief, is the soup of norms, patterns, expectations, language, and incentive systems surrounding and embracing us in ways that fundamentally shape our behaviors and beliefs. In my personal memoir, *Confession of a Clueless Rebel*, I muse how I broke away from my youthful, limiting culture . . . Catholic, working class, tribal, and insular to become a radically different adult. The notion of culture has so fascinated me in recent years that it became a central theme in my first two fictional works, *Tenuous Tendrils* and *Palpable Passions*, both published in 2017. In each novel, I explore how one's cultural environment shapes choices, possibilities, and attitudes.

I start with one of my favorite vignettes involving my good spouse. In earlier times, she labored in a high administrative position with the Wisconsin court system. Many years ago, the Wisconsin legislature, in its wisdom, decided to kick the state Supreme Court out of the Capitol building. They wanted the space. The justices said, "No way, unless you build us a *palais de justice* overlooking one of Madison's lakes." My wife would have had to manage such an undertaking and came home all upset. How can we build a Palace of Justice with seven corner offices, each of equal size and shape, and all on the same floor overlooking the lake? She knew that no sitting justice would accept even the slightest hint that one of their colleagues had been treated preferentially. I had a good laugh, in which she did not join. Academics (at top research universities) and justices share a common cultural attribute . . . their egos are continually stroked and thus risk inflation. This gives them a sense of entitlement which makes walking through doorways without bruising the sides of their heads an iffy proposition. Culture is a powerful force. By the way, in the end the justices stayed put, at least while she held that position.

This notion of culture represents an omnipresent reality in our lives. It shapes our understandings of our wider world, our perceptions and normative beliefs, our communication preferences, our ambitions and purposes, and just about everything else that counts. Many things go into shaping our dominant personal perspectives and world views. What is important to realize is that we often fail to fully apprehend the world in which we are immersed. Below, I do some complaining which admittedly is obsequious but not irrelevant. I look at how one small part of the academic community and I interacted with dismal results. In retrospect, I find that sad story very illuminating, as I do with all the counters in my candy store. My own experiences reinforced some broader implications for cross-cultural understanding and communication in general. I remain grateful for all the epiphanies and insights that came my way.

In all the important ways, my entire professional life has involved negotiating a demanding tightrope between the academic and the policy worlds. I nominally had a position in one while predominantly working in the other. Is that even legal? It certainly is not wise. Anyways, this is like living in a bicultural world which, I have discovered, is excellent for those preferring to accentuate their bipolar, even schizophrenic, dispositions. In layman's terms, living in these two worlds can drive you nuts. Those wishing to lead sensible and sane lives are well advised to choose a single dominant culture in which to spend most of their waking hours.

Unfortunately, I have never been a wise person, a fact not in dispute among my acquaintances. While foolish, this high-wire act between the academy and policy worlds offered me one clear advantage. My bicultural immersion helped me understand each culture much better than if I had chosen to live within one and study the other. I often felt like the proverbial anthropologist living among primitive cultures. Total immersion helps the observer to better understand a foreign world. However, I could never quite decide which was my native tribe and which the primitive one. In any case, this has given me insights into what it takes to communicate across these two very different cultures where any interaction can be awkward at best. Unfortunately, I see the chasm between those in the academy and those in the real world widening, not closing. This is a sad trend in my opinion, if true.

First, a moment on terminology. I call one tribe the academy since their members largely identify with the function of knowledge-production or the creation of new theories and insights for the betterment of mankind, or the advancement of their careers, whichever comes first in their own minds. The other tribe I refer to as members of the policy-world (sometimes referred to as the real world) since they tend to be knowledge-utilization junkies as they seek ways to improve society and people, if that is even possible. They are the policymakers and implementers and managers that we tend to associate with public bodies like legislatures and executive agencies as well as many think-tanks and trade or interest groups that dot our national and state capitals. In fact, both tribes produce and consume knowledge and each side evidences considerable heterogeneity within their ranks. That is, not all knowledge producers and consumers are identical. Still, this is how Karen Bogenschneider and I have created a boundary between communities in our writings on this topic.

Second, an important caveat or two. Below, I descend eventually into the depths of that most mysterious of all rituals within the academy . . . the tenure process. I do so by exploring my own experiences with this ancient rite of passage. In truth, my aborted effort at securing an academic position, not my idea to begin with, needs to be seen in context. My perceptions of the academy are historical in character. However, I discuss the issues in a way that implies contemporary validity about how things are done in the academy. As such, I risk mischaracterizing some since, while my example may be historically accurate, it is about two decades old after all.

In fact, I have been informed that changes have been made to improve the processes I touch upon more below. I have no idea whether the situation is materially different now, but some believe that to be the case. My story is also written about a single departmental process, which might be misleading to a casual reader. What I write about below, to the best of my knowledge and based on discussions with colleagues across the disciplinary spectrum, taps what historically has been some of the more universal aspects of the academy's dominant culture. My rhetorical victim, the University of Wisconsin Department of Social Work in this case, is only a convenient illustration of what is, or had been, things common among research universities. I have been informed that the School recently has taken steps to better integrate research with teaching and application within the tenure seeking ordeal. Again, more later.

Despite my whining below, I loved living mostly among members of the academic tribe. Despite their idiosyncrasies, I enjoyed romping in a university playground among the intellectual elite. Most of them commanded mental quickness, substantive knowledge, and analytical depth. I found that my own cognitive and analytical competencies improved merely by proximity, if not intimate association. Then again, they hardly could get worse.

Importantly, the academy provided an opportunity to pass on what little knowledge and insight I possessed to the next generation of young students. The real problem was this: I was not, by disposition or preference, a scholar. Thus, a certain amount of cleverness was required to make this tightrope-walk work. I almost pulled it off but, alas, not quite.

You probably have heard it said that three factors are important to academic tenure and promotion decisions—research, teaching, and public service. That is not quite right. During my day, the three that really counted were research, research, and research . . . at least at those institutions where teaching is viewed at best as an unavoidable nuisance. Of course, not all research counted equally. Research, in this context, only means articles published in peer-reviewed journals.

In my long experience in the academy, good teaching would not hurt your cause unless you worked at it too hard. It would not be wise to be seen with students too often, certainly not undergraduates, nor should you express much enthusiasm for the classes you are stuck teaching. Atrocious student reviews will never be a mark against you if your production as a researcher is exemplary. If your research production is exceptional, no one will even notice rampant student drug use or waves of suicides following their attendance at your lectures. If your research is not that great, however, you best do well in the classroom though that is unlikely to save your fanny.

I recall an assistant professor in Social Work once telling me that she had been cautioned about spending too much time with students. Now that I think on it, she did not get tenure. I made the mistake one day of casually mentioning this vignette to a powerful state legislator with whom I was working at the time. I thought he was going to jump out of his pants. Here was proof that the university did not care about teaching undergraduates, not exactly the best kept secret in the world but hard to prove. I had to beg him to back off by mentioning how much trouble I would get in with the UW administration before he would back down. Thank god he liked me.

In research universities like Wisconsin, teaching is at best tolerated. At least that was my experience associating with IRP affiliates for over four decades, most of whom had faculty positions in mainstream departments. I cannot recall any discussions about teaching, or at least so few that they made no impression on me. in all that time. If it did come up, the discussion mostly ran along the lines of the misfortune of getting stuck in the classroom. Very recently, I was having lunch with two long-time IRP colleagues. One had recently retired and accepted Emeritus status. I expressed surprise, believing she would remain a faculty member somewhat longer. "Well, they expected me to teach a service course the next semester (usually a larger, lecture course for undergraduates). That prospect pushed me out the door." This was on the extreme side but I heard such sentiments for decades.

Public service, on the other hand, is always a loser. Teaching is something woven within the rationale of a university but public service strikes many in the academy as a frivolous add-on. You cannot be a serious researcher if you care about the real world, the so-called Wisconsin idea notwithstanding. While the sentiment most associated with the Wisconsin ideal is "the boundaries of the university are the boundaries of the state," this catchy phrase has little currency in the academy of today. Back in the days when the Wisconsin Idea emerged, scholars from the University of Wisconsin easily moved up and down State Street betwixt the academy and government. Respected members of the academy such as John Commons, Charles McCarthy, and Richard Ely worked with Wisconsin legislators on several ideas that eventually became national initiatives including a worker's compensation program, a progressive income tax, and various labor market improvements. Perhaps more importantly, they helped elevate the professionalism of the state legislature by developing an independent staff capability, on occasion taking staff positions themselves. They wrested control of the bill writing process from the powerful corporate special interests who previously drafted legislation for friendly politicians that favored their own narrow business interests. The academy and the state were true partners. Given that the corporate interests once again have seized control of the legislative-writing process in Wisconsin and other states, we need that state-university partnership to make a comeback.

That sense of collaboration lasted for decades. In the 1930s, Ed Witte was summoned by President Roosevelt to head the committee that created the Social Security Act; and in the early 1960s Robert Lampman did the key analyses that provided the conceptual foundations for the War-on-Poverty. Throughout this period, there existed a dominant ethos that scholarship had a moral component dedicated to the public good. An early University of Wisconsin president, Thomas Chamberlain, captured this underlying foundation of the Wisconsin Idea as follows.

Scholarship for the sake of scholars is refined selfishness.
Scholarship for the state and the people is refined patriotism.

A wonderful sentiment to be sure but probably a tenure-killer in today's academic climate. As the social sciences chased the methods and respect enjoyed by the physical sciences with rapt adoration, their interest in and connection with the real world faded from view.

I loved Irv Piliavin, the faculty member who brought me into the academic world. He was a funny, engaging, and very bright man though I suspect many students found him most intimidating. We talked a lot over the years and I found his biases illuminating. He would characterize colleagues who decided to become administrators within the University as selling out their true calling for mere money. He really could not understand why they would abandon research. And those that drifted toward public service were a bigger mystery to him. While I am certain he liked me personally, I am convinced I disappointed him terribly. Rather than following in his footsteps, I had gone over to the dark side. In truth, I never left the dark side.

I was never shy about expressing my opinions on these matters. Still, there were these inexplicable pushes to get me on the faculty. The faculty of that period presumed that this is what I must want since this is what all members of the academy want. The first ill-fated attempt landed me as an assistant professor in something called the Department of Governmental Affairs, which sounded okay at first blush. I was sent over for an arranged meeting with the head of this small department, a meeting arranged sometime before I headed off to D.C. to help with welfare reform. The more we talked, the more I realized that accepting this position held absolutely no advantage whatsoever for me. I could not even figure out why this department existed. But I went along with the program because I am a nice guy, and I knew that my colleagues went to some trouble to set this up. It turned out to be the fiasco I anticipated it would be. I basically had no contact with the place and my association with them disappeared seamlessly in a couple of years, one of which I spent in Washington.

The next push came while I was working on Clinton's welfare reform bill in D.C. I ran into some UW colleagues from Social Work in an airport who told me of the push to get me a faculty position. They seemed so excited about this. Why won't these people just go away I thought? But all I did was smile. Part of the push, according to Bill Wambach (then the associate director for administration at IRP), was coming from UW administration. The higher powers apparently argued that I had been teaching so much in Social Work that I should be a member of the faculty. I concluded that the real reason was that it would be cheaper for the university if I signed on, though the mechanics of that theory eluded me. Okay, I thought once again, whatever!

When I returned to Madison in June 1994, I had a half-time appointment as a clinical assistant professor in Social Work and a half-time appointment as a senior scientist for the work I was performing through IRP (mostly research and consulting) including my role as associate director. I did assess one thing before letting the faculty part of this arrangement happen. I calculated when my tenure clock would expire assuming it ran at half-speed, which it did. Better still, it would stop altogether when I served as acting IRP director, which I also did for a year.

No problem, then, I thought upon finishing my calculation. Most probably, I would retire before the tenure decision arrived, so what could be the harm in letting this happen. Tenure, after all, would never mean the same thing to me as it did to others who, upon failing to get the brass ring, would need to leave the university to seek a position elsewhere. At that point, there was no way in hell I was going anywhere else. Nothing would change, I would continue to be a policy wonk operating out of IRP and I cannot imagine Social Work would get rid of such a popular teacher. After all, by now I was fully entrenched in a rewarding career and enjoyed the status of a well-known figure on the national policy scene.

As I now write these words, the back-forty quality of my passive acquiescence to this faculty scheme astounds me. What an idiot! I really should have been taken out and shot for allowing myself to be pushed into this position . . . a misbegotten adventure from the get go. For one thing, most of my fellow faculty in Social Work did not know me or what I did. This was a significant problem. Mark Courtney, a child welfare scholar now at the University of Washington, was one of the senior faculty members who was punished for some infraction and had to serve as my tenure advisor for that year. These poor schmucks turned over on an annual basis as I recall, probably because the hopelessness of my situation was obvious to all. But all I can really say is that it was obvious to me.

I can only imagine that senior faculty must have drawn straws to determine who would get stuck with me for the upcoming year, unless the role really was doled out as punishment for a major transgression as I surmised at the time. Mark was so traumatized by this duty he left Wisconsin, though perhaps there were other reasons. When he did escape, I was instrumental in helping Mark land the head job at Chapin Hall for Children at the University of Chicago. To assist his cause, I endured the longest reference call of my life. We had to reschedule the final half of it for a second day when I ran out of time as the initial call dragged on and on. I must have been quite talented at telling lies on behalf of colleagues, he got the position.

In any case, Mark was my only mentor who appreciated the ridiculousness of my seeking a faculty position in Social Work. Well, that is the way I remember it. He put it this way, "I know that you work with the very top poverty scholars in the country, but their names mean nothing to most of the social work faculty here. You have a helluva selling job to do." I wanted to say that they should get out more, but I remained silent.

Outside of Social Work, I was a player. Therefore, unsolicited job offers from other places came my way on occasion. Al Kahn (eminent Social Work faculty member at Columbia and IRP Executive Committee member) tried to get me to New York; Rebecca Maynard (economist and long-time affiliate at IRP) tried to lure me to the University of Pennsylvania; Judy Gueron offered me a position at MDRC (Manpower Development Research Corporation), a prestigious evaluation firm located in New York; Kris Moore asked if I would come to Child Trends in D.C., to name a few I can recall. It was always flattering but I never was really interested, nor did I care to exploit the time-honored game of securing an outside offer to put the squeeze on your home institution. Again, money never held any charm for me.

In addition, several headhunters inquired about my possible interest in foundation positions. I recall two contacts that did command some of my attention, one for a spot with the Annie

E. Casey Foundation and one with the Ford Foundation. I did not think very seriously about the Casey position, but the Ford possibility was the one that, in truth, strongly captured my interest. You know what they say about philanthropic positions . . . everyone laughs at your jokes and you never have a bad meal. I wound up flying out to New York three times for extensive interviews. But in the end, Mary (my spouse) made that decision for me. She repeatedly told me to have a good time in the Big Apple. There was no way she was going, and we had already done one long-term commute during my year in D.C.

My appointment in Social Work was only as a clinical assistant professor. This is some junior league faculty member position and it was only half-time, I cannot imagine being lower on the faculty prestige ladder. To be honest, it held no prestige whatsoever in my eyes. It would be the equivalent to Tom Brady, perhaps the top NFL quarterback of our era, hooking on with a local semi-pro team named the Hoboken Steamrollers. From outside the academy, it looked ridiculous next to my senior scientist title and associate director status. Inside the hierarchical world of the academy, however, even the lowest faculty position rises well above any other professional title. The scientist and faculty positions are supposed to have a rough equivalency (with distinct duties) but they do not in reality.

I spite of all this, a clinical position was perfect for me, at least that would be true in any rational world. Being a good clinical faculty member involved doing outreach, translating research for broader audiences, and looking for useful applications for what the academy produced. It is what I did every day. I still could not estimate the expected duration of the boat captain's lunch break, but I could do these other things better than virtually anyone else. Interpretation, translation, and communication were my strengths. Few did these things better or with more flair. Moreover, given the pace at which my clock was running, my tenure decision would hit about three or four hours before my anticipated retirement date, not the three or four decades typically remaining in the career of a senior faculty member. As it turned out, I never did hit the end of my tenure clock. It was still running when I nominally retired, even though I continued to maintain a robust research and consulting schedule for years after that.

Now, the truth is that I would not vote to give someone like me tenure as a real faculty member. I had never been acculturated properly for that role despite my decades-long dalliance in the academic fold. At the same time, this half-time clinical thing they cooked up should have been a no-brainer. From my biased perspective, there would have been zero risk in just giving me tenure for a clinical position. I had earned it long before this position was created for me. There were two issues, however. First, all my prior work did not count, weird but true. An entire career within the academy was irrelevant. More importantly, the tenure decision would be made by the senior faculty in Social Work. Now that second point *was* a real problem.

First, the small issues! It is possible that I had alienated one Social Work colleague. She indicated to me that she wanted to become an IRP affiliate. When I approached Bobbi Wolfe, who was director at that time, she displayed no interest in extending such to the faculty member in question. In fact, Bobbi was rather against it, though the reasons were not terribly clear to me. I could always tell when Bobbi really didn't like something, she would give me her look . . . the "you are nuts" look. For a moment, I hesitated, realizing that not extending affiliate status to this person would likely come back to bite me in the ass. Just for that one moment, I considered asking Bobbi to bend on this one and telling her why. Then I stopped, reminding myself that my tenure vulnerability should play no part in any IRP decisions. All I can say is that I was told later that this woman was in the anti-Corbett camp though I never bothered to gather intelligence on what specific faculty thought of me.

For some senior Social Work faculty, I suspect I was thought of as one of those poverty boys from IRP. Worse, I was one of Irv Piliavin's boys; and Irv did leave a few burned bridges in his wake. Again, this is mere speculation on my part since I never asked. I had long heard that some faculty felt they had been forced to accept these poverty-types onto the faculty in the past even though they were not real social workers. Resentments had lingered.

Technically speaking, I was not a social worker either since I never did bother to get an M.S.W. on the way to my doctorate, though I took most of the required courses. For sure, I did not take the Interpersonal Skills course, an omission reflected in my current paucity of friends. This tiny omission should have prevented me from teaching the policy practicum courses in the school. Only bona fide social workers were permitted to teach these practice courses. Chalk up another ethical lapse for me though there were many co-conspirators in this transgression. We always prepared a song and dance routine when accreditation time came around but never had to use it.

There may have been one final impediment. The number of clinical faculty had been trimmed over the past decade or so. This meant letting people go, which always creates hard feelings. I am sure those who might have seen their beloved comrades being put out to pasture were a bit angered by the creation of a new clinical position for this Corbett character. It wasn't my idea I wanted to say, but I suspect that would have been a futile gesture. Ah, yes, there is nothing like academic politics.

All these might have been valid points. However, I suspect my ultimate challenge, and the real issue, lay elsewhere. I will describe it by example. One day, a small issue arose during a Social Work faculty meeting early in my tenure-seeking era. I have long since forgotten what it was. Still being relatively new to the faculty governance process, I was stunned at how long the discussion went on. Not only did everyone get a say but everyone got the opportunity to repeat what everyone else already had said. As I sat there, contemplating the different ways I might take my own life, the following hit me. My tenure prospects were absolute toast. At the time, I was the acting director of IRP and had use of the director's office just down from the associate director for administration, Bill Wambach. In my head I calculated that if I threw out this small issue being discussed that day as I passed Bill's office, he might throw something back for me to ponder. Still, we would have resolved the thing before I arrived at my office some seven seconds later.

Now, I entertained the following horrific possibility. Consider what likely would happen when the Social Work faculty confronted my fate even if it only meant that I would be made a half-time associate clinical professor, not even a real professor, for maybe a couple of hours before retiring. They would get all tangled up in what a clinical position meant, whether it justified considering factors other than pure rigorous research published in peer reviewed journals (which I had done on numerous occasions but always jointly with others), and what their bending of time honored tradition would mean to the future of all tenure decisions, the integrity of the academy, and to the very fate of Western civilization.

Such conundrums, I feared, would paralyze them. They would have to be secluded in that walled up Sistine Chapel vault where the cardinals are sealed until they choose a new pope. In this case, however, they would never reach a decision, their bones to be retrieved at some point in the distant future. I could never have that on my conscience. After all, many had spouses and children. So, right from the start I knew I would retire from Social Work before my tenure clock would run out. No problem there, I could keep on working at IRP as long as I wished and even after formal retirement. Moreover, I would do my IRP work, as it happened, at a significantly higher pay level. Oh yes, my pay rate began to deviate between my two appointments with my compensation as a scientist increasingly outstripping my pay as a faculty member.

Yes, I am such a numb-nuts that, in the end, it cost me money to walk into a classroom, to do committee work, and (worst of all) to attend faculty meetings. It is hard to imagine a more deadening experience than faculty meetings. Henry Kissinger was right that faculty disputes are so "vitriolic because the issues are so trivial and the egos so massive." Social workers are, I admit, nice to each other but that also could present a problem. Everyone was so nice that they danced around issues forever rather than make decisions that might disappoint someone. I spent much time looking about the faculty meeting rooms for a beam that might support my hefty body as it swung from the end of a rope.

I am not totally sure why I had such difficulty with my social work colleagues. The economists I worked with seemed to like me and respect me, even the tough ones who generally were considered difficult, which is putting it mildly. Earlier, I mentioned the dean from the School of Human Ecology looking over my curriculum vita in his office. I sensed he was concerned by my prominent position on the governor's hit list. At one point, he stopped and said, "I am sure we can get you tenure here in the school." Once, upon meeting a university dean as acting director of IRP, the man shook my hand vigorously. "I am so happy to meet you. I have heard so much about you." His enthusiasm seemed very genuine. Once again, I was stunned. Everyone seemed to respect me except those in my so-called home department. What was with that? My initial response to that puzzle is that they knew me better, to know me is to realize I am a fraud. The thing is, though, they didn't know me very well at all.

To be fair, I do think the Social Work faculty quite strong today. And they do a good job of educating the students. In the end, the students were worth all the aggravation of being a pretend academic though I started my teaching career long before this ill-considered effort. I yet send the school a decent annual contribution to support their work with students. Still, the fact that they knew me less than others in the university, and in the broader policy and academic communities, remains a nagging conundrum. That puzzle, in the end, likely is mostly my fault. I could have done much more to reach out to them, but those were such busy times and I was reluctant to market myself. By instinct, I was always more comfortable working behind the scenes, the guy who made things happen without taking much upfront credit. But success in the academy demands selfishness and self-promotion. In retrospect, I might have attached my name to various products and projects in which I played a significant role but doing so would have made me very uncomfortable. Sad but true!

I still recall one evening during those frantic days when I was balancing teaching, administration, research, public speaking, and several other roles. I got a call from my tenure mentor, or whatever they called these individuals burdened with such an onerous task. It probably was the third or fourth in the round-robin parade of losers in the annual straw-drawing contest to determine who got stuck with me. This woman went on about how to improve the organization of my tenure package that would go to senior faculty for the annual review. I am sure she was correct and doing her best to be helpful. I simply dug up as many of my annual products that I could find in the moment and stuffed them into a folder. As she droned on, I felt myself reaching a breaking point. I came within a whisker of saying, "Hey, let's end this now. I just don't have the time. Damn it, I am doing way too many things that are important. This is just crap. Let's just agree it was a bad idea. No harm, no foul." But I did not. I regretted that lost moment ever since.

I had one more lost moment to end this charade. Irv Piliavin caught me one day. He said, "Tom, go over and talk to Mel Morgenbesser (school director at the time) about your tenure situation. They should be past ready to give it to you by now." I was dubious but thought he must know since he was senior faculty who had been around forever. It turns out he did not know a thing. Poor Mel squirmed in exquisite anguish as he went on about how much I was liked in the department but . . .. Somehow, I diverted Mel from having to complete the sentence. I knew the substance of all the buts from the get-go. I felt so bad for him and secretly cursed Irv. I knew I was an issue, why didn't Irv know that from the inside. For the second time I came within a whisker of just ending it as I watched Mel's agony that day. In truth, I know why I never pulled the plug. I liked teaching and there might be a tiny chance that walking away could impact those opportunities to work with students. Not at all likely since finding willing faculty to teach all the courses was a constant struggle, but the prospects of being shut out of the classroom remained above a zero probability in my head. Then again, I was never good at math.

Perhaps I can attach one moment of regret to my failure as an academic. Bob Haveman and Bobbi Wolfe once sat me down for a serious talk. I suspect it was toward the end of Bobbi's tenure as director and before we began to full-court press Karl Scholz into taking the position. They asked me if I would consider becoming the next IRP director, essentially moving up from being associate director. After all, I had already run the place for a year while Bobbi had been on a sabbatical and had been a very hands-on Associate Director. It seemed like a great idea to me, a natural position given my skills at schmoozing all kinds of folk and cross-walking institutional cultures . . . the academy, government, evaluation firms, think tanks, interest and trade groups, the media, and others. Besides, I was good at thinking strategically and seeing the big picture.

The catch, they said, was that I would have to be tenured. I smiled but said nothing in the moment as I recall. Tenure would never happen. I knew that from that early faculty meeting where the agonizing paralysis of faculty governance hit me upside the head like a two-by-four. I suspect that the discussion of the directorship was genuine on their part though it did occur to me that this might yet be another ploy to motivate me toward tenure. Others always seemed far more interested in my status than I ever was. If the motivational theory were correct, it was doomed from the start since that ball was not really in my court. Still, this lost opportunity to lead IRP did constitute a small regret for me.

Even after I formally retired from teaching and IRP management, this tenure farce would pop up at unexpected times. I was sharing a taxi with Maria Cancian in New York. It was 2004 and we were on our way to a conference at Columbia University. Suddenly, she mentioned the fact that Dan Meyer, who started out as an RA on the child support project Irv Garfinkle and I had put together years earlier, was now department director. Getting tenure could happen now, she argued, though did not elaborate on how things had changed so dramatically. I tried not to laugh as I thanked her and declined her offer. Many years later, the current director raised the possibility very casually as we were having lunch at Blackhawk Country Club, which has the best view in town from the terrace. She is a very nice person, a great director, but I had no idea what she was thinking on this one occasion.

It might surprise some that I accepted a monetary sacrifice to become a pretend academic. To repeat, I was paid quite a bit less for my role as a traditional academic. My colleagues in economics would disown me for this. The thing is, money never motivated me. The reason is quite simple. My mother obsessed about not having enough money and she became a rather bitter, unhappy woman. I promised myself early on that the pursuit of wealth would never dominate my life. Besides, my spouse made considerably more than I, so we always were quite comfortable financially, thanks to her. I recall concluding once that, even though I was acting director of IRP one year, I was very likely the lowest paid affiliate associated with the institute. I suspect I won that award, so to speak, with considerable ease. Fortunately, our needs were never great in any case. I only wanted enough to cover the basics and, beyond that, to enable me to call someone to fix anything that broke in the house. Now, that *was* very import ant to me, given how inept I was at life's everyday tasks.

For me, the academy remained the best platform from which I could erect my policy candy store. I was surrounded by whip smart people, I had almost total freedom to pick and choose what policy delights to put into my various store counters, and I enjoyed passing on my policy knowledge to students, some of whom might even follow in my footsteps. Specifically, IRP enabled me to connect with the best and the brightest in my areas of interest from across the nation and even beyond our borders. It also brought so many unsolicited opportunities my way. Most of us policy wonks want to be players…to get a chance to participate in the next great adventure. Being at a place like IRP, I never had to worry about being shut out of the fun, policy adventures kept falling into my lap. Make no mistake, I do love the academy, even the not so good parts. Still, while I was in the academy I was never fully of the academy.

Irv Piliavin once told me that I had problems with authority. If I had just played the game, all would have been okay. I never thought of myself as being that rebellious. Well, maybe just a little. Oh hell, I titled the recent republication of my personal memoir *Confessions of a Clueless Rebel*. So, perhaps I am one of those. In any case, I am clearly too selfish and perhaps a bit too stubborn to follow all the rules. I simply enjoyed playing in my candy store way too much. After all, I am still just a kid at heart who has never really grown up! And what kid doesn't love to be surrounded by a lot of candy!

There is, however, a larger story associated with this bout of narcissistic whining. As most acquainted with me know, moaning and groaning is a peculiar strength of mine. A former neighbor, a social worker herself who worked with teen delinquents rehabbing houses for the needy as a treatment modality, once bought me a shirt that said, "No Whining." Apparently, I would go on and on about my dislike of yard work. I was a big fan of artificial flora and Astro Turf, but I could not get the neighborhood to agree. They preferred the real stuff. Go figure!

Perhaps the biggest critic of my "poor Tom" theme is the current director of the Wisconsin School of Social Work, Stephanie Robert. She is, hands down, one of my favorite social work types and a great head person for the school. Better still, she reads my books. My best guess is that she did something truly despicable in her prior life and this is her karmic penalty, reading my books that is. She praised my first fictional work, saying that my rendering of female characters was so authentic despite my being a clueless male. My point is that I must possess a strong feminine side...a claim that, when made by me, results in most women present losing their lunch. On the other hand, she believes that the story of woe regarding my experiences in the social work school is way too chipperish. On that point, I suspect she is bang-on. Like I said, I am a whiner.

Nevertheless, here is how I look at it. Bottom line, I fully agree that I am not suited for a conventional faculty role. As I keep saying, I am not a traditional scholar, far from it. A clinical position, though, is much different. Such a position reflects the rhetoric that could be found (and ignored) in many university mission statements of my era. Among other things, these often call for faculty to synthesize and translate research for the public good. That is what I did all the time. I pushed to realize that part of the university mission that gets overlooked given that traditional faculty do not get rewarded for doing it. If you don't reward something, it won't get done.

I can state, even without too much blushing, that I contributed much to the academy. I excelled as a teacher, helped manage the premier poverty research entity in the country, brought in millions of dollars either directly or indirectly, worked my fanny off flying around the country giving talks, consulted on a variety policy and programmatic matters at all levels of government, maintained an exemplary reputation in the policy and philanthropic worlds, wrote reams of papers and reports on policy and program evaluation matters that were very well received, maintained a place on the speed dials of media types from around the country, and developed networks for bringing research and researchers to policymakers. That is just a partial list. For a scholar, however, only narrow, technical peer-reviewed papers count and those bored me to tears. They always struck me as being as being narrow, ritualistic, and excessively selfish.

In the end, this is a story about more than me. It is about the notion of culture and fully appreciating the professional environment in which we function. So, let me now broaden out my personal whining in a way that embraces more important, or at least more universal, issues. I start this more significant, if somewhat pedantic, story by noting some wider implications of professional culture on the policy world. There are two primary inputs to the creation of our personal world view . . . professional training and institutional position. Training is never only technical. You learn both substance and preferred styles for dealing with the world. That is why Law students spend at least one-year learning how attorneys think and write while social workers spend their first year being indoctrinated into the ethos of that profession. Positional influences, your institutional home, recognize that you typically are surrounded by similar types of people in your work setting. Your organizational peers are likely to be very much like you in important ways and thus reinforce the dispositions you bring into a setting through training and background.

Older theoretical positions tended to see the world rather simply, within a more dichotomous framework. There were academics and policymakers…knowledge producers and knowledge consumers in our lexicon. Karen, who spent a great deal of time working with legislatures, and I quickly recognized that the real world is far more complicated. Initially, we developed several major categories that could easily be positioned along a theoretical continuum: basic researchers, applied researchers, intermediaries, policy doers, policymakers. It doesn't take rocket science to postulate that those positioned at the extreme end of the continuum would be most unlike one another and have the greatest difficulty communicating or even understanding one another. Those residing in the middle are operating in institutions that incorporate features of both worlds. For example, knowledge brokers like trade organizations and issue-oriented agencies (e.g., child poverty) want to use evidence and analysis that passes the methodological sniff test but are acutely aware of the complexities that make the doing of policy far from a purely academic exercise.

Let us take two actors, one from each end of the continuum. At one end would be your typical academic toiling in a major research university. At the other might be a legislator or a politically-appointed executive agency head. The possibilities of misunderstanding and miscommunication between these two worlds are endless including breakdowns in information needs, work cultures, and communication preferences, among other areas. But an important question remains . . . what do these hurdles look like? Experience in this regard is a great teacher, and I saw a lot walking back and forth between these two alien worlds.

Let's look at a graphic employed in a paper we just finished that focused on how state legislators viewed research and researchers, using responses from state politicians from Indiana and Wisconsin. The graphic lays out the critical dimensions of culture:

Domains and Themes of Professional Culture

Domains	Themes
Work Context	**(A) Decision-Making Process—** How does the decision-making process work? What factors and processes influence how decisions are made and the ways the work product gets done? **(B) Work Environment—**What kinds of pressures do inhabitants face in this professional world? What is the dominant pace of activity and to what kinds of time pressure are they exposed?
Interaction Preferences	**(A) Preferred Communication Style—**What communication channels are preferred? How important are interpersonal relationships and how do relationships compare to other influences on getting the job done? **(B) Preferred Interpersonal Qualities—**What qualities or style contribute to productive interactions? What qualities of style can interfere with effective communication?

Epistemological Frameworks:	(A) Credibility of Knowledge—What processes and methods do individuals use to know what to believe. (B) Decision-Making Criterion—How does this individual make decisions about what types of evidence to acquire to factor into decisions? How do inhabitants screen and sort out conflicting information?
Influence Loops	(A) Effectiveness Strategies—How do inhabitants shape the attitudes and beliefs of others and how are their attitudes and beliefs shaped by others? What ways of presenting information are being most effective? (B) Organizational Signals and Rewards—What defines effectiveness in their professional world? How does an individual define success? What institutional cues do they respond to and which indicators signify success?
Focal Interests	(A) Salient Topics—What substantive topics or challenging problems attract interest and attention? (B) Salient Goals—What is the nature and purpose of policy goals? From whom do ideas come?
Salient Stakeholders	(A) Salient Targets—What constituencies are of prime interest? At whom is the work product aimed? (B) Salient Actors—To whom do inhabitants pay attention?

Like all tables, this one is as boring as hell, but it is critical to my narrative. It provides clues as where to look when trying to understand miscommunication and misunderstand across actors in different systems. It is along these dimensions that friction points exist between dwellers in separate cultures, or islands as my colleague Karen Bogenschneider puts it. When you run into the natives from a different island, look out for problems. In addition, it might help us see where members within the academy might misunderstand one another if they come from different cultural traditions even if they nominally are from the same general tribe. How effortlessly can scholars from the hard sciences get along with social scientists or university scholars with evaluation-firm researchers?

How do we make the above table come to life? Easy, we draw upon a wealth of real life experiences for stylized examples. Take your typical academic, sitting in their ivory tower laboring away toward the discovery of ultimate truth. Naturally, they see this quest as timeless, nor do they want to arrive at any ultimate answer. Were that to be the case, they could not end their most recent paper with the standard caveat that more research is needed, accompanied of course by a request for further funding. Normally, our truth warrior would only care what his anonymous peers would conclude as they reviewed the paper for inclusion in a top journal. Beyond the limited group of similarly-situated academic elitists, why would any real academic care? It would do them no good. It could do them harm.

For the sake of argument, let us assume this paragon of the ivory tower is moved to take his insight to the real world. Perhaps they lost a bet, and this was the penalty imposed on the loser. He or she would approach any meeting in the real world using the same techniques that had always worked in the past. Hell, it always worked before. They would focus on the methodological rigor employed and the lengths they went to ensure that the resulting statistically significant results possess internal and external validity. Just before their audience of policymakers lapsed into a full coma, they would use their assumed hubris to convey the fact that anyone who did not agree that their results deserved immediate policy consideration clearly had to be a cretin and a Philistine deserving immediate approbation.

The legislator, if that is whom they are addressing, is sitting there looking across the table with increasing incredulity. He or she has concluded that the first order of business after this meeting is to fire the idiot aide that scheduled this clown in the first instance. If the legislator were savvy enough, they might point out that statistical significance is not the same a substantive significance. The former could represent rather small differences when larger sample sizes are employed. Why wasn't this clown informing them about relevant findings in a clear manner that might have applicability to the issues on their plate.

Policymakers focus on the issues relevant to their world and in ways that stress applicability and not abstract additions to our theoretical understanding of things. The two worlds talk past one another. Okay, this egghead might have a point but why am I listening to him or her. The underlying issue is not of concern to his constituency back home, no one has brought a compelling story that might elicit action on his or her part. Besides, no one is pushing this in the legislature no matter the merits. Finding co-sponsors would be a pain and might demand that he give up chits he needs for his priority items. There are only so many favors you can call in. What time is my next appointment?

Furthermore, the egghead has not considered the immediate fiscal implications. Sure, there might be savings down the road, but the political world is dominated by the next election. The policymaker could already envision oppositional ads from his next opponent decrying the expansion of unnecessary government during these difficult economic times. It makes no difference whether there is significant money involved, the big-spender label is almost impossible to shake once established and remains no matter the worth of any costly proposal. The policymaker cannot envision this egghead engaging the typical voter with his complicated charts and graphs in a convincing way. By this time, communication surely has ceased.

I can well remember attending a university-sponsored event where several leading academics were discussing a very controversial topic ... whether there was scientific support for racial differences in intelligence. The book *The Bell Curve*, had recently been published, placing this explosive topic back on the political screen. I was standing in the back with a sociology colleague who would later become the dean of Letters and Sciences when we realized that our congressional representative, a Republican, was standing next to us. I had met the congressman before when Bobbi Wolfe and I tried to secure his support for continued IRP funding, a rather hopeless quest though he was quite courteous as he turned us down.

The former director of IRP, an eminent sociologist, was one of the main speakers. His presentation would have been dynamite for an audience of his peers. This, however, was a mixed audience that included undergraduates and many members of the public and press along with the usual array of eggheads. The topic, as I said, was topical. As he droned on about methodological and statistical issues, I could see our congressman slowly falling into a deep stupor. Let me stress that politicians listen to crap all the time, you are really doing something special when you get one of them to tune out visibly. I began to panic, why would he ever expend political capital on a research institute where their better representatives could easily compete with nationally known sleep aides. I wanted this man to think good things about IRP. In desperation, I pointed out that the current speaker was a member of the National Academy of Sciences which seemed to impress our congressional representative not at all. Once again, I felt like the idiot I fully knew I was.

The point of this extended discourse is that the professional silos are becoming narrower and narrower, the communication between the silos less effective. The traditional academic departments are separating from the professional schools (e.g., economics and political science from public policy schools) and universities are increasingly distancing themselves from the real world. I suspect, rather I know, that the gap between my policy and academy worlds grew further apart during my long tenure at the university. I could see it in who was hired and promoted in the several departments associated with IRP. The troubling part of this evolutionary tale is that the breakdown in understanding and communication occurs not only between members within and outside the academy. I had been in the academy for a long time. Yet, because I did not follow all the cultural expectations, I felt misunderstood and, in the end, rejected, though never formally. Make no mistake, you are punished for not following all the rules, even the unstated ones. Sadly, even within the academic culture, the barriers between silos are becoming increasingly rigid, the ability to communicate and understand the other less likely. Not surprisingly the chances of effective communication from those ensconced within the academy with those in the real world is becoming increasingly remote.

I can still recall a conversation with Bob Haveman one day. He told me that the Economics Department had treated him well over the years. At the same time, he would not be hired now nor, if he had, could he possibly have achieved tenure. This department was desperately aping the theoretical aspirations of all the other top disciplinary departments. That is understandable though there is a cost. The Wisconsin Economics Department no longer has many faculty that might contribute to solving a major societal problem like poverty. Applied economists no longer need apply. I still vividly recall a brownbag where a hot economics faculty recruit was making a presentation to the IRP family. He was being touted as a future affiliate. Toward the end of his highly theoretical talk, the IRP editor turned to me and exclaimed with more than a little anguish, "How the hell could we ever turn something like that into a *Focus* article?"

The story embedded in this chapter saddens me, rather deeply, though not from a personal perspective. I love the old stories about how academics were heroes on the other end of State Street when scholars would willingly expend time and energy to tackle policy problems. Doing the public's good was once something of value. We should never lose that sense of sacrifice and commitment. To recapture those halcyon days, though, we must get inside our own cultures and better understand how they shape who we are and how we think. Perhaps, in the future, we can once again entertain the possibility of permitting someone like myself to sit down at the main table in the academy.

I don't want to be overly pessimistic. There may be some hope in that regard, as I suggested earlier while pointing out caveats about the vignette employed to make my earlier points. Perhaps small steps are being taken to make the academy more inclusive. Wisconsin's tenure process in the School of Social Work now permits what they call an "integrated tenure" case to be made. From what I understand, this is designed to accommodate tenure-seekers who evidence balance in their scholarly pursuits between knowledge production with application and distribution. Those budding scholars who wish to synthesize existing research, or bring it into the real world, or find ways for educating broader audiences about what we are discovering within the academy no longer need to hide their secret proclivities in a sock drawer or under the pillow.

It is a small step and I hope this innovation succeeds. I have no idea whether it is a sufficient step. The whole point of my essay on institutional and professional culture is to emphasize how sticky and impervious this phenomenon can be to change. Embedded cultural norms and tendencies are remarkably resistant to change. I recall the time when the need to upgrade the quality of undergraduate teaching became the cause *du jour* among the university community. Such fads seem to spontaneously erupt on occasion. The fear was that the obsession with research had led to neglect of the basic teaching mission at elite universities, at least for undergraduates. Mission statements were rewritten, and new reward systems were sought out. Amidst all this, I recall one eminent scholar from Stanford saying, "The administration can make all the noise about this they want but, if they get serious about prioritizing undergraduate teaching here, all the top researchers will just leave." More than once, pessimists have argued that the cultural divide between the teaching and research cultures is too wide, that we need to separate these two functions and have them operate as distinct entities, each with their own personnel. Perhaps that overstates the challenge, I don't know. My point—substantive cultural change ain't easy, that is why it is so important to understand.

Ultimately, my belief is that we need for members of the academy to look about the world with way more imagination than they currently do. Albert Einstein, the one member of his university physics class not to get an academic appointment upon graduation, transformed our understanding of the world because he integrated imagination with analytical skills like no one else. He employed what we call lateral thinking to understand the world about him. Time to take off the blinders and see opportunities to do things differently for once, as Albert did. Time to take a chance or two. Academics like to believe they think outside the box. True, that does happen, but there remains a helluva lot of encrusted, traditional thinking. Think about the following for a moment. What other professional group still wears robes harking back to the fourteenth century?

I truly was a wayward academic. I fell into the arms of the academy without ever intending to become an academic. I simply found it a great institutional base from which to ply my policy skills and to impart my knowledge to the next generation. It was all serendipity and opportunism. Looking back though, I provided the academy with a perfect role model for addressing the cultural drift that was separating knowledge producers from knowledge consumers. At a time when more bridge builders are desperately needed, at least part of the academy could not see nor appreciate someone who was uniquely suited to perform this role of communicating across the cultural divide.

That saddens me. Unfortunately, I can be overly passive when it comes to pushing my own causes. I find selling myself unsettling at best. Still, I remain disappointed that those about me back then apparently could not see the need for my potential contributions nor the opportunities I offered them. If Stephanie Robert is correct, my experience would be different now. But that is a counterfactual we cannot test. It is now up to the next generation to find a way forward.

CHAPTER 12

THE "SHELTERED" WORKSHOP

*But the Wisconsin tradition meant more than a simple
belief in people. It also meant a faith in the application of
intelligence and reason to the problems of society. It meant a
deep conviction that the role of government was not to stumble
along like a drunkard in the dark, but to light its way by the
best torches of knowledge and understanding it could find.*

—Adlai E. Stevenson

I often have called the Institute for Research on Poverty (IRP),
my professional home for over four decades, a sheltered workshop.
That term, as you may recall, typically is used for places where those
with diminished capacities are given an opportunity to perform
useful tasks for society and to hopefully realize some measure
of independence and self-respect. As such, they are worthwhile
institutions indeed for those challenged in some fashion. Does IRP
fit under this rubric. Barely, I suspect. Many would argue that the
work performed has little societal value, but the tasks performed

do keep the affiliates occupied and therefore from doing more general harm.

Now, think about this! Where else could I have been kept productively focused, busy at least, for over half my life? With respect to keeping the marginally employable out of mischief, it has been a wonderful institution. In fact, over the years I have noticed that people are loath to leave the place. When they do, they often return, for good or at least for visits. There is something comfortable and soothing and safe in its venerable halls, attributes often associated with many sheltered workshops.

I consider IRP to be the physical location for my allegorical policy candy store. True, it is primarily an academic institution but has served as an ideal site from which to sate my favorite private vice . . . mucking around in matters about which I am clueless as I seek to improve society. Still, I must say that the setting of my private sweets-filled paradise is ideal. The main offices are on the third floor of the Social Science Building which is situated along the shores of Lake Mendota on the University of Wisconsin-Madison campus. For six, maybe seven months a year, it really is an Eden-like place, until arctic blasts turn the lake into a frozen tundra akin to wastelands of outer Siberia.

As my career wound down, I would drive from our home to my campus parking spot in twenty or so minutes, with most of the journey taking place adjacent to serene Lake Mendota in Shorewood Hills. Along this idyllic road, I would weave past lakefront mansions and along the pristine, green fairways of Blackhawk Country Club where my wife and I played golf for many years. Then I would pass through Eagle Heights, the graduate student housing complex, before descending onto the west end of campus. Eagle Heights is a mini-version of the United Nations where kids can grow and play in an international community composed of young families drawn from around the world to complete their graduate educations.

After meandering through one of the more beautiful campuses in the country, I would settle into lot 34, perhaps 300 or so yards from my destination, the Social Sciences Building. Typically, I would get there very early on most days, long before the campus came to life. In mid-summer the sun might just be peaking over the eastern edge of the lake. Yet, the UW rowing crews already would be out practicing for their next competition. There was nothing quite like it, walking along the shoreline path adjacent to a calming lake touched by the amber blush of dawn as sleek boats skimmed over the water's surface guided by the encouragement of the coxswain or the instructions of a coach from an adjacent boat. Is there a better place to study poverty and societal dysfunction? Really, you never have to see any of the poor, unless you count students up to their eyeballs in debt among the nation's destitute. I doubt they count though.

Once, we held a conference at the historic Edgewater Hotel which is situated on Lake Mendota not too far from the campus. A local media wag drew up a cartoon making fun of this conference on poverty being held at a somewhat upscale hotel. I am not exactly sure why this one was selected from the hundred other gatherings IRP had convened over the years, but there you have it. A cartoon was published in the local paper centered about a tramp dressed in hobo-looking clothes with flies buzzing around his head. Some officious-looking character looking like a moderator was at a podium with the Institute for Research on Poverty prominently displayed on the front. The moderator, referencing the bum, is saying, "Our next speaker needs no introduction." It was funny, if a bit demeaning to the poor. We had the cartoon blown up and prominently displayed for many years at the institute. I am afraid it is lost now. I should look for it one of these days

There have been other political shots taken at IRP. Bob Haveman told me that a reporter looked up his salary when he was IRP Director in the early years, even before I got there. We are talking the very early years. The reporter pushed the story line of the "scandal" that some academic was making so much money from studying those who had so little. Apparently, this was considered fair game at the time.

Similarly, a reporter sought me ought when I was acting director and wanted to know what the position of director was paid. Knowing Bob's story, I suspected where he was going with this question. The conversation could have been ended if I simply told him my salary, which barely put me above the poverty line. That would have been disingenuous, though, since all other directors did receive decent compensation. So, I chuckled lightly as I explained there was no salary as such for being director. The position reduced your teaching load by one course per semester. In truth, being IRP director was taking on more work than you got paid for, sort of like picking the short straw when the general was looking for a suicide volunteer. I could literally hear his disappointment on the other end of the line. No story appeared in the paper.

For me, and others I believe, IRP has become an iconic institution. Not that long ago, it celebrated its golden anniversary, fifty years of doing cutting edge research on one of society's most compelling and enduring issues. William Proxmire represented Wisconsin in the U.S. Senate for several decades. He was known as a fiscal hawk always campaigning against pork-barrel spending and budgetary earmarks. He was also known for spending virtually no money on his own campaigns. I recall some of his later campaigns when he listed total expenditures of a few hundred dollars at most. That is inconceivable in today's electoral climate where campaigns for county coroner seem to cost more than the GDP of smaller countries.

Proxmire was best known for his "golden fleece" awards where each month he would select some federal expenditure for scathing ridicule. Once, he focused on a UW sociology professor who had a federal grant to explore equity theory as it applied to love relationships. Apparently, Bill was not a romantic. I found it noteworthy, then, when I examined the only two projects the senator pushed for his home state, the kind of pork that is a staple of most politicians. One was some boat project in Manitowoc, Wisconsin, located on Lake Michigan. The other was for this little-known research entity, according to the article on this topic, called the Institute for Research on Poverty at the University of Wisconsin. We must have done something right to deserve such a singular honor.

While IRP may not have been a household name to the public, it was quite well known among the rather large set of social scientists and policymakers interested in poverty, inequality, and issues related to the social-safety net. As I traveled extensively around the country during my career, I seldom had to say more than I was from the Poverty Institute. Everyone seemed to know what that meant. The mere mention of the name would open doors.

Not that many years ago I looked up a good friend from college and my childhood neighborhood after not seeing him since the early 1970s. He had been a sociology professor at Providence College in Rhode Island for decades. During my visit, he and his spouse, whom I also met in college, both mentioned how they kept seeing a Thomas Corbett in *Focus* (the IRP publication I have noted throughout). They were avid readers of our publication and had wondered if that was the same guy they knew from the old days. It was indeed, I affirmed, basking in the glow of reflected glory. Yet, I could see a look of amazement in their eyes. I had seemed like such a loser back in college. While they were not wrong, I was clever in fooling folk.

Speaking of *Focus,* I was always taken by how popular it was. One day, during the time I served as acting director, I was off to Washington for another of the seemingly endless trips there. Someone, probably Betty Evanson who was our top editor, stuffed a draft copy of the next *Focus* into my hands as I left the office. I was to look it over one more time and call back with a final blessing before it would hit the streets. I recall standing with several high-level analytical types from a couple of federal agencies (Census and Labor Statistics I believe) when one asked if that was the new *Focus* I was holding. I said yes but cautioned that it was not final yet since I was doing one last proof. "Could I make a copy anyways?" she asked. As she ran off to a copy machine, the others in the group shouted out their order for copies. Their enthusiasm made me feel so good about the care that went into its production and about its impact on the policy community.

I first learned of IRP when I was working in state government in the early 1970s. I had been sent to D.C. on some state business. As I waited for the return flight, I noticed a guy sitting nearby. To pass the time I often like to guess something about the people I observe around me. Obviously an academic, I mused. Either that or he was an accountant suffering from a bad hair day or perhaps a mad scientist whose latest experiment had gone terribly awry. I was proud of myself when my guess was confirmed as we were seated next to one another on the flight. The "obvious" academic turned out to be Irv Garfinkel who was then director of IRP. Being anti-social, I don't normally chat on airplanes, but this would be an exception. I mean, we were both in the welfare business and it occurred to me that this place he ran might be a good resource for my state work. It never occurred to me that I would be situated there in less than a year and never leave except for brief excursions.

When I first stepped into the Social Science Building in 1975, I was not cognizant of the significance of IRP or of the long history that the University of Wisconsin played in the development of the country's social safety net. On the other hand, I surely was aware of the beauty of the place. There was a carillon located outside the sixth-floor entrance (the building is nestled into the side of a hill that slopes down to the lake) from which emanated lovely chimes several times a day. I was also aware of the fierce anti-war demonstrations that had broken out in front of the then Business School located across the street. The spark for the protests was a visit by Dow Chemical, the maker of napalm used in Viet Nam. They were recruiting students about to graduate. On that day, the long-time future mayor of Madison, Paul Soglin (mayor once again and candidate for governor), would be bludgeoned by police and dragged off to jail along with hundreds of other students. That had happened less than a decade earlier than my arrival.

What made U.W. a perfect place for the study of poverty was a history of social experimentation and activism that can be traced back to the turn of the twentieth century. Charles Van Hise, a university president of that era, and fighting Bob LaFollette, a fierce progressive politician and reformer, were classmates and good friends. Their close bonds helped generate a synergistic connection between the university and state government that would grow with time. The 'Wisconsin Idea,' most succinctly expressed in the phrase "the boundaries of the university are the boundary of the state," really took off during the Progressive Era. John R. Commons developed what he called Institutional Economics while working on numerous Wisconsin reforms including Workers Compensation and the Progressive Income Tax. He also supervised many Ph.D. students who furthered the Wisconsin Idea including Edwin Witte who was tapped by President Roosevelt to lead the committee that generated the Social Security Act and other key New Deal ideas. Other acolytes of Commons and Witte flocked to D.C. to help implement and solidify New Deal reforms including Arthur Altmeyer, Robert Groves, and Wilbur Cohen.

Robert Lampman had also studied under Ed Witte. Bob was a classic Midwesterner growing up in a smaller northern Wisconsin town and getting his Economics degree from U.W. He happened to be serving on President Kennedy's Council of Economic Advisor's Committee in the early 1960s when he and Burt Weisbrod authored what turned out to be a seminal chapter in the annual economic report to the president. Bob had been tracking the downward trend in poverty during the post-World War II economic expansion in which all segments of society benefitted. But he cautioned that this rising economic tide would not necessarily lift all boats as Kennedy had once suggested. Some groups, based on physical limitations or racial segregation or geographic isolation, might be left behind. For these remaining boats, further targeted government help would be needed. Many concluded that this chapter served as the intellectual origins of the War-On-Poverty (WOP) that would be declared the following year.

Shortly after, when President Johnson began pushing a poverty agenda far more aggressively than Kennedy probably would have, his generals in the WOP looked around for a place where the heavy intellectual work might be done. Wisconsin seemed a likely candidate with its long history of contributing to progressive policy ideas and given Bob Lampman's return to the Economics faculty there. The story I heard from those around at the time was that the university did not jump at the idea when it was first presented. Today, if a random federal dime rolled down Bascom Hill, where the campus leaders hide, several U.W. administrators would hurt themselves chasing it.

But those were flush times and there probably were some legitimate concerns about academic freedom or getting too close to government and perhaps risking excessive oversight. Part of university's initial reluctance involved uncertainty about how to structure such a research entity. Then Chancellor Robert Fleming issued the following directive.

Madison has a great tradition of policy analysis and government service. The Madison campus has an outstanding cadre of researchers dealing with welfare issues, each working in his or her own sphere. Yet, such problems do not fall neatly along disciplinary lines. Policy development and evaluation can only be effective if it is approached in a multidisciplinary way. Let us see if we can bring faculty efforts together in some synergistic way.

In 1966, the Poverty Institute was born. Poverty related research exploded in the next few years. Whereas one would need no more than two or three pages to complete an exhaustive bibliography of poverty in the early 1960s, IRP published some 35 books, 650 discussion papers, and 18 special reports in the first decade or so after its inception. Federal support was generous in those early days, with some $20 million federal dollars alone being allocated over the first several years to support this work (worth over $100 million today).

I walked in the door just as the first decade of IRP's existence had ended. I was about as low as you could go on the order of merit as they say. In the academy, there is a huge distinction between the regular faculty, where those with and without tenure are ranked accordingly, and the academic staff who barely rise to the rank of noticeable mammals. But even within that lowly species I was without a doctorate at the time. If I were back in India, that would put me among the ranks of the untouchables.

Still, I immediately enjoyed the energy of the place. There was always a buzz of excitement. Papers and reports were being produced at a dizzying pace. I loved going to the brown bags where researchers would talk about their work and where a spirited dialogue would often occur. I loved the team that worked on Irv Piliavin's welfare decision making project including Stan Masters, a Princeton-trained economist doing a post-doc at IRP, and Tom Macdonald, Irv's top graduate student. I also got to know many of the other male researchers since I wound up hiring several their spouses on Irv's project as data collectors. It proved a nice way for them to reenter the work world after helping their husbands through graduate school and raising young children. This got me integrated within the social structure of IRP as I probably would not have done otherwise. It also put me in a touchy situation. I could hardly reprimand most of my staff for poor performance since they were related to the powers that be. It was fortunate that I had no need to do so.

It was a busy place. There were queues to get work done by the large typing pool (in the pre-word-processing era) or to get a document copied, or any of the other staff services such as editing and so forth. I learned early on to appreciate those who can make your life easy or miserable. Walking around as if life owed you everything, which some at the top of the pyramid are tempted to do, is not always a wise policy. Jack Sorenson was the associate director for administration in those days, the man who managed the money. People would often go in and ask for something, often demanding it as the entitled are disposed to do. He would say no almost as a matter of course depending, of course, on the status of the supplicant. I noticed that if you were nice to him, and chatted for a while, a no might turn into "I will see what I can do."

I was always nice to the administrative staff like Joyce Collins who made the place run on most days. Joyce was as smart as a whip and had an acerbic tongue with quick put-downs. We got along famously. Long retired now, Joyce still, on occasion, looks after my dog when we are out of town. Again, for those readers just starting out in life, be nice to the people who may not look powerful but who are positioned to make your life easier or a living hell. Surviving in a bureaucracy is hard enough. Don't make it even more difficult by being stupid or arrogant beyond all possibility of remedial help.

In the very early days I recall being reticent to speak up at brown bags or other public events. I always figured I was on borrowed time. Somehow, they let me in this hallowed place and I was getting by with it, at least so far. So, if I were to publicly display my ignorance, as was my wont, I would find a new name on my door and the locks changed. In retrospect, there was probably little real chance of that happening. Irv Piliavin hated the detailed tasks of data collection and that first project of his that brought me to IRP was a data collection nightmare. My reticence did not last long. For all my insecurities, I was seldom shy about engaging even well-known scholars or high public officials. I wonder where that hubris comes from?

We would have these meetings about Irv's project at 8:30 in the morning, at first to make plans and later to deal with management issues. At these meetings would be the usual suspects . . . Tom Macdonald, Stan Masters, and few others waiting for Irv to arrive. He inevitably would arrive late. Upon rushing into the room, he would claim once again that his car would not start which eventually became as believable as the dog ate the homework. After a few minutes of him fidgeting in his chair, he would suddenly jump up and say, "I think that is my phone ringing," before dashing out the door. On cue, Tom Macdonald would shout out to him, "Nice of you to stop by, Irv." But we managed to keep this complex project on track, and I did come to believe Irv was very thankful to have me around.

In fact, he later put me in day-to-day charge of his next big project, a longitudinal study of the homeless in the Twin Cities. He would be doing this project with Michael Sosin who would eventually leave for the University of Chicago. Now, in some ways the data collection demands were less complex since virtually all of it would be collected through survey instruments that we would design and thus control.

In other ways, the challenges were far more daunting. Think about this, you are trying to do a longitudinal survey of a homeless population. Obviously, I would not testify in court as to the representativeness of the sample. We had to work with those people frequenting selected soup kitchens and homeless shelters who were willing to work with us. Not an easy task since paranoia ran high within this population. We also had to find some way of tracking those who drifted continuously from place to place and tended to fly under the radar. Getting cooperation from a population that is wary of authority was not always easy to say the least. But we did a pretty good job, I must admit.

Between figuring out clever ways to capture needed data and managing project staff, I became increasingly useful to the Institute, at least in my own head. Apparently, though, my most significant contribution to the homeless project was keeping Irv and Mike Sosin from killing one another. Irv was gregarious, outgoing, energetic, and bored by details. Mike was serious, conscientious, disciplined, and paid a lot of attention to details. This was not a match made in heaven. One day, Sheldon Danziger thanked me. "Why?" I asked. "You kept Mike and Irv from killing one another." I figured preventing a homicide was yet another reason for keeping me around IRP a little while longer. Think of the mess with the blood and all as well as the scandal.

During those early years, there was one person who was unfailingly nice. It was the man most responsible for the institute being at Wisconsin in the first place. Bob Lampman occasionally would catch me in the hall, or stop by my office, and ask if he could pick my brain for a minute. My brain! I can no longer recall what kinds of questions he asked, though I do recollect that he wondered if I might hire a relative of his for some low-level project data position. Most of his questions involved substantive issues though, and I never ceased to be astounded that this icon of poverty research thought I had anything at all to contribute to him.

I recall one day when I was walking along the path that bordered Lake Mendota just outside the Social Science Building. My name was called out and I turned to see Bob moving quickly to catch up with me. He obviously wanted to chat about something. He began commenting on a piece I had written for an obscure IRP series at the time called *Notes and Comments* where people could articulate emerging ideas that might become actual research projects or papers. I can no longer recall what pearls of wisdom I had committed to paper though I believe the topic had something to do with the relationship between workforce development systems and the welfare system. He went on to praise what I had written and asked a few questions. As we parted, he turned and said to me, "Tom, you keep writing. You have a lot to say." I was flattered beyond words and surely found some way to dismiss such praise at the time.

Sometime in the 1990s, when it was becoming apparent that Bob's health was declining, we started chatting in the IRP hallway one day. It turns out that we had both read Nicholas Lehman's book on the great migration north from the Mississippi Delta to Chicago and other northern cities and how this transformed

America as we knew it. Somehow, we convinced each other that this book contained a set of issues that deserved broader discussion. In fact, at some later point we invited the author to IRP to discuss this book.

In any case, Bob and I decided to do a brown bag on this work, we somehow concluded that the ideas it contained were provocative. As the day approached, it was clear to me that Bob was declining fast and I was having second thoughts about this joint venture. No one had brown bags like this one, which struck me as little more than a book report. On the day of the event, I probably carried a bit more of the water but thankfully the dialogue was brisk and stimulating, even carrying over to some holiday parties later that same week. I was grateful it did not turn out awkward in any way. I felt honored just to be able to share this moment with him.

That brown bag was, to my knowledge, Bob's last public appearance. He would die of cancer not long after in 1997. Soon after his passing, I got on the Social Sciences Building elevator and realized I was standing next to two Nobel-Prize laureates in Economics. James Tobin and Robert Solow had come to honor their respected colleague. As I sat listening to several noted IRP affiliates talk about what Bob meant to them, I thought on what he meant to me. Bob was the intellectual godfather of the WOP and spiritual creator of the Institute. Beyond that, he simply was one of the nicest people I have ever come across in my life. He treated me as an equal when I was clearly not. He made me sound wise and profound when I was little more than incoherent. He made me feel important at a time when few knew of my existence or cared. When I think back on his infectious smile, it is hard for me to admit that he really was an economist. I did not think God made them so human or so kind.

IRP now sponsors an annual Lampman lecture where some notable scholar is invited to give a talk. I recall the time that Sheldon Danziger, who most recently headed the Russell Sage Foundation in New York, gave the talk. Sheldon, like many of us, considered Bob a father figure. His voice cracked several times as he tried making a few comments about Bob. I know mine would have as well.

As I think back, there were so many small memories that intrude. One day, Bobbi Wolfe, the director, called me and said to come to the conference room immediately. There were some issues involving IRP that we needed to discuss right away. *This must be important to interrupt my nap,* I thought as I rushed to the meeting. Perhaps, at last, they realized what an imposter I was. I just knew it could not last forever, but how did they finally figure it out after all these years? When I walked into the crowded room, a hearty happy birthday rang out. My spouse had conspired to surprise me on my fiftieth birthday.

It turns out that her fiftieth would be coming up in a little over two months. Not surprisingly, she was on high alert. "Don't you dare do this to me," she said. "I wouldn't think of it," I lied. As the day approached, she asked if I had reneged on my promise. I had learned much from spending so much time in Washington. I looked at her without blinking and asserted in my most nuanced Clintonian language, "You have absolutely nothing to worry about." With her being trained as a lawyer, I thought this ruse had no chance whatsoever. But it worked! After I got my revenge, she accused me of engaging in an untruth. "Perish the thought!" I exclaimed, explaining. "I never said I wasn't planning a party, I merely said that you had absolutely nothing to worry about." She gave me that one though there was a moment or two when I feared losing the family jewels.

I loved the rich intellectual life of the place. We had so many conferences and workshops and other events on the eighth floor of the Social Sciences Building and elsewhere on campus. The view from the eighth-floor conference room was particularly breathtaking. You had a panoramic vista of Lake Mendota along with the countryside beyond. You could also see picnic point, a thin peninsula that darted out into this large body of water. As you stroll to the point itself, you can see the State Capitol and city skyline shimmering across the waters.

My cousin's daughter, Sharon Hennessy, once sent me a magazine article that had a list of the twenty or so most romantic spots in the world. I am not talking about just Madison, or Wisconsin, or even the United States, but the whole world. Picnic point made that list. This seemed a bit of a stretch to me, but I must admit it is a very nice place to walk and does possess romantic possibilities. I also suspect that a few young people probably lost their virginity there including, most likely, the author of that article.

I still smile at the memory of one event there on the eighth floor. The deans of Social Work doctoral programs from around the country were meeting on the Madison campus. An old classmate and officemate of mine from early on, Ann Nichols-Casebolt, then headed the doctoral program at Virginia Commonwealth University. She also was serving as head of this national organization of doctoral program deans. Since the deans were very interested in visiting IRP, Bobbi and I were glad to oblige. We, of course, brought them up to the eighth floor for the spectacular view and I, as associate director and a nominal Social Work type, gave the opening remarks. I have a general stump speech I can rely on in a pinch but do try to tailor my remarks to the audience if I have time. On this fine day, I decided to emphasize a theme in which, amazingly, I believed. I went on about how welfare reform was moving in a direction that would potentially benefit from the contributions of social work and social workers.

"Policies were moving away from cash transfers to issues involving family integrity and independence," I intoned solemnly. "This represents a return to the Kennedy call for social workers to solve the growing welfare crisis in the early 1960s." That was okay, but then I got carried up in the moment and let my rhetoric go just a bit. I went on to assert that the days where economists dominating poverty policy were past. They had failed and now it was our turn. Social Work would take its rightful place at the table once again. Of course, I had forgotten that Bobbi, a dyed in the wool economist, was waiting to make a few remarks of her own. When I caught her out of the corner of my eye, she was looking at me as if I had totally lost my mind. Once again, I was getting her "look." When it was her turn, she said something about an unemployed associate director needing work. There were no takers!

I never did much with social work or social workers. I never attended their conferences or networked to any degree. I stayed with the policy and poverty groups. But I did take my basic message about an expanded role for social work in welfare reform on the road. At one point, I spoke to another influential social work group of academics . . . the Midwest deans of Social Work schools. I did believe, starting as early as Learnfare and really picking up with the passage of PRWORA, that the social work profession might play a bigger role in this new face of social assistance that was emerging. What had been strictly welfare agencies were increasingly focused on all kinds of family-stability and family-functioning issues as they tried to move clients toward self-sufficiency and independence. Which discipline should know more about these issues than social work? What interventions should be applied to these issues other than those perfected by social workers?

In two talks to the Midwest deans, one in Madison and one at the University of Chicago, I gave my pitch. I also tried again during an invited talk at the School of Social Work at Case Western. But the magic never took. People were polite enough but there was undercurrent of resistance. The overriding narrative was that welfare reform simply was evil, that any cooperation toward making it better might be construed as a form of implicit endorsement. A deeper message might well have been a continued reluctance to engage the poorest segments of society. The profession had always struggled for respect. It was harder to get that respect if you were dealing with those considered basket cases by the broader society. If true, I understood the impulses that motivated their concerns. It was still a bit sad though.

Another benefit of being at IRP was the continuous flow of visitors and speakers that came through the Institute. Virtually everyone who was anyone came by at one point or another. But I found the foreign visitors more interesting, in part because I was less likely to run into them during my typical round of conferences and workshops and other poverty events. There were too many to mention individually but a common theme among them struck me. First, they often wondered when IRP affiliates would sit around and just chat, or brainstorm, or exchange ideas. Brainstorm, that must be a personal vice peculiar to foreign universities. It struck me that no one had time to properly take care of their personal hygiene never mind sitting around chatting. Apparently, our foreign peers find the time. I could only wish we did. Culturally, I do belong in Europe.

A favorite story of mine came from a casual one-on-one I had with a visiting economist from Poland. Being of Polish extraction myself (on my mother's side), I was curious about his background, and how Poland had emerged from Soviet domination. So, one day I asked him about that. It turned out that he had been in the thick of things as the Solidarity movement unfolded, the first act in the final fall of Communism. He was a prominent member of a group of academic dissidents who were in support of the Solidarity labor movement. He knew he was under surveillance and worried each day that his freedom would come to a swift end.

One day, he was alone making copies of some statement that would be distributed later by members of the movement. If I recall correctly, he mentioned using a mimeograph machine, remember those? In any case, he heard the outside door burst open and the heavy boots of the police rushing up the stairs. There was no mistaking the sound, his time had come. They burst in and pointed their guns at him. He wondered at that moment if he might be executed on the spot. Rather, they took him off to be "interrogated." He felt certain he would either rot in prison or perhaps even "disappear" in a more final way. To his surprise, he was released not long after.

Later, he learned that his fellow academics got in touch with those lawyers who were part of the movement when his detention became known. These were difficult times and his plight was very uncertain. It turned out that Polish lawyers had formed a labor union of sorts as part of the Solidarity movement. They banded together to surround the building where he was being kept and interrogated. If he "disappeared" it would not be in silence nor without witnesses. As an organized force, they put such pressure on the government that his continued incarceration might prove too inconvenient. He was released.

"Lawyers!" I exclaimed in disbelief. "My wife has a law degree and I know a bunch of them in this country. You mean they helped without being paid? I am positive they would first demand a hefty retainer here." Despite my effort to lighten the mood, I knew I was talking to a brave man who tested his beliefs and convictions in a far more compelling way than I would ever be required to do. I felt humbled.

Then there was the story of Luke Geohegan. I was asked one day if I would be a mentor for a Harkness fellow who was interested in social policy. The Harkness fellow program sent mid and early-career professionals to the States for educational and relationship-building purposes. This was a request that had come through the School of Social Work as I recall. He and his family would spend six months at the university. Sure, there was always room to squeeze in one more task. When the time came I was supposed to fly to Pittsburgh for an event where all the new Harkness fellows were to meet their mentors. I was so slammed at the time I begged off, which did not help my guilt level that always was at a high level. One late Friday afternoon, there was knock on my office door and there stood a dark-haired young man with a broad smile and a decidedly British accent. It took a second and then it hit me . . . oh, my mentee!

Over the next six months, my wife and I became good friends with Luke and his wife, Charis. Like all Brits, it seems, he came across as intelligent with a very droll wit and an easy manner. He did not quite look British, and it did turn out that his mother was from India. Like most foreign visitors, he was rather shocked at how undeveloped our safety net was and how negative the typical American was to the plight of the disadvantaged. He visited social agencies while here and attended my policy class which he complained was scheduled at an ungodly hour of the morning. I did make it to the wrap-up session for the fellows in Texas where he and I made remarks to the larger group.

We stayed in touch after his return. He later became a member of the clergy in the Church of England and assumed several high positions in various service agencies. I took note that he became the warden, head person, of Toynbee Hall, the prototype for settlement houses in the nineteenth century that later spread across the U.S. He suggested Mary and I spend some time there but, to my regret, we never made that work. During his tenure as warden, Prime Minister Tony Blair used Toynbee Hall as a venue to make a speech announcing a war on child poverty in the U.K. We continued to see each other when he visited Hull House in Chicago or when we got over to the U.K. One of his children now works for the royal family but I forget in what capacity. This was a connection I have always treasured.

While IRP provided me with a marvelous sheltered workshop through which to ply my craft, there are two areas in which I may have made some small contribution to the institution. When I arrived at IRP, there was no relationship with the state of Wisconsin. IRP might well have been located near Salumbar, India (my old Peace Corps site) as far as Wisconsin State government was concerned. The Welfare Reform Study group that Mary Ann Cook roped me into in 1977 proved the first substantive opportunity for IRP affiliates to become involved in Wisconsin issues. Out of that flowed the extensive child support work, the involvement with the legislature in developing the Work Experience and Job Training pilot program, a survey project called the Wisconsin Basic Needs Study, an evaluation of a pilot State health insurance concept, and extensive work with the development of the State's first one-stop agency in Kenosha. By the mid-1980s, more than a few affiliates were involved with the state and there were several IRP-Wisconsin contracts.

Everything was looking up until the election of Tommy Thompson as governor. Relations quickly soured after that. This did not interfere much with my work, or that of Mike Wiseman, with the various county agencies we were helping. These locals were rather perplexed about the whole situation, wondering aloud why the governor hated us so much since we were helping locals implement parts of his agenda. Good relations with locals continued despite a visible increase in tensions with the state powers as the Thompson administration settled in. The state had agreed in principle to financially support the continued work of Mike Wiseman and myself in Kenosha County. Suddenly, however, I was having all kinds of trouble getting a signed contract out of them.

I knew that Mike was getting nervous and so I called my state contacts one Friday afternoon to get a status update. State officials were still raising nitpicky issues but, considering the overall tone, I remained confident we would be all right in the end. I had never failed before. Still, I thought it best to let Mike know what was going on and called over to the LaFollette Institute of Public Affairs which was located right across the street. I tried to sound upbeat as I told him of the most recent delay. There was silence on the line. "Come over," he finally commanded icily. By this time, I knew Mike's temperament and thought, *This is not good.*

I slowly, very slowly, walked across Observatory Drive, so named for the former observatory that yet adorns the highest point on campus. I think Mike was already on the third page of a scorching letter to the secretary of Health and Family Services, Tim Cullen. He was a former Democratic legislator that Tommy lured from the State Senate either in the spirit of bi-partisanship or to take one more Senate seat from the Democratic side of the ledger. Both theories were circulating at the time. Mike said that as soon as he finished his written tirade we were going up to the other end of State Street and sit in the Secretary's office until he agreed to see us.

Oh, no, I said to myself. I had visions of what would happen. Mike would storm in and demand to be seen. Secretary Cullen, not nearly as impressed with the credentials of any academic as the academics in question were of their own, would probably call security and have us thrown out on our behinds. This probably would result in a severe case of brain damage for me, always a concern. It took me the rest of the afternoon to convince him to wait until Monday morning, by which time he had cooled down. Fortunately, my minimal optimism proved correct and I soon managed to pry a contract out of them.

Relations clearly were on a downward spiral though. The breaking point would come with Irv Garfinkel's effort to pilot the child support Assured Benefit (AB) guarantee. The governor had appointed Jim Meier to head the key division through which we would have to work if the AB pilot programs were to be tested as planned. As mentioned earlier, this was Garfinkel's pet dream and everything was set to go. We had federal waivers, Foundation help, state legislative support, and two counties willing to try it. One of the counties was Dane, where Madison is situated and where Carol Lobes, a good friend of mine, headed the human services agency. Child Support, in addition, was a special interest of Tom Loftus, Democratic leader in the assembly and the most likely gubernatorial opponent for Tommy in the next election. Jim obviously knew of his boss's feelings and, as a former County Child Support attorney, also had set ideas about any kind of assured child support benefit. He thought the concept a big pile of doggie doo-doo.

I assumed we were dead in the water. Irv, though, was not likely to give up, so I played the good soldier. At first, the IRP-State relationship was not quite dead but obviously on life support, no real need quite yet to put a fork in the turkey to see if it were finally done. We were getting closer though. One day, I was asked to accompany Jim Meier, Mark Hoover (the State Department's budget wizard), and a representative from the governor's office to visit the federal regional office in Chicago. I don't recall the details but there was an apparent dispute about how federal child support pass-through dollars might be used for the pilots.

My recollection is that they originally asked Sheldon Danziger to go as director of IRP. That was probably protocol given the rank of the state people. "No way," said Sheldon, "Corbett, you go." I always had this feeling of being expendable. We used a state car for the trip, but I ended up driving. Good idea, I thought, they are less likely to attack me physically if I am in control of the car, just out of self-preservation. I must say, though, the drive down was frosty, but absent any outright physical hostility. I couldn't quite shake several scenes from the Godfather trilogy where the mobsters would take their intended victim for his last ride.

The meeting with the regional federal officials went as I expected … poorly. If you are trying something new, and IRP often pushed the envelope, you should never work with the regional federal officials. They will say no, since saying yes is more risk-taking and dangerous. They were particularly obnoxious on this day. I recall posing a hypothetical at one point and getting the response that they don't deal with hypothetical situations. I called this version of federal behavior, which I had seen before, the Woody Woodpecker effect. When you posed a question, their heads would bob up and down into the federal regulations where they would always come up with some justification to turn you down. The up-and-down motion reminded me of the woodpecker attacking a tree. I must admit I did not run into this effect with the people I worked with in Washington. I suppose that is why they had regional offices, to do the nasty jobs and protect them from befuddled academics.

On the way back to Madison, the mood in the car had changed dramatically. They were so appalled by the rigid, bureaucratic demeanor of the feds that they suddenly saw me as an ally. The banter back and forth was now light and friendly. At one point, Jim Meier, who was seated next to me, said with a big smile, "Tom, I bet you have seen assholes like me come and go." I paused for a moment, but my darn wit got the better of me once again. "No, Jim, not like you, you are the biggest one I have ever seen." But I said it with a smile! A moment of regret was followed by relief as everyone in the car gave out with a hearty laugh. It was a moment of levity that was not to last long.

Tensions between Irv and Jim continued to escalate. At one point, Jim lost his temper and grabbed Irv's tie, there was some concerns about physical conflict. Despite all the work that had gone into the pilots, there was no way to get around the hostility within state government. The concept would die a slow death. A few years later, Jim Meier was being considered for an appointed position that would require legislative assent and thus required a public hearing. Irv by then held a faculty position at Columbia University in New York. He flew back to Madison to testify personally that Jim was temperamentally unsuited for this appointment. Feelings ran deep.

All State-IRP contracts were to disappear except for the child support research and analysis work. That effort initially was launched under the agreement Sherwood Zink and I had negotiated years earlier. It was later revamped by Maria Cancian and Dan Meyer, who have headed that initiative for many years now. That child support work survived my Learnfare testimony before Moynihan's sub-committee, the agonizing demise of the AB pilot initiative, and all the other hostilities associated with our atrocious relationship with the governor. I suspect it survived because the staff in the state child support bureaucracy wanted the work done. In addition, Maria and Dan probably were viewed as relatively apolitical while I was the son of Satan. More to the point, the two of them did not pop-up in the media all the time. Thank God the child support research survived since it became the foundation for a deeper relationship when the cold war thawed some decade or so down the road.

When the thaw did come, it might have started with a series of small steps. Gerald Whitburn, the secretary of the key state bureaucracy, got in touch with me on several occasions. Once, he called me at home at 10:00 PM on a Friday night to talk about a book he had just finished. I thought his choice of literature rather strange for a Republican appointee. It was Francis Fox-Piven's quite radical treatise on welfare as a sop to the poor to prevent the radical uprising society really needed. Another time he called to see if I would write an editorial on some child support topic. I was happy to oblige though I cannot recall if it ever was published. A third call was to have lunch with him at the Madison Club, an exclusive eatery where the downtown power brokers meet. The food was good but the discussion apparently forgettable since it is long gone from memory. Finally, he called to have a meeting on some other child support issues. I brought Dan Meyer with me since I was moving on to other issues (I still had the attention span of a gnat) while Dan, along with Maria Cancian, had already taken over the reins on all things child support. The secretary did have his idiosyncrasies. Though I explained the rationale for Dan's presence, he acted as if Dan were not even in the room, physically positioning himself to exclude Dan from the conversation. It was awkward in the extreme.

Then the steps got larger. Soon after J. Jean Rogers, who long had disliked IRP, resigned as head of W-2 to take another state position, I got a call from the secretary of the Department of Workforce Development, where W-2 was now housed. Linda Stewart wanted to meet with me. I was intrigued, to say the least. When the appointed time came, I told Bobbi Wolfe that I was headed up for this meeting and would let her know what was up upon my return. However, when I arrived and informed the secretary's receptionist what I was there for, she gave me a blank stare. No such meeting was scheduled. The secretary wasn't even in Madison that day.

What was going on? Did someone play a malevolent joke? Did I dream that such a meeting had been planned? Had I finally lost what was left of my mind, which was never particularly robust to start with? The heavy betting was on the last option. I had to drag my fanny back to IRP and explain there was no such summit meeting. I got another one of those "he is finally losing it" looks from Bobbi. A couple of weeks later, the mystery was resolved. The secretary had not gone through the regular channels to put the meeting on the calendar, and then was called out of town suddenly. Perhaps she wanted to keep it somewhat secret. In any case, it was rescheduled.

Fearing another dream or hallucination, I kept the second appointment secret. But they knew what I was talking about when I arrived, and I was ushered into a small meeting room. Soon, in walked a tall, attractive blond. I knew this was not the secretary who was a short, black woman. This mystery woman turned out to be Jennifer Noyes who had just replaced J. Jean Rogers as head of W-2. In fact, it was her first day in the new position. We introduced ourselves to one another and waited, neither of us knew what was going on. Then Linda walked in and the meeting began. Yes, the secretary wanted a new relationship between her department and IRP. Were we interested? I assured her we were and would be most willing to work with her. We agreed to keep in touch. Not much happened for a while. I believe the secretary began to hit a rough patch politically and became distracted. However, I did run into Jennifer once or twice and we did have that disastrous trip to D.C. where we exchanged life stories during the long delays. Perhaps it is more accurate to say I told her mine as she proceeded to slash her wrists in despair.

Around this time, the state put out bids soliciting proposals to write White Papers on some of the challenges facing W-2. They offered modest amounts of money and, given that I was over funded in any case, the work was not that attractive to me. But I really wanted to know if I was still blacklisted. So, I bid on one of them. When I got it, and eventually a second one, I had real tangible evidence that the world might be changing. Evidence of a real thaw came about when I invited Jennifer to a meeting at IRP. By this time, I was sufficiently encouraged to seek a new understanding. She agreed and Karl Scholz (then IRP director) and I went up to pick her up and bring her to our place.

A brief note about Karl before continuing. Karl was raised in one of those Midwest farming states that all look alike to me, rural and flat and boring. I do believe his parents were academics though he does possess that look of a fresh-faced farm boy who had spent the morning slopping the hogs. He typically had a wide grin and a friendly demeanor. Growing up, Karl was more interested in basketball than academics. He chose a small school in Minnesota, Carlton College, because that would give him the best opportunity to play college ball. Apparently, he was good, or so he claims, but realized his future lie in scholarship and not professional sports.

He switched his focus to hone his incisive mind and excellent scholarly skills as an economist. He also had sharpened his policy skills with two tours in D.C. For some reason, Karl and I have been trading insults in a good-natured way since the day he arrived on campus. I recall the day when he must have thought I had gotten the upper hand in our ongoing banter. So, he reached back for the best invective in his arsenal. "You . . . you . . . social worker . . . you," he sputtered from the other side of Observatory Drive. I hung my head in shame with that one, hoping that passing students and faculty had not heard what he had just called me.

On another occasion, I was teeing off on the tenth hole at Blackhawk Country Club. Karl was the guest of another member that day, Mike Knetter, who was dean of the Business School at the time. He has since become a member. In any case, they passed behind me as I addressed my drive, Karl tried to throw me off by yelling out as I swung. No need for that, really, I suck at golf on my own without any distractions. He told me later that Mike chastised him, saying that was quite improper behavior at a Country Club!

Someday, however, I will find this picture I have of Karl, the current dean of Letters and Sciences, and Gary Sandefur, his predecessor in that office. Both are wearing silly costumes and mugging for the camera when they were much, much younger and even more foolish than they are now. The event was some mystery game where you were supposed to play a part in costume while identifying the guilty party. My wife and I had sponsored this fun-filled evening at our house. When I find it, I am sure the National Enquirer will pay me big bucks.

But back to Jennifer and the State-IRP cold war! To this day she says it was an act of courage coming to the institute on her own. Her staff apparently cautioned her against doing it. Either they thought it would get her into political difficulty with the governor, or they believed the rumors that we had instruments of torture somewhere in the basement of Social Sciences explicitly set aside for Republicans and other such enemies of truth and justice. It is true that we have a room called the mole hole where copies of old IRP publications are stored. However, never did I see a single rack or other form of torture there. Admittedly, being forced to read some of those old documents just might constitute torture under the articles of the Geneva Convention.

We chatted loosely for a while. She had not been around when the IRP-State relationship darkened into political hell. But she admitted that her staff had filled her in on the rocky relationship of the past dozen years or so. She was curious as to how we saw things. I was more involved in all this than Karl had been, so I spoke for several minutes about the sad situation. I tried to stress that the animosity was largely one-sided, that most affiliates here had no political agendas though, of course, had opinions. These were scholars first and foremost. They would be guided by evidence more than anything else. The bottom line, as I saw it, is that IRP would welcome any thawing in this cold war and a return to normalcy.

She listened politely. When I finished, she got up and closed the door. "Okay," she started, "I am willing to take a chance on you guys. But if you ever screw me over I will find out about it and you will be sorry." Wow, she looked so young and attractive, but she came across like a Mafia hit man. I loved the honesty. This is a woman I could work with, that was for sure. And work together we did. Besides putting the IRP-State relationship back together again, we became good colleagues and friends. As life has a way of working out, Jennifer is now an associate dean working directly for Karl who, as noted, is now dean of Letters and Sciences.

IRP is perhaps the only university-based research entity that had direct access to state automated case files of selected public benefits programs. I helped bring in a talented state worker named Ingrid Rothe who was critical in setting up mechanisms for permitting IRP programming staff to access automated state data files. Some of these technical staff had split appointments between the state of Wisconsin and the university which enabled us to address certain privacy issues. This synergistic arrangement is a stellar illustration of the Wisconsin Idea in practice . . . the state and the academy working in concert to address public concerns.

Cooperative research and policy analysis now goes on in several program areas including child welfare and child support. I went out to the University of Washington in 2011. At the time, they also had a poverty research center supported by ASPE, much like IRP. The conference was on how to facilitate evidence-based policy making and improve relations particularly with state policymakers. The issue of Wisconsin's now close relationship with state government was raised several times. I told them that one critical factor is that, for the past two decades, there has been an IRP associate director who had been recruited from state government. I was the first, Tom Kaplan was the second, and Jennifer Noyes held that position until very recently.

My other contribution to the institute was in the keeping alive the relationship between IRP and ASPE. I recall a question I asked Irv Garfinkel when I first met him on that plane ride sometime in 1974 or 1975. I wondered if federal funding had been jeopardized at all when the Republicans had taken the presidency and began dismantling some parts of the WOP. He replied that they had not experienced any budget problems during the Nixon years. Of course, Nixon turned out to be a rather big spender on social programs even when his rhetoric was tough. Fast forward to the Reagan presidency, now the rhetoric about minimal government and budget austerity had more bite. First, the new administration argued that funding for a federally supported poverty research center ought to be awarded through a competitive process rather than a targeted earmark.

Fair enough, earmarks were not good government. Competition is necessary to keep you on your toes. When IRP subsequently won the competition, the Reagan administration decided to sequester the money or simply defund any poverty research center. This was the first crisis. I recall having to drop something off at Gene Smolensky's house during this period, perhaps 1982. He invited me in and looked rather down, not surprising since he was IRP director at the time. In fact, either just before or after my visit, he cut a bit of his finger off while mowing the lawn. He was simply too preoccupied by the impending collapse of IRP to focus on what he was doing.

Geno, as he was known, obviously wanted to talk. My memory is that we sat in his darkened house for some time. He had none of his normal mirth and humor. At one point I asked what he thought would happen. He thought the party was over. The institute would have its name and perhaps the university could pick up a few support staff but, without federal funding, they might not even want to do that. He ended his monologue with a little shrug. He certainly looked like a defeated man to me.

Rumors of IRP's demise were a bit overstated, however. It turns out that Bob Haveman had served a stint as senior staff on the Joint Economic Committee of Congress just before coming to Wisconsin. While there, he got to know Senator Proxmire's staff very well. With this access, he asked if an earmark was possible to save the institute since the senator now was a member of the powerful Appropriations Committee. No was the response! The fiscal hawk would hold to his position against earmarks. He did, though, agree to put strong language in the committee report about the value of the Institute and that continued support for its work was both essential and warranted. For the administration to ignore this language would be to pick a fight and there were other fights to be fought. For over a decade, a line was inserted in ASPE's budget that specified a certain dollar figure that would go to the IRP.

IRP would live for another day though the Republican administrations remained suspicious of the place. It was getting easier to be tarnished politically and conservatives saw the institute as a supporter of big government and discredited ideas like the Negative Income Tax even though many conservative intellectuals such as Milton Friedman endorsed that very concept. ASPE now required a say in the composition of the National Advisory Committee that would comment and even approve, to some extent, the research projects supported by the institute with federal dollars. This was less alarming in practice than it might sound in principle. These were academic appointees. Though some were conservative, my memory is that none were total ideologues. I was not in management during this period but never sensed great tension between the ASPE overseers and IRP leadership. I did hear one assistant secretary half-jokingly say on his first visit to IRP that it was nice to finally see the place to which he was forced to send such a large chunk of his budget.

The bigger problem was that IRP's budget was shrinking over time in both nominal and real terms. If you looked closely, you could see the changes. There were fewer and then no post-docs. The personal secretary to the director, the typing pool, the gal who did the photo copying all went away. Most significantly, there were fewer and fewer IRP grants to support research and research assistants. IRP did continue to make small grant awards, many to external scholars, but they were very small indeed. One might also think that the overall level of activity would be in decline. This was undoubtedly true but probably not as much as would be imagined.

Outside grants began to replace federal dollars. The university picked the costs associated with some of the support staff. The place remained exciting and viable. In fact, some administrative positions lost during the lean years are back in some form or another and other lost support staff are no longer needed.

The Clinton years brought another more serious challenge. I will say one thing for the Democrats, at least the appointees I worked with in the executive agencies, they did believe in good government and in playing by the rules. They looked at earmarks and said this is not the way things should be done. We should have an open competition for university-based poverty centers. I am speculating here, of course, since any such deliberations took place after I had returned to Madison. But given that Donna Shalala, the former chancellor of the Madison campus, was secretary of the department at the time, it is not likely they wanted to simply move the function to another institution as was likely the motivation in the Reagan administration. This was a good government move.

Thus, we geared up for a major competition for both federal blessing, as well as their money, as the poverty research center. At ASPE, the details of managing the national competition were assigned to Don Oellerich and Matt Stagner. I suspect that the appearance of balance played a role here. Both men were very smart and capable. Don, whom I described earlier, had received his doctorate from the University of Wisconsin. No one wanted to put him in the position where favoritism might be playing a role.

Matt, on the other hand, earned his doctorate at the University of Chicago which, in fact, would be one of our main competitors. Matt had distinctive red hair and round face that easily broke into a pleasant smile. He had a quick wit so made a good partner for the playful banter I always enjoyed. We grew into good friends over the years.

In the run up to and during the competition, we all had to walk on eggshells. No one could talk about anything that could be interpreted as advantaging one competitor over the other. Since it was natural to run into Matt or Don this made conversation strained indeed. "How is the weather there in Washington?" "Hot and humid, you moron, what do you think?" As the competition approached, I increased my presence out there in the so-called real world. I wanted to make the Institute as visible as I could. I was painfully aware that things had changed drastically since the place was established in 1966. Back then, there were a paucity of think tanks and evaluation firms to which the federal government could turn for rigorous analytical work on social issues. By the 1990s, the Washington landscape was dotted with such organizations, most of which were more responsive than any university could be and peopled by staff who were accustomed to interacting with policymakers. On a day-to-day basis, the ASPE staff did not think of IRP or any university for that matter as a go-to place.

Putting together the proposal was a painful process. In retrospect, I imagine it is easier to write a proposal from scratch, with a clean slate so to speak. You do not have to incorporate a lot of the baggage accumulated over the years or make what you have been doing for so long seem fresh and exciting. How do you balance the tried and true with the innovative and provocative? In the end these are subjective decisions. It is a good thing that Bobbi Wolfe and I worked so well together. Had we not, this would have been a total nightmare.

We did employ a rather democratic approach to writing the damn thing. Bob Haveman wrote the long introduction that summarized what we knew and didn't know about poverty. We then brought in affiliates to do first drafts of sections where their individual ideas and strengths might be highlighted. Bobbi Wolfe was scheduled to participate in an international conference in Portugal in the middle of all this. We faxed a draft copy to her which came out the other end in one long script with increasingly larger print size for some reason. She spent all her free time editing this long, continuous scroll that wound throughout her hotel room. After all this, we tried mightily to weave the whole buffet into an appetizing entree that we hoped made some sense.

The process was a tense, grueling ordeal. With so many cooks stirring the pot, there were numerous disagreements about approach and tone. Egos were bent as various affiliates felt their ideas were not prominently displayed or their contributions to IRP sufficiently appreciated. It was like walking on eggshells to keep everyone happy. I was very glad when Dan Meyer, an IRP affiliate with business in D.C. at the time, hand delivered the proposal to ASPE officials. After the first blush of relief, however, I found the waiting much worse than developing the damn thing in the first place. I would be in D.C. for some event and run into some of the ASPE folk. Since we could not discuss the competition, I would try to tease something out of their expressions and body language. Did Don or Matt or Ann or Wendell or Canta look me in the eye or not. Was that an expression of sympathy I just saw? Am I a total paranoid nutcase or what? My concerns, however, were not frivolous. Some thirty years of history were at stake as were the jobs of numerous staff.

The end came in an unexpected way. My phone rang one day. It was Don Oellerich from ASPE. What could we do with half-a-million per year over several years? What could we do? Not much, I thought! Now what should I do? We obviously did not get the big prize but what was this, the consolation prize? This was surprising, no consolation prize ever was mentioned. Should I start by negotiating for more, sound outraged, sound grateful? I must have signaled someone to get Bobbi because I recall she appeared in my doorway. I mouthed the offer and she looked as stunned as I was. Then I just went ahead and carefully told Don we would do the best we could, watching Bobbi as I said the words to see if she disagreed. She didn't correct me or, if she did, forgave me quickly.

The big grant went to Northwestern-Chicago. They were our natural competitors though other strong institutions had entered the fray. Their team was led by Rebecca Blank and a host of other heavy weight researchers such as Greg Duncan. They were clearly capable of beating us in a straight-out competition, and probably did. However, we later found out that we were handicapped from the start, perhaps fatally so. Our old friend, Larry Mead, was on the external review committee. Larry had said more than once that his work with Mike, Bernie, and I in Kenosha was one of his favorite projects. Apparently, though, he felt slighted by many of the mainstream economists at the Institute. He later wrote that IRP was too wedded to the anti-poverty agenda of the past. He felt the Institute was overly attached to the Negative Income Tax and other income transfer schemes as a solution to poverty.

Our methods and our predispositions, he argued, did not permit us to fully explore the behavioral and cultural dimensions of poverty nor solutions that went beyond manipulating economic incentives in conventional ways. His strong views swayed others on the review committee, Wendell Primus much later obliquely hinted as much to me. While there may be some truth in what Larry believed, he did go astray in one way. Every other serious competitor would rely heavily on the same type of economists, the same methods, and the same substantive priors as did IRP. That is simply where the world was in the mid-1990s.

I recall a lunch I had with Larry several years after the competition when he was in Madison for something or other. I did not raise the sensitive issue of the competition, but I was fascinated by where he took the conversation. He was deeply unhappy professionally. He felt disrespected by his peers at New York University and believed he had been treated badly by the number crunching economists and political scientists who now dominated life within the academy. He had a point, his name did not come up a lot when organizers of events were pulling together "experts" on various poverty topics, at least not as often as you would imagine given his national reputation. Ron Haskins, a conservative icon, once expressed to me his ire that Larry was so often overlooked in poverty discussions.

Larry expressed himself well both verbally and in writing. In fact, he may well be the most articulate man I know. But he also was somewhat narrow in his approach to issues. He argued that government programs should be used to reward and facilitate appropriate behaviors. It is not a bad point at all. He simply had trouble moving on to other perspectives and issues. My guess is that people did not invite him to things since they knew what he was going to say no matter what the issue of the day was.

Since no second prize had ever been discussed there was much speculation on why IRP got this Miss Congeniality award in the first place. Some felt that no one wanted to go to Donna Shalala and tell her that they were putting IRP out of business. Perhaps there was a realization that the review process had been biased or tainted a bit. On the other hand, perhaps ASPE had grown to like IRP and those of us who spent time there. I recall a couple of ASPE staff mentioning how much they liked Dan Meyer and myself (Dan also spent periods of time at ASPE) and thought that proof that IRP must be populated with nice people. Obviously, they had not met many of the economists (Dan is a Social Work professor).

On the other hand, maybe they did not want to lose the institutional capacities and human capital that had been built up over some three decades. There is at least one small piece of evidence that ASPE did not want to lose what IRP had developed over time. Don Oellerich and Becky Blank (from the winning team) were in Madison for some IRP event soon after the awards were made. Bobbi, Becky, Don, and I sat on the deck of Bobbi's house which lies on the shore of Lake Mendota. It was a lovely spot for an awkward set of negotiations. Don was hoping we would share mailing lists and perhaps other goodies with our competitors. Feelings were yet a bit raw, but we ended up being quite cooperative. There really isn't anything personal in all this nor is there much to be gained by stonewalling at this point. I do recall Phil Certain, the Letters and Sciences Dean at the time, asking me to nose around to see what might have happened. I never did since what is done is done. The role Larry played eventually came out in any case. But as I mentioned, Chicago-Northwestern was a powerhouse competitor. Perhaps they would have won without any help.

Day-to-day, you could not see all that much of a difference in the aftermath of the bad news. The university kicked in more support for the key staff members. The belt was tightened even more. And everyone went out to more aggressively seek external funds. For a while, I did run into some embarrassing moments in the outside world which thought that IRP was about to go out of business. I would run into people at conferences who treated me as if my pet dog had just died. There was pity in their voices as they expressed their condolences. "But we are still there," I would say, and I just knew they thought I was in denial of the inevitable. They would pat me on the head and mutter, "Of course it is."

One day, I was serving on a panel for the plenary session at APPAM (the national public social policy organization). Judy Gueron, the CEO of MDRC (arguably the leading welfare evaluation firm in the country) was a co-panelist and seated next to me. Before we started she turned and offered me a job. I had spoken at MDRC, had run into Judy who knows how many times in the past, and now she is offering me a job out of the blue? I thanked her for her gesture but really, IRP is alive and well. Eventually people got with the program and the expressions of sympathy died out. It was a consolation to know, however, that if I had been booted out of the UW as a fraud, I might have had opportunities to fool other institutions for a while.

Fast forward a few years and we had another competition. Karl Scholz is now director and I am still associate director. First, another quick digression on Karl as director! Karl is a proficient technical economist who is also interested in policy having served in staff positions for the Council of Economic Advisors (CEA) and the Department of the Treasury. I knew Karl had served at CEA under Bush the father and assumed early on he was a Republican. During a conversation about whether we had any Republicans at IRP I offered up Karl Scholz as an example of one. This was early in his tenure at UW. My observation brought forth much hilarity from the economists in the room, particularly Art Goldberger, just about the Economics Department's premier econometrician at that time. As a junior faculty member, Karl also thought his love for policy surely would doom his tenure chances at UW where, as mentioned before, the economics department had swung toward the theoretical side of things. As his tenure decision approached, he started looking for where to land next after the ax fell. I recall him once mentioning the University of Oregon as a place he was considering. Then, to his surprise, he received tenure. Even so, I sensed he had some reservations about staying in Madison.

When Bobbi was about to step down as director, we put together a search committee for her replacement. I recall trying to sell Dan Meyer on the prospect. He felt he wasn't quite ready to take it on or simply was too smart to take the job, it was never clear which. There were a couple of economists who expressed interest but neither of them generated much excitement on the committee. Karl's name kept coming up. Unfortunately, he was off in D.C.

serving a stint as Deputy Secretary for Tax Analysis at Treasury. Bobbi and I concluded that he was the man we wanted. We just have got to convince him of that fact. The problem was that Karl, as I had long suspected, was not sure he wanted to return to Madison after his D.C. stint was over. He was talking about heading to the Dartmouth Business School. In a very recent conversation with Karl, he now expressed how happy he is to be at Wisconsin.

Undeterred at the time, Bobbi and I set up a dinner with him and his wife, Melissa, while we both were in D.C. on other business. He was in a great mood. The federal budget had just passed after the usual political fights, and he had been named by Vice President Gore as a key player in the Rose Garden celebration. When Melissa left the table for a moment, Bobbi and I pounced, he was the man for the job as our next Director, the savior of IRP. He didn't quite see it that way though. His head dropped on the table and he kept repeating . . . no, no, no, over and over!

I piped up with "Perhaps this was an inopportune time for us to raise the issue. We can come back to it later." He gave us no hope that later would make any difference as he raced back to Treasury after dinner. There really is no rest for the wicked who take these high-level Washington positions. Bobbi and I were not to be deterred by this tiny setback. She opined that we had to work on Melissa. After all, everyone knows that women make the big decisions, men just think they do. It was inconceivable to us that Melissa would want to leave Madison for Hanover, New

Hampshire and Dartmouth College unless you like the wilderness. Okay, Karl's best friend was there, and it is an Ivy League school. But really, Hanover? You might as well be on the other side of the moon. We worked on Melissa and, lo and behold, Karl returned to Madison and became the next director.

For this next competition there would be a national poverty center (the big prize) and three regional centers. You could apply for either the big or secondary prize or both. Applying for both meant more work but you hedged your bet somewhat. What you did not know is whether simultaneously applying for both would diminish your chances for the big prize. Presumably the review processes were independent but still. Karl wanted to go for broke and only apply for the big prize. I, being more cautious by nature, argued that we should go for both, just in case. We went back and forth, eventually my opinion prevailed.

This time around we were less democratic, or at least Karl was as I recall. We solicited input, but the writing was more closely held at the center. No matter, the outcome was essentially the same. We got one of the regional poverty center designations while the big prize went to the University of Michigan. Can you guess who now headed the Gerald R. Ford School of Public Policy at Michigan . . . the same Becky Blank! She was ably helped by Sheldon Danziger, a past IRP director. Sheldon and his spouse, Sandy, moved to Ann Arbor several years earlier when it became apparent that Sandy would not land a faculty position at U.W. On the other hand, the School of Social Work at Michigan was happy to have her.

Could I have argued the wrong position? Perhaps our going for both prizes diminished our chances for the big prize somewhat. We will never know, and I will always have that doubt in the back of my mind. I sense that Karl felt quite bad about not getting the big prize. For me, IRP was still alive. I ran into Greg Duncan soon after at some conference. Greg was still at Northwestern, one of the two institutions that had just lost the big prize. He asked me to join him for breakfast and poured out his disappointment at losing the main poverty center brass ring. Everyone is very good at this level. These competitions are fierce and the final decisions always a close-run thing.

The continuing designation of IRP as a federally recognized research center still had benefits, even with a minimum-wage level of funding. It opens so many doors. The university still kicked in and the IRP name yet had much credibility out in the wider world. Though IRP was technically a regional research center, most outsiders never made that distinction. IRP was IRP. My WELPAN work and my other work on service integration in the surrounding states, as well as Dan and Maria's work on child support in Wisconsin, made it look like we were focusing on the Midwest region while business as usual could prevail for most in the IRP family.

There was yet another competition in 2011. This time there was no big prize. Three institutions would be named as Poverty Centers. Tim Smeeding (the new IRP director), Jennifer Noyes, and Kathryn Magnuson led the IRP for this round. Again, IRP survived while Michigan as well as the other existing regional centers such as the Universities of Washington and Kentucky lost out. The other two centers winning in this round were located at Stanford and the University of California-Davis. In the end, all the other big names such as Northwestern, Chicago, and Michigan faded had from sight. IRP kept chugging along as the little engine that could.

Finally, there was one last competition in 2016 which coincided with the fiftieth anniversary of the creation of IRP. This time around, Lawrence (Lonnie) Berger, Jennifer Noyes, and Kathryn Magnuson led the charge. Before the competition, I had a lunch with Jennifer who set up a meeting with Lonnie based on our conversation. My point was that there was not enough money to support original research. That research would happen in any case, just be supported by other sources. The institute ought to focus on complementing the work of ASPE to stimulate more useful research both by better connecting the knowledge production and consumption communities and by translating that work more effectively for decisionmakers. Lonnie was interested but cautious. I don't blame him. No one wants to be the last director of IRP.

When the Request for Proposals (RFP) came out, I had nailed it. It was merely a hunch on my part but sometimes you get lucky. Perhaps this gave IRP an advantage going forward by getting them to think about such themes early on. In any case, the institute won this last competition to become the one and only poverty research center once again. After a half century, we are back to the beginning. The analytic center for poverty research is back in Madison, the only site to have endured in this role continuously since the inception of the War-on-Poverty.

A while back, I glanced over the IRP staff directory. There were over eighty on-campus affiliates listed from a variety of campus schools: Economics, Political Science, Sociology, Social Work, Law, Consumer Sciences, Education, Women's Studies, Population Health, Public Policy, Education Policy Studies, Commercial Arts, History, Business, Human Development and Family Studies. In 1969, there were some thirty campus affiliates mostly drawn from two departments—Economics and Sociology. In addition, the IRP of today had almost fifty staff members including graduate students who helped with various research projects. Obviously, the small federal investment leverages much more in outside research support.

The reach of IRP beyond the university is broader than ever. The Institute oversees a network of research centers known as the U.S. Collaborative of Research Centers. The participating universities are: Columbia University, Howard university, Stanford

University, the Universities of Kentucky, Michigan, U.C.- Irvine, U.C. Davis, and the University of Washington. Many of these formerly were federally sponsored research centers. Moreover, there are over ninety off-campus affiliates associated with IRP. Their home institutions represent a who's who of top research entities: University of Chicago, Massachusetts Institute of Technology, Brookings Institution, University of California-Berkeley, Harvard, Yale, Princeton, Columbia, Cornell, University of Pennsylvania, University of Michigan, Michigan State University, New York University, Cornell, UCLA, and so many others. There is even a foreign presence with affiliates from the University of British Columbia, the University of Western Ontario, and Cambridge University.

I mention all this only because I take some small measure of pride in being there when it all could have unraveled. There were dark moments when I could easily see the lights being turned out and the name becoming a mere memory. Did IRP solve poverty? No, of course not! In fact, a small joke I often used in talks and lectures was to show the aggregate poverty rate from 1959 to the present day. Then I would point to the year on the horizontal axis when IRP came into existence. The poverty line had been declining to that point and then flattened out for a time before rising and falling over the succeeding decades. See, I would tell the audience, here is proof that the worst thing you can do is research a problem. I always go for a laugh.

I came to love the place . . . the people, the work, the vision and principles that motivated all of us. It surely was my special 'sheltered' workshop. Really, just think about it a minute, who else would have put up with me so long? Okay, my spouse has!

Well, you now have taken a tour with this wandering academic through his policy candy store and, in this chapter, spent time in the edifice where it is located. Of course, that is not correct since this is a virtual store that lies in the mind. I hope you found the offerings worth a visit, if not enticing. I enjoyed my time in the store very much. Sure, as a kid, I wanted to be a writer and, even now, that strikes me as my natural niche. Still, I cannot think of a better fallback vocation to keep me fed and housed than being a policy wonk. Doing public policy never got old . . . the quests remained complex, intriguing, and even dramatic at times. I can say one thing with conviction, I never got bored.

What a way to fill up a life!

POSTSCRIPT

I hope the joy and satisfaction I experienced throughout my career has come through in the preceding pages. In recent years, I have enjoyed many discussions with peers who grew up in the post-World War II period as I did and came of age in the 1960s. While we faced some angst generated by the Cold War and the Vietnam conflict, we also considered ourselves extraordinarily fortunate for one reason on which we all seemed to agree. We emerged into adulthood at a time when opportunity seemed endless.

In college, I cannot recall ever taking a class because it was essential to my future employment prospects. In truth, I never worried that much about the future other than not being sent off to fight in a conflict I desperately opposed. We had an implicit faith that if we prepared our minds as best we could, and if we honed our cognitive abilities in a way that fostered critical thinking, the rest would fall into place. I took courses that interested me. I spent hours debating the great issues of the day. I devoted great energy and much time doing things I thought might make the world around me just a little better. Despite such self-indulgence, it never occurred to me that I might be sacrificing my future. Such a naïve faith would seem ridiculous today. Somehow, though, it worked for me and I suppose most of my peers back then.

We emerged into adulthood when America was yet a land of opportunity. A totally unremarkable working-class kid like myself could work his way through college all the way to a Doctorate absent any help from my economically struggling family. No question, hard work was involved. I started delivering papers as a boy of ten or eleven and never stopped working after that. Now, I look back and wonder who that young man was that headed off to his morning college classes after working the eleven-to-seven shift at a hospital. It simply was what you did.

As it turned out, all my various and eclectic experiences as a young man served me well in recent years. As I stress in chapter ten, being a great policy wonk is more than numbers. You need a breadth of experiences that provides a broader perspective. You need to see issues and possibilities in a holistic way. Without knowing it, I managed to create an array of experiences that would serve me well. It was another piece of serendipity.

If there were one piece of baggage I brought with me into adulthood, it was the dreaded "imposter syndrome." I could not accept the feedback I started receiving in college that I was smart, even a leader that others might follow. After all, I had once been put in the slow class in elementary school and did not graduate in the top quarter of my high school class. There were scant indications of any future academic success in my performance as a young man. The strong sense that I was just the most average of working-class kids, faking it in academia and among the policy elite, stayed with me far too long in life. I don't believe I ever fully shook off the crippling residual harm that came with embracing that script. Fortunately, I managed to achieve much despite that enervating impediment.

In the end, I cannot overstate how fortunate I feel. Sure, I wish I had done more non-academic writing earlier, but I am making up for lost time now. I am now moved to repeat something I have uttered so often that I fear putting readers into a coma from endless repetition. I was this damn lucky guy who literally fell into a career that perfectly matched who I was. I flew around the country and worked on many of society's most complex and controversial issues. In doing so, I had an opportunity to interact with many caring and competent people from all walks of life. I had the opportunity to engage the most brilliant social policy minds and researchers of my generation. And somebody paid me to do this. That was better than stealing. Come to think of it, maybe it was a form of stealing.

Amazingly, I did all this absent much observable talent, a statement of fact and not my imposter syndrome rearing up. Real life skills have always eluded me. An example from early in my marriage, I foolishly tried to put oil in our car all by myself. I did this just once, to save a little money. When the oil immediately gushed out, I realized I had poured it in the wrong hole. Who knew I had a decision to make about this or that I should have looked at some manual? So, I dragged myself in the house and asked my long-suffering wife to call a garage. I begged her to tell them she did it, and to ask if this was a fatal error of some sort. Amazingly, she did this for me. She still liked me back then. That may very well have been the final practical task I ever attempted in my life.

All in all, though, erecting my allegorical candy store has been a marvelous run. Now, at the end of this run, I think back on what I did bring to the table, what I think those most successful as policy wonks need to bring to the table. I have long considered some of these essential softer skills and dispositions. Here is the list of what I have come up with and which I promised to share with you back in chapter one:

Humor. I think being able to laugh at yourself and with others is important to doing policy. While the issues are critical to the well-being of society, and the debates can be so vitriolic, humor helps us keep a sense of perspective in an otherwise deadly endeavor. I have prided myself on bringing laughter wherever I have worked. Really, how many times have I heard people say, "Corbett . . . that guy is such a joke!" Once, when I was in a very serious meeting in the old executive office of the White House, chaired by Clinton's Chief Domestic Policy Advisor (DPA), I had just finished up a dress rehearsal for my part of a critical meeting that was coming up. The DPA said my remarks were very good but needed to be shortened. "No problem," I quipped, "I'll just cut out every other word." She stared at me blankly, not the slightest hint of a smile. *This town*, I said to myself, *really needs to lighten up.*

Inquisitiveness. It is helpful if you are always seeking out new things, never being quite satisfied by your known and comfortable world. I am reminded of Irish twin girls who grew up in a Chicago Irish neighborhood. When very young, they would spend many an hour looking out their front window at the busy street below. As adults, they realized they were looking at different things. One did look down at the street below, happy with the doings of her Irish neighbors. Her twin sister, in contrast, recalled always looking up the street and wondering what was around the corner. The inquisitive one grew up to get a Ph.D. in Russian studies and spent her life as a policy wonk in D.C., including heading Senator Ted Kennedy's staff for a while. The other spent her life as a wife and mother in Chicago. Here they were, biological twins, same family environment, yet so different in perspective, and yet each happy with their life choices. One knew from early childhood that she wanted to push the envelope and explore new challenges. She was born to a life of public policy. Her twin was happy with the world as is. It was as if they were wired differently.

Conceptual elasticity. You need to be able to adapt when your givens are challenged by new information, new theories, and new ways of looking at things. I read a memoir by Claire Conner about her childhood. Growing up in a John Birch household, her father was a founding member of this ultra-right-wing group. As an adult, she pulled away from her early indoctrination and started asking questions on her own. She lamented the fact that her parents were stuck in the same place. In their world, there were communists everywhere, and America would go down the drain in six months unless they did something drastic. When six months had passed, and the apocalypse failed to arrive, the day of doom was reset to another six months out. Their script never, ever changed, they were bound in a rigid form of structured, self-reinforcing paranoia. The ability to absorb new information and adapt accordingly is critical to doing policy work. Rigidity of thought or personality is the death of a good policy wonk. The ability to absorb and integrate conflicting input is essential. You must accommodate new things from the world around you.

Caring. I think you must care about things outside yourself, perhaps another trait that is internally wired at birth. I recall listening to radio talks by Dr. Tom Dooley, a Catholic physician who worked in South East Asia where the communists were making inroads in the 1950s. I can vividly recall wanting desperately to grow up to live a life of equal sacrifice. Of course, this was before I realized how cowardly and debauched I was. It is quite easy to be a technical policy wonk and not really care about the issues and people who are the objects of your efforts. You can strive to contribute, but not get overly involved.

Sense of tribe. I think having what I call a large-tribe perspective is critical to doing policy. By that I mean having an ability to think beyond yourself, your family, and the intimate groups you identify with. Many people fall into the "us versus them" perspective very easily, and I don't feel they make good policy types. As I see it, they have a harder time seeing the big picture. Again, a vignette from my sordid past! Even as a very young teenager, perhaps a pre-teen, I recall thinking that we should share more of our agricultural abundance with those in need around the world. It really bothered me that we had so much and others so little. Really, given the tribal attitudes of those around me back then, where in the world could that sentiment have come from? In fact, I recall wanting (and I think I did) to join something called the World Federalists Society—a bunch of one-world types. It was probably a communist front organization, but it made sense to me. As I recall, it was one of two organizations I joined in my early years; the other being the Boston Celtics Junior Booster Club, not quite on the same level as a bunch of one-world advocates.

Imagination. I also think that doing policy demands a lot of imagination. Some people may call this lateral thinking, or the ability to see beyond the obvious or outside the box. It may involve seeing relationships among disparate things that are not obviously connected or perceiving causal connections that others miss. It may involve leaping to new explanations where others are stuck in old ruts. This is less an ability to integrate conflicting input as opposed to bringing together facts and ideas that don't seem related to one another at all. For that, you need to be able to dream. Perhaps there even is a bit of the Celtic muse in this trait, or the ability to express things in a compelling manner. Now, is there any evidence that I had a touch of this trait in my early years? Perhaps this is a stretch, but I remember my mother telling me to take out the garbage. This meant taking it down three flights of stairs and putting it in the garbage pail for pick up later that week. In that short trip, I would often slip off into my overactive imagination somewhere; coming back to reality a block or two away, still carrying a load of garbage to some unknown destination. I would scurry home, hoping the neighbors were not shaking their heads going, "Poor Mrs. Corbett, there goes her addled boy again. She has such a hard life." Having survived adolescence without being committed as delusional, I found a vivid imagination to be able to let my mind wander, to be helpful in thinking through difficult issues and seeing possibilities others don't.

Adaptability. You need to be able to listen to those who have different points of view. You don't have to change your world view, but carefully listen to others; even if on first blush, you don't agree. Seek out both ideas and people that contradict your priors, don't be afraid of debate whether it is out in the open or within your own private thoughts. We get better when we can confront diverse and conflicting input and still come out of the process with a coherent world view. When teaching, I would often assign readings from conservative authors to the more liberal students, and the more liberal screeds to the more conservative students; and make them argue the positions expressed in the paper or book. Yes, sadism came easily to me. It really can be fun being the teacher.

Guilt. Let me end my short list with the attribute of guilt. Is this really an essential trait for doing policy? Hell if I know! It just seems to me that many who try this avocation have guilt to spare. I recall my Peace Corps group, we spent two years in India back in the 1960s; more than once talking about why each of us had joined up. We kept returning to the guilt we often felt at having so much while others had so little. We often noted the predominance of Catholics and Jews among us—two groups known to make excess guilt a matter of personal pride. I myself have gone through life waking up and immediately beginning to apologize to no one in particular ... well, to my wife, I suppose. *Mea culpa* (my fault or sin) became my personal mantra. If I hadn't yet done anything wrong that day, it was only a matter of minutes until I did, perhaps even seconds. It could be that the felt need to do good in some larger sense was a way of expiating all the bad I had done—real and imagined. In the end, just a little bit of guilt may well push you to remedy the things you see as wrong with the world.

It is a list that not many possess. Great policy wonks, to some extent, are born and not made but you can do a lot to refine these attributes. At the end of the day, the best part of my career was the many laughs along the way. I was introducing several federal officials to a group of state officials one day. The federal folk included Don Oellerich, Howard Rolston, and Ann Segal. I started by saying how too many people view federal workers negatively. In my experience, however, I found most of them to be very intelligent, highly competent, hardworking, and totally dedicated to doing the best possible job. Then I paused as I felt that little devil inside getting the best of me. Out it came, "Unfortunately, none of those good people could be with us today." I could not help myself. I never could help myself. You can stop wondering why I get no cards at Christmastime!

They threw me a retirement party as I stepped down from administrative work and teaching. It was a rather lavish affair. I suspect they wanted to guarantee that I did not change my mind. I recall telling those assembled that I had enjoyed a dream career beyond anything I had any right to expect. It was like romping through a policy candy store with no adults to keep me in check.

Yes, I enjoyed the students (most of them anyways) and I found teaching very rewarding. I even tolerated the administrative duties at IRP, mostly because of the superb staff I had to work with and the knowledge that I was helping to sustain a worthwhile institution. I also enjoyed the onerous but necessary task of fund-raising to an extent, perhaps because I proved better at it than I ever would have imagined. And I admit to enjoying some of the research functions attached to my position in the academy, though I was not by disposition a natural researcher. I am merely a guy beset with natural curiosity. Mostly, of course, I enjoyed tilting at all those 'wicked' policy problems that seemed to elude easy solution. I cannot say I solved many of them, but I gave it a good shot in most cases.

One last thought! Now it is the time for another generation of younger, less weary, adventurers to tilt at windmills and try for their own version of the holy grail. Yes, it will remain a difficult, frustrating avocation but so much remains to be done. Fortunately for the next generation, my colleagues and I have left many windmills out there for besotted young knights to tilt their lances toward. Some bright young men or women with passion and the right values need to step up and take on such issues. Don't be afraid of failure. In the end, the reward comes from the effort, the journey itself. Trust me on that.

If students were to find their way to my door these days and ask me if they should pursue a career doing policy, what would I now say? I might just say what I said so many years ago. If you care about the rules we live by, about everyone getting a fair shot in life, go for it. If you have guts, a high tolerance for pain, and can see the big picture, then let no one stand in your way! If you can imagine a just and more equitable world, permit nothing or no one to divert you from your vision. Besides, it sure beats the hell out of working for a living!

KEY SOURCES AND OTHER RESOURCES

BOOKS REFERENCED IN TEXT:

Campbell, D. and J. Stanley. *Experimental and Quasi-Experimental Designs for Research.* Boston: Houghton-Mifflin, 1963.

Conner, Claire. *Wrapped in the Flag: A Personal History of America's Radical Right.* Boston: Beacon Press, 2013.

Confessions of a Clueless Rebel (Hancock Press, 2018)

Palpable Passions (Papertown Press, 2017)

Tenuous Tendrils (Xlibris Press, 2017)

The Boat Captain's Conundrum (Xlibris Press, 2016)

Ouch, Now I Remember (Xlibris Press, 2015)

Browsing through My Candy Store (Xlibris Press, 2014)

Return to the Other Side of the World with Mary Jo Clark, Michael Simmonds, Katherine Sohn, and Hayward Turrentine (Strategic Press, 2013)

The Other Side of the World with Mary Jo Cark, Michael Simonds, and Hayward Turrentine (Strategic Press, 2011)

Evidence-Based Policymaking with Karen Bogenschneider (Taylor and Francis Publishing, 2010)

Policy into Action with Mary Clare Lennon (Urban Institute Press, 2003)

Ellwood, David. *Poor Support: Poverty in the American Family.* New York: Basic Books, 1988

Handler, Joel and Ellen Jane Hollingsworth. *The Deserving Poor: A Study of Welfare Administration.* New York: Academy Press, 1971

Mead, Lawrence. *Beyond Entitlement.* New York: Free Press, 1986

Moffitt, Robert and M. Ver Ploeg. *Evaluating National Welfare Reform.* National Academy of Sciences Press: Washington D.C., 2001

Murray, Charles. *Losing Ground.* New York: Free Press, 1984

Piketty, Thomas. *Capital in the Twenty-First Century.* Cambridge Mass: Harvard University Press, 2014

SUPPLEMENTAL READINGS BY AUTHOR

House Training a Policy Wonk (Chapter 2)

Worker-Client Interactions and Case Level Decision-making: An Exploratory Study. (February 1988) Report to the Wisconsin Department of Health and Social Services. (With Irving Piliavin.)

"Errors in AFDC Payments." (Winter 1979) In Social Work Research and Abstracts. (With I. Piliavin and S. Masters.)

"Administrative and Organizational Influences on AFDC Case Decision Errors: An Empirical Analyses." IRP: DP #542-79, University of Wisconsin–Madison. (With I. Piliavin and S. Masters.)

"An Introduction to CHIPPS: The 1985 Wisconsin Survey of Children, Income, and Program Participation." (February 1986) IRP: University of Wisconsin–Madison.

"Public Sector Innovation: A Case Study of the Child Support Data System." (1984) IRP: University of Wisconsin–Madison. (Report for IBM Corporation.)

Welfare Wars (Chapters 3-5)

"Recreating Social Assistance: Perspectives of the WELPAN Network." Institute for Research on Poverty, University of Wisconsin (2002).

"The New Face of Welfare: From Income Transfers to Social Assistance?" Focus, Vol. 22, no. 1 (2002).

"The New Face of Welfare: Perspectives of the WELPAN Network." Institute for Research on Poverty, University of Wisconsin (2000).

"Reallocation, Redirection, and Reinvention: Learning from Welfare Reform in an Era of Policy Discontinuity." An unpublished paper first presented at the American Sociology Association meetings in San Francisco (1998).

"Changing Family Formation Behavior through Welfare Reform." Rebecca Maynard, Elisabeth Boehnen, Tom Corbett, and Gary Sandefur with Jane Mosley. In Welfare, the Family, and Reproduction Behavior. Washington, DC: National Academy Press, pp. 134–176 (1998).

"Informing the Welfare Debate: Introduction and Overview," in Informing the Welfare Debate: Perspectives in the Transformation of Social Policy. (University of Wisconsin–Madison: Institute for Research on Poverty), IRP Special Report #70, April 1997, pp. 1–24.

"Moving Families Out of Poverty: Employment, Tax, and Investment Strategies," a briefing report edited with Karen Bogenschneider, Mary Ellen Bell, and Kirsten Linney. (University of Wisconsin–Madison: School of Human Ecology), April 1997.

"Wisconsin Works: A View from the Ground" in Evaluating Comprehensive State Welfare Reform: A Conference. (University of Wisconsin: Institute for Research on Poverty) IRP Special Report #69, March 1997, pp. 117–138.

"Work-Not-Welfare: Time Limits in Fond du Lac County, Wisconsin" with Elisabeth Boehnen. Focus, 18:1, Special Issue 1996, pp. 77–81.

"Revising Child Support Orders: The Wisconsin Experience" with Kate Kost, Dan Meyer, and Pat Brown. In Family Relations, 45 (1), January 1996, pp. 19–26.

"Developing a Child Support Assurance Program for Minnesota" with Dan Meyer and Tom Kaplan. IRP Special Report no. 66 (August 1995).

"Immigration and Social Policy: New Interest in An Old Issue" with Thomas Espenshade, Michael Fix, Wendy Zimmerman. Focus, 18:2, Fall/Winter 1996–97, p. 1–10.

"Welfare Waivers: Some Salient Trends" with Elisabeth Boehnen. Focus, 18:1, Special Issue 1996, pp. 34–37.

"Understanding Wisconsin Works (W-2)." Focus, 18:1, Special Issue 1996, pp. 53–54.

"Welfare Reform in Wisconsin: The Rhetoric and the Reality," in The Politics of Welfare Reform, Donald Norris and Lyke Thompson (eds.), (Sage Publications: Thousand Oaks Cal.) pp. 19–54, 1995.

"Why Welfare Is Still Hard to Reform?" In Welfare Reform: Can Government Promote Parental Self-Sufficiency While Ensuring the Well-Being of Children? Wisconsin Family Impact Seminars Briefing Book, Karen Bogenschneider and Tom Corbett (eds.). School of Family Resources and Consumer Sciences: University of Wisconsin–Madison (January 1995).

Final Report of the Order Revision Pilot Project. A Report to the Office of Child Support Enforcement, Division of Economic Support, Wisconsin Department of Health and Social Services. Daniel Meyer, Kate Kost, and Pat Brown (December 1994).

"Changing the Culture of Poverty," in Focus, 16:2, Winter 1994–95, pp. 12–22; a lengthier version of this article was presented as a paper at the October, 1994 APPAM conference in Chicago.

"Child Poverty and Welfare Reform: Progress or Paralysis?" Focus, 15:1, Spring 1993, pp. 1–17.

"The Wisconsin Child Support Assurance System: From Plausible Proposal to Improbable Prospects," in Child Support Assurance: Design Issues, Expected Impacts, and Political Barriers as Seen from Wisconsin (1992). Irwin Garfinkel, Sarah McLanahan, and Phillip Robbins (eds). Washington, DC: The Urban Institute Press.

A New Way to Fight Child Poverty and Welfare Dependence: The Child Support Assurance System (CSAS) (1992). A report published by the National Center for Children in Poverty. New York: Columbia University School of Public Health (with Irwin Garfinkel and Elizabeth Phillips).

"The Wisconsin Welfare Magnet Debate: What is an Ordinary Member of the Tribe to do when the Witch Doctors Disagree?" in Focus, 13:3, Fall and Winter 1991, pp. 19–28.

Final Report on the Wisconsin Order Revision Pilot Project (1991). A report to the Wisconsin Department of Health and Social Services.

An Evaluation of the State Health Insurance Pilot Program. (June 1991) A report to the Division of Health, Wisconsin State Department of Health and Social Services. (With Karen Holden and Pamela Spohn.)

A Preliminary Assessment of the Order Revision Pilot Project. (October 1990) A report to the Bureau of Child Support, Wisconsin Department of Health and Social Services. (With Pat Brown.)

"Income Support and Welfare Reform—Wisconsin Style." (1990) In Dollars and Sense: Policy Choices and the Wisconsin Budget. La Follette Institute for Public Affairs, University of Wisconsin–Madison. (With Robert Haveman and Michael Wiseman.)

The Wisconsin Learnfare Program: A Mystery in Three Acts. Written testimony to the Senate Subcommittee on Social Security and Family Policy (June 1990) in Washington, DC

"Learnfare: The Wisconsin Experience." (1989) Focus. IRP: University of Wisconsin–Madison.

"Reflections on the Work Experience and Job Training Program." (May 1989) IRP Notes and Comments.

"Assured Child Support in Milwaukee: Problems and Prospects." (September 1989) A report prepared for the Milwaukee County Department of Social Services.

"The Welfare Magnet Issue Revisited." (December 1988) Paper distributed by the La Follette Institute of Public Affairs, University of Wisconsin–Madison. (With Robert Haveman and Paul Voss.)

"Public Opinion About a Child Support Assurance System." (December 1988) In Social Service Review. (With Nora Cate Schaeffer and Irwin Garfinkel.)

Evaluation Design for the Wisconsin Child Support Assurance Demonstration (June 1988). Report to the Wisconsin Department of Health and Social Services. (With I. Garfinkel, M. MacDonald, S. McLanahan, P. Robins, N. C. Schaeffer, and J. Seltzer.)

"Managing Workfare: What Are the Issues?" (February 1988) IRP: DP #859-88, University of Wisconsin–Madison. (With Michael Wiseman.)

An Evaluation of the Use of Immediate Income Withholding to Collect Child Support Obligations in Milwaukee County. (Spring 1987) Report to the Wisconsin Department of Health and Social Services. (With Ann Lewis.)

Report of the Welfare Magnet Study Committee. (December 1986) A report to the Wisconsin Expenditure Commission. (With Bernard Stumbras and Paul Voss.)

"Respondent Judgments about Components of the Child Support Reform Program." (Fall 1986) IRP: University of Wisconsin–Madison. (With N. C. Schaeffer.) Report presented at APPAM Conference.

"Child Support Assurance: Wisconsin Demonstration." (Spring 1986) <u>Focus</u>. IRP: University of Wisconsin–Madison.

"Assuring Child Support in Wisconsin." (Winter 1986) In <u>Public Welfare</u>. Pp. 33-39 (With I. Garfinkel, A. Skyles, and E. Uhr.)

"A Design for an Economic Analysis: The Wisconsin Child Support Demonstration." (June 1986) In J. S. Catterall (ed.) <u>Economic Evaluation of Public Programs: New Directions for Program Evaluation</u>, No. 26, San Francisco: Jossey Bass.

<u>The Child Support Assurance Program in Milwaukee County: Prospects for Implementation</u>. (Summer 1985) IRP: University of Wisconsin-Madison. (With Sandra Danziger.) A report to Wisconsin DHSS.

"Child Support: Weaknesses of the Old and Features of a Proposed New System." (February 1982) IRP: University of Wisconsin–Madison. (With I. Garfinkel, et al.)

"Tax Credits to Stimulate the Employment of Disadvantaged Workers." (April 1981) IRP Special Report #31, University of Wisconsin–Madison.

Searching for the Holy Grail (Chapter 6)

<u>Integrating Human Services: Pursuit of Public Policy's Holy Grail</u>, with Jennifer L. Noyes, work-in-progress, Institute for Research on Poverty.

"The Family Impact Lens: An Evidence-Informed, Family-Focused Approach to Policy and Practice" with Karen Bogenschneider, Olivia Little, Theodora Ooms, Sara Benning, and Karen Cardigan. Forthcoming in *Family Relations* (2011)

"Family Policy: Becoming a Field of Inquiry and Subfield of Social Policy" in the *Journal of Marriage and Family*, (June 2010), pp. 784-804, with Karen Bogenschnieider.

"A Progress Report on the Wisconsin Family Forward Initiative" a report prepared for the Wisconsin Departments of Health and Family Services and Workforce Development, with Jennifer L. Noyes (December 2006).

"Toward a Comprehensive Definition of Service Integration" a working paper with Jennifer L. Noyes, (July 2006).

"Integrated Human Service Models: Assessing Implementation Fidelity through the 'Line-Of-Sight' Perspective" a working draft (July 2006).

"Cross-systems innovations: The *line-of-sight* exercise, getting from where you are to where you want to be, in *Focus*, Vol. 24, No. 1, Fall 2005, with Jennifer L. Noyes.

"The Challenge of Institutional "Milieu" to Cross-Systems Integration.." *Focus*, Vol. 24, No.1, Fall 2005, with James Dimas, James Fong, and Jennifer L. Noyes.

"Service and Systems Integration: A Collaborative Project." *Focus* Vol. 23, no. 2 (Summer 2004) with Jennifer L. Noyes.

"The Service Integration Agenda: Political, Conceptual, and Methodological Challenges." *Focus*, Vol. 22, no. 3, (Summer 2003) with Jennifer L. Noyes.

"Eliminating the Silos: Perspectives of the WELPAN Network." Institute for Research on Poverty, University of Wisconsin (2002).

"Strategies for Coordination at the Local Level," in Welfare System Reform: Coordinating Federal, State, and Local Programs (1992). Ed. Jennings and Neal Zank (eds). New York: Greenwood Press.

"Interstate Migration and Public Welfare: The Migration Decision Making of a Low Income Population," in Community, Society, and Migrating (1992). Patrick Jobes, William Stinner, and John Wardwill (eds). New York: University Press of America (with Paul Voss and Richard Randall).

Doing JOBS: A Comprehensive Research and Demonstration Program for Kenosha County, Wisconsin. (1991) A report prepared for the Kenosha County Department of Social Services.

A Management Assessment of the Dane County WEJT/JOBS Program (1991) A report to the Dane County Department of Social Services. (With Michael Wiseman.)

A Management Assessment Report on the Pilot Work Experience and Job Training Program in Kenosha County. (January 1988) A report to the Wisconsin Department of Health and Social Services. (With Lawrence Mead, Bernard Stumbras, and Michael Wiseman.)

A Failure to Communicate (Chapter 7)

"Welfare Reform and Family Well-Being: Apocalypse or Opportunity." A paper prepared for the Midwest Meeting of Social Work Deans and Chairs, Madison WI (September, 1999).

Welfare Reform: Challenges or Opportunities for Philanthropy, edited with Karen Bogenschneider and Mary Ellen Bell, Donors Forum of Wisconsin: Milwaukee, WI, June 1997.

"The Midwest Welfare Peer Assistance Network (WELPAN): A Model" with Elisabeth Boehnen and Theodora Ooms. Focus 18:3, Spring 1997, pp. 64–66.

"The New Federalism: Monitoring Consequences." <u>Focus</u>, 18:1, Special Issue 1996, pp. 3–6.

"Background and Context for the Forum Series," in <u>Welfare Reform in the 104th Congress, Congressional Forum III</u>. IRP Special Report #65 (May 1995), pp. 1–13.

"Welfare Block Grants: Concepts, Controversies, and Context," in <u>Welfare Reform in the 104th Congress, Congressional Forum I</u>. IRP Special Report #61 (April 1995), pp. 15–24.

"State/University Relationships: Problems and Prospects." (September 1982) Center for the Study of Public Policy and Administration, University of Wisconsin-Madison.

To See Things, You Have to Go Out and Look (Chapter 8)

"Evaluating Welfare Reform in an Era of Transition: Are We Looking in the Wrong Direction?" <u>Focus</u>, Vol. 21, no. 3 (2001).

"Implementation Analysis: From Intention to Intervention" with Tom Kaplan. An unpublished paper prepared for the conference on Process Methods held in Washington DC (October, 1999); also "INTRODUCTION AND OVERVIEW: Social Policy Devolution and Process Studies." with Mary Clare Lennon, for the same conference.

"The Next Generation of Welfare Reforms: An Assessment of the Evaluation Challenge," a chapter in a proposed book titled Evaluating Comprehensive State Welfare Reform: The Wisconsin Works Program, Burt Barnow, Tom Kaplan, and Robert Moffitt (eds.) To be published through Rockefeller Institute at SUNY-Albany.

"Social Indicators and Public Policy in an Age of Devolution." With Brett Brown, forthcoming in Trends in the Well-Being of Children and Youth. Roger Weissberg, Carol Bartels, and Herbert Walberg, eds. Thousand Oaks, CA: Sage Publications.

1999 WISKIDS Count: A Portrait of Child Well-Being in Wisconsin . Prepared with Elisabeth Boehnen and Cynthia White . Wisconsin Council on Children and Families, Inc.: Madison WI (September, 1999).

"Poverty: Improving the measure after Thirty Years" in Focus Vol. 20, No. 2 (Spring 1999), pp. 51-55.

1998 WISKIDS Count Data Book: A Portrait of Child Well-Being in Wisconsin. Prepared with Elisabeth Boehnen and Pat Brown. Wisconsin Council on Children and Families, Inc.: Madison, WI (1998).

"Working Around the Official Poverty Measure." Focus Vol. 19, no. 2, pp. 21–24 (Spring 1998).

Welfare Reform: How Will We Know if it Works? A publication of the Midwest Welfare Peer Assistance Network (WELPAN). This publication was prepared by Theodora Ooms and myself with editorial and stylistic input from Valery Denney Communications of Chicago, IL (January 1998).

State Capacity Study—The Wisconsin Report. A report prepared for the *State Capacity Study* being conducted at the Rockefeller Institute of Government: SUNY-Albany, with Tom Kaplan and Elisabeth Boehnen, November 1997.

The Foreword for Indicators of Children's Well-Being, Robert Hauser, Brett Brown, and William Prosser (eds.), Russell Sage Foundation: New York, 1997.

The Foreword for IRP Special Report #72, B. Brown, G. Kirby, and C. Botsko, "Social Indicators of Child and Family Well-Being: A Profile of Six State Systems," 1997.

The Foreword for IRP Special Report #73, J. Koshel, "Indicators as Tools for Managing and Evaluating Programs at the National, State, and Local Levels of Government—Practical and Theoretical Issues," 1997.

"Social Indicators and Public Policy in the Age of Devolution," with Brett Brown. (University of Wisconsin–Madison: Institute for Research on Poverty), IRP Special Report #71, Summer 1997.

"Improving the Measurement of American Poverty," with Gary Burtless and Wendall Primus, unpublished working paper (University of Wisconsin–Madison: Institute for Research on Poverty).

"The Next Generation of Welfare Reforms: An Assessment of the Evaluation Challenge"in <u>Evaluation Comprehensive State Welfare Reforms: A Conference</u>. (University of Wisconsin: Institute for Research on Poverty) IRP Special Report #69, March 1997, pp. 7–24.

"Research and Evaluation Issues Relating to W-2" with John Witte. <u>Focus</u>, 18:1, Special Issue 1996, pp. 74–76.

"Third Annual IRP/ASPE Conference on Evaluation: Reflections on the Conference." In <u>Focus</u>, 14:1, Spring 1992, pp. 25–28.

<u>Coordination: A View from the Streets</u> (1991). A paper prepared for the National Commission for Employment Policy and discussed at a conference held in San Diego (July, 1991).

<u>Coordination: A View from the States</u>. A paper prepared for the National Commission for Employment Policy and presented at a conference held in May 1991 in San Antonio, Texas.

"The New Face of Welfare: From Income Transfers to Social Assistance?" <u>Focus</u>, Vol. 22, no. 1 (2002).

Values and Other Inconveniences (Chapter 9):

The Other Side of the World. With Mary Jo Clark, Michael Simonds, and Hayward Turrentine (Strategic Press, 2011).

Return to the Other Side of the World. With Mary Jo Clark, Michael Simonds, Katherine Sohn, and Hayward Turrentine (Strategic Press, 2013),

Ouch, Now I Remember. (Xlibris Press, 2015).

Confessions of a Clueless Rebel (Hancock Press, 2018)

In Darkness, Some Light (Chapter 10)

The Boat Captain's Conundrum. (Xlibris Press, 2016).

A Wayward Academic (Chapter 11)

The Rise and Fall of Poverty as a Policy Issue, Vol: 30, no. 2, *Focus*, Fall-Winter 2013-14

Evidence-Based Policymaking. With Karen Bogenschneider. (Routledge Press, 2010).

The Boat Captain's Conundrum. (Xlibris Press, 2016)

The Sheltered Workshop (Chapter 12)

When Researchers Delivered Evidence to Policymakers, chapter 3 in <u>Evidence Based Policy Making</u>, by T. Corbett and K, Bogenschneider, (New York: Taylor and Francis, 2010)

<u>The Rise and Fall of Poverty as a Policy Issue</u>, Vol: 30, no. 2, *Focus* , Fall-Winter 2013-14

ABOUT THE AUTHOR

Thomas Corbett, Ph.D. is an Emeritus Senior Scientist with the Institute for Research on Poverty where he served as Associate Director for a decade before his retirement. He earned a Ph.D. in Social Welfare from the University of Wisconsin-Madison and taught various Social Policy courses at the undergraduate and graduate levels in the School of Social Work. He has long studied social assistance systems that affect the well-being of disadvantaged families. In addition, he has explored methods for assessing program effectiveness and strategies for monitoring the status of vulnerable populations, including service on a National Academy of Sciences expert panel examining methods for evaluating contemporary welfare reform. He co-edited a book with Mary Clare Lennon (Columbia University) titled *Policy into Action,* an exploration of methods to evaluate the implementation of innovative initiatives. More recently, he published a book with Karen Bogenschneider (University of Wisconsin) on evidence-based policymaking. Over the years, he has worked on poverty-related policy issues at all levels of government, including a year as senior policy advisor at the U.S. Department of Health and Human

Services where he worked on President Clinton's welfare reform bill and other policy issues. Among many other initiatives, he has worked with a number of senior state officials in the Midwest on various welfare reform issues through the Welfare Peer Assistance Network (WELPAN) and has consulted with numerous state and local sites in the U.S. and Canada who are developing integrated human service models in their jurisdictions. Beginning in 2010, Dr. Corbett has published nine books distributed across the fiction, memoir, and public policy genres. Now retired, he resides in Madison, Wisconsin.

CPSIA information can be obtained
at www.ICGtesting.com
Printed in the USA
FFHW01n1017040818
47600427-51113FF